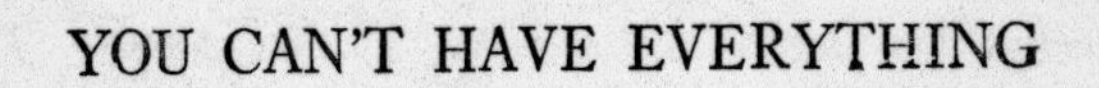

YOU CAN'T HAVE EVERYTHING

YOU CAN'T HAVE EVERYTHING

BY
KATHLEEN NORRIS

PALO ALTO EDITION

New York
P. F. COLLIER & SON CORPORATION
BY SPECIAL ARRANGEMENT WITH
DOUBLEDAY, DORAN & COMPANY, INC.
NEW YORK

MO

★

MANUFACTURED IN THE U. S. A.

The quotation from "The Way Through the Woods," from *Rewards and Fairies* by Rudyard Kipling, is used by special permission of Mrs Kipling and The Macmillan Company of Canada, Ltd.

YOU CAN'T HAVE EVERYTHING

CHAPTER I

BREAKFAST IN THE SYLVESTER HOUSE was supposedly served at eight o'clock. But no matter how promptly Cam descended the stairs she was apt to find Bob and his mother halfway through their meal. Old Mrs Sylvester would be deep in her morning paper; a silent, grizzled woman of sixty-five, she had a strange gift for digging news items out of a dull paper. Bob would be equally deep in the stock-market reports, sometimes muttering to himself and making brief notes on a scrap of paper.

Cam always said good morning cheerfully to both, and sometimes they added something to their monosyllabic recognition of her greeting. But not often. As a rule Bob muttered the middle syllables of the words "Good morning, dear," and Mrs Sylvester's answer was lost in an embarrassed murmur. If Cam went down alone, from this point on there was silence.

Usually, however, Jane and Joanna, aged four and a half and two, came into their mother's dressing room in the mornings and accompanied her down to the dining room; she could always make a little noise and fuss then over getting them into their chairs. The grandmother, too, would turn adoring faded, deep-sunken eyes toward them with the nearest thing to a smile that her face ever wore, and their father quite often had some facetious greeting for them: "Well, here are the Misses Jackson of Sylvester Street!"

Jane always laughed gaily at this and said, "No, no, Daddy!" and of late Joanna would echo "No, no, Daddy!" too, but before the little protests were finished Bob was back in his paper. He read the headlines first then glanced at the sports. The remaining fifteen minutes of his time in the house were absorbed in the market reports.

After that he folded the paper, finished off his coffee, arose, kissed his mother and his wife with abstracted brevity and was gone. Cam's query would follow him:

"Bob! Dinner tonight?"

"Oh—what's today? Friday? No. I can't get here. Good-by, girls. Take care of your cough, Mother."

Or it might be: "I'm not sure, Cam. Nelson's here. I'll have Miss Freeze telephone you."

Sometimes on a Friday she would say: "Any chance for the Fieldings tomorrow, Bob?"

"The whos?"

"Larry and Nance. They want us down tomorrow night—there's a dance."

"Oh, Lord, no!"

"And it's Edith's lunch Sunday."

"Get me out of it, will you?" That was all he had to say; she'd get him out of it, of course, and probably herself, too. It was not much fun driving alone down to Burlingame, having Elsa somehow get "a nice man" to sit beside her at dinner. Cam got very tired of saying to everyone: "Oh, Bob was so sorry! He's working terribly hard, you know. He can't manage dinner; he truly can't."

If she did decide to go alone, she would arrange that on Sunday Mabel would come down on the train and bring the little girls to the club. Everyone would exclaim over their taffy-blonde beauty that was so like their mother's beauty, and Jane and Joanna would walk about stiffly with Mabel, being polite, and presently join the other children in the sandbox or on the lawn, and have their luncheon with Mabel in the children's dining room. Cam would lunch with Edith, at whose gay Sunday table under terrace awnings rich young men would talk of polo and yachts, rich young women display the fashions of month after next, rich food be assiduously served by quiet maids in gray moiré.

Afterward there might be a rubber or two of bridge among the women; the men would be off for more tennis or golf, and at the end of the game they would all wander out to watch last shots and separate in time to get home and change for dinner engagements.

Cam would perhaps see Bob himself playing golf, arguing as he stepped along boldly in the hot sunshine, browner and noisier than the other men, his thinning hair plastered to his forehead. Then they would disappear, their brightly colored sweaters turning to dots of red and yellow on the far-away greens. If she was ever near enough to ask him if she might take him home, he invariably declined; he'd be late, he was going to sit in a poker game.

So Cam would rejoin Mabel and the children and drive them back to the city. Fog would come streaming down over the Millbrae hills as they drove northward; Jackson Street would be blanketed in it; the shelter and warmth of the house would be grateful even on a July afternoon. It was always pleasant to find a coal fire in the upstairs sitting room and take off the tired children's garments and let them go leaping about for half an hour, getting ready for baths and bed. Often Cam's mother-in-law would come upstairs from her eternal quiet vigil in the library to watch the nursery revels, although she never took even the slightest share in them, never told a story or explained a toy. When the little girls were in bed the two women would descend through the quiet house to have their Sunday supper together in the big dining room.

Immediately after supper the elder Mrs Sylvester always returned to her room upstairs, and Cam was entirely alone.

There was a radio close to her bed; she liked to establish herself comfortably in pillows with a book and turn the dial to something interesting. Long before Bob came home at twelve or one o'clock she would be sound asleep.

They were in different rooms now; that was funny, too. It all began to seem very funny—no, that wasn't the word, it was all far too serious for that. Cam pondered the situation; the consciousness of it underran every other thought she had. What was the wrong between herself and Bob, if anything was wrong? What was the matter with the whole scheme, anyway? Or was this rather dull state of affairs just what any woman should expect, when she was approaching her twenty-seventh birthday and had been married for six years?

"Perhaps it's something wrong with me," she said half aloud one evening, when she was changing her dress for dinner and at the same time amusing the little girls while Mabel had her own dinner.

"Joo say, Mummy?" Jane asked, looking up from the dressing-table drawer that she was carefully putting into complete disorder.

"Mummy was talking to herself. You can't have that, angel," Cam said, removing an open jar of cold cream from the small brown hand of Joanna. "Oh, no—that isn't to eat—no——!"

Joanna gave a roar of rage, was instantly quieted with the little hinged mirror. The two little sisters worked along busily, their fair heads bent in absorption. They were very nice, Cam thought, in their soft flannel wrappers of pale pink, with pink cords tied about their sturdy little tums. Somehow the children always were sweetest at this going-to-bed hour; they became affectionate, gentle, confidential. Her two were as wild as little Indians by day, but after their evening baths they were quieter. They ought to have more open air, then they would not be so uproarious. But Bob did not want to take on the expense of a country place yet awhile.

She sighed. Her thoughts were back on Bob again. What had happened to him and to her, what had changed the relationship that only yesterday had been that of lovers? They were completely out of touch with each other somehow; they were almost strangers, living in the same house.

Cam shuddered as the phrase formed itself in her mind. It might apply to other women, never to her. Strangers, she and Bob! It was ridiculous. And yet, of late, whenever they had found themselves alone together, there had been a queer little sense of stiffness about it; she had felt it, and she imagined that he had.

"Will you be home early tonight, Bob?"

"I can be, if you need me."

"Oh no, not at all."

That was not the way for a man and his wife to talk to each other. How had they ever gotten to it? Cam frowned, trying to remember the exact stages, came out of her revery with a gasp, removed the open stick of lip red from Joanna's little red mouth and turned both daughters over to Mabel, who came in still panting from a hearty meal, smelling of coffee and onions.

With many kisses and promises the little girls straggled away. Cam finished her dressing, sat down at the dressing table and put it into order and sat looking at her own reflection in the mirror, her elbows resting amid the pretty little jars and trays. The bedroom behind her was large and old-fashioned, furnished with big heavy chairs and an enormous double bed and curtained thickly against the dark of a cold spring night. A fog was blowing in from the sea on a roar of whistles and horns; bay traffic would be slow tonight. Bob was coming back from an appointment in Oakland—he might be late.

But even as she thought it she heard him come in and went out to encounter him as, red-faced and chilled and disorderly, he came running up the stairs.

"Hello, Cam. Is it seven?"

"Not quite. Take your time. I'll go down and talk to Granny."

He rushed past her, and she descended to the old-fashioned back-parlor library, where, beside a coal fire, her mother-in-law was sitting, staring at the coals. Mrs Sylvester always wore black silk to dinner, with prim lace or embroidery at throat and wrists. Her lank, sad-colored hair was looped and twisted plainly, her colorless, long-featured face devoid of artifice. She smiled at Cam as Cam came in, blonde and fresh and at her loveliest in dark blue velvet. The two liked each other.

"Was that Bob?"

"Just back from Oakland. He'll be right down."

"Little girls get to bed? I heard them laughing."

"Oh, yes, bustling about in my room. They had my dressing table in a complete mess. They were particularly adorable tonight."

"Miss Beatrice Cline came in, and I had May bring her up some tea. She feels miserably, poor thing."

"Isn't she going to have an operation?—Here you are," Cam interrupted herself as Bob came down. "We can go right out."

They went together into a dark room looking out on a narrow strip of evergreens and the walls of the next house. Tonight curtains were drawn at the windows, but Cam knew exactly what would be shown had they been opened. The old Sylvester house was shut in between other old houses; ugly, heavy, bay-windowed places that had proved the possession of wealth in the late 'eighties, and that had not been changed since. Cam meditated sometimes upon the state of mind, the point of view of the men and women who could complacently erect these dull places, scores and scores of them, and fill them with carpets and tremendous tables and chairs, brown marble washbasins, curtains of painted velours. And her mother-in-law loved every inch of the place and would have nothing changed! Well, this was only a temporary arrangement, anyway, this combination of the two families; someday she and Bob could go house hunting down on the Peninsula again and find a home with a garden and a patio, oaks and roses and a fountain for the children.

Shaking out his heavy napkin, Bob said:

"Lord, I'm tired. It's a mean night. Are we supposed to be doing anything?"

"We said we'd drop in at Aline's late, after the concert, if we could. She's got Martino there, and he's going to sing. They were fixing things up for a Spanish supper—red tablecloths and yellow plates—when I was there this afternoon. Tamales and red wine and cheese pancakes."

"Not for me. Bed for mine. I was up until four o'clock this morning," Bob said, finishing his soup with a few hasty mouthfuls, pushing his plate aside. "You want to go?" he asked suddenly.

"I don't care much about it."

"What was it last night, Robert?" his mother asked, in a grave hoarse voice. "Poker?"

"No; we got into a long rubber, and then Morris got talking. He goes tomorrow, and I wanted to get some things straightened out. I'll get some sleep tonight; I've got to get away early in the morning. Howard's driving to Del Monte, and I'm going with him."

May brought roast lamb from place to place, gravy, mashed potatoes, string beans. There was currant jelly at Cam's place; there were finger rolls.

"Is it golf at Del Monte?" old Mrs Sylvester asked.

"Yep. It's going to be kind of rotten because a lot of the men are bringing their god-awful wives," Bob said, "and they've got up a fancy-dress dance or something; I know Howard's wife isn't going. She came into the office today and said she'd bought caps and souvenirs and rattles enough for ten parties, but she'd have no lot or part in it."

"Joan isn't going?" Cam said.

"No. Why, you didn't want to go, did you?"

"Heaven forbid! I hate that sort of party."

"Well, I only go for the golf," Bob said on a note of apology. "This feller Cutter's going to be there. I'd like to see that feller shoot. What were you doing today?" he added, with a swift glance at his wife. Was Cam "off him" for some reason or other?

Cam pulled herself together, forced herself to answer brightly and amiably. Well, she had gone downtown and gotten some yarn, and shoes for Jane, and she had met Aline at the club and heard some details of the Spanish party, and she had stopped in the park on the way home and taken the girls away from Mabel for a little extra walk. And they had walked to Aline's, across the park, and seen the red and yellow flags and the little tables and the jars of marigolds and yellow daisies, and then—let's see—come home. And that was about all.

"No German today?" But he was not interested, he was not listening; he told May that he wanted a big cup of coffee, and to ask Wong to have some breakfast for him at seven. And almost immediately after drinking the coffee he jumped to his feet, flung his crumpled napkin on the table, pressed his brown cheek for a moment against his mother's silver-and-gray locks and announced that he was going to turn in.

The women lingered for a few minutes over their coffee and fruit. Cam observed that Jane was so large that she wore six-year-old sizes already, and her grandmother said with pleasure that children were much healthier than they used to be.

"You didn't eat much dinner, Granny."

"No. Tomorrow will be the anniversary of Larry's death," the older woman said, folding her napkin scrupulously, putting it into a heavy chased silver ring. "My little boy that I lost when we were in Rome before Esmé was born."

There were a great many anniversaries in her year. Cam, respectful and sympathetic, tried sometimes to remember some of them, but they usually escaped her. Bob's father's birthday and the day of his death, similar days for his sister Esmé and his brother Fred, Esmé's brief little calendar, old Mrs Sylvester's wedding day, her mother's, father's, sisters' anniversaries—all these were occasions when the old woman grieved and was silent for an entire day.

"You won't be down to breakfast, then, Gran?"

"No. I'll——" A dark flush came over the old face that was wrinkled like the wrinkles in soft leather, and spotted with dark brown spots on paler brown. "I'll not come down," said Jane Sylvester with difficulty.

"He was seven?"

"Yes. It was the day after his birthday. He'd been so happy; we had our Carlotta make him a real American cake with candles. And then—suddenly——"

She fell into silence. Cam knew that once again for her mother-in-law the chilly sun of a Roman February was shining, the bells were sending their golden notes across the heavy stone walls, the vine-wreathed roofs, the cobbled streets. Once again afternoon light was sharp on the dome of St. Peter's, and the doves were flying up in soft explosions of frightened wings, settling again on the wide steps. Once again they were coming to her, lying idly resting and thinking of the baby so soon to be born—coming to her carrying something that had fallen, living and eager and sweet and small, from the high hotel balcony and that would never be eager and living again.

And Cam, thinking of Jane and Joanna, felt her heart contract with the undying pain that was wringing the older heart.

After dinner they looked into the back parlor. The coal fire was laid behind the polished steel bars of the grate, the blower stood at hand to help it get started, but they decided against a fire tonight. More comfortable to have fires in their own rooms, if they needed them, but Cam said she thought she would read in bed for a while and be quite warm enough.

CHAPTER II

WHEN BOB'S MOTHER had gone her way to her own room, Cam reflected upon Aline's party. Aline Chard was a three-times-divorced woman, amusing, spirited, bitter. She had had a child by each marriage, and to hear Aline tell her children of their fathers' respective shortcomings was one of the delights of Aline's group. She was lawless, but she was funny, Aline, and Cam thought it might be rather fun to go to the after-concert party; she would know everyone there, and everyone would be glad to see her. If Bob had wanted to go, she thought, she would really have liked to go, too. But Bob was rather bored by his old friends in these days; he had known them all his life long, whereas Cam had met them only after her marriage. To her there was still something of novelty in them; but he asserted that he despised them all, and except for occasional poker or bridge encounters had little to do with them.

The party would begin somewhere around midnight, for all the women would want to go home after the concert and beautify themselves, perhaps change their costumes entirely. Cam glanced at her mantel clock! it was not half past eight. No; she certainly was not going to stay awake for three hours just to go see the crowd at Aline's and hear Billy Martin sing. He was a great radio success in these days; he had made his good American name Italian; but he really didn't sing well or choose interesting songs. And besides that he was unbearably complacent, and the women made an embarrassing fuss about him.

Cam prepared herself very carefully for bed. Cold creams, soft pink tissues, hairbrush, net, all were in requisition. She put a new book and a German grammar on her reading table, opened windows, extinguished all the lights except the soft pink lamp beside her bed. And at this point Bob called her from the adjoining room.

They had the two big bay-windowed rooms on Jackson Street; a dark old bathroom was between them. Cam went to her husband's door.

He was resting on his elbow in bed, looking tumbled and flushed.

"Damn it, I can't get to sleep, Cam, I'm too tired," he said. "You haven't got a pill or anything, have you?"

"I have that stuff the doctor gave your mother."

"Have you? That 'd do it. I've been fooling around with Morris since he got here, not getting any exercise. Bridge and dice last night until four o'clock, and three rubbers at the club at noon before we went to Oakland. I can't do it. I've got to get exercise."

She brought a glass of water to the bedside, two flat small pills on the palm of her free hand. He gulped them down, lay back panting, and she shook up his pillow and pulled his sheet straight.

"Thanks, Cam; you're a peach. I'll be all right now."

She sat down on the bed beside him, her serious eyes on his face, and he freed his arm and put it about her.

"Gosh, you're a sweet woman," he said; "you're a sweet little Danish milkmaid, that's what you are."

"Bob, how long will you be at Del Monte?"

"Tomorrow's Friday, we get there for dinner, play all day

Saturday and Sunday, and home Monday sometime. Why? Want to go?"

"No; I don't want to go. Arthur's driving you, for one thing. Then I'd have to take Mabel and the girls to have any fun. I don't get much out of those women who sit on the porch knitting and talking."

"They are certainly a hot bunch of babies!" Bob said with a grin. He settled his big frame on the pillows, looked appreciatively at his wife. "Do you know you're a pretty girl, Cam?" he asked.

"Am I?" she countered unsmilingly; and a little wryly she added, "So what?"

"Well, you're easy on the eyes, that's all."

There was a pause during which she looked steadily at him. Presently she said:

"Bob, I'm terribly unhappy."

She had not meant to make the statement so strong; it shaped itself into words in spite of her. She saw the familiar little cloud darken his eyes and felt her own sting with self-pity and hurt.

"What's the matter? Tired of living here with Mom, eh?" he asked.

"Oh no; it's not that. It's not any one thing; it's everything!" she said, regaining her self-control and trying to smile. "It's *us*. We seem to have come to the—the edge of a desert. We don't do things together any more; we sleep in different rooms; we're drifting away from each other every minute, and I don't know whether it's your fault or mine, or how to stop it!"

There! It was said. For months she had been trying to gather courage to say it; for months mood and opportunity had always failed her. Now he knew what she was thinking about as she went through her lopsided days without any husband, any companionship, any love.

He lay looking at her steadily as if considering. After a moment he said speculatively:

"How d'you mean we're drifting away from each other? We're married, aren't we?"

"Yes, legally," Cam agreed with a desperate little shred of laughter. "But that isn't all marriage, Bob. We used to want to do the same things; we used to go off to movies nights, and go down to the club on Sundays and fool around. And sometimes—*sometimes,*" she added, "we'd have evenings at home. I mean when we had the little Hillsborough place. I loved that place. Everything seemed so much simpler; you saw more of the girls. I don't know. Life seems to be getting entirely out of control!" Cam concluded, putting her hand on his as she spoke.

He patted it, looking thoughtfully into space.

"It was a hell of a note for you to have to move in here with Mom," he said. "I know that. But—damn it!—the way things were we couldn't do anything else. I've been cleaning up just about half a million dollars' deficit in the last eighteen months; d'you get that?"

"I know. And I was glad to come here, and I like her, and it's carried us over the bad time," Cam assented eagerly. "But to be either in the office, or entertaining New York brokers like Morris, or playing golf *all* the time——" she began again, and stopped.

"Golf kinder rests me, honey," Bob apologized.

"I don't want you to stop your golf. I simply—well," Cam persisted, her eyes watering again, "I simply don't—like my life. I adore the girls, but they're with Mabel more than they are with me. I don't like going to dinners and lunches alone; I can't spend all my time having my hair done or playing bridge with Edith and Annette. I'm restless, Bob. I want to get away, and yet I don't want to get away. Edith says to go to Paris, but Jane and Joanna are too young for that; I hated Paris when I was little, and I think they would. I don't care much about Europe, at least for a woman with two small girls, and to take them to London, away from this climate and into that one, seems perfectly idiotic——"

"Listen here," Bob interrupted her flow of words, his tone and look amazed ,"what are you talking about? Are you leaving me?"

Again she gave a forlorn laugh.

"No, I'm not leaving you. I'm just—trying to reach out, I suppose, for a life of my own. I'm trying to find something that will occupy me and interest me as business and golf do you. And I want you in it, Bob."

"Business hasn't been much fun in these last years, Cam," the man said, looking away, but stroking the hand that touched his. "We've had a pretty poor time of it, by and large."

"I know you have. But it is coming back now, Bob?"

"Oh, sure. Morris has worked us out a scheme that practically takes care of it—takes a big load off me, anyway. I'll square things up with Mom sometime this year—November, probably—and then you can get the kids back to the country again, if you want to."

"What do *you* want to do?"

"You fix it," Bob said. The opiate was beginning to work now, and his eyes were pleasantly heavy and smiling.

"But I like to do things *together!*" she half wailed. "In the Hillsborough place we had one room," she reminded him, her face suddenly rosy.

"Well—when I come in I wake you up," he said. "I sleep better and you sleep better this way. What's the great point of one room?"

"It makes a person feel more married," Cam began, in a low tone. "It's more—*companionable.*"

"Well, you can come in here whenever you feel like it, Cam, and then if I do get snoring and wake you up you can beat it to your own room." He yawned tremendously, put a big hairy brown hand up over his mouth, laughed in apology. "Lord, that stuff's wonderful," he said.

His eyes were smiling at her lazily; the lids came down.

He turned on his pillows with a sleepy, comfortable sigh. Cam snapped off the light and went away.

In her room she stood quite still for a while, thinking. She saw nothing that was about her; her thoughts and eyes were far away. After a while she glanced at the clock, took a book and settled herself on the couch. Time went by. It was after ten o'clock when she roused herself from a half-sleep and took from her closet an evening gown of silver brocade shot with lines of pale blue and cherry. Deliberately, slowly, she began the pinning of curls and strapping of slippers; she touched her cheeks with carmine and piled the gold glory of her hair into a crown of glittering ringlets. Her blue eyes watched the process soberly in the mirror; she had small heart in it after all.

A little before midnight, wrapped in a great cape of fur, she walked down the dark silent block and across the empty park that was lighted with cold moonlight. Aline's house was not far away; it could be easily identified by the cars that were already arriving at the curb, the muffled forms that went laughing up the steps. Cam joined them, was welcomed, and went on into a place of noise and lights; radio music was going loudly, and some of the early arrivals were dancing. Red Japanese lanterns swung over the little gay tables; certain guests had come in Spanish costume; Aline herself, a sharp-faced brunette, was earringed and shawled and fringed in true señorita fashion. She screamed something ecstatically to Cam; everyone was shouting and screaming now; the noise-makers were croaking and clacking and buzzing and hooting. The party was certainly starting off with a bang.

"Where's Bob?" everyone asked, sooner or later.

"In bed with a blazing headache. He was up until all hours last night playing bridge. His partner is here from New York."

Everyone was nice to her, and walking home very late with Van Moslyn for escort, she agreed that it had been a wonderful party; all Aline's parties were. Martino wasn't so good; Cam didn't like his voice, somehow. Van couldn't stand him or his voice.

"Where's Betty now, Van?"

"She and the kids were in Vienna, last I heard."

"Come up and have dinner with us whenever the spirit moves you, now that you're a bachelor. This is it—here we are."

"I'll do that very little thing. Is this where you live?"

"Bob's mother's. We moved in on her—she was darling about it—when Venable-Stacks went to the wall."

"Lord, what a crash that was!"

"Very costly for the Sylvesters. However—things are looking better now."

She had said it ten times that evening—a thousand times since the beginning of the year. Everyone else had said it back to her. Van said it now.

"Looking better. You bet your life they are! Well, good night. See you soon."

"I mean that about dinner."

"Thanks." She had let herself into the house. He turned now and went down the dark street. Cam reflected that she liked Van Moslyn. He was so dull that the mere thought of his coming to dinner appalled her, but he was nice. He was just back from a year in New York. He had sent Betty and the children abroad to economize. Van did things on rather a handsome scale, as Bob did. He might be broke, Bob had once said of himself, but he would never be poor. And Van was something of the same type. Financial reverses did not frighten men as they did women; they seemed rather to challenge them and spur them on.

Well, here she was back in her room, the sound of Bob's snoring coming rhythmically through from the bathroom side. She was going to bed at quarter to three instead of at nine. It had not really been worth while, the whole thing. She would tell Bob at breakfast tomorrow that she had gone to

Aline's party after all. He wouldn't care. That was just the trouble; he'd be glad in his kindly patronizing way that she had had a good time. Had she danced with Kent Ferguson? Good for her! Could he make love off the screen as he did on?

"What's the matter with me that I can't keep my husband in love with me?" she thought. "What's the matter with my marriage that I can't make it seem alive?"

And she looked at other women in the shops and streets. They were alive. Or were they? After the first intoxicatingly happy years of marriage did all women go into this half-living and half-dead state, automatically moving through their days, robbed of everything that made them complete?

Campbell Sylvester, spending her mornings in the old house in Jackson Street, sending the children out into the sunshine, climbing the stairs to her mother-in-law's big back bedroom on the second floor, felt herself dazed with the change that had somehow crept upon her so insidiously. Bob did not love her any more. He liked her well enough, had no animosity, no ugly feeling toward her. But Bob, who so short a time ago had actually trembled when the lovely Campbell Bayne of Baltimore had smiled at him, had surrendered her ruffles and gardenias to his arms for a dance, Bob just did not love her any more! He took her for granted. There was to be no more thrill, no more compliments and laughter and little parties for just themselves. She was just "my wife," now. "My wife has taken the children to Tahoe. . . . My wife knows that I don't care for large parties. . . . I asked my wife to let me off."

Considering it, she felt herself shaken with deadly fear. She was not yet twenty-seven; life couldn't stop right here and leave her stranded. And yet for weeks—for actual months, since before Christmas, indeed—every overture she had made toward Bob had made her feel only more clearly that his life had separated itself from hers, that he really did not need her any more.

She had her children, of course. But their lives went on very smoothly in the dim, dark old house under Mabel's supervision. They loved Mummy best, and Mummy managed to see them at various intervals during the day, to have them with her for bedtime romps at night. But little girls whose added ages did not total seven years could not be expected to give real companionship to an eager, vital, lonely woman of less than thirty, who felt herself still so unsatisfied at the table of life and love and delight. And the children always were in bed at seven o'clock. Seven o'clock, with the long evening and the dull dinner still ahead for Cam and Bob's mother!

And other people were beginning to notice it, of course; notice the golf engagements and the business engagements that so constantly separated Bob and Campbell Sylvester. Cam knew that there was talk.

One day not long after Aline's party, when she came suddenly into Elsa Fielding's for tea she suspected that the whole group—Elsa and Annette and Larry, Irvington Brown and Betty O'Connor, Edith and Jean—had all been talking about her.

They were drawn into a tight knot about Elsa's fire, and someone—it looked like Larry—had been talking in an undertone; their heads were all together. There was no mistaking the flutter with which they broke apart when she came in; there was no mistaking the utter unnaturalness of Larry's voice as he said: ". . . and I say that when a horse does that he's no more good for polo or anything else!"

After that dominoes and backgammon were resumed, and Cam had a big chair and a glass of something to drink, and everyone was especially charming to her.

"Were those your adorable kids with you in the park yesterday?"

"They were. We saw you and we waved to you. Aren't they cute?"

"The little powder-blue coats and the bonnets," Edith said.

"And the gold hair fluffing out around their little pink faces! I could eat them."

Dice rattled; dominoes clicked; a maid came about to collect glasses and offer fresh ones. Cam loosened her furs and sat back in her big chair, listening, looking at the fire. But she knew they had been talking about her!

By degrees the group melted. It was getting toward dinner time. One by one there was mention of dinner engagements; everyone had drifted away except Elsa when Cam suddenly came out of a dream, got to her feet, gathered her furs about her.

"Cam," said Elsa then, "I want to speak to you."

Cam had gone to the window of the high apartment to look out at the view. The long strip of the city beneath Elsa's windows melted into the green pines of the Presidio, and beyond these lay the waters of the bay and the glittering windows of the prison island and the line of the hills beyond.

"Lovely, isn't it?" Cam said. "I wish we were on the view side of the street. As it is, only the windows in the mansard roof at our house have view, and the servants are in those rooms."

"Couldn't you do anything with that upper floor, Cam? I mean, make a porch up there and have a sort of game room? That is the dismalest old house of theirs!"

"It's the way Mrs Sylvester likes it, and she's had so much sorrow, poor thing, and she's at home so much, that I never suggest any change. You see," said Cam, very lovely in the little hat that curved so closely over the rich gold of her hair, her blue eyes dark and wide and serious, "you see, Bob and I only meant to go there as a makeshift. It's more than two years now—we didn't think it would be more than two months. Things simply—collapsed, and she was loaning him a great deal of money, and it seemed only sensible to cut down everywhere we could. But we've always said that we were going to buy a place in Hillsborough as soon as things got better."

Elsa stood quite close to her; they were both looking out of the window.

"I wish you could," said Elsa, with a hint of significance in her voice.

"I don't think," Cam answered quietly, "that it would make any difference."

"I do." Elsa took a chance. "Is it so bad, Cam?" she asked lightly.

"Why, I don't know," Cam said very evenly and carefully. "I don't suppose there's anything very bad about it. It's just that Bob worked too hard for those years after the crash, and that now he's in the habit of being completely wrapped up in business and in golf. He says he loves me and the girls, and I think he does. But I don't believe a man as busy and as amused as Bob is really needs a wife and children. He's often at the office at seven to get the opening of the New York market; he goes to the club and plays bridge or dominoes every afternoon, and very often he has to take a man somewhere to dinner and isn't in until late."

"Why doesn't he bring the man home to dinner?"

"Well, there's his mother, you know. She hates strangers, and although she's perfectly polite, she doesn't make things very easy. It's a—funny situation," Cam said, trying to speak carelessly and lightly.

"You could go out to dinner with him and his man, Cam."

"Well, of course I could! And in the early years of our marriage I did. We were always entertaining these business acquaintances. I'd come up from Burlingame, when Jane was a tiny baby, and meet him at the office, and we'd plan——" Cam's voice thickened suddenly, and she stopped short, looking out of the window. "But I don't play poker and I don't talk business," she presently added, "and in some funny sort of way I seemed to have just—stopped registering, with Bob."

"I think it's an absolute shame!" Elsa said warmly.

Cam spoke over her shoulder.

"Were they all talking about me when I came in?"

"Well, yes. That is, Irvington was saying that he didn't know what had changed Bob so completely, and that he couldn't understand why Bob wasn't interested in the Mardi Gras this year."

"I wonder if Bob has changed," Cam said thoughtfully.

"Some women wouldn't put up with it, Cam. I mean, never to go anywhere together any more."

"Oh, well——" Cam said. "I suppose I'm very silly to complain; there's nothing unusual in the situation. Only—only one gets so tired of apologies and excuses. Bob has a headache—Bob has an important business engagement—Bob is going to try to get in later. And yet, you know, Elsa," Cam went on, "the alternative to my going places, and being the odd woman, is simply to stay at home night after night after night. And I assure you that that house is like a tomb after nine o'clock! It's all so stupid—and so lonely!"

"That you, of all women, should have to complain of being lonely!" Elsa said in the pause.

"I've been spoiled, I suppose," Cam said; "everyone's always been so kind to me. My mother and father and brother, first. They're both dead now, and Edward's married. But for the first twenty years of my life it was as if they couldn't get enough of me. They really loved me. Perhaps nobody deserves to be loved that way, but it was so sweet! And then to come out here visiting and have big Bob Sylvester, who was the football idol that year—remember?"

"Don't ask me," said Elsa. "I was cracked about him."

Cam laughed; her voice dropped again.

"I thought he and I would always love each other," she said. And then, in a resolutely brighter tone, "And of course we *do,*" she added. "It's only a phase. He'll get over it! But I wish we were down in a country house somewhere—where his friends would come in on Sundays, where he'd be home sometimes."

"It's all a part of that rotten depression!" Elsa said.

"When I think of my beautiful bonds—that I used to go cut coupons off of—hundreds of them!"

"Life seems sort of mixed up. Well—it 'll all work out!" Cam suddenly kissed her hostess, said gratefully: "Thanks, Elsa. You always do me good," and went on her way.

CHAPTER III

SHE WALKED HOME BRISKLY in languid spring twilight; the girls would still be awake. There was no getting them quieted down in these first long warm evenings. Furs were much too warm for this weather. Cam's mind went to her old English suit; she would get it out again. She had had it three years; it dated from a flying glorious trip to London in the year before Joanna's birth; she remembered the little shop in Farm Street and the big eyes of "Miss Rose," who showed her one beautiful tweed and homespun after another. She had chosen the brown check with a blue line and a red line faintly hinted here and there. It was still smart; it was still the right thing for midseason wear, especially if she could find a hat that matched it and a brown bag, and those plain square-toed brown shoes that Joan was wearing . . .

Oh, why couldn't she think of clothes as she once had thought of them, enjoy planning her wardrobe, love to go in and out of the morning shops? Why was it so drearily hard to think of anything now, except that she was lonely? Joanna had a way of saying, "Oh, dee-dee-dee!" when she was in desperate straits, and Cam found herself saying it ruefully, too, as she walked along. "Oh, dee-dee-dee!"

Bob was stretched on the couch in her room when she got there, his small daughters rollicking about him. It was somehow extremely pleasant to find them so, and Cam kissed them all three, touching her cold cheek for an instant to the top of Bob's head, throwing aside furs and hat to drop into a low chair and take the little wrappers and the little flushed faces and the tumbled gold curls into her arms.

"Have you been taking good care of Daddy? If I'd known you were coming home early, Bob," Cam said, "I'd have been here. Headache?"

"No. I've got to go to Los Angeles tonight, and I thought I'd get here in time to pack."

"I thought you were going to fly tomorrow or Thursday?"

"Newton's going down tonight; he won't fly. And we're going to have a bull session on the train. He's got all the figures from Morris."

"That means a mean night for you."

"Oh, well, I'll see Flood tomorrow and maybe go to the races with someone. I ought to be back Sunday."

"Sunday?"

"Got to. Yacthing season opens and Greg is trying out the Zuleika. We went over to Sausalito the other day and took a look at her—I told you that. He's taking six of us out on Sunday night, all men; we may sleep on board. And you, Pinkeye," Bob said to his youngest born, who was astride him now, using a hairbrush with a tortoise-shell back as a spur, "you may never see your Daddy again, how'd you like that? Daddy may be washing about in cold green slime, with little crabs crawling over him, this time next week."

"Yittoo trabs?" Joanna asked interestedly.

"Why should little crabs crawl over you, Daddy?" Jane asked, laying aside the hinged fire screen with which at this time of day she always built herself a "housie," and coming to stand beside him. Her beautiful round blue eyes, exactly like Cam's, were fixed upon him anxiously. "I'd hit them!" she added, her little face suddenly very red.

"Here, give me that hairbrush Joanna; that's my very prize possession!" Cam said, taking it away. "You can have this one. It seems to me," she went on, at her mirror now, loosening her hair, "that you're having a rather easier time of it this spring, Bob."

"Yep, I am," he agreed, his big hands under Joanna's armpits, his chest giving the baby a ride as it rose and fell. "This trip to Los Angeles is business, of course, and one reason I'm going with Greg is because I'm pretty sure that I can sell him a slice of the Morris-Sylvester thing. In fact," Bob said, thinking it out as he talked, "that's the *only* reason I'm going. I'm not so keen on yachting, especially the way he does it. He's got this crazy Swede for a mate, and the rougher it is the better they like it. Say, go easy, woman! Don't hurt Daddy. Lord," Bob went on, tying the tassels of Joanna's wrapper above her gold curls, "I wish the days were five times as long as they are! D'you realize I'm going to be thirty-one on my next birthday, and it seems yesterday that I was a soph, and old Pop put me on the squad. That was the year the Trojans——" He fell silent, remembering, and gently jigging the baby up and down. "By gum, I'm seventeen pounds heavier than I was then!" he said suddenly. "I was on the scales at the club yesterday. I'm getting to be a fat old man."

"Fat old man, oh, fat old man!" Jane said in an undertone of deep, sophisticated amusement, as she rattled a poker in the bars of the grate.

"Jane, don't get ashes all over yourself, now. You've had your bath."

"I won't, Mummy. Mummy, why can't you eat your sponge cake if you squeege it into putty?"

"Because it's too heavy then.—Jane, put down that poker. You nearly hit Daddy in the head with it. Fix a nice housie for Joanna. I thought," Cam went on, speaking to Bob now, "that we were going to house-hunt, one of these days?"

"Were we? Did we have a date about it?" he asked, taking

the baby's warm little palms from his eyes to give his wife a surprised look.

"No, we didn't have a date, exactly. But Joan and Arthur said that they had a place in mind, and that we might leave the children with her boys and go take a look at it on Sunday."

"Well, Lord, Cam," he said, settling back again, "you go look at it. If it suits you, it 'll suit me. I've got to go to New York in August—rotten time to go—but that's when the new company gets going, and I'll be in Los Angeles a lot now that we've opened a branch down there. You pick it and I'll like it fast enough."

"I was thinking it would be rather fun if we did move back to Hillsborough to have it understood—informally, of course—that we always would have open-house supper on—say, Sunday nights. Then if we got a place with a patio——"

"Oh, Lord, you'd have the whole push coming in, and cocktails until nine o'clock, and the maids going crazy. Last time we were at Madeleine's—remember? I never did get any supper."

"Ah, well, but that was Madeleine's."

"Let's go somewhere else. Over the San Rafael way, maybe."

Cam composedly continued her dressing. The San Rafael way, indeed! She knew nobody in that direction; she would be completely alone, with two small girls digging in a sandbox and taking naps on porches. She'd talk him out of that.

But when she came back ten minutes later after escorting the small girls to the nursery, he was sound asleep on the couch. The clock said five minutes to seven.

"Bob, come down to dinner, and I'll help you pack afterward," Cam said. He started up dazedly.

"I don't want any dinner, Cam. Tell Mom. We didn't finish lunch until three o'clock. Set my alarm for eight, will you, and put something over me? Nat's coming to get me at half past eight. I'm pretty well packed, just got to—throw—a few . . ."

His voice died away drowsily. Cam spread a light rug over him and went down to dinner. Today was the anniversary of Esmé Sylvester's birth, thirty years ago; Mrs Sylvester would not come downstairs. After her solitary dinner Cam went to the older woman's room.

She knew that although her mother-in-law never would have asked her to come in, yet she was glad to see her, for she made certain little awkward gestures of friendliness, pushing a chair forward, asking Cam if the light was in her eyes.

"Bob home for dinner?"

"Not for dinner, no. He and Mr Newton left for Los Angeles a few minutes ago."

"You had your dinner alone?"

"I didn't mind. I had a book."

"Of course you minded," said the older woman in an undertone. She was knitting now; she did not look away from her needles.

"I wish you could have seen your granddaughters at the Aquarium," Cam said, determinedly cheerful. "Jane's one prayer was to be allowed to get right into the water with the baby seals."

A smile lifted the sad old face.

"What a lively little thing she is! She's like Esmé. Esmé was always so full of fun, even as a baby.—Would it help, Cam, if I talked to Bob?" his mother asked, bravely yet shyly, not stopping her knitting.

"What could you say?" Cam countered after a moment in the same embarrassed tone.

"That he is neglecting his dear, good wife."

"And would that do any good, do you think?"

"No, I'm afraid it wouldn't. That's why I haven't said anything. But there's always the chance. I'm sure—because he's so like his father—that he doesn't realize it."

"You can't talk anyone into loving," Cam murmured, as if she thought aloud.

"But of course he loves you, Cam. It's just that he's so absorbed in other things."

"Well," Cam said, looking into space with a rueful smile that was half a frown, "being absorbed in other things isn't loving, is it? A man who loves his wife *isn't* absorbed in other things; he's absorbed in her. What worries me," she went on as the other woman made no comment, "is that I know I must be the one to blame somehow. And yet I can't see just where."

"Robert," said his mother, in her sad, toneless voice, "and his father before him, aren't loving men. They don't need women. They need nurses and cooks and housekeepers at times, like everyone else, but they very quickly get over their lovemaking, and after that it's only a matter of being kind and nice to the woman who happens to be living with them."

Cam's heart sank as she listened. Sank. It was like raising a stone to make her voice speak.

"Then what is the wife, if she happens to be young and loving, to do?" she asked.

"What I did, my dear. I had my church and my books and my children. After Esmé was born—and she was the youngest of my four—I don't think my husband ever opened my bedroom door at night. He never said an unkind word to me; I could have everything else I wanted—except the one thing I wanted. I wanted—God knows how I wanted!—my husband's love, his companionship, the feeling that he wanted to tell me everything—share everything with me. I was thirty-five when Esmé was born, but it began—the gulf between us—long before that. And I loved Lawrence Sylvester as much on the day he died as on the day I married him! I lay on the bed beside him, when they told me he was dead, and put my arms about him," Jane Sylvester said, in a dreadful voice that Cam had never heard from her before, "and I said to him in my heart, 'You can't push me away now, Lawrence! Wherever you've gone you must need the woman who's been beside you for twenty-three years!' "

There was a silence. In the deeper enfolding silence of the big room and of the city beyond it, Cam felt suddenly afraid. Life could stretch long and lonely before one at twenty-seven!

She did not know what to say. Perhaps there was nothing to say. After a long time she began to talk of Jane's approaching birthday party, and Jane's grandmother, composed and interested, said that her present was going to be the little scalloped green tent. They could put it up in the playroom, next to Mabel's room, for the present, and when the family moved to the country it would be just the thing for any strip of lawn.

"I'm giving them both presents," Cam said, "because when I just give them to one there is such an uproar from the other. They are wild girls, that pair!"

She was laughing as she crossed the dimly lighted upper hall to her own room; she held tight to the rare mood of gaiety and courage; she would carry off the honors in this affair yet. It would be sheer cowardice to give in, as poor Granny had, to years of loneliness and hurt. Times had changed; women could do things now that they couldn't do thirty years ago. Bob was only a human being, like other human beings, and his affection and interest could be trapped if his wife were smart enough to trap them.

"We live in such a silly crowd," Cam reflected. "Everything's artificial; nobody's in earnest. If someone says a witty thing—like Irvington, for instance—they repeat and repeat it as if there weren't people hungry in the world, and great changes going on! We're not real, and that's why men don't need their wives any more! It's not Bob's fault, really, that he has money enough for races and poker and golf and yachts. But if he had to come home tired and hungry every night to a supper I cooked, it would all be so different!"

And she thought with a great longing how wonderful it

would be to have him love her again as he had loved her once. To have a little home together, to have him always near her, to sleep in his arms at night, ah, that would be heaven!

She was still reading, comfortable in pillows, a few nights later, when she heard him come in. Cam just of late had determined to be interested in his business affairs, to learn something about them, and if possible to make him interested in what she thought and said of them. That was one avenue of approach she had ignored; she had always felt that she could not grasp the complicated details of the stock-and-bond market. But she must leave nothing untried now.

"Is that you, Bob?" she called. "What sort of a trip?"

He came in through the bathroom, yawning, disheveled, undressing. Cam looked at him from the circle of rosy light thrown by her reading lamp. Her gold hair glittered above her serious blue eyes.

"Aren't you in bed early?"

"It's eleven. I was kind of tired."

"I took the six-o'clock plane," he said, "and had dinner at the club."

"Come in here and sit down a minute, I want to talk to you."

"Will breakfast do? I'm half asleep."

"Oh, come in, Bob, and sit down—sit down there in that chair," Cam commanded impatiently. "I never get a chance to talk to you, and I never see you alone. Here it is May, and we go to the Lake in about three weeks, and you're never at home!"

He looked at her, surprised, stooped over and began to unlace his shoes.

"Shoot," he said.

"It's this. How much are you going to be up at Tahoe this year?"

"Oh, Tahoe? Oh? Well, I'll get up whenever I can. I'll be up week ends."

"That means just never at all, Bob. You were there twice in nine weeks last year."

"Well, doesn't Blanche go up, and Joan, and Edith? Don't they all get up there sooner or later?"

"I'm talking about *you,* Bob," Cam said patiently. He laughed.

"Honey, give me two more years to lick my affairs into shape and you can have any diamond bracelet Shreve's got," he promised.

"I don't want diamond bracelets, Bob. And I don't want to drive over to visit Joan or Edith. So it means day after day with only the girls and Mabel. It's lovely, of course! It does us all good. But when I feel you're coming up there's always a kind of excitement. It's something to look forward to. Can't you understand that?"

He went away, carrying his shoes, came back after a minute tying the cord of his pajamas.

"I know how you feel, Cam," he said. "I've had to keep at it pretty hard these last years. But I'm winning out. When you go house-hunting in Burlingame, or wherever you say, next autumn, you can pick out any house you like. Just give me a couple of years——"

"And then what?" she asked, as he sat down at her dressing table and began to comb back his thick black hair with her tortoise-shell comb.

"Well, then we'll show 'em!" he said.

"Show 'em what?"

"Oh, a handsome place, and all the clothes you want, and the kids to Europe, if you say so—anything. Howard was trying to talk me into buying a boat, but I don't want a boat. Nothing but a nuisance now. But next fall, if I get Mom's affairs all straightened out—that's what's taking me to New York this trip——"

"Bob, you're not going to New York again! Why, you're just back."

"I'll only be there three days this time. I'd need a private plane if this was going to keep up. Nat and I were figuring it out in the office this morning, and I've been to New York four times in the last twelve months."

"I'd go with you, and see a play, if it weren't for Jane's tonsils," Cam observed, watching him to see the effect of this.

"Not this time, you wouldn't. No decent plays, anyway. And you hate flying."

"Then you won't be here when poor little Janey has her operation?"

"It isn't much of an operation for a kid her size, is it?"

"No. She comes home the next day. But Bert tells me she'll be a month or two picking up."

"She'll pick up all right, at the Lake."

"I wish you were going to be here, just the same. I'll hate that hospital day and the responsibility."

"Mom 'll be here." He had faced about on the dressing-table bench now; his hands were loosely locked before him; he yawned.

"Bob, why do you want to be so rich?" Cam asked suddenly.

"Well, doesn't everyone?" he countered, with a surprised and heavily sleepy glance.

"Everyone wants enough. But not to be so terribly rich—not to be cutting everyone else out—not to have to work so hard all the time. These are such good years, Bob," Cam went on, warming to her subject, and remembering some of the phrases that were sounding in her heart all day long. "It seems such a shame to waste them—to be so busy making money that we haven't time to enjoy our money! I wish we could take it a little easier."

He looked thoughtful.

"It's like a game, Cam. You size up the field, and you think you can gain here by giving a little there—solidify this and let that go. And, by George, when it begins to work out, and a few of your hunches turn out right, you get excited. It's exciting in the office; sometimes you go out to lunch feeling as if you'd been put through a wringer. And then if some feller wants to play a couple of rubbers of bridge, or you can get out and do eighteen holes, and let the wind blow it all away, why, you can't wait to get back to it the next day!"

"If I came down to the office every morning, Bob, and looked at that big blackboard with you and Nat, and read the ticker ribbons, would I understand it?"

"You wouldn't at first. You might after a while. But I don't know that it's the sort of thing that would interest a woman," he said. He got to his feet, stretched again in a yawn. "Don't you worry, Cam," he added, going toward the door, "things are coming our way. You're going to have back everything we lost and then some."

"Come here and kiss me good night," she said suddenly. He came over and knelt down beside her, and she drew a great breath of satisfaction as the black head went down on her shoulder and his arms were about her. She laid her fragrant cheek against his; her gold hair was loose on his shoulder.

"Gosh, you smell sweet, you little Danish milkmaid!" he mumbled. He dragged himself to his feet. "I'd go right off to sleep there," he said. "I've had a long day."

"Good night," she said, reopening her book.

"Good night.—Oh, and say, Cam! Will you get me out of that Golden Wedding thing at the Hunters'? I saw George Moran today, and he said they wanted me to give the toast. Well, you know me. I'm no good at that sort of thing. I said I'd let him know. But while I'm in New York you get me out of it, will you?"

"Robert Sylvester," Cam said, startled and impressive, "what are you *talking* about? Not go to the Hunters'? Your mother 'd never speak to you again if you didn't, and neither would I. This is a *Golden* Wedding! You don't get asked to many in these days. And Mrs Fenton's your godmother, and they sent Jane that magnificent English pram, and everyone's going. Don't you think for one instant," Cam went on, spacing her words emphatically, her bright blue eyes fixed upon him, "that you can get out of it. We'll all have to go, even the children. Margaret Fenton married Terry McQuaide, who was our best man, and Joan, whose mother was Lily Hunter, is about the best friend I've got, and married Arthur Howard who's *your* best friend——"

"All right, all right, all right, I'll go!" Bob interrupted her hastily. "When is the damn thing?"

"June nineteenth, the day before we go to the Lake. It's a Sunday."

"Oh, Lord, Cam, I can't go on a Sunday. No golf? I think that's the Sunday we're going down to Pebble Beach to play that course."

"Sunday or Christmas or Fourth of July, you're *going* to the Hunters'!" Cam said.

"Maybe they'll die before it comes round," Bob muttered, departing. Cam lay quite still in the pillows, in the rosy circle of light, looking thoughtfully at the door through which he had disappeared.

CHAPTER IV

THE HUNTERS had a great side garden surrounded by a stone fence and a wall of exquisitely graded shrubs. Granny and Cam and the children were a little late in arriving, and found the place well filled. There was an awning down at the end of the path with pots blazing flowers shutting off the space beneath it into a little bower of color and sweetness, and here the happy old couple stood, with daughters and sons-in-law and grandchildren all helping to receive the guests on the great day. Blooms were massed everywhere, the garden was framed in roses, the hawthorns were in wild pink-and-white bloom, and the women guests themselves looked like flowers as they drifted about in their light frocks and wide hats. Music was playing; the air was filled with laughter and voices.

On the terrace and in the tennis court scores of little square tables had been set; the luncheon was late, but by two o'clock waiters were going about with laden trays, and everyone stood to drink the health of the bride and groom. It was Arthur Howard who gave the toast; it wasn't the sort of thing Arthur could do at all, Cam thought.

"I'll never forgive Bob for this!" Arthur said.

"Ah, don't be mad at him, Arthur," Cam told him. "He

really had the most frightful cold; he would have been an idiot to come out and give it to everyone else!"

"I don't believe a word of it. I'll bet his mother tells an entirely different story."

Cam laughed, her blue eyes moving amusedly to the spot where old Mrs Sylvester, having paid her compliments to the hosts, was sitting in a little group of elderly men and women, her sad eyes moving from face to face as they talked. But under the laugh Bob's wife was conscious of despair. Bob had failed her again.

She was too much absorbed in the business of making the anniversary party a success to savor now the full strength of her anger at Bob. That could wait. Meanwhile the music played and the sun shone, flowers blazed in the light and shone richly in the shade, and the ruffles of her flowered chiffon trailed on green grass as she went to and fro. Everyone was especially nice to her, or she imagined so, and presently, she told herself, she and Mabel and Granny and the little girls would be driving home, and people would have other things to think of than that Bob Sylvester had treated Cam badly again and had not shown up at all at the Hunters' party.

"Cam, will you take him on?"

"Who?" Cam asked, pausing with a tray of tiny cakes as Joan, one of the daughters of the house, passing her, put a hand on her arm.

"Over there, with Grandfather. That's John Kilgarif—why he came we don't know, for he never goes anywhere. And what to do with him now he's here we don't know."

"The writer?"

"Oh, you know that? Well, then you're the girl for him, for I didn't know it," Joan said, "and I introduced him to a bunch of those fool girls over there and *they* didn't know it! He's very picky and choosy, and he's been bored by Grandfather long enough. Come along and be an angel."

"Why, he looks like a perfectly delightful person," Cam said reproachfully. "Here, Betsey, take these cakes and pass them round," she said to another Hunter granddaughter as she and Joan turned toward the round main table. "I've known his stuff for years," she added. "I love it! And I like his looks, too."

"Like whose looks?" said the object of the remark with a keen smile as he got to his feet.

"You've got good ears," Cam answered, smiling. "Brooks of Sheffield, it was."

"Oh? Good old Brooks!" said John Kilgarif, nodding thoughtfully.

"Mrs Sylvester, Mr Kilgarif," Joan said. "Grandfather, you've seen Cam?"

"Seen him?" Cam's blue eyes, under the light circle of a transparent pale straw hat with great blue poppies sprawled upon it, were filled with laughter. "I kissed him about seven times."

"And for what, if I may ask?" said John Kilgarif.

"For being married, and being a good boy and everything," the woman answered, shifting her blue gaze for a moment to the writer's face.

"I've been married, and I'm a good boy, and everything," he said instantly.

"Ah, well, wait until it's fifty years!" Cam smiled.

"Wait forty years?"

"I can't see any way out of it."

"At that," he said, his eyes upon her, "it might be worth it."

Other guests had come up now to greet the silver-headed old pair. Joan had gone away. Cam and John Kilgarif walked across the lawn together. Cam, who had been busily helping the young women of the family in the passing of plates and successful seating of guests, realized suddenly that she had had no lunch. It was obvious that John Kilgarif had had none, for he had just arrived.

"What about food?" she asked him.

"I'm hungry," he said. "Have you had anything to eat? I haven't. Let's sit down."

A table for two had been wedged in between a white fountain of bridalwreath and the straight wall of the box hedge. Cam seating herself there with the man opposite her, signaled a tall girl in a pink frock.

"Connie, tell someone we're starving!" she said.

Constance, showing proper concern, lingered for a moment, one of her big, brown young hands resting on the table.

"Mrs Sylvester," she said, flushing and smiling, "may I say something to you?"

Cam moved her surprised blue eyes, smiled back as she nodded.

"I think in that blue-and-brown thing that you're the most *beautiful* person I ever saw!" Constance stammered, laughing and embarrassed. "I really do. All the girls do. And another said 'Cam gets prettier every minute.' There!"

"I hope you're right!" Cam said, adding as the girl went away: "That was a nice little unsolicited tribute, wasn't it?"

The man was looking at her curiously; he seemed not to have heard her.

"You're Mrs Sylvester. What did she call you—Connie?" he asked.

"No, I called her Connie; she's Constance. Constance McQuaide. She's only fifteen—isn't she enormous?"

"But I thought she called you Con, too."

"No, Cam. Campbell. My real name is Mary Campbell. But I've always been Cam."

And they began to talk about themselves, exploring those new fields that make the beginning of any friendship fascinating.

The June sun shone on serenely; the sound of music and laughter and happy voices reached them in their leafy, scented retreat; platters of sandwiches, salads, coffee and ices arrived in due order; friends stopped on their way toward departure to have a word or two with Cam. And it was all to her like a pleasant dream, just because this man was making it so plain that he found her charming.

"Have you children, Mrs Sylvester?"

"I have two little girls."

"I have a boy of two. My wife—I don't know whether you knew that?—my wife died last year."

"Oh-h-h!" The beautiful face under the light shadow of the big hat was filled with sympathy. "Poor little fellow!" Cam said.

"He's happy enough. He's with my mother and my sister in Philadelphia. My sister's at Bryn Mawr."

"Philadelphia! Not so far from Baltimore."

"Is that home for you?"

Presently she was saying: "No, of course my husband isn't sick. I'm just telling people that to save my face—or his. He simply hates affairs like this, and he won't come. But what makes it inexcusable—what makes it absolutely criminal today," Cam went on, with a serious look, "is that these are his mother's oldest friends, and he was to have made the speech. Arthur gets an impediment, you know, when he talks in public, or gets nervous, and Doctor McQuaide isn't here. And for Bob to fail them—it's dreadful."

"A recluse, your husband?" John Kilgarif asked.

"A recluse—Bob!" She laughed. "He's not as tall as you and he weighs two hundred," she said. "He was end on the Stanford team for three years, and he's held the amateur golf championship of the state for four. He plays polo, and he won the swimming race down at Catalina year before last. Bob," said his wife, "likes everything men do. Wrestling matches and prize fights, races, poker, dominoes, dogs and so on."

"What's he do? Raise cattle?"

"He should. I think he'd like it. But as a matter of fact he's a broker."

"And what do you do while he's tearing around snatching cups?"

"I? Oh, I'm lonely," Cam said and could have bitten her tongue out for mortification at the quaver that would come into her voice and the sudden tears that were in her eyes.

"I see," John Kilgarif said thoughtfully, looking away. And for a moment there was a silence. Then, his arms locked on the table now, his eyes not leaving her own, they began to talk again. Cam had one elbow on the table, her chin resting on her palm, the delicate chiffon of her frock sleeve falling back from an arm as smooth as pale-brown ivory.

What made the talk especially thrilling was that she really did know something about the man, or about his work at least. For several years, in the lonely woman's wistful, unguided search for culture, for interests, for avenues of self-expression, she had turned toward essays and poetry; in the soberer type of magazines she had often seen John Kilgarif's name, and more than once had told herself that she liked everything he wrote. It was delightful now to be able to tell him so personally and to prove her own sincerity by being able to quote this line and refer to that article specifically.

He had come to California to have a talk with the movie people about a poem that was to be filmed. He did not know what they were going to do with it, and he did not much care, and had presently deserted Hollywood to come north to see San Francisco. There he had chanced to meet Joan McQuaide, who, as Joan Fenton, had been his sister's close school friend.

"And now I'm buying a place back of Atherton," he finished.

"Oh? In the hills?"

"Very much in the hills. I want to work there, and I believe I can coax my mother to spend some part of the year with me anyway."

"And the boy. He'll love it!"

"Even when he gets to school age he'll have his vacations here; there must be good schools near. It 'll be the very thing for him, build him up. He's a delicate little monkey at the moment. Well, look at the delphiniums coming along!"

Cam turned to look; laughed.

"Those are my daughters; they do look adorable!" she confessed, watching the progress of Jane and Joanna across the grass. Clad alike in microscopic butterfly dresses of pale blue, with blue socks on their round brown legs and blue ribbons in their shining gold hair, the little sisters were at their loveliest. They were tired now, their blue eyes shadowy, their small cheeks flushed; they tumbled themselves against their mother's knee, and she put her arms about them and rested her cheek against the blue hair ribbons.

"And did you have a nice time at the party?"

"We had oyes-cream," Jane said, in her deep voice, with a suspicious look for John Kilgarif.

"Eyth-kweem, kweem-caketh, choklit!" Joanna added. And to the man she added confidingly, "Dokker took my tonthillth out and I bleeded!"

Mabel, who had followed the children, stood respectfully near.

"Mrs Sylvester thought that maybe me and the girls and her would go on with Mrs Butler," she suggested, "since your car is here, too."

Cam, who was down on the grass between the children now, straightening ribbons and fluffing curls, looked up and met John Kilgarif's eyes. And quite suddenly, with a warm rush of feeling at her heart, she knew what he would say to her as soon as he dared. Splashes of sunlight and shade from the mighty oak overhead were over her and the little girls in the green sweetness of the garden; the three pairs of blue eyes, the blue frocks, the golden heads were close together.

She sent Jane and Joanna off with Mabel, stood watching them go, turned and sat down at the table again.

"The little Butler boys will be with them; they'll have a nicer time than if they waited for me," she said. "But it always kills me when Jane says, in that barroom voice of hers, 'Joo too, Mummy?' "

John Kilgarif cleared his throat.

"Does he know how lucky he is?" he asked.

"Bob?" she asked, laughing. But suddenly the betraying color was hot in her face. "He thinks they're very nice," she said, in a sensible voice. "You were speaking of Robinson's poetry," she said. "I must go at him again."

He looked at her so steadily that she had to meet his eyes. She laughed again.

"But you like Frost?"

"I love Frost's stuff."

"And Emily Dickinson?"

"I don't know her things at all. Is that criminal?"

"It's suicide." He took from his pocket a small black book, made a note. "I'll send you some things," he said carelessly. "Lindsay—ever read much of Lindsay?"

"The jungle stuff?"

"Well, I don't think that's one of the best. But it's all readable; it's like Kipling. You like to read it."

"Do you know this one of Kipling's—'The Way Through the Woods'?" She recited it soberly; her eyes far away. Her voice was exquisite in its hoarse softness on the last lines:

> "*. . . you will hear the beat of a horse's feet,*
> *And the swish of a skirt in the dew;*
> *Steadily cantering through*
> *The misty solitudes,*
> *As if they certainly knew*
> *The old lost road through the woods. . . .*
> *But there* is *no road through the woods!*"

The man listened until she had finished. Then he said, "My God, that is lovely! He'll live for that sort of thing when they've forgotten all about Danny Deever and Gunga Din. I've never found that one."

"Don't you read *Rewards and Fairies* to your little boy? By the way, what's his name?"

"David. We call him Taffy, but he's as dark as a Mexican. No," John Kilgarif said, "I've never read to him; he's only a baby yet. I'm stupid with children. I am blind, crazy, intoxicated, and in a fever!" he added steadily. "You know that, of course."

She glanced at him, got to her feet. The frail blue ruffles trailed on the grass. Neither man nor woman spoke again as they walked toward the tent on the far side of the lawn.

When they reached the group in the garden everyone was going home. It was five o'clock; oak shadows were long across the flowers and shrubs; the roses stood in a sort of glassy light; bees zummed by like flying bullets. Aline Chard drew Cam aside.

"Cam, is Bob Sylvester *crazy?* He was at the club playing golf today."

"Bob?" Cam echoed, her eyes blank, her color fading.

"Yes. Finished up at about three, and said he was going home to get some sleep."

"Who told you?"

"Phil Wymans. He had to go up to the club on his way over here to get Rosemary, and he saw Bob there—just leaving in his car. And Walter and some men were there playing bridge; they'd just come back from here, and they said Bob had been playing golf."

Cam looked into space through narrowed lids.

"I know how you feel," Aline said.

"I hope you don't!" Cam said, with a brief laugh. "Oh, it's not murder; it's not as if he hurt the children," she went on, in an undertone, and without meeting the other woman's eyes, "but it's so—so unkind, it's so unnecessary!"

"Don't cry, Cam. Not here."

"I'm not going to cry. But it's all so—so senseless!"

Cam went to old Mrs Hunter and kissed her again for good-by; she was caught in a little group of friends; someone said that it was to be hoped that Bob's cold would be better. "He would have come if he could, I'm sure," Cam said. "But he is working hard, and moving about so fast that he can't take care of himself. Good-by, everybody!"

"How you getting home, Cam? We're going right straight in and you can sit in Richard's lap."

"Oh, thanks, it sounds terribly tempting! But I've my car parked right down the lane."

CHAPTER V

JOHN KILGARIF was walking beside her. She wished fervently that he had not waited. She was badly shaken and not at all sure that she could conceal her feelings. But she glanced at him with what composure she could muster when he spoke to her.

"Did it matter so much, his not coming? There seemed to me to be about a thousand too many persons here as it was."

"He was expected. He was to make the speech. They love him," Cam said simply.

"And why didn't he?"

"He's grown tired of it all."

John Kilgarif spoke kindly, reasonably. His pleasant voice came like a soothing breeze across the hot desert of her thoughts.

"Well, I don't know that I can blame him. I don't often do this sort of thing myself—a big mixed luncheon with five or six hundred people at it. I wouldn't be—cross, if I were you. I can't think of anything quite so terrible as your being cross with anyone."

"Oh, it isn't that!" she said unguardedly. His quick glance met hers obliquely again.

"What is it, then?" he asked, in the unalarmed, affectionate tones of a big brother.

"Nothing. And thanks——" Cam said confusedly, reaching her car, taking the big white coat from the front seat.

"Thanks for what?" he asked.

"Why, for——" She looked straight at him, and he saw diamonds on the thick black lashes of her blue eyes. "For holding my coat," she said.

"Oh! You're very welcome. And now when do I see you again?"

"Not for ages, alas. We leave for Tahoe tomorrow. The infants and I have a cabin there."

"I don't know Tahoe at all. Where am I to send the books, then?"

"The books? I'd forgotten them. But don't *you* forget them. Send them to Bob's office—Sylvester, Morris & Company. Can you remember that?"

"I can, this way." He was writing in his little book again. "And will Bob take them up?" he asked, slipping the pencil into its strap, putting the book away again. Cam laughed. "What's funny?" the man questioned.

"The calm way you say 'Bob.' "

"Well, I'll hope to call him that, sooner or later. He goes up week ends to his three yellow-headed women, I take it?"

"When he can, he does."

"And don't worry about this—here, today, I mean," John Kilgarif said. "Those things will happen, you know."

"They shouldn't," she said gravely, buttoned into the big, white coat now, and behind the wheel. "Good-by, Mr Kilgarif, and thank you."

"Now for what?"

"For being so kind," Cam said and drove away with her heart in a glow. He *had* been kind, this stunning new man, this poet and essayist whose name she had known for so long. And how women did like men to be kind to them! Just companionable and kind; that was all they asked. It made life different, somehow, that this one man had seemed to like her and to understand her.

Very handsome, Mr John Kilgarif. Handsome in the nice way that was so close to ugliness. Jaw a little too firm, eyes a little too deepset, cheekbones a little too high, and skin burned just too brown. But stunning-looking, and perfectly dressed without the slightest hint of affectation. Easy and considerate in his manner, too, this John Kilgarif who had stepped right out of the pages of a romantic novel into the Hunters' garden. Cam congratulated herself upon being the only person at the big party who really had known anything about him. A flaming sort of person, for all his gentleness; there was fire in the brown face and in the flash of the hazel eyes. His hair was really lighter than his skin, a sort of sunburned light brown. "He's nice!" said Cam aloud, as she drove past the Airport and up the hill into the gore at Mission Street. She crossed Market, was passing the big municipal buildings before she knew it; the late afternoon was cold, with driving fog, but her coat was soft and warm, and her thoughts kept her so occupied that she hardly noticed the trip.

She had put the car away and was going into the house by the side entrance before her anger at Bob began to creep back, and she wondered what his excuses would be. Her heart sank at the thought that there might be a scene; scenes sickened and exhausted her. And yet one could not let that sort of thing go absolutely unnoticed; it was too flagrant, too unnecessary, too rude.

He was lying on his bed, reading a newspaper, when she went upstairs. Cam, quite without intending to begin in this way, suddenly found herself pouring out to him all she felt. Words ran away with her: she began to tremble and feel frightened.

He lay listening, his eyes not leaving her face, his expression changing from one of apology to one of resentment.

"Listen, I tell you I completely forgot it! I was so late at Graham's last night that I stayed in Piedmont, and this morning I had to meet Wilkins—that's the fellow who came up from Los Angeles—at the club and play off a match! It never occurred to me that this was the Hunters' day."

"Well, it *should* have occurred to you, and you had no *business* to forget it and play golf with a man you never saw before, when *everyone* was asking for you, and Doctor Carter and Arthur had to give the toasts, and everyone expected something wonderful from you! And your mother, too; do you think *she* liked explaining to everyone that you were in bed with a cold——"

She had touched him at last, and she saw it, and through all her excitement was hurt afresh that the thought of his mother's disappointment meant more to him than that of his wife. But she pursued the advantage none the less:

"In fact she wouldn't lie about it—you know that she never will—and yet she wouldn't tell people that we didn't know *where* you were last night or where you were today, and when anyone would say to her, 'Cam says Bob has a terrible cold,' she would sort of smile and say, 'Well, he was out in the rain all day Sunday!' and let it go at that. I can tell you, Bob Sylvester, that it spoiled our day! It completely spoiled our day!"

But even as she spoke she thought of the new friendship that had made this day already unique, and, her voice and manner softening in spite of her, she turned away and went into her own room.

"What difference does it make, not going to a lunch where there were five hundred people!" Bob muttered unrepentantly, as she closed the door.

Cam changed her clothes and went into the nursery, meditating upon exactly what her attitude should be at dinner. The elder Mrs Sylvester was there to share the before-bedtime hour with the little girls, and looked at Cam rather anxiously as Cam sat down, dragged Joanna into her lap and began to fit on her small, fur-edged bedroom slippers.

"No supper yet?"

"It's all there on the table, but she hurt her foot and Granny had to look at it."

"Mummy, I throwed a cracker box in the fire and it blazed!" Jane announced excitedly.

"Has Mabel gone down to her supper? Both of you go over there now and get started. Bob's home," Cam said to his mother, when the little girls were busy with cereal and milk.

The apprehensive look on the sad old face did not lessen.

"Did you see him?"

"Yes, he was lying down reading the paper."

"He was asleep when I came in." Old Jane Sylvester sighed deeply. "I don't know what *possesses* Bob," she said. "He has everything in the world to make him happy, and he acts so —strangely. Well, it's just the way men are, I suppose."

"I hate to go away tomorrow cross with him," Cam said, steeling herself against weakening into kindness, "but I do think he behaved abominably, and there's no use my pretending that I like it! He said just now, 'What difference does it make, not going to a lunch where there were five hundred people?' Well, it *does* make a difference, it makes a great difference, and I'm deeply angry with him, and I don't care if he knows it!"

In answer the other woman only sighed heavily again. Cam, with a sudden rush of pity for her, went over to kneel for a second beside her chair, her arms about her.

"Don't worry, Granny. It's only Bob's way, you know. He's like that, and I suppose I'll have to get used to it! I'll be decent to him at dinner."

"I don't think he's going to be here for dinner," the older woman said. Cam's face wore an odd expression for a moment, then without comment she went out of the room.

In her room trunks were open and half packed; she heard Bob moving about in his room as she went to and fro. She was standing with the cobwebby orchid softness of a dressing gown in her hands fifteen minutes later when he came to her door, looking his handsome best in impeccable dinner clothes.

"Don't be cross with me, Cam," he said; "what are the old Hunters to us? I don't ask Arthur and Joan to go to parties at my grandmother's, do I? What's the difference? I'm sorry if I threw you and Mom down, and I'm darned sorry that I've got to go to this Jinks Committee meeting tonight. I'd have gotten out of it if it hadn't been for Reg. Be a sport about this, Cam, and don't go away tomorrow mad at me."

"It's only one more thing, after all," she said, in a tired, cold voice. "You'll be here in the morning to see us off, I suppose?"

"Oh, sure. I'll be home early tonight." He came to her, and she raised a cool unresponsive cheek for his brief kiss. "Don't be mad at me," he said again, in a little boy's tones.

"I'm not *mad* at you." His use of the childish phrase offended her. After all, she and Bob were not children. "It's simply that I never seem to know where to find you these days," she said wearily. But he didn't need this; he was not listening.

"You're a swell little sport!" he said. "I'm going in to make the peace with Mom." And he was gone.

But somehow her heart felt quieter at dinner, and afterward, when she was in bed and reading, it was pleasant to review the events of the lovely summer day, to think complacently of the blue frock and the wide frail hat, to remember the moment when Joan had turned over to her the square-shouldered, handsome tall man in the brown tweeds.

The little table by the hedge—that had been fun! Fun to talk of Patmore and Kipling and Frost with someone who was as interested as oneself. Wonderful to meet anyone who could be so friendly and interesting and—yes, obviously admiring, at such short notice! Cam went off to sleep planning other talks with John Kilgarif; talks in which he said just the right things and she made the right replies. All life, she thought, took on new color with a new friend.

CHAPTER VI

Bob, repentant, and at his nicest, saw them off the following morning. The long day's trip to the Lake would be taken in Mrs Sylvester's big car, driven by the children's adored old Fred. Mabel, elated and all but useless in her excitement, got into the front seat with Joanna in her lap. Joanna and Jane were to take their naps like good girls in a nest of rugs and pillows on the back seat, when the time came; meanwhile Jane shared the seat with her mother. Crackers and a thermos bottle of cool water were duly prepared in advance, coats were to remain buttoned until they reached the first moment of warmth on the other side of the bay, and finally the party started, with good-by kisses for Granny. Granny was to have a week of peace and quiet at home before going down to the warmer airs of Palo Alto, where she and a few old friends would be comfortably housed in a girls' school during the summer. May would follow to the Lake by train in a day or two and be Cam's cook for the summer.

Cam loved the Lake and always found it good to reach it, especially now, when the girls were reaching ages to remember it from season to season, and love it, too. Jane distinctly recalled falling into it, and her red bathing suit, and the boy who had the nosebleed, and Joanna shrieked with joy when first she saw the water. They were all tired and dirty when at five o'clock they finally walked stiffly into the little cabin under the great red shafts of the pines that were blood red in clear sunset light, but Mrs Lusky, the owner, had gotten everything clean and sweet, had made up the beds and had a good wood fire in the tiny stove.

In no time at all Joanna and Jane were out on the rocks in Mabel's charge, not too tired to shout in ecstasy at the rippling clear green waters that lapped all day long within a few feet of the door, and the jays that were flying home, and the pipers whose pink feet hemstitched the little strip of wet strand. Cam scrambled eggs and sliced bread, going to bed after supper as soon as the children did, with only one look for the rising moon and the faint shadows of the pines and the metallic ripples gleaming far out on the Lake.

Lazy days followed. Sometimes she played bridge or rode with women from the hotel a mile away; once there was an evening picnic at the Fords', on the other side of the Lake. She could always go to the Fords' or the Fieldings' to see who had come up for the week end, and hear the gossip, drink cocktails, and eat marvelous summer meals.

But she rarely did. It was pleasanter to idle away the time with agreeable little English Mrs Scott, whose cottage was near by and let the girls paddle and dig with the three small blond curly-headed Scott boys for companions. Mrs Scott's husband was in distant Brazil, in the export and import business.

"On account of my having had such a frightful time getting Terence through his second year in Pernambuco, I came home before Lloyd was born, to Victoria," the little Englishwoman said. "Then when everything was arranged for our going out to poor Evelyn last March, little Miles here must get whooping cough. But now they're all quite fit, and we shall be off directly Evelyn can arrange passage for us. I shall take Nurse, and go second—it's quite as nice as first class and quite a bit cheaper!" Irene Scott ended cheerfully.

She had had less than four years of her husband's company in the nine years of her marriage, Cam discovered.

"It's dreadful, isn't it? Evelyn and I had to wait seven years to get married, too," she told Cam. "It was that after-the-war time, everyone so poor, and jobs so frightfully scarce. Evelyn went away, and I lived with Grandmother in London, and pretty dull years they were for me, too. I'd four sisters, all unmarried, and we'd really nothing to expect. And then Constance and Marigold married quite suddenly, and both came to Victoria to live, and Margery and I came along. Now Margery's married, too, so it's all turned out quite well, hasn't it? But I was thirty-four when Miles was born, and it went very hard with me. Evelyn had to leave me in England for a year with the baby, and then came all the worry about Terence. However, we hope everything's all right now! One can't have everything, can one? I mean one can't have both babies and husband and old friends."

"You really think one can't?" Cam asked, struck by the other's cheery philosophy and common sense.

"Well,"—Irene Scott gave an eloquent shrug—"one must sacrifice the old friends first of all," she said with a laugh. "Men do act so stupidly about *that*—about being dragged places and made to be polite! Then when the children come along, that's a problem, too. If I'd not had any I'd have been with Evelyn all these years, and of course it would have been easier. We've never had a penny to spare, what with doctors and trips and the expenses of kiddies. Worth it, of course, especially as there aren't any boys in Evelyn's family, and there's an uncle in Carnarvonshire. But," she ended with a laugh, "Miles put it very well the other day when he said, 'We do quite use up your life, don't we, Mummy?' "

Cam looked at her thoughtfully, looked away at the water. The two women had brought a basket of sandwiches and the old chocolate pot down to the very edge of the Lake and were meditating presently the exertion necessary to a beach supper. The five children, digging, shouting, panting as they dragged driftwoods and stones to and fro, were half in and half out of the water.

Before them the Lake stretched a placid wide sheet of blue to the rising tiers of the dark pines on the Nevada shore. Back of them the great trees rose gaunt and red in the last crystal light of the lingering summer day. Birds whizzed in short flights from bush to bush; from the little summer cottages scattered among the mighty boulders thin spirals of smoke rose against the sunset sky; white figures wandered on the trails through the woods between the tremendous shafts of the tall pines. Children, far down the Lake near the hotel, were shouting and splashing in a last ecstasy of swimming.

A man was coming across the rocks to the Sylvester cottage; just one more tall man in white, picking his steps. Cam watched him idly. In a minute he would say "Venables?" and she would say, "No, next house to the pink one, around the bend. . . . You're very welcome!"

She did not look up until he was quite close. But when she did her face changed to an expression of amazement, and she got to her feet.

"Mr Kilgarif! What fun! I didn't know you were anywhere in the neighborhood."

"I didn't get here until about three." He was introduced, sat down easily with his back against a great rock and sighed in complete content. "I see the delphiniums have picked up some gents as blonde as themselves," he said.

"Mrs Scott's property," Cam explained.

"Aren't they nice?" the man said. "Brown little boys and girls with yellow hair. That's the way they all ought to be."

"Mine are just as homely as the Sylvester girls are pretty," said Irene Scott, "But they're good boys, and strong, and that's all that matters."

"Nobody ought to have children as pretty as Mrs Sylvester's children," John said, in his pleasant way. Cam had forgotten, in these three weeks since the garden luncheon, just how pleasant it was. Her heart was suddenly light because he was here; life took on values.

"We're having a picnic," she said, as he glanced at the pans and basket.

"Oh?" he said, approvingly. "Am I staying?"

"If you want to," both women said, laughing.

"If I want to!"

"It's only sandwiches and chocolate. But we'll ask May to make you a cup of coffee and bring down some bacon."

They sat on, talking, comfortable. The children splashed and chattered; the blue sweet water lapped gently on the rocks. Mabel and May came down with reinforcements of food; went back to the house again. Irene went to the shore to examine a bite on Lloyd's brown hard little cheek.

"What brings you here?" Cam said to her companion then.

He did not answer audibly, and she raised her eyes to look at him in surprise. The query had been commonplace enough. But the look in his face brought the hot color suddenly to hers, and she laughed on a shaken note that had pleasure and panic in it at once. Just a long thoughtful look, but Cam was to remember it all her life.

CHAPTER VII

JOHN KILGARIF stayed three days at the Lake and then departed to meet his mother and his little boy, coming West from Philadelphia. They were to take immediate possession of their new home, which was really an old home, in the quiet hills behind Atherton. Cam promised that when she and the children came back to town in early September she would make her first call on Mrs Kilgarif and meet Taffy.

Meanwhile she and John had their three days at the Lake.

He was staying at the little hotel two miles away. It was a quiet place, patronized principally by mothers, nurses and children, and enlivened only on Saturday nights and Sunday nights with dances and movies. On the five week nights it went dark at about ten o'clock, when the women finished a second rubber of bridge. Cam walked over in soft twilight to dine there on the second night. She and John presently walked back to her cottage, and the two miles might have been so many yards for anything either felt of fatigue. There was a July moon high in the clear dark blue sky; there were stars. Cam looked up at them and at the glimmer of moonshine in the Lake, and something of their pulsing light got into her eyes.

Life did pulse and throb with John there. But it was not

anything that he said or did that worked the miracle. He spoke very little, and they were almost always with the children, he and she, and with Irene Scott and the maids. They sat on Cam's steps above the water, on all three nights, and talked for a little while when all the rest of the world was in bed, but it was not lovers' talk, though it trembled near it again and again, and was broken by those silences that only lovers know.

They talked of their childhoods, nurses and stories and schools they had liked and hated, and of books and plays and places. London both loved; both had chanced to have more than one happy holiday in Connecticut. John detested Palm Beach; Cam had never been there. She spoke of Hawaii; she had gone there for her honeymoon.

"I always knew I would detest the place!" John said at this, and they both laughed.

Some time between the quarter- and half-hour after eleven he would get to his feet and make her a little bow, standing straight and tall in the moonlight.

"Good night, my dear!"

"Good night, John!" And before the echoes of his footsteps had died away among the rocks she would have mounted to the porch, the dim red light from the little sitting room silhouetting her slender figure among the other shadows.

"Breakfast?" he would call back.

"Any time! Nine-ish."

"Nine-ish!"

And that meant that the next morning, at about nine, he would come strolling onto her rocky little terrace, perhaps with the children trailing him, to find Cam lovely in linen shorts with a white hat on her gold hair. After that it was all so simple, laughing over coffee, laughing at the children, parting to get into bathing suits, and laughing again as they climbed in their rope-tied cork slippers down among the rocks. Irene would come wandering down her own steps, guiding the staggering Lloyd; the blue water was always waiting, always quivering with sapphire light above the clean white sand. It was shallow here, but before they reached the sunbathed rocks two hundred yards from shore Cam and John would be swimming in fifteen feet of crystal.

Here they could lie and look down at the bottom, where clean seaweeds waved against rocks, and tiny schools of minnows jerked to and fro. Cam would stretch her splendid young body gratefully in the sun; Tahoe waters were always cold. She loved to feel them streaming away from her, to smooth the hot rock with her bare hands and warm her palms against it.

He loved her as no man had ever loved her before, as she had not thought any man ever loved a woman any more. It shone out of every casual word he said, out of every look he gave her. He came as early as he could every morning and did not go home until late at night, and in all that time there was not a thought of his that was not of her and for her. When she talked of the opera, or of dances or dinners to come in the next winter, he merely asked if she was going to be there. When she said that unfortunately she must go and have supper at Madeleine Deems's, he said quite simply that he would go, too; he would telephone Mrs Deems and say that he knew her husband and would like very much to be included in the invitation so that he could bring Mrs Sylvester home.

And go he did, behaving so charmingly, dividing his attentions so agreeably between all the women that everyone wanted to see more of him; he was asked to a great many lunches and dinners instantly. But he declined them all. He might have to go back to the city the next day.

He never offended; she never had the sense of keeping him at bay. But Cam knew, when she stretched her brown firm hand for his so that he might help her negotiate a difficult passage across the rocks, what the touch meant to him. She knew that her shapeless old white hat, her sandy beach shoes, the expressions she used when she was discussing meals with May, were sacred to him, and that tones of her voice had power to make him tremble. It was delicious after the lonely years, it was intoxicating to feel her power!

"Tomorrow's your last day," she mourned on their final evening together. "Oh, dear!"

"How polite you are! How terribly kind you are!" John said.

"Polite? Can you possibly think that I haven't enjoyed every minute of this?"

He was lying in the sand, scratching furrows with a bit of velvet-soft driftwood. Her knee was only a few inches from his gravely averted face.

"I wish I might think you had."

"You must think I'm a wonderful actress."

"I think you're a wonderful everything. However, that's neither here nor there." The late afternoon was sultry and dull; it had been a sticky day of unbearable heat, but Cam had hardly noticed it. When the children had all been taking naps after luncheon she and John had gone for a long ride, following the winding piny roads under the great trees, and had come back for another plunge into the rather quiet and lifeless water; now they were lazily watching storm clouds pile up in the south and shadows darken over the Lake, and deciding every moment that before the first drops fell they must join the children indoors.

"These have been happy days, my dear."

"Haven't they been? They've done me good, John. I feel better for them—younger, somehow."

"You're not so very old, you know."

"Not so very, no. But I'd been feeling so—groovy."

"There's the lightning. We'd better move."

He gave her his hand; she stumbled against him a little as she got her footing on the rocks. The sky above them was electric blue now; little gusts of wind smote sullenly on the leaden surface of the Lake; thunder smashed about them like the gigantic crashing of wooden boxes. Cam laughed in excitement; still holding John's hand, turning back to show him blown golden hair and flashing white teeth, as they mounted to the house.

"I love it!" she called.

"You—Valkyrie!" he shouted back.

Then they were crossing the porch, he had torn the door open and Cam slipped inside, and they were laughing at the amazed children. The little Scott boys had been rushed home just before the storm; Irene's mother had come down to be with her, and M'ma, she said, didn't like thunder.

Jane, Joanna, Cam and John clustered at the window and watched the tempest race across the Lake, and turn the world dark, and beat the water into foam. Lightning split the clouds. "Oo-oo, that was a terror!" Mabel and May, at the other window, said with ecstatic shudders at every jagged thrust. They would all wait a moment, expectant, and then the punctual roar of the thunder would be located, and crack upon crack shatter the ominous silence of the darkness without.

"Come, it's not so bad now, the children must have their suppers," Cam said. "Get them some bread and milk, Mabel, and I'll sponge them off." John waited, smoking, by the wood fire, until she led the small nightgowned pair forth; he watched her tie on bibs and superintend the meal. The lightning was infrequent now; the thunder had rumbled far away, but the whole outside world was caught in the fresh rush of the rain. It beat upon the roof of the cabin; they could hear it splashing and gurgling about the shutters and dripping from the trees.

Presently the children were in bed, and May was bringing in cold chicken and a hot Spanish dish made of tomatoes and corn, and the wooden bowl of salad. Cam and John dined close to the wood fire, almost in silence as far as words were concerned, but with the sleepy crackle of wood and the constant steady fall of the rain for accompaniment.

"Mrs Sylvester, shall we fix Mr Sylvester's room for Mr

Kilgarif?" Mabel asked, when the girls had taken away everything but the coffee and fruit, and Cam had dismissed them for the night.

"No, I think this will clear. It's stopping now."

"Then is that all?"

"That's all, thanks, Mabel. You girls aren't nervous?"

"No, ma'am. We like it!" Mabel and May retired on a series of titters; clashing and rattling of plates and pots in the kitchen was heard for a little while. Then there was complete silence.

Cam sat back in her chair, the little coffee cup in her hands. John was sitting deep in a low wide chair opposite her, his arms crossed on his breast, his long legs stretched out and crossed, his head resting back against his chair, and his half-closed eyes fixed upon her.

"This is one of the hours that come once in a lifetime."

"Somehow the storm seems to end your visit on a good dramatic note, John. This *is* lovely," Cam conceded, looking at the fire.

"They've been intoxicating days. And it would have been fun to be under the same roof with you tonight. I know, I know, I know!" John added hastily, as she moved her eyes toward him. "But I say it would have been pleasant."

"You'll not be over for breakfast?"

"No. The plane leaves at eight. I'll look down at you."

He was silent for a long time, and Cam was silent, too. It was a peaceful silence; she felt no need to talk. She was thinking that she would miss him, and wondering if he might be thinking that he would miss her, too.

"And when does Bob come up?" John asked suddenly, out of revery.

"Not this coming week end, but the one after it, if he can."

"If he can!" the man echoed, under his breath.

"Why do you say that?"

"Because—— No reason."

Again there was silence, while the thunder muttered

farther and farther away, and the tapping and gurgling of the rain grew less. The plain little cabin room was charmingly fresh and simple in design and finish; there were open redwood rafters overhead; the fireplace had been built of great rounded rocks from the near-by shore. Cam herself had chosen the red-checked tea-towel curtains, and she and Bob, in earlier days, had together painted the chairs and tables lacquer red. Bob! He seemed as much out of it now as a person in a long-ago dream. A clock somewhere unseen struck a long number.

"Well, I've got to go!" John said, getting up. Cam stirred herself from a dream, crossed the low-roofed room and opened a closet door.

"There must be some old coat of Bob's here."

She came back with two garments displayed in her hands.

"Here's a sweater, John, and this frightful old Burberry. But it doesn't matter, if it keeps you dry."

He slipped his long arms into the stiff old thin brown coat.

"It's perfect. It isn't raining now, anyway—it's just the branches dripping. Good night, my dear."

She walked out to the porch with him, and they looked into the darkness together, trying to distinguish the surface of the Lake and the pines across the water. Everything was a black pit, except where the dim light of the room sparkled on wet leaves and dripping eaves. Clouds were moving in great masses of blackness on the blackness overhead; somewhere the moon was struggling to break through; the rainstorm was over.

The man and woman stood for a long minute, watching, breathing the freshened ether of the air, not speaking. Then John caught at her hand and pressed it against his lips, and immediately turned and went up across the rocks and between the tufty young pines, and was gone. Cam stood quite still for a long while. Then she lifted her hand and laid it against her cheek.

CHAPTER VIII

After that, for a few days, time seemed to drag heavily, and the days were duller than she could bear. John's voice, his presence everywhere were continually escaping her; every ring at the telephone, every clink of an unexpected foot on the rocks might have been he, and never was! Certain places along the shore, where they had sat talking, watching the children, basking in the shade, were sacred to him; one certain rock, where he and she had rested after a long swim, staring down through the clear water, feeling the good sun bake their wet shoulders, seemed to have moved away to the center of the Lake again; she could not believe that she ever had reached it.

Life went flat. There was no more thrill to racing for bathing suits and towels, no more laughter at the children, no more poetry in the moonlight, or joy in her own tingling young health. She was simply a broker's young wife, up at the Lake with her little girls, idling the weeks away until autumn should bring the world back to town.

Then Bob arrived, and all the memories and dreams of John were scattered and destroyed. Bob always demoralized the little household of women; it was not that he took it for granted that Cam and the little girls and the maids should instantly readjust their schedule for his comfort; she knew that he never thought of their side of it at all.

He was there two days and two nights; flying up on Friday and flying back to town again on Sunday afternoon. Two men friends of his had recently arrived at the hotel, it appeared, and they immediately came to call, backing a smart cream-colored roadster over Cam's carefully reared bed of gilly-flowers and awakening Joanna, roaring, hot and cross, from her nap. They swam violently, as men swim, charging across the blue water to the rock, shouting and dripping there for a few minutes, tearing in again, and lying for an hour afterward on the little strip of strand, with sand on their hairy dark bodies and in their wet hair.

Afterward there was a long cocktail session on the porch terrace. Joanna and Jane came forth, clad in snug white sun suits, and were regaled upon chocolates from a tremendous box that Bob had brought. Cam had already decided that the box should be given to the Buckner children who brought the milk every night. Candy only upset Joanna and Jane, made their skins feel tight and hot and their mouths furry.

"Bob, not just before their dinner, *please.*"

"It won't hurt 'em once in a while, and they don't see their Daddy very often! Lord, they're nice and brown, Cam."

"All I'm giving you men is stew and biscuits for dinner, and I think there's a watermelon."

"Oh, listen," Bob said, "we're all going to Reno for dinner at the swellest place you ever saw—Rod says it is, anyway. What's the name, Rod? 'The County Jail.' That's it. Steaks and beer and spittoons and sawdust, eh, Rod?"

"Not quite so bad," Rodney Fairchild said deprecatingly, with a smile for Cam. "But it is awfully good food and afterward we're going to play 'borli-borli.' "

"Madeleine's going and she's got a girl friend; they came back to the inn for the week end," Bob said. "They were on the plane."

"Bob, I hate roulette!"

"This isn't roulette. It's lotto, really, just good old-fashioned lotto."

"Just a simple nursery game at which you lose your shirt every hour on the hour," Ned Quinlan said in explanation.

Cam laughed. And after a while, when the girls were rushing about in the usual bedtime excitement, she got herself into an appropriate frock of pale blue linen, with a small linen hat to match it, and a white coat. Her long wrinkled gloves, her blue-and-white bag, final instructions as to fire or attack to May and Mabel, and she joined the men and was wedged into the cream-colored roadster.

At the hotel they all moved into a larger car; it was six o'clock now; they had seventy miles to go. Madeleine Deems, a handsome woman with a square stocky figure, the voice of a bartender, and the reputation of a good sport, was accompanied by gentle Ethel Moorehead, unmarried, poor, grateful. Madeleine was always being tremendously generous to someone like Ethel. Ethel made the men laugh by saying that she'd never seen a roulette wheel and just knew she'd win, because you always were lucky at a thing when you didn't know anything about it.

Cam had never been to Reno. She looked with keen interest at the boiling little Western city with the walled river charging so freshly and noisily through its very heart. The streets were gay at eight o'clock, but the men and women in the throngs that went to and fro tirelessly seemed to her all to wear the same expression—a hard, nervous, feverish look of dissatisfaction.

In the smart cocktail bar where the party waited for their especial dinner to be made ready at "The County Jail," several groups of quite beautiful women, most of them in the mid-thirties or a little younger, were scattered about, attended by young men of the Adonis type, college graduates, stunning great fellows in their early twenties, who went from table to table and were affectionately greeted, who drank temperately enough but never paid the checks.

The women's jeweled hands, with their nails polished into blood-red talons, reached for these; and the costly bags were opened, and the rolls of bills came out.

"Bob, how magnificent this bar is!"

"There are fifty like this one up here."

"And that's roulette, down there at the end of the room, isn't it?"

"Yep. Tables everywhere. This is a wide-open town, you know."

An exquisite little girl of perhaps seven was sitting next to one of the handsomest of the young women. She was evidently tired; her rich, soft red curls were resting against her mother's shoulder. When the mother lighted a cigarette or raised her cocktail glass the child's little head was disturbed. Once Cam heard her say, "When's Dad coming, Mother?"

"Come on," said Madeleine, in her hoarse deep voice. "Let's try three spins."

They went down to the roulette table. Madeleine put a hundred-dollar bill on a column; as soon as the ball stopped rolling the croupier laid two more on top of it. Madeleine laughed, and under the envious eyes of two stout, nervous, jeweled women who were the only other players at the table at the moment, folded the bills and put them into her bag. At that moment a little boy in dirty shirtsleeves, with a spotted apron tied high under his armpits, tugged at Bob's arm.

"Mr Sylvester, sir? Dinner's ready, sir. Right around the corner to your left and across the alley."

"Oh, all right! Wait a minute." Bob fished out a big hard silver dollar and put it into the messenger's hand. He and Rod had each gingerly placed a quarter on the double zero; they assured the croupier that now they wouldn't be able to buy their girl friends any dessert after dinner.

"We get you all, sooner or later, sir," the croupier said, raking in the chips that the stout women had so carefully placed on this number and that.

"Are they all crooked, Bob?" Cam asked, as they walked

up a dark little alley toward a hanging boxed light of red glass. On the glass, dimly etched, was the one word "Jail."

"They don't have to be crooked!" Bob said, with a laugh.

On a dirty wooden table, whose furnishing of spoon holder, catsup bottle, pepper and salt shakers was all equally sticky and spattered, they had incomparable steaks, a small thick steak apiece, with a bone in it, and a border of crisped blackened fat. Cam had to concede that she never had tasted anything so luscious; the accompaniment of plain salad, toasted French bread, sour, and dripping with hot butter, and plain red wine, was perfect, too. "The County Jail" never served anything else; seats at the grimy table were in demand from New Year's to Christmas and all the days between.

After the meal the men sat back, sipping clear hot coffee, tired, happy, lazy. They smoked, and the women idly smeared cheese back and forth on their plates. The talk turned on duck hunting; Bob had a membership in one of the best clubs; some old man's membership was for sale; Bob would have liked Rodney Fairchild to buy it.

Then suddenly everything was disrupted again. The check was paid in a wild rush, coats were hurried on, and they were all out in the street, walking briskly past one gambling hall after another. Bingo and Ringo and Reno and Kongo all were games; games played in long rooms open to the streets like shops; games into which players drifted and from which they drifted away in an unending eddy.

Long ovals of narrow tables filled these places almost to the walls; about them were the seats: revolving chairs with padded backs. In the center was the mechanism, whatever it might be, that decided the winner. Cam saw the old-fashioned game of ball rolling, saw marble games and baseball games and football games, and the players, men and women, crowding in, were paying out their dollars and half-dollars for the privilege of sitting in every one.

Roulette was on all sides. In the "borli-borli" hall where Bob finally brought his party to a halt there were two roulette tables, and there were a dozen other games beside the one that gave the place its name.

"Borli-borli" was merely a glorified lotto, the old Italian game of tombola. The numbers in this case were cut deep into small balls of clean white wood; they were mixed in a round cage of wires; Cam studied the hard and haggard and stupid and undeveloped faces that looked from the numbered cards to the whirling balls, watched the expressions in the eyes of these men and women as the "mixer" clicked the mechanism that dropped a ball into a pan of white sand just under the machine. Where did they all come from, she wondered, and where did they get the money they were spending? Many looked poor, desperate indeed, and yet the game went on and on, and the bright big dollars for the thumbed, thick old lotto cards were always forthcoming.

"This is a very swanky game. There are lots of fifty-cent ones, and some quarter ones," Rodney told her. Cam had duly bought her card with the rest; she had taken her seat on one of the padded stools that ringed the long counter. A hundred and forty persons were playing; that meant that the winner would get ninety-eight dollars. The house took thirty per cent; modest enough it sounded. But the games went fast, the adjustments between the games were transacted with incredible rapidity; before she knew it Cam had played ten games, and got up to wander about to see what else was interesting in the place. Ten games in thirty-two minutes; yes, she could see that the management was not exactly losing money on "borli-borli."

"Six-*teen!*" shouted the mixer; "number one—seventy-six!" The players, their hands full of large red beans, moved their eyes anxiously over their cards. They checked nervously whenever any delay gave them a moment's opportunity. Beans were laid tenderly on such numbers as came up: as these were called a great glass chart hanging in the center of the room recorded them.

Cam watched another game or two. There was one very

simple game of which the base was five cards, set under glass. They were the ace, king, queen, jack and ten of spades. Cam could not understand what was going on, for the crowd about the table was three deep, and the dollars were flying fast. She rather shyly tried another game, and won three separate times, and felt all the gambler's satisfaction.

In this game the croupier merely dealt four cards, any four cards in a row. The players could play each row high or low as he chose. If the cards were high he might put up as much money as he liked that the cards presently to be turned would be lower than the one already shown in that suit. Or he might bet that the cards would be low. Sometimes he was nonsuited. Sometimes a card as high as a queen would be played high, only to be topped with king or ace. Gasps of excitement went up from the rather limited group that was playing this game, as fortune wavered to and fro.

Each player placed some token of his own upon the money he wagered, so that there would be no confusion as to paying off. Cam put her enameled cigarette case on the dollars she put down; it was fun to have the croupier lift it and the wager and the payment back into her hand. A win paid three dollars for one.

"Bob," she said, weaving her way through the milling crowd to his side. "I won! I won twenty-four dollars!"

"Good for you, honey. You and your luck stay right beside me here, I need you!" Bob said. He was playing roulette, as was Madeleine. The other three were still absorbed in "borli-borli." Madeleine had been to Reno for a six-months' stay some years earlier, when her divorce from Pemberton Gerrard was under consideration; she knew the ropes. She was playing hard, with keen concentration; her handsome dark eyes shooting from the green cloth with its heaped and scattered chips to the revolving bowl in which the little ivory ball spun and sang and was silent, sang and spun and was silent again.

"Hell!" she muttered good-naturedly now and then. Once

she put a heavy hand, glittering with gems, over a little column of chips. "Mine," she said.

The croupier, dispassionately drawing them toward him with his rake, raised indifferent eyebrows, nodded. She might have those few dollars; there would be no dispute.

"Yours were on the red," a pimpled, thin young man said to Madeleine casually.

"I played both!" she answered quickly, with a glance for the croupier. "Did you notice, Cam?" she asked.

"I didn't."

"I played red, and then I had this little heap and shoved it onto the black," Madeleine said. No one seemed interested now, and with a rather flushed face she began to drop chips here and there on the numbers. Cam quite suddenly and rather shyly put half her winnings on "Odd." They were instantly lost, just as she was beginning to think it would be rather fun if they won. She was more particular playing the columns now, trying the zero. When all her money was gone, she gave up her chair, for at midnight the place was packed, and began to wander about, looking at the faces that showed pale and wet with perspiration in the thick air. Smoke moved in blue drifts through the room; there was little noise, except for the rattle of chips and the click of the flying balls. Bob was more absorbed than ever; Cam satisfied herself with watching, now and then putting a silver dollar on this table or that. Twice she won her money back, doubled, on the columns, and had an odd sense of gain. Roulette could be rather fun! She had lost only twenty-two dollars on the evening, after having bet at least four times that, and by the strange psychology of the gaming tables, she felt that she had won.

Presently the crowd began to thin, and on one or two tables the men stretched oilcloth coverings. Cam gravitated to the corner where play was still going on, and found Bob winning, and Madeleine apparently a winner, too, for there was a little colonnade of neatly stacked chips before her. A man who had leather money cases strapped to his belt came and spoke to Bob, and Bob glanced at Madeleine and laughed.

"No, sir," he said good-humoredly to the man, "Mrs Deems pays her own bills! What's the big idea," he added to Madeleine, "roping me in on this?"

"There's nothing the matter with my check," Madeleine said heavily, in an amused voice.

"I thought since the gentleman was a friend——" the man began. Cam's eyes widened; Madeleine evidently hadn't been winning, then? She had written a check!

It became painfully evident after a moment that Madeleine was indeed losing at a good stiff rate. She gave a short angry laugh as the stubborn numbers evaded her; when eleven came up she had a stack of chips on each of the eight numbers surrounding it. A column bet succeeded, and she muttered a word of satisfaction, but on the next turn, when by some oversight she had not put the usual twenty on number three, three came up, and the watching crowd groaned in sympathy.

"No luck!" Madeleine said in disgust.

"Better quit," Bob said. He was playing along lightly beside her, dragging his winnings in carelessly with his big brown hand.

"*Now?*" she said, with a brief scornful laugh.

Few others were playing, but from the thin fringe of watchers a man or a woman would occasionally lean forward and venture a bet in currency. When they won the croupier always paid in exactly the same money; one by one they stopped, and Madeleine was playing alone.

She gave the croupier a fevered glance.

"How late can I play?"

"As late as you like."

CHAPTER IX

FOR THE FEW HOURS that were left that night Cam lay wakeful thinking about—indeed, haunted by—the wretched scene. The players had one by one gone away; she and Madeleine and Ethel and the three men had stayed on. Ethel had looked exhausted and frightened; the men had been embarrassed and uncomfortable.

They had not gone back to Tahoe, when at last they were all out in the cool dark street. Reno had been very quiet in the early-morning hours; the party had gone to a hotel, where Bob had registered for them all, and where the women had pretended to laugh at the cotton pajamas, toothbrushes, combs and Japanese slippers that, for a dollar and a half, could be bought, neatly wrapped in glazed paper, in just such emergencies.

But no one had been very much amused. Madeleine had talked more than the others. She had said that she could easily raise any amount of money on her watch and rings. They were worth thousands.

"How much was it all together, Bob?" Cam had asked cautiously, when he and she were alone in their rooms.

"Something over seventeen grand, the poor sap! She was up to twenty-two once," Bob had said, yawning.

"Where 'll she get it, Bob? Has she anything but her alimony?"

"I don't know where she'll get it."

"You wouldn't back her check?"

"I would not. I've got two checks of Madeleine's now, marked 'no funds.' She owes me about six hundred; she knew damn well why I wouldn't back her! Lord, I'm dead!"

Their rooms adjoined. Bob had tumbled into bed, just as dawn had been breaking, leaving the connecting door open. But he had been instantly snoring so deeply and loudly that Cam had gotten up and quietly closed it. Afterward she had lain awake, still breathing the hot, smoky, smelly air of the gambling palace, smelling the stale drinks, seeing the pale, tense faces. Even men who could well afford it and who were lucky, like Bob, wore strange expressions when they were playing roulette. And the others—the ones whose chips were melting away, melting away—were sickening to see!

It was six o'clock when at last she fell asleep. But she slept late. The party straggled downstairs to a midday breakfast and lunch at one. Cam's head felt heavy; she wanted to escape to the children and the clean green water. Madeleine, who had telephoned her insurance man and had had a low-voiced conference with the three men, wanted to play again. She said she felt lucky.

"Suppose we each back you for a hundred, Mad," said Rodney Fairchild, who was extremely wealthy. "Start off with three hundred and see what you can do."

"Three hundred!" she echoed scornfully, pouring herself a second cup of coffee. "You big ass!"

"Well, you started with one, and look where you got going the wrong way," Ned Quinlan said pleasantly. They could all afford to laugh at poor Madeleine, who was in such desperate straits. The men had won only a little or lost only a little. "Roulette," said Ned, sententiously, "is the only game in the world where, if you break even, you think you win!"

"I've got to get that money in the bank before they try

to cash my check," Madeleine said. "He let me date it Thursday."

They went to the tables again after lunch; it was three o'clock now and very hot. Cam wandered away and took a look at the town; it was a dreadful place, she thought, for all its continual air of gaiety and recklessness and extravagance. There were a great many beautiful women and handsome young men; magnificent cars flashed in the sleepy summer-time streets, and the shop windows were filled with fineries from Paris and New York.

There were children, too. Cam's heart, for some reason she would not quite analyze, ached for the children. Such brushed and groomed and well-frocked darlings, with nurses, playing in the shade of the park near the curbed rushing river that bisected the town. Big changes hanging over their small shining heads; no more Daddy in their small scheme of things. Going back to live in houses they never had seen before, with new persons to live with. . . .

At four o'clock she told Bob that she really wanted to get back to the children. Bob said he'd had enough, too, but unluckily they hadn't come in their own car; they couldn't drag the others away.

"Bob, is Madeleine winning? I don't like to go over and watch."

"She may be now. She wasn't when I was watching her."

Eventually Bob engaged a taxi; at six he and Cam were at the cottage. The brown little girls were digging on the beach; Mabel was on guard; Cam had arranged that there should be provision for dinner; everything fell comfortably into line. She and Bob had a swim, Bob outswimming her with brutal joy in sheer strength, and going so far out into the Lake that his head was a mere speck on the afternoon waters. Then the Crimminses came over from the hotel and were kept for dinner, and there was bridge until two o'clock. By this time Cam felt positively ill with fatigue, and the men, who had been drinking highballs, were truculent and argumentative.

"God damn him, he has to have the four trumps! No other combination could lick me!" Bob said, when the guests were gone.

"Maybe I shouldn't have doubled?"

"On my two bid with two aces? You're cracked! You had a peach of a double. No, it was having the trumps bunched that sank me. Damn him!" Bob said good-naturedly, under his breath.

He went away on Sunday morning, and peace and quiet fell upon the cottage and the pines and the Lake. Cam drowsed almost all day in the shadow of a great rock on the beach. The girls brought her treasures: shells and tiny dead crabs and fringed seaweeds. High up in the blue, airplanes occasionally winged their steady way north or south; motor-boats occasionally cleaved the still waters, echoed and were gone.

When the girls went to take their naps, she napped, too. She felt wearied and jaded after Bob's visit, and the magic of John's presence was completely destroyed. There was nothing left of it. Life was all money and waste and noise and hurry and people being stupid and unkind to each other. It was only after a long night's sleep that Cam felt like herself again.

The morning brought a letter from John. There was nothing particularly significant in it. In the shop where they had been making him a croquet set he had seen an amusing rubber duck with straps on it; he was sending it up for the children. They could easily get to the flat rock on it, escorted, of course, by some grown-up guard.

A croquet set for the new house in Atherton! Cam amused herself with a dream in which she and the children spent an autumn Sunday with him there, met his mother and the little boy. He would be as proud as a child showing her things; she would wear the stiff, gauzy, old-fashioned green dress and the big green hat. And the girls would wear their microscopic green linens.

There was a certain niceness in everything he did. To put

in that line about a grown-up being with the children—that was thoughtful, charming. He did not want her to forget that, shallow as the water was over the white sand, small children might easily get panicky in it.

He was sending her the amusing letter his colored cook had sent him from Baltimore, and a book was coming. He thought of her, she told herself, all the time. Whatever pleased or interested him he wanted to share with her. It gave her a comforted feeling; she could not be lonely while John Kilgarif was somewhere in her life.

She wrote a letter acknowledging the rubber duck and describing the children's excitement over it.

"*The girls are getting so companionable, and it is such fun to see their joy in things,*" the letter said. "*The power to make children unhappy or to raise them to the heights of ecstasy is really too great to be vested in any man or woman. If I am going to dine at the hotel they are so sorrowful, and if, on the other hand, I tell them that we are going to have supper down on the rocks the delight is all out of proportion. For the first time this summer I've begun to realize the privilege it is to give two little human beings a completely happy childhood. I'm planning for their college days already! The clothes they want to wear, the places they want to go, the friends they want to entertain—it's going to be such fun to work it all out!*"

When John wrote her that he was coming to the Lake again she experienced an emotion that surprised her. It seemed a thing that could not happen; that a car would drive in to the hotel yard, and a man get out, and the magic begin all over again. People were coming and going all the time, but not John. Cam thought of the moment when the tall lean figure should come along the path under the pines, and take the little trail between the rocks, and her heart closed on a sort of spasm of joy. Her friend, coming back again!

This time he brought his mother, the little two-year-old

Taffy, just Joanna's age, and Taffy's nurse. His sister was still in the East. Cam liked the pleasant, fragile old lady and made love to the shy little dark-haired boy. Taffy played with the children on the strand, and Toomey, his devoted nurse, watched over them all, leaving Cam free to spend much of her time with John's mother, who rarely left her cottage porch.

It had not the flavor of the first visit, this three-day stay, but in one way it was almost more satisfactory, for there was something rather impressive in this meeting of the whole clan. It was as if John had wanted her to know his mother, and his mother to know her; his own pride and delight in the women's liking each other, his cleverness in keeping the conversation moving between them, were obvious.

And his feeling for Cam had deepened rather than lessened with the three-weeks' separation. She saw that and felt it in everything he said and did. Any wish that she expressed as to riding, dining, planning for the children's days was instantly sacred to him; he would move heaven and earth, but things should be as she wished them. Any casual little word of affection for him, the "dear" she dropped as if unthinkingly, the monitory touch of her hand on his when Taffy was in danger of sliding off the rock, by these he was completely shaken; he would maintain a trembling, grateful silence, unable to speak at all for moments. When he did speak his whispered "Ah, you darling!" warmed the very center of her heart.

They were to leave on an early evening train; he walked over to the cabin late in the last afternoon to say good-by. The day had been perfect and was dying in exquisite beauty; long shadows were slanting through the pines; the Lake was a sheet of glass; every flower stood erect in a bath of pure light.

Cam and John waked down to the shore and stood there talking. She told him that she and the children had only three weeks more of holiday and promised to get in touch with him when they came back to town.

"That is, unless you get up here again," she said.

"No, I don't think I will," John answered, after a moment.

"You like the Atherton place?"

A silence. Then: "I didn't hear what you said, dear."

"Is it going to be nice at Atherton?"

"Lovely. Just what I need."

Beauty—beauty—beauty was all about them. Beauty of the quiet water and the giant bare shafts of the pines, rosy in afternoon light. Beauty of the paths through the trees, with blue Michaelmas daisies and golden wild sunflowers starring the dark background of the rocks. Little shafts of midges buzzed and spun in the warm sweet air. A mile away, around the curve of the shore, children were bathing and screaming on the hotel beach.

"Cam," John said in a troubled tone, speaking out of a musing silence, "I think I had better not come again."

"It's a long trip. It's a hard place to reach," she said, fluttered.

"Yes," he echoed deliberately, "it's a long trip and it's a hard place to reach."

Neither spoke for a moment or two.

"Isn't it too bad?" John asked then suddenly. And without explaining or elaborating his remark he turned abruptly, and they walked up the natural rocky steps together.

"You're dining on the train, John?"

"Mother and I, yes. The youngster will have some supper before we start and Toomey 'll get him right into bed."

"It's been lovely to have you here."

"Well, I don't know," he said. "It has been maddening, too. I've wanted every minute alone with you. I've wanted talks—our old talks, such as we had the night of the big storm."

"Ah, that storm!"

"That was a wonderful night. They don't come often like that."

"I hate you to go away, although we'll see each other so soon," she said. "Send me a book. Write me."

"I think perhaps I won't, Cam. I've got to get over it, you know. The sooner I begin, the easier for me," John answered.

She felt her heart stop for a moment, begin pounding again. The enchanting summer sunset seemed to break into stars and lights. Cam could not speak; she raised her eyes to his.

"So good-by, my dear," he said lightly and levelly, and he turned and walked slowly away. She stood looking after him, every fiber of her being longing to reach out for him, to call to him that he could not go away. There was a ringing emptiness in the world as she went slowly into the house. Loneliness such as she had never felt before in her life possessed her. Life at the Lake cabin seemed unendurable; she did not know what to do with herself. She went out and sat alone on the terrace and looked at the Lake in the dusk and the early stars, and heard the far scream of the seven-o'clock train tearing on its way south.

He loved her. He had told her so in those few last awkward words; but she had long known it. She held this very important man in the hollow of her hand. And life was all different because of it.

What would Bob think—Bob who was so indifferent to her love and her claims—if he knew it? Cam's first reaction to the situation was a sort of angry pride. Other men found her charming, if her husband did not! For a few days she went about thinking constantly of the two men, her feelings hardening a little when she reflected on Bob, weakening when the memory of John's glances and words ran through her whole being like reviving wine.

But when John came for a third time to the Lake all reasoning power was submerged in the rare, heady delight of his presence. He came unannounced, about ten days after his last visit; came straight down to the strand, sat there talking with her for three unbroken hours.

The day, its crystal light thinning into autumn already, was hot and sweet, and scented with aromatic weeds and with the oil of the pines. There was not a breath of air on the water; the figures of the children were reflected clearly in afternoon shadows as they waded and plunged in the long shallows near the shore. Irene Scott was with them for a while; then she engineered the three sandy, weary, hungry little boys up the steps, and May and Mabel came down to get Jane and Joanna.

After that Cam and John had the place to themselves. Their voices went on and on, lowered, hesitant, with long pauses between sentences. Now and then Cam laughed, a brief low ripple of laughter. Now and then the man, shifting his position to stare out over the Lake, flipped a little stone at the quiet water.

Cam, clad in a blue bathing suit and beach shoes, with her shoulders protected by a loose crash coat, was wedged comfortably into her favorite seat, with one carelessly flung and deep-implanted boulder for a back rest, and a smaller one just beneath the crook of her elbow. John half lay, half sprawled beside her; sometimes he twisted his lean cheek a little to glance up at her; mostly he looked out toward the Lake.

And still it was not lovers' talk. Yet every word thrilled them both, and the simple, unimportant things of which they spoke took on rare meaning and significance. John did not explain his coming; Cam asked for no explanation. He might stay all of the following day, then he must go back, he said. She made no protest; she did not say, as she would innocently have said a few weeks ago: "Ah, don't go back. We're having such fun!"

"Shall we ride tomorrow morning?"

"I told them at the hotel to keep Betsey and Nobby for us."

"At seven?"

"And then have breakfast here about nine."

"And swim."

They planned their hours jealously. And each, as it came, was more perfect than they had dreamed, and each left a memory that so haunted the beach and the trails and the Lake for Cam that it was a relief presently to be packing for the return to the city.

CHAPTER X

AGAIN they were established in the grim old house on Jackson Street, and again its strange stuffy odors, its shadows, its echoes enveloped Cam like a spell. After the freshness and freedom of the Lake she somehow could not settle down to it with any philosophy. The little girls felt the restrictions of city life, too; the prim paths of the park were a poor substitute for their beloved rocks and sand. Granny was not very well. Cam felt obliged by affection as well as duty to spend what time she could in the older woman's room; altogether the early winter began in general dullness and discomfort.

Bob was happy. He went to New York to conclude a most satisfactory business deal; went on to Florida for some fishing. He came back brown and contented in time to get into the golf tournaments. When he was at home he was good-natured, gay with the children, kindly with his mother, quite his easy self with Cam. But he was rarely at home; his business and the social obligations connected with it, his clubs, his golf, fishing, hunting, bridge, kept him completely absorbed. He came home occasionally to eat, often to sleep, aways for clothes, shoes, guns, golf sticks, camera, fishing tackle.

Cam had never cared very much for her engagements with women, nor did she ever spend much time in beauty parlors.

The conversation of Edith and Aline interested her now only when it occasionally touched on John Kilgarif. He was away all through October and November, writing articles about some social movement of the government in Washington; he did not write to her.

She filled her days as best she could with the children's company. Just because she was bored and lonely there was no reason that Jane and Joanna should not be happy. She took them, sometimes with another child or two, sometimes with Granny, to the big park, and the zoo, and the beach. They had their lunches in cafeterias, when the children filled their own trays, or in tearooms where there was whipped cream on the chocolate. They went into five-and-ten-cent stores and bought all sorts of fascinating things and brought them home for rainy days.

It was oddly satisfying. She had not known how fascinating the company of eager little girls and boys could be, how delightful to make them happy. Their adoring love, their strangling hugs and wet kisses, their new passion for Mummy's society deeply gratified her. They were much nicer than Joan and Aline and Elsa; they never bored her as rich, stupid Larry and Arthur and Sam did. She let them have their friends in for supper and to stay overnight; there were pillow fights and weepings and rejoicings, and the wiping of sticky, jellyish fingers on all the chairs.

Old Mrs Sylvester liked all this. The children would go in to say good night to her, their hair in wildly tossed mops, their faces flushed, their small breasts heaving.

"Are you having a nice time, darlings?" she would ask, before Cam shepherded them all away to bed.

It tired Cam, but she knew it was good for her. She tried to put her resentment of Bob's treatment, her aching loneliness for John's company, out of her mind.

On a clear warm December day she announced to her mother-in-law that she was going to take the children down to Menlo Park to look at a house.

"Margaret Coates was telling me about it. It has a big garden, fruit, it's up on the hill, and it's going for a song. Come on, Granny, you go with us!"

"Oh, my dear child, it tires me to think of it."

"I'm taking Peter Howard and the little Ford girl, and Mabel, of course. We'll have peanut-butter sandwiches and chocolate, and it 'll be fun."

"You'll be so far away from me, if you and Bob buy down there, Cam. And yet it's lovely country. I went down about two years ago and had lunch with dear Rhoda Freeze. I remember such lovely oaks. Whose place is this?"

"It was the Burns place, and they sold it to the Purdees. But it's too big for Mrs Purdee, and she wants to get rid of it and go East and live near Rose. It sounds lovely. Margaret said that she'd go with us, but she's got her arm in a sling and it's so awkward and gets so tired. I'm going all over it, and I'm going to tell Bob that if we like it, it's a deal!"

"Cam, I think you're right, dear. The children need more space to spread in."

"And I think you're very generous," said Cam, kissing the top of the lifeless, oily braids of gray-brown hair. "You'll come to us for long visits, and we'll have dogs and cats and canaries and everything else, and you'll love it!"

The children, already excited, were in ecstasies when Minna Ford and Peter Howard arrived. Sweaters were buttoned up, for there was not much warmth in the December sunshine, the lunch basket was placed in the car, arrangements as to who should sit first in the front seat were concluded, and at eleven they were all off in great spirits.

Cam found her old house without much trouble and interested herself in it, or rather in what she considered its possibilities, at once. It was old-fashioned to the point of colonnaded and bay-windowed ugliness, but it was roomy, sunshiny, surrounded by trees and garden, and there were five orchard acres ready to supply the little Sylvesters with apple sauce and prunes.

They ate their lunch on the chipped old shabby veranda, in the sunshine, after which Joanna frankly went "seepy-by" in Mabel's arms, and Jane and Peter promised to be very quiet for a while, resting on the dry brown grass. Cam and Minna meanwhile explored the garden and sheds and presently followed a path through the rose bushes to the side gate.

There was a little lane beyond, with another side garden gate opposite. And on this gate was the name Kilgarif, neatly lettered, and the words "Deliveries."

Cam stood quite still in the sunshine, looking at it. Of course, Atherton and Menlo Park ran into each other. Only she hadn't thought of it. This was John's place.

"Let's take a look at this house, too, Minna," she said.

"Do we know the lady what lives dare?" asked Minna, mannerly at seven.

"I think we do, and I think she's a very nice old lady, with a little boy named David," Cam said encouragingly. She and Minna went along a path between leafless, well-tied berry bushes and into a space where clothes were drying on a line. They could see the house now, a low-roofed place with red chimneys, snuggled down among giant oaks that spread their great branches over its silvery shingles. A dream house. A house that said to Cam everything that pictures of country farmhouses ever had said to her since babyhood. Her heart began to beat fast.

In utter silence, the child's little hand in hers, she went on past flower beds and past a light green lattice fence and came out on an open lawn that sloped away in a shallow bowl from an awninged veranda. Here a setter met her, wagging his red-gold tail, and she and Minna stooped to pat him.

When she straightened up she saw John standing a few feet away, an old white shirt open at his throat, his loose old cords earth-and-water stained, a trowel in his long lean hand.

"You can't say he's a watchdog!" Cam observed, with a broken laugh, her hand still on the dog's silky head. For a moment she and the man stood looking at each other.

"He wouldn't bark at you," John said then in the voice she remembered, the voice for which she had hungered. "Hello, Cam," he added, wiping his hand, extending it. "This is—who? Minna, is it? Hello, Minna."

Cam explained why they were there and what an odd chance had brought them into his garden. John listened, looking at her, his expression like that of a man walking in his sleep.

"Mother and Taffy are in town. Taffy had to see a doctor about his feet; he's got some twisted trick of walking," John presently said, speaking as dazedly as he had looked. "Toomey and the man took them in an hour ago. Let me show you my place."

He guided them about. Cam approved of everything; John had very little to say. She exclaimed at the oaks, at the riding horses idling in the sunshiny paddock, at the long low farm-house parlor with its big fireplace and small-paned windows through which garden flowers were peeping. Minna, tiring, had a drink of water and a cookie, and waited for Aunt Cam downstairs, and John and she went on to look at his study, at the businesslike plain bedroom that yet so spoke of him. Books, rows of them everywhere; brown blankets stripped in darker brown; a working desk wide and flat, a typewriter holding a half-written sheet of yellow paper, a camera and riding boots and a worn old stick carved and weather-stained with a leather strap on it.

"Is that actually a manuscript getting itself born?" Cam asked.

"It actually is. And I'm afraid it 'll be a long time getting itself finished now."

"Oh, why?"

He did not answer.

"Come here to the window and look at my view," he said.

Cam went to stand beside him. They looked out together at the bare garden and the clean shadows. He dropped his big lean hand to his side, and her fingers fitted into it. Neither spoke.

After a long minute she freed her hand and turned and walked about the room, glancing at books and pictures, touching the paper in the typewriter.

"To have you here in my room!" John said.

"I—apparently—came straight to you," Cam said dryly.

"And you might be next door this summer." He stated rather than asked it. Cam's eyes came to his.

"I don't know," she said. And then, with a change of manner: "We mustn't keep poor little Minna waiting forever!"

They went downstairs, and Cam took the child's hand again, and John walked with them along the path and across the lane. Mabel and the younger children were all ready to start for home; Cam got them properly distributed in the car, turned and extended her hand, raised her blue eyes.

"When do I see you again?" the man asked.

"Oh, I was going to say—and I forgot. Could you dine with us on Tuesday, a week from today? Bob and I are having a dinner for four or five persons who don't play bridge, and you would be the fresh meat!"

"I'd love to." He bowed a little over her hand. Cam took her place at the wheel. When they were well down the road she could see in her car mirror that he was standing perfectly still looking after her.

Bob asked her a day or two later what she had thought of the Menlo Park place.

"It wouldn't do, Bob. Too old-fashioned. It needs too much repair. I'd be afraid of the plumbing. Oh, and by the way, the night you're having the Bullards here," Cam said, "I've asked John Kilgarif."

"Oh? You told me who he was."

"The writer. You've seen his name in magazines a hundred times. Sociology—essays on sociology, that sort of thing. He's just back from Washington; he went on there for the international congress thing."

"He and Bullard ought to hit it off, then." Bob went on shaving as if the idea were quite natural. To Cam the sound of John's name seemed to echo in the room like the clamor of a great bell.

She found herself a little fussy about the appointments on Tuesday night; ordered the flowers herself, instead of leaving it to May, and discussed the meal more than once with the Chinese cook.

"They must be pretty important people, the Bullards," Mabel observed.

"They're Mr Sylvester's London representatives—or rather, he represents them here," Cam explained. She studied the seven names carefully. Derrick Bullard on her right, of course; Mrs Bullard on Bob's right. Mrs French, Mrs Bullard's daughter, on Bob's other side, and young Arthur French next to his wife. That put John on Cam's left, next to Mrs Bullard; that was really the only way to arrange it. Cam felt like a bride giving her first party when the evening of the dinner came, and she found herself flitting about from the dining room to the sitting room, glancing at candles, flowers, lamps, anxious that everything should be perfect.

John was the first to arrive, ten minutes before the hour. He said that he had expected to sit downstairs alone waiting for his hosts, but as Cam was already downstairs she took him into the library and they waited together for the Bullards. Cam had never seen him in dinner clothes before. He seemed to her very handsome—no, better than that, distinguished-looking. Her own gown was not new, but it had always been extremely becoming, and she knew that she looked her best now. She sat with her satin skirts spread about her, petal fashion; the pearl and gold and silver rose that was the gown's only decoration opened at the delicate line of her breast.

"I've never seen you as a great lady, Cam."

"I was thinking that I'd never seen you except in summer things before. You like me as a great lady, I hope?"

He raised his serious eyes from the fire, looked at her. "I like you."

The Bullards came in, and Bob joined the group at the fire.

Bob had been drinking that afternoon; he was not at his best tonight. Cam struggled valiantly with the familiar situation, interpreting his remarks, laughing away what was utterly inept and unfortunate. But as usual when she was being admired and made prominent in the conversation, he was perverse, willfully interrupting, misunderstanding, silencing her.

There was no help for it; there was no reaching him when he was like this. Derrick Bullard had known Bob for years, she reflected; he would understand. Young Arthur and Phyllis French were too happily absorbed in their honeymoon joys to care; Mrs Bullard was kindly and sympathetic. But what John was thinking she dared not surmise. She must carry on as best she could and let him think what he must!

After dinner he suddenly took charge of the entertainment, to her unspeakable gratitude and relief. It was not much after nine o'clock when they all went back to the library. Cam, surreptitiously glancing at the clock, thought despairingly that the Bullards could not possibly go home until half past ten; indeed their car had been called for that hour. And Bob was heavy with sleep; he would go to sleep the moment he got into his chair.

But John saved the situation. He had heard of a questionnaire in one of the magazines; it was found, pencils were found, and they all settled down to work. When that was over, Derrick Bullard remembered a puzzle that could be done with pencils and paper; Cam recalled another test, and before she knew it the clock was blessedly striking eleven, and the visitors were apologizing for staying so late. Bob, who had been keeping glasses and cigars moving, gave a series of yawns that were like shouts when they were gone and observed that that was one of the ghastly dinners, but that thank God it was over for another year.

"Did you think it was ghastly, Bob?" Her tone was a little hurt.

"Thought it was awful! All our dinners are. No bridge. Hate talk."

Lights were out; they were going upstairs.

"And what did you think of John Kilgarif?"

"He's all right. Has he got a crush on you?"

"What makes you ask that?"

"Because it's pretty plain. Well, all right," Bob said, going into his room with a last rending yawn. "Let him have it! Was I sunk without a trace after dinner?"

"You seemed terribly sleepy."

"I wasn't sleepy. It was something in the dinner that doped me. I think it's the way he makes that stuff on the steak. Too rich. You looked swell. Wonderful how that old dress holds up. Oughtn't you have a new formal?"

"I don't go to many dinners now. Other things interest me more." She said this much aloud, her thoughts racing on: to hours in the spring park with the children when John's car would slide up against the green lawns and John come walking slowly over to join them; to two stolen exquisite tea hours when he and she had talked together in a dim corner of a big hotel tearoom; to telephone calls and almost daily notes and gifts. These things made dinner parties seem dull and lifeless indeed.

But she could not tell Bob that. Bob seemed not to be in her scheme at all these days. He did not matter any more. There was no one in the world anywhere except John.

CHAPTER XI

ONE EVENING when Bob's mother had gone to bed and Cam was quite alone, John came to call at about nine o'clock. Cam was expecting him; she opened the door to him; Mabel and May had gone to a movie, she explained. They went into the library and sat at an open window looking out at the city streets under the night lights and the stars above the park. The evening was sticky and close; there was no breath of air stirring.

"Is it getting lovely in Atherton now?"

"Beautiful. Roses simply going mad, hawthorns, lilacs; every word that ever fitted into spring fits in down there now."

"And little Taffy, has he fitted in, too?"

"Well, we gave up the kindergarten idea. He's too young, Toomey and Mother think. He digs around, and wheels his little wheelbarrow about, and seems completely contented. I write all morning and walk around the hills in the afternoons. But my horse is over his lameness now, and next week I'll get into a routine."

"How's the cook?"

"Mother's delighted with him."

"I had our Wong talk to him. When they're good they're very good."

The man was not listening; he brought his eyes from the night panorama outside the windows and glanced at her seriously.

"Have you thought about it, Cam? What we talked of out on the beach yesterday?"

"John, as if I could think of anything else!"

"Said anything to him about it?"

"No."

"And when are you going to?"

"Well, this is only April. We don't go to the Lake until late June."

John folded his long arms on his chest.

"I can wait," he said briefly.

"I'm glad to wait, to have time to think it over."

"You don't have to think it over, Cam. It's predestined."

"I wonder if it is. I think of the girls. He loves them in his casual sort of way, and of course his mother loves them."

"That can all be adjusted. If people are only decent about these things, not trying to revenge themselves on each other, those things fall into line. It 'll be a hard time for you when everyone's talking about it, but after all, what does it matter what other people think? You and I aren't going to have much to do with them, anyway. Certain ones will criticize you, and others will understand. And you and I," John continued, shifting his chair a little so that he might reach for her hand, "will be down in Atherton, watching our peaches ripen and our children grow up, and we won't care! I'm going to have a pool made there for the kids," he went on. "They'll live in it, summers. I'll write, and Mabel and Toomey 'll take care of the youngsters, and Mother 'll go around the world—that's what she wants to do, with this new German nurse of hers, Prague. Mildred Prague. She's done such wonders for my mother that Mother feels actually young again.

"So that's what we'll all do, and you'll take care of us all!

Read my proof, and let me talk things over with you, and ride in the early mornings, and go on holidays to Mexico or the High Sierras. And what does he lose?" John concluded, speaking in a sensible yet impatient voice, and still holding her hand. "He's going off in July with a lot of men on a yacht. He doesn't care what you do!"

"I don't see why he should care," she said thoughtfully, as if she were thinking aloud and speaking to herself. "I don't see why, since women do it for such little reasons, I shouldn't do it, when it's so obvious that he doesn't care."

The man did not answer. Instead he moved to put a firm square leather pillow on the floor beside her and sat upon it, his head resting against her knee, her fingers on his hair. They sat so for a long, long time.

"I wish it was over!" said Cam.

"The fuss? It 'll be over so long by this time next year that you'll forget it ever happened."

He twisted the palm of her hand about and kissed it, and she felt electricity run through her like a fire.

"Do you know I'm going to be terribly jealous of you, Cam?"

"It 'll be strange," she said dreamily, "to have anyone jealous of me. I don't think anything would ever make Bob jealous. He's completely sure of himself."

"Where is he tonight?"

"Golf semifinals tomorrow at Pebble Beach. Everyone's there. Movie stars, Hatchett, everyone."

"Wish you were there?"

"I could have gone. At least I could have gone down in the train and joined them. He was in Los Angeles night before last and came up in Jim Wilkins's boat. I thought there might be some business reason for my going down, to talk to dull wives, so I wired him. He answered, 'Your coming inadvisable. My time jammed. Many thanks.' "

"Ha!" John said abruptly.

"But I don't want to go," Cam assured him. "I'm too

happy fooling about with the children, reading books, waiting for the telephone to ring. My whole life's changed since you came into it. I like different things. Or else," she continued thoughtfully, "I was fooling myself when I thought I liked the things I was doing. It's the children and the garden and you that I really wanted. And d'you know, John," she concluded, with a sudden change of manner, "that I'm happier, even with all this muss of the divorce ahead, I'm kinder, I'm more like what I used to be when I was a little girl, since you came into it all! I mean, I want to do generous things for Mabel and your mother and everyone. It's like a sort of enchantment."

"It's an enchantment all right," he said. After a while he added: "You're not afraid?"

"No," she answered. "I'm not afraid, because I'll belong to you. That's all that matters. That's the happiest destiny anyone ever could have. I can't think of any woman alive who wouldn't change places with me then, John. I can't think of anything ever happening to us that won't seem wonderful, if we're together."

"I love you," he said. And in her sweet, faintly hoarse voice, with her fingers touching his hair she answered:

"And I love you, John. I didn't know I could love anyone this way. I can't believe that we're ever going to be the Kilgarifs, belonging to each other."

"We'll be married in September. And for a little while they'll talk; but after that nobody 'll care. We'll live in our farmhouse, in the garden, and we'll go to New York and sell books, and it 'll be happiness—just sheer unearthly happiness—for us both."

Before she and the little girls went up to the Lake in June she had her talk with Bob. Cam approached it with trepidation and doubt. It was impossible to imagine in advance just what Bob's attitude would be. But he must know, and the sooner he knew the better for them all.

"Bob," she said, on a foggy soft June morning, when they were alone at breakfast, "would it surprise you very much to know that I want a divorce?"

He put his paper down; stared at her.

"What you talking about?" he demanded.

"I'm serious. I've been thinking of it for more than a year. Thinking that you and I have grown completely away from each other, that we have nothing in common, and that we'd be happier apart."

A silence, while she faced him squarely.

"Where 'd you get all this stuff?" Bob demanded then, displeased.

"Does it surprise you so much?"

"Yes," he said scornfully. "You bet your life it surprises me. What are you talking about? What is all this?"

"You've not been home for the last five week ends," Cam said, her ammunition ready. "You're going off now on a yachting trip. I'm not in it at all. I'm left with the girls, week after week and month after month. Well, that's all right; I like it. But it's not marriage, and I don't see any use going on with it. Everyone else we know, practically, is divorced. There doesn't seem to be any reason why we shouldn't be."

"What do you want to do?" he asked, watching her, when she had finished speaking. And she felt that he was putting a constraint upon himself.

"I want to go up to the Lake—our cabin is on the Nevada side, you know—and stay there quietly for the six weeks that are necessary, and then drive into Reno and get my divorce in a few minutes. There needn't be any publicity or any recriminations."

Bob was looking at her steadily.

"Ha!" he said finally, in a dissatisfied tone. And then, more sympathetically: "I'm sorry you feel like this."

"Well, maybe it's my fault," Cam said, feeling her eyes water, "maybe I ought to have known how to hold you. But I didn't. I've felt—oh, ever since we started sleeping in separate rooms—that we were drifting further and further apart from each other. There didn't seem to be anything to do about it."

He was silent, scowling into space, his forehead wrinkled.

"Wait a minute," he said. "Wait a minute! Don't go too fast on me. What about the kids—my mother——" He interrupted himself, stopped short. "You don't want to do this, Cam," he said in a troubled voice.

It shook her as no violence could have done. She forced herself on.

"Your mother had very much the same sort of thing to stand, Bob. Your father was like you. After a few years his wife simply didn't count with him. You know it's true! Your mother will understand."

"She'll feel pretty sick losing the kids."

"She won't lose them! I'll keep Mabel. Mabel will bring them in to see her whenever she wants them. Every week."

"Bring them in, eh?" he said in a musing voice. "From Menlo Park, is that it? It's Kilgarif, isn't it?"

She could not lie. Her eyes were riveted to his, and he saw the hot color creep up into her face.

"He's in a swell business," Bob said bitterly, "coming to a man's table to eat his food and then trying to steal his wife. I don't know what I think about this, Cam," he said gruffly. "I'll have to have some time on it. We'll talk about it some other time."

He went away, a big bulky figure in coarse homespun. She saw that the thick bull-like back of his neck was red. She had hurt him and humiliated him and surprised him; there was no help for it. Cam felt a great relief; he knew now, anyway. He knew. He might rage and grumble for a while, but in the end she thought that he might give her her way.

He came to her late that night when she was reading in bed. He looked flushed and even sulky, but he spoke with a sort of gruff generosity.

"I've thought this all over, Cam. I think you've had a rather rotten deal. I suppose I've been playing too much golf, thinking about myself more than I have you. You make whatever arrangements you like. Only—I was talking to Fitzgibbons about it today—only I'd like the kids now and then. Mother could rent a little place for them in the country somewhere, take Mabel and May, and I'd be with them whenever I could work it."

"Well, certainly!" she said, feeling suddenly touched and sad and ashamed, all together.

"You'd agree to that?"

He had taken all the wind out of her sails. Her voice was low and troubled:

"I'd agree to anything, Bob."

He went to the door of the bathroom that connected their rooms.

"I suppose I ought to have seen this coming," he said.

Cam remained silent.

"I mean," Bob continued, turning, fixing his eyes on her, "I suppose that if I had seen it coming I could have done something about it. I suppose it's been working up for a long time."

"I've been lonely," Cam said simply.

"I thought," he went on, as if he were thinking aloud, "that it was just that I'd gotten to like one sort of thing and you'd gone in for another. I thought a house and kids and her friends and all that were enough for a woman. Maybe I didn't think much about it. Anyway, I was wrong. D'you want me to move to the club?"

"We start for the Lake tomorrow."

"Train?"

"No. Driving."

"Oh," he said expressionlessly.

He went away, and Cam continued to read, but with an excitedly beating heart, and a tendency to let her attention wander from the page and her thoughts churn about in a wild confusion that had no starting point, no sequence and no end.

Suddenly Bob, still dressed, reappeared in the bathroom doorway.

"I'm going down to the club," he said. "You'll be off in the morning. Good-by."

Cam's throat contracted; her heart seemed to stand still. "Good-by, Bob," she said.

Was that all there was to it? A desolating feeling of blankness descended upon her. He and she had been married seven years ago. A church wedding it had been, with bridesmaids and flowers and solemn organ music. They had shared one room for years; he had been the only person admitted to her hospital chamber on the dreadful night when Jane had been born. Quite suddenly now she remembered that night, and her utter weakness and peace after so much pain, and his tears hot on her face as he bent over her. She thought of her honeymoon in Hawaii, of their laughter as they went hand in hand into the blue breakers, of her pride in her big athletic husband. The men had circled about Bob Sylvester, talking to him of long-ago games of golf and football and of games yet to come, and when Bob, on a blue Sunday morning, had gone out with his golf sticks to play Johnny Cates an admiring little field had followed them, and Cam had been most admiring of all.

All of this went through her mind as Bob stood looking at her. She felt frightened. Had she any right to do this? What was she doing with her life, anyway?

"I'll bring Mother up to the Lake to see the girls about the fifth," he said. "We go off on the Zuleika on the tenth. Can you send them over to the hotel?"

It would be horrid. Everyone watching the Sylvester smash-up, she thought rapidly. But of course she had no choice. He seemed to know what she was feeling.

"I'll have Mother with me. Nobody 'll know it then," he reminded her. "She's had it all arranged for weeks."

"Nobody need know—of course! That 'll be all right, then.

I'll come over and see her anyway. I'm very fond of your mother," Cam said uncomfortably.

"Yes, I'm sorry on her account," Bob said briefly.

"Are you sorry on any other?" she asked, steadily. But she was sorry herself the minute she had asked it. He might try to dissuade her from the course she was determined to follow.

"Yep. I think you're making a mistake," he answered. And immediately he added: "But I wish you luck! I thought—or maybe I thought——" He stopped, began again: "Maybe I think you could have done it differently—given me a chance——" he said, formulating the words slowly. "But that's all right. I'm in wrong; I ought to have known it! But here's something," he added, with a sudden change of manner. "It's Mother. D'you want me to talk to her?"

"Unless you want me to." How amiable they were, now that they were parting! But then she and Bob never had quarreled.

"I'd be awfully glad if you would!"

"I will, then. Tomorrow. She's going to Palo Alto on Friday; she can talk it over with old Mrs Putnam and Auntie Reese."

Bob lingered.

"This is the way they do it?" he presently mused aloud.

"I was thinking that."

"Well, I wish you luck." A moment's pause. "Good-by. I'll see you at the Lake," he said.

"Good-by."

The bathroom door closed. Cam lay staring vaguely into space. It seemed to her that her chief emotion was heartache—heartache for all the stupid and unnecessary pangs of life. Why should it trouble her so to take the sensible and obvious step? She had been leading only half a life with Bob; she had meant little or nothing to him. They were independent human beings; they had free will. Why *shouldn't* they avail themselves of their natural rights? Why this wretched sense of doubt and guilt?

CHAPTER XII

SHE TRIED TO TELL John about it when they were driving to the Lake the next day. Mabel and the small girls, the latter in blue-dotted swiss frocks and hats, were on the back seat; Cam, also in blue-dotted swiss, was beside John in front. They drove up—up—up through the sweet June country, now passing through a hot little town whose sidewalks were shaded by roofed arcades, now stopping beside a roadside fruit stand for figs or ripe apricots. They lunched on the rocks beside a stream; both little girls went to sleep immediately afterward, sunk into small blonde heaps upon pillows and upon Mabel's knees, and Cam, glancing back, saw that husky young Mabel was sound asleep, too.

"I had a session with my mother-in-law this morning, Jack."

"I love to hear you call me Jack. No one else ever has. You see it's Johnson Kilgarif, really, and the nickname is John. You had a session with your mother-in-law. Was it awful?"

"It was awful because she was so nice. She said that she knew it was coming and had warned Bob. And *that* made me feel better, because he intimated last night that I was taking him unawares. And she said that she had done the other thing, and she had been a lonely woman for many, many years. 'Many women used to be, as their husbands' interests expanded,' she said, 'and they used to go melancholy as the years went by.' But she said the spiritual element troubled her. She said she felt Bob was almost entirely to blame——"

"She must be quite a remarkable old woman."

"She is. She is really generous in her sad old way. Yes, she said she felt Bob was to blame, but that nevertheless divorce was a sin."

"A sin?"

"Yes; and she asked me to talk to Canon Hicks."

"Who's he?"

"He's her clergyman. She's known him forty years. He's out here for his lungs, or something, and he lives down at Watsonville or one of those warm places."

"Cam, my dear, what could he say?"

"Well, exactly. Just that we must sacrifice our lives for the better part, and discipline ourselves, or something like that! I was baptized; I was married in church," Cam said, "but I don't go to church. He'd talk about breaking a vow, I suppose. Well, if you take a vow when you are too young or too unthinking to know what it's all about, it seems to me honest to break it, to say, 'I made a mistake, and it's making me and several other persons unhappy. So I'm going to annul it.' "

"How smugly the churches condemn one to unhappiness!" John mused.

"One wonders why. Canon William Frederick Coles Hicks—he's an Englishman—has no idea of what my life is in that Jackson Street house. He never thinks of the emptiness of my days there, talking about meals with Wong, sending the children out in the park with Mabel, going up to Granny's room for a visit, Bob perhaps gone for three days, and then a message: 'Mr Sylvester would like his golf bags sent to the club by two o'clock, please.' What does Canon Hicks know about that?"

"He expects you to go down to Watsonville to discuss it with him?"

"Well, I don't think so; no. He and Mrs Hicks and Emily and her boys come up to Fallen Leaf Lake every summer, and I suppose he would drive over to see me and wrestle for my soul."

"I wouldn't see him."

"I won't, if I can help it. Do you suppose your mother has any such ideas?"

"I don't imagine so."

"And what about your sister Amanda? She's as old as I am, and she sounds rather forbidding. Amanda Kilgarif."

"Amanda?" He laughed. "She's a bird-brain," he said affectionately. "You'll like her. She writes poetry. She misses trains and forgets to do her hair. You don't have to be afraid of her."

"You know, Jack," Cam suddenly began, after a silence, "if you hadn't come into my plot I believe I'd have left Bob anyway. Seeing your place down there made me realize that I could have been happy in such a place, with just the girls and a puppy and perhaps a cat and my freedom. But not—not with Bob in it, always keeping me wondering if I ought to accept invitations on his account, and then wondering why he didn't show up to keep his engagements. Going places without him and having the hostess shift all the places at table to make room for me, and then hearing that he was going places without me. Perhaps I was stupid about it, but I didn't seem to be able to manage it."

"It simply wasn't marriage," said John; "that isn't companionship, that isn't sharing."

"Well, part of it, I suppose, was to make money for the girls and me. It was after the stock-market smash, when we all lost everything, that he began to live so completely apart from me. Perhaps," said Cam, thinking aloud, and speaking in a troubled low tone, "I should have taken a cheap little apartment somewhere, done my own work, cooked his dinners for him. But he didn't want that. He didn't want his friends to know what a complete smash it had been. Some of his mother's money was in Venable-Stacks, too, you know, and when she asked us to combine with her he jumped at it. Perhaps it was partly our being there. But then I don't think that," Cam interrupted herself to say, "because even before the crash Bob was never at home. Only I was younger then, and Joanna was coming, and Jane was quite a troublesome baby, and I didn't notice it so much!"

"It simply wasn't marriage," John said again, and for a little while they were silent, driving along the lovely winding roads near the Lake and letting the peace and beauty of the spring afternoon influence their roaming thoughts.

May was ready for them at the cottage when they arrived; the children were too tired for anything but supper and bed, but John and Cam had a wood fire after dinner and sat by it talking for an hour or two before he left her. And to them both there was something utterly satisfying in this quiet time together by the fire, with the waters of the Lake lipping at the piles of the Scotts' little wharf, and the wood sleepily answering from the lazy flames on the hearth.

"Do you suppose we'll have our troubles like other people Jack, after we've been married awhile?"

"I hope so," he said, his serious fine face breaking into a smile.

"Hope so!"

"Well, I'd so love to solve problems for you, Cam. If your brother Ned, for instance, got into trouble and was tried for murder, it 'd be fun to move heaven and earth just to please you."

"Fun except for Ned. But Ned isn't the kind to commit murder. He's a research man, and if I know any one thing about doctors it's they're too much absorbed in what they're doing to murder anyone. They work, and come home to eat and sleep, and while they're eating and sleeping the telephone rings. My father was a doctor, and I remember that we had a telephone always on the dinner table."

"Well, maybe he won't get us into trouble, then."

"How about your sister? Is she the kind to murder anyone?" Cam asked.

"The Mouse? Well, wait until you meet her. She wouldn't murder an unusually large bumblebee. She's always afraid that the servants' feelings will be hurt, or that the little boy selling newspapers hasn't had a rightly balanced lunch, or that she's said something mean in a letter. I don't suppose the Mouse ever sent a letter yet that she didn't worry about."

"She sounds cute," Cam said, pleased, her dreamy eyes on the fire. "Do you call her Mouse?"

"We've always called her that, and Tiddy, for Tidbit, and Mike, for Microscopia."

"She sounds darling! Is she so small, Jack?"

"Well, she isn't big. But it's more for something spiritual than anything physical. And by the way, Cam, I've not gotten this far without thinking about Mother and Tids. As soon as we're married—as soon as we're married—I'll keep repeating this until you stop me because it makes me feel intoxicated——"

"Go on, idiot!"

"Well, just as soon as we come back to Cherry Ridge—by the way, that's the name of my place."

"I like it," Cam said, out of a happy daydream.

"Just as soon as we come back, Mother and Tidbits will move into some place near, in Menlo Park or Palo Alto. Mother likes a village because of clubs and church, and Tids doesn't mind, because she never knows anyone anyway, and she can have a back garden and fool along with cats and pigeons and so on to her heart's content. So that's the present plan."

"Your mother isn't dependent on you, Jack?"

"Oh, Lord, no; nor the Mouse, either. Why, were you worrying about finances?"

"Not worrying, dear. But I'd hate to feel that our marrying was going to make a difference to them."

"Not a scrap. But they love the kid, and if you want to be generous, you can be generous there, sending Toomey and Taffy over to see them."

"Every day," she said, still deep in dreams. "Oh, Jack," Cam said, "it's going to be so wonderful! Do you suppose any two persons ever went into marriage so confident of each other, so sure that everything was going to be right? Tell me——" She had reached the words impulsively; she stopped suddenly upon them.

"Tell you what?"

"Whether you felt this way when you married Margaret?"

"No; not this way," he said. "I was a very much younger man, younger even than the few years stand for. She was vivacious and childish and affectionate, and I remember the afternoon we got engaged. She had her arms locked on mine—we were skating—and she said, 'Before you go back to college tonight I'm going to tell Mother that we're engaged! You've kissed me, and we're crazy about each other, and we don't like anyone else, and then I'll be the first girl of my crowd to marry!"

"Little-girl stuff."

"Well, exactly. I don't know," John said thoughtfully, "that I really thought it would go through. I remember saying to her mother that night that it was to be a great secret, because my people naturally wanted me to finish my law work—I'd been out of college nearly three years, but because of one thing or another I'd not taken my bar exams. And Mrs Booth, I remember, gave me a queer look, and said very gently, 'John, it shall be exactly as you decide.'"

"Meaning," Cam said with a shrewd quick look, "'I am so glad to have my little girl bag you that you can make your own terms as long as you'll continue to consider yourself engaged to her!"

"Listen, that's smart," he said admiringly. "How on earth could you put your finger on that?"

"Because it's going on all the time! I could tell you of a dozen marriages that are arranged like that. Didn't you see it?"

"If I did later, I certainly didn't at the time. And Margaret was a gay little thing, audacious, you know, always making everyone laugh. She used to say she loved me more than I did her, and perhaps it was true. But anyway, we didn't quarrel, and those weren't bad years."

"What was it, at the end, Jack?"

"She dived—we were up at Bass Rocks, and she dived from someone's boat. She must have hit her head; she came up, but we could see she was groggy, and when I brought her in she was unconscious., There was a compound fracture, and what they call *contre-coup;* she lived four days—poor kid."

"Was she pretty?"

"Oh, no. Saucy-looking, with a wide mouth like Taffy's, and round frog eyes. Yes; she was kind of pretty sometimes. I don't know whether she was or not—anyway, she always got what she wanted. I was trying to get started writing, and like a fool took a little place out in the country near Trenton. She didn't like it at all, and after a while we moved back into town. I don't think I ever would have gotten going if Margaret had lived; she always had a plan. We were going to Florida, we were going to Newport, we were going to London. 'The Snowdens and the Harrisons are going and we're going!' she'd say. And if I protested she'd say, 'Talk all you want to, but get the tickets.' "

He laughed, remembering it, and Cam laughed, too.

"We went to Europe," she said. "I wish you and I could go somewhere when we're married that neither one of us has ever been before."

"And do you think we're not, Mary Campbell?"

"Ah, you've thought of it!" Her face flushed with sheer pleasure.

"Thought of it? Thought of the night I shall have you for my wife?"

"Well," she said, in a small subdued voice, looking back at the fire, "I didn't know."

"We're going to take the children down to Cherry Ridge—shall we go on calling it that Elsie Dinsmore name, Cam?"

"Oh, why not? It sounds as if we ought to have a nurse called Nana, and the curate in for tea."

"Cherry Ridge, then. After you've been to Reno in September we'll take the children and Mabel to Cherry Ridge, and get them settled, the day before. Mother 'll be there, and the Mouse, and you'll sleep in the spare room, like the guest of honor you are. Then the next day, or after a day or two, when they're quite happy, we'll slip away to San Francisco in the blue car and be married. Then we'll send telegrams, you to your brother, and to Mother, and whoever else you like, and off we'll go—north along the Redwood Highway to Ben Bow and Victoria and Banff and Lake Louise. We'll slant down to New York for a show or two, and I'll buy you something grand to remember me by. What would you like?"

The question brought her up with a laugh.

"Oh, let me see. Oh, I know what I'd like. A really swanky evening coat. Brocade, sort of goldy and reddish and bluish, with pearls or something embroidered into it, and a chinchilla collar."

"You shall have it. And we'll buy presents for all the kids, boots for Taffy—he's dying for rubber boots—and Joanna wants a hammock all to herself."

"You heard that? I heard her holding forth to Mabel in the back seat. It seems she has a grievance because Jane has a hammock all of her own, and Joanna never has had one. Three years old!"

"She couldn't be more cunning, could she?"

"Well, she's the loving one—she always waits for someone's lead. But I love my bold Jane, too."

"They're both darlings. You like this plan, sweetheart?"

"I like that plan." She had come to sit on the broad, low arm of his chair. He had an arm braced about her; her fair head drooped until it touched his own brown hair.

"I love you, Cam," he said. "I suppose the days will go by and the weeks will go by, and somehow September 'll get here. But it seems as far away as the world to come, now."

"You'll be up again?" she asked, when he was going.

"In about three weeks."

"Only let me know. Bob's bringing his mother up in about three weeks."

"Will it be hard for you?"

"I won't like it. But it won't be too hard."

"And be sure," John said, "if the Canon comes, to give him my kindest regards."

CHAPTER XIII

THE CANON DID COME, riding over in good neighborly fashion upon a stout cob, accompanied by two jolly young grandsons. Mrs Hicks, the Canon explained, was being very lazy this summer, still tired out from her remarkable work with the girls' recreation winter camps, but he and George and Herbert were beginning to be famous riders.

Cam suggested grape juice. They all sat on the terrace drinking it. The day was burning hot and still. The little girls came down dewy and rosy and aggrieved from their naps, and the Hicks boys escorted them down to the shore. Cam had known that some such opportunity would have been arranged by their grandfather in advance.

"May I say something very frankly to you, my dear?" said Canon Hicks then, with his pleasant smile. "I stayed in San Francisco several days on my way up, and had more than one talk with your husband's good mother. And may I say that she feels, and that I very definitely feel, that you have been most unfairly treated!"

Cam looked at him, and he laughed cheerfully.

"That surprises you, doesn't it?" he asked. "You thought I was going to pull a long face and begin to scold you for your sins, didn't you? Not at all. I've known Robert Sylvester since he was a small boy, like my boys here. I love him. Frankly, I love him like a son. I knew the father. He has magnificent qualities, Robert. But he has been an inconsidate husband—yes, he's failed you. It's a very sad thing when really fine people fail each other, I always think. But that doesn't mean that you are going to fail him, does it? I mean," the clergyman went on, spreading his fine, well-groomed hands in an eloquent gesture of appeal, "I mean that marriage is a matter of give and take, isn't it? You forgive me today, and I forgive you tomorrow. Why, my dear child," he went on, warming to his work as Cam made no protest, but continued to regard him with a steady, reflective gaze, "no marriage would ever continue if we were reasonable folk. You have good reason to be angry with Robert. But we're not going to go by reason; we're going to go by faith. We're going to say, 'What? Am I going to be so weak, and so self-centered . . .' "

He talked along earnestly, and Cam watched him earnestly. After a while she moved her eyes from his face to the blue Lake, and watched the afternoon shadows gathering there, and the children wading and splashing. She looked at one particular stubborn little pine, springing up between two boulders, and wondered at its tenacity. She heard May rattling down the ashes to start the supper fire. Now and then she conceded him a monosyllable.

"Yes, yes, of course. Yes," she murmured from time to time.

But when he and his boys had ridden away she brushed the memory of him from her as if it had been a tangible thing, covering her flushed uncomfortable face with her hands, pushing her hair back from her temples.

"Oh, b'r'r'r!" she said. And then, "I call it *nerve*. What right has he to come preaching at me!"

And late as it was she ran for a bathing suit, plunged into the Lake and shook away the last humiliating memory in the clean waters.

The rather dreaded visit from her mother-in-law and husband never took place. The older Mrs Sylvester was injured in a motorcar accident on the peaceful drive along the Monterey shore, and never recovered consciousness. Cam wrote to Bob, expressing what she truly felt, a genuine sense of loss, for she had loved his mother. That she also felt a certain relief and freedom because of her going she kept to herself.

"But it does clear the way," she confided to John. "It almost seems like a sign. He can't have the girls now!"

The weeks ran their appointed course, and Cam idled them away in pine-scented security under the green tassels of the trees and beside the blue waters of the Lake. Her children became more and more companionable to her, and she wrote John that she found their company completely satisfying; "if I can't have you," she added. Jane was a bold, strong, original child, devoted to her mother with a stormy, passionate affection that made Cam's guidance very simple; little Joanna was tender, loving, sensitive and willing to cuddle against anyone who would be kind to her. Each one, in clear, fair, baby beauty, was a conspicuous figure among all the children at the Lake; when they were together and dressed alike, Cam had trouble in keeping away from them the attentions of everyone who saw them.

In mid-August she drove quietly with John to Reno, and in a few seconds her case was quietly handled, and she found herself again a free woman, in name at least. That she was not actually free, that seven years of marriage could not be so easily annulled, she had proof. Bob was away with friends on a long yachting cruise; his mother was dead. But his lawyer had adjustments to make, rights to handle for Bob; Cam's face flushed with nervousness as she signed papers, saw the names of her "minor children" incorporated in impressive documents. Bob was to have the girls when he wanted them, for periods not totaling more than nine weeks annually. He would place certain sums in the bank quarterly for their maintenance.

"That won't be necessary," Cam said to the lawyer. "I can very well manage their expenses."

"Let him do it," John said to her later. "It will make him feel better, and it can very well pile up against the day they'll want to use it."

All these arrangements were unpleasant, but they did not take very long, and the day came when the Lake cabin was closed, and when Cam and Mabel and the little girls went down with their beloved "Uncle Jack" to the city. Here Cam had a suite at the Fairmont for the few days during which she had to settle several affairs of her own in town.

Bob had left the Jackson Street house untouched since his mother's death. His lawyer informed Cam that she was to have a key and take anything and everything she wished from the place. May was living there and would give her any assistance she liked, if she would take the trouble to let May know when to expect her.

Once again in the shadowy, richly furnished, empty old place Cam decided that there was little she wished to take. Her books, her clothes, some of the presents her mother had made her, the table linen an aunt had sent her from Italy seven years ago, the portrait of her brother and herself as children, and a few frames and vases were all she set aside. The Sylvester treasures of deep-colored delicate dinner plates, countless heavy spoons and knives wrapped in red flannels and packed away, rows and rows of engraved gold-rimmed glasses, mahogany, tapestries, onyx and ormolu must come to the girls through their father, if at all. A beautiful portrait of Bob's mother as a bride, with wrist-length gloves and bustled creamy satin evening dress, looked down at her as she worked. There were fresh roses in the lovely crimped and piled auburn hair; the young soft breast of the bride had been pushed up and tightly bound by the whaleboned, gusseted gown.

Somehow the one day she spent in the old home made Cam feel sad and uncertain. She had had happy hours here, despite the gathering shadow of Bob's increasing indifference, his lengthening absences. She had come home many a late afternoon, exhilarated from walking in the cold, blowing fog, to run up and discover the babies warm and sociable in their little corded wrappers beside the coal fire in the nursery; she had felt pleased with herself, in her own soul, somehow, when she had gone in later to spend a daughterly hour with their grandmother.

Bob had been a disappointement and a problem, of course, but in many other ways life had been serene enough. It had been at least free from the scared, doubtful emotion she sometimes had now, the awesome feeling of having taken life into her own hands.

And then there had been the thrilling days of last winter, to make this house forever sacred ground in her memories. Even now, with the actuality of marriage—the breath-taking ecstasy of the prospect of belonging to John Kilgarif, and having him belong to her—drawing so close, Cam could look back with a pang of longing at that time when they had been first finding each other, first discovering the kingdom that was their love.

She remembered days when she would have an engagement with John, perhaps as late as the tea hour, perhaps even later, and that the thrill of it would be with her when she awakened in the morning, and go with her through the quiet routine of the children's and the household's demands upon her time, coming nearer and nearer as eleven o'clock, one o'clock, three o'clock struck. She remembered the excitement of making herself lovely for John, getting into the checked heavy suit and the big furs, careful with touches of rouge and powder and lipstick. Then would come the commonplace departure from Mabel and the children that yet was like the ringing of bells all over the world, and a dizzied trip somehow through the city that was so oblivious of what was going on, and the final moment of something like vertigo when she went into the hotel and heard the music lazily playing, and smelled the combined scent of flowers and of the perfumed women, and saw him, lean and grave and tall, waiting for her.

Ah, those had been hours of enchantment! Leading, they always said, to today's more definite bliss, to the complete fulfillment of joy in a few days more. But like everything else that had been sweet, it was hard to let them go even for things more sweet. Cam would have had the coming glory of consummated love and the hours of wooing, too, last forever. She seemed to say good-by to that uncertain, exquisite time when she left the old Sylvester house behind her, and John, coming to the hotel that evening, found her in rather a sobered mood.

"I wish I were a rigid Catholic, Jack, believing in everything, from the Fishermen's Ring to Saint Rita of the Impossible!" she said on the last night, when he came to dine with her at the hotel.

They were out on a green iron balcony, relaxed in green iron chairs cushioned in gay chintz; below them glittered the lights of the piers, and the tiny lights that were little boats crossing the bay, and the far sparkling line of diamonds that were Oakland and the Berkeley hills. The dark silhouettes of the hills themselves could be seen in warm starlight; to the left the profile of Tamalpais showed against a west that had not quite lost the glow of a perfect September day.

"Then you couldn't marry me, sweetheart."

"Well, maybe I couldn't. But I'd know, you know. I'd know definitely that if I did I'd be an outcast. It would be sort of satisfactory."

"To be an outcast?"

"Not to be this half-and-half way about it. Some persons thinking it's awful, some thinking it's the most natural thing in the world to fall in love while you are still someone's wife. Old Mrs Cathcart, for instance. She talked to Joan Howard, and Joan talked to me. Arthur Howard is Bob's partner, and they're off me for life. Joan said old Mrs Cathcart said that while all divorce was tragic, somehow there was something more respectable about people who didn't meet each other until they were separated. Joan says lots of people think I was jealous of Bob's tennis and golf!"

"Not much to pay for Jane and Joanna," the man said, watching her. Her face brightened.

"Oh no; not much to pay for Jane and Joanna!" she echoed eagerly. And he knew that she was quite herself again.

Or rather, he told her, she was more than herself. Never, in his knowledge of her, had he known her to be quite so sweet, quite so endearingly young in her shy questions, her musing replies, as she was tonight. They sat, occupying one big chair now, with his arm locked about her and her head on his shoulder, and talked of their marriage and of their life together, and to both the hour was filled with an unearthly beauty that comes rarely in a lifetime, and seemed to become a part of the dark bay waters and the eternal hills and the starry sky that encompassed it.

The next day they went down to a glorious welcome to Cherry Ridge. The farmhouse windows and doors were wide open, the rooms were filled with flowers. Taffy was in white, his broad little frog face one beam of welcome; Mrs Kilgarif was on the porch, her own face radiant; and Cam met for the first time the slender shy girl with the nervous beautiful brown eyes who was John's sister.

Cam's little girls ran eagerly to see the puppy that Taffy was carrying. Mabel and Toomey spoke in guarded cordial tones to each other. There was everything to see, everything to rejoice over, everything to share for the rest of a perfect day.

Luncheon was laid on the terrace in a dapple of tree shadows; there was a smaller table near the large one, where the nurses could take charge of the children unobtrusively; there was a smiling Chinese bringing out popovers and baked crabs and blackberries. Zinnias and phlox and hollyhocks blazed in the garden, where water sprinklers were lazily whirling, flinging arcs of diamonds into the warm autumn air; blue jays flashed in sharp notes of color and chattered in the oaks.

They pushed their chairs back after the meal and sat on, talking in the afternoon shade. Joanna came to climb into her mother's lap and went to sleep to the sound of lowered voices and bees murmuring over the garden, a delicious little warm lump of brown satin skin and tangled, pale gold hair. A hummingbird shot near, hovered over the tiger lilies in Cam's hat, whirred away again on invisible wings.

"This place is heaven," she said.

"Now," John said significantly. Amanda laughed a delighted little nervous laugh.

After a while Mrs Kilgarif went upstairs to lie down, and Joanna awakened, hot, prickly, tearful. She was taken upstairs to the big guest room adjoining the little one, sponged, settled off to finish her nap. Cam glanced into the next room to see Jane heartily asleep, almost as violent in relaxation and unconsciousness as she was when awake, and then decided for a rest herself. She got into a thin batiste wrapper, creamed her face and wiped it fresh and soft, loosened her hair and brushed its soft corn-gold lengths to coil them loosely about her head. Then she stretched herself flat on the hammock on the sleeping porch and locked her hands behind her head.

Autumn afternoon sounds were going on in the peaceful world below her. Birds stirred the high shadows of the pear and oak trees that were patterned on the patterned linoleum of the porch. Now and then an apple dropped in the orchard with a thud; now and then horses whinnied in the paddock beyond. Bees buzzed; sometimes one bumped against the netting near her head with an angry banging for a few bewildered seconds and was gone again. In some shady spot in a lane, unseen chickens fluffed and talked to themselves—a sound infinitely farmlike and homely and pleasant in the crystal warmth of the day. Cam sighed for sheer felicity; this was a pleasant bit of life to be living. She closed her eyes; she was asleep.

CHAPTER XIV

It was more and more like a beautifully staged play as the enchanted hours went by. She walked about the place with John before dinner, and the ruffles of her lavender-striped gown brushed against the flowers, and she gathered them into her hand to cross the bit of oak wood to the barns, to wander with him up the path to the real woods.

The children, who had had their suppers, joined them as they came back, Taffy clinging to his father's hand, Joanna holding tight to her mother's, Jane strutting independently ahead, shouting aloud a sort of jargon of triumph and carrying the puppy undisputably.

"Ah, she got it away from him," said Taffy's father.

"Of course she would! She'll get his teeth away from him if he doesn't keep his mouth shut," Cam conceded in comic despair.

They dined at seven, Cam and John, Tids and their mother, and that was like a play, too, for the low-ceiled dining room was paneled in plain Spanish gumwood, a wood fire sparkled behind old brass dogs, and candles were the only light that showed the pink china and the old silver, the fine linen and heavy chased candlesticks. This was the way life ought to be,

Cam thought, with harmony and friendliness making every meal an event, and beautiful things used in their proper old places, and not set about merely as heirlooms. She thought of the ponderous horrors of the Jackson Street house, the terra-cotta Neapolitan girls, the lampstands and cushions, the chests and chairs, and once again shook it off with a little shudder and determined not to think of it again.

Amanda, never called anything but Tids, Tidbits or the Mouse, was not only acceptable as a new sister, she was actually lovable. Cam laughed at her, teased her, liked her from the moment of their meeting. Except for beautiful shy dark eyes, rather like Taffy's eyes, there was nothing beautiful about her. She had the sensitive splay mouth of the poet, thin dark hair in loose curls, a colorless skin, a thin neck, and nervous bony hands that were rarely still. But her voice had appealing cadences, and she was so timid and so loving that Cam found herself reassuring Tids rather than being reassured by her in the new relationship.

"Campbell, you're very—*beautiful,* you know," Tids said on the day before the wedding, in a fluttered voice. "And John—but I think John's handsome, too, don't you? I'm his sister, of course. But I've always thought John had something really beautiful in his face."

"John has absolutely the loveliest face in the entire world," Cam answered this calmly. Tids was in ecstasies.

"Campbell, he *has,* hasn't he? He's really handsome, isn't [illegible] And you love him, don't you? Do you know the night [illegible]as married to Margaret I cried all night—I was only [illegible]een then, but I hated her. But I'm not going to cry to[illegible]w night, though I'll know you two are driving away [illegible] your happiness—and it must be such happiness! For [illegible]w if a man even kisses you, and you love him, that's [illegible]s, isn't it? And marriage—to really belong to each [illegible]why that must be just so much more wonderful! Just [illegible] your things this morning, the lovely lacy things, made [illegible]ze what a paradise you two are going into!"

"Tids, draw it mild!" Cam said, laughing, but with sud denly self-conscious cheeks. "When you love a man as much as I do, it frightens you to think how different you are from what he thinks you are," she added, more reassuringly, as Tids drew back in shy alarm, thinking herself reproved. "But one can't be afraid, with Jack," she added, looking, from the upper balcony where she was drying her corn-gold hair in the sun, down to the garden where her husband-to-be was playing with all three children. "He's so wonderful with them, and they do adore him so," she said.

"And don't you think that the way a man is with children is sort of an indication of the man himself?" Tids asked.

"I think it is. But a man could be quite satisfactory and yet not have John's instinct for dealing with children."

"Oh, Cam, you are quite right!" Tids said fervently. "I'm horrible with children," she added, under her breath.

"I don't believe you are."

"Yes, I am. You see, I treat them as if they were grown persons, which of course they *are,*" Tids said in her bewildered gentle way, "and then grown-ups punish them. Toomey, you know, she doesn't like me to have much to do with Taffy."

"I think she's jealous of Taffy, and naturally enough, too. She's had him so completely since he was born," Cam said pacifically. . . . "And that's one of the things I'll have to do when I get back," she thought. "Put that priceless Toomey into her place. They're all afraid of her, and she man them all. It's ridiculous how she demoralizes Taffy, ju hold her influence over him, and sooner or later I'll lose if it keeps up. But while we're away perhaps it's bet to break anything up."

She spoke to John about it that evening.

"Jack, was Toomey with your Margaret when T born?"

"Oh yes; saved his life. He was a miserable little th

mother was ill, and Tids never has been much of a hand with him. She was only a girl of twenty, anyway, and young for that. Toomey simply took charge of him, and she's never let him go."

"She runs the house, too?"

"Well, in a way. She's rather a superior person, you know, not any too friendly to the Chinese boys, and she's gotten into a way of being rather waited on. But she's indispensable. You and I'll be away a good deal, and we'll always know that old Toomey is at the helm."

"They'll outgrow nurses pretty soon, anyway. At least Taffy will."

"I don't know. He's mad about her. And I'm mad about you," John said. "I'm going to want you all to myself, so it's lucky we have a person like Toomey to take charge when we're away."

"How long will we be away, Jack?"

"Oh, not long. Couple of months. Then we'll come back here, and I'll dig in for the winter."

"I hate to leave the girls so long. I've never been away from them before."

"My dear, they'll have Mabel. And Mabel 'll have Mother and Toomey if anything goes wrong."

"They know there's something up. They're uneasy," Cam said. "Tonight when I sent them up to supper Jane came back and put her arms around my knees and said, 'Oh, don't go 'way, Mummy. We really truly need you.' And of course at that Joanna clung to me and began to weep."

"They'll be all right. We'll get them presents in New York," he said easily; "they're only babies."

"I feel as if, in a way, I'd robbed them of their father."

Cam thought it; she did not say it aloud. They were sitting on the terrace, she and John, watching the great September moon rise in a clear, dark blue sky. There were no stars yet in the early evening; only the arch of cobalt that thinned into mauve in the still warm west, and the great rising globe of gold over the haystacks. The moon lessened in size, strengthened in light; oak trees dropped a faint lacework of shadows; silver trickled down through the dry gold and brown grape leaves on the trellis. From the nursery windows upstairs a pale oblong of light lay on the path.

"Tomorrow night you're mine, Cam!" John said.

She did not answer in words, but he saw the clean line of her chin turn in the soft gloom and caught the glitter of deep light in her eyes.

"God, that life can hold an hour like that!" he said. Her hand hung lax by her chair; he moved his own chair a little, and caught at her warm smooth fingers, and felt them living and responsive in his own.

There was an interruption. From the open hall doorway a small flying figure came across the terrace; Jane, in her pajamas, with her gold hair tumbled and her voice tremulous.

"Mummy, I was asleep and I dreamed you went away! Mummy, you aren't going away, are you?" she faltered.

Cam gathered the small bundle of girl, the mop of bright hair, into her arms.

"You silly, you know you oughtn't get out of bed! Wasn't Mabel reading up there inside?"

"Mabel went downstairs, and we were out alone on the porch. Mummy, you aren't going away, are you?" Jane was exquisitely comfortable in her mother's arms now; she was drowsing even while she waited for an answer.

"Not for long, my dearest darling," Cam mumbled into the soft hair, pressing little kisses on it, resting her face against the child's head. A pain as keen as the agony that had brought this child into being stirred at her soul. They were little and loving, her baby girls, and she was failing them. For the moment John was forgotten, and she was all mother and all suffering.

Then she looked up with an apologetic smile, to see him watching her steadily, a smile in his own eyes.

"They don't love you the way I love you," he said.

Cam made no answer. She held the child's soft little yielding body close to her, she looked up at the moon, now riding proudly over the highest oaks, and in her heart was a feeling that she wished she knew how to pray.

CHAPTER XV

THEY drove into a lovers' heaven of autumn beauty. The twinkling new car went on and on up the wide highway, came out on level roads beside the sea, turned back to mount twisting grades under solemn miles and miles of redwoods. They had left Atherton at ten in a cloudless, soft sweet morning; by midafternoon they were in a part of the world neither Cam nor John had ever seen before. In utter peace and content they traveled through the bright colors of the maple leaves and the cathedral shafts of the tall conifers, sometimes coming out on a headland beneath which the sea washed on a long curve of sand, sometimes reaching a hilltop and looking off at a hundred other hilltops clothed in the rising tiers of the hemlocks and spruce and juniper trees.

The exquisite shortening days of the year flew by, finding them only deeper and deeper in the happiness that seemed to have no limits and no measure. When they went for an early-morning ride, and Cam came back with him to the hotel, her gold hair disordered, her cheeks glowing, her slim young body ready to spring from the horse, her riding glove snatched off so that her warm hand might find his as they walked into the breakfast room together, he told her that no man in the world had ever had a companion like her. When they took their fishing rods and a basket of lunch up into the autumn woods and sat dreamily silent beside a stream, listening to the plop of trout and the quiet swirling of the sleepy currents, to bird calls in the woods and the occasional crack of little branches when some small furry thing went cautiously by, the harmony between them was so perfect that perhaps for an hour neither would disturb it by a single syllable. Just to be dressing in the same room with John for dinner was joy to Cam; to have him come and balance on the edge of a near-by chair and watch her at her dressing table made the routine processes of powdering and brushing exciting. And in the evening hours when, bundled up warmly against the chill of a Canadian October, they sat on some lodge porch, watching the moon rise and the stars come out, going up at last to the warmth and sanctity of the room that was their room, helping each other kindle the wood fire and draw the curtains, wandering about, talking by its kindly light, the love that had glorified all their hours was with them still, and at its holiest time.

The first snows found them in Montreal, each day an adventure, each meal welcome, each museum or curiosity that they could find to explore an untiring interest. Sometimes they took the car and cruised about the surrounding country. Sometimes they walked; Cam erect and stunning in her tweeds, with a rough-brimmed hat turned up against her bright hair, and her square-toed, heavy little shoes keeping gallant step with John's larger ones. Sometimes over some casual luncheon they would fall into talk that lasted well into the afternoon. And on a morning when she was tired and wanted to rest, he made her stay in bed, brought her her tray himself, gathered in an old Montreal bookstore enough odds and ends of amusing reading to keep her busy for hours.

Coming down through the New England towns they brought the winter with them; snows were already deep in Connecticut; New York, seen by Cam from the high warm bedroom of the great hotel, was delicately powdered with it on the day they arrived. All the way from the grapes and warmth and moonshine of Atherton to this heart of the greatest city, and every hour of the trip, she wrote Tids, happier than the one before it.

"And you can't think of the grandeur of belonging to John!" her letters said. *"He knows so many thrilling persons —everyone, in fact—and they're all so nice to him! We go to dinners—not that he likes them very much, but he knows they amuse me, and we go to play openings, tremendously thrilling, even when they're poor, and we walk up Fifth Avenue late in the mornings and buy each other ties and sweaters and things, and are very silly."*

And, at the end of every letter to Tids and John's mother, to Toomey and Mabel: *"Tell my darling girls that Mummy will soon be on her way home."*

She dared not say more; she never said even to herself that she missed them. That was a door in her heart that must not be opened, ever, until she saw them again. Ah, what a meeting! Cam would think, as she flashed through the brilliant life of the city at John's side, hearing only that she was beautiful, that John was a success, that their finding each other was one of the miracles that sometimes happen in life. What a meeting, to have golden vital Jane and loving little soft Joanna in her arms again, and to say to them between laughter and tears: "Mummy said she'd come back, sillies! Here she is now, and not ever going away from her girls again!"

The thought of them was always with her. They rose like golden-mopped little ghosts between her and everything wonderful and happy that she did; not reproachful, not suffering, but yet her own little Jane and Joanna who were missing Mummy. A hundred times a day she told herself that they were well and happy in their California garden, no one was oppressing or disciplining them; Mabel, if something of a fool, was competent and devoted. And a hundred times a day, as she and John got into a car to drive down for a Sunday on Long Island, or when she returned to her room to find that flowers arrived and tea ready, the quick stabbing thought came: "How they'd love it!"

The Singletons, John's publishers, entertained the Kilgarifs at Huntington; there were four princely children in the big house, brunette children with dark eyes. Cam thought of her blondes; their small white buckskin oxfords would have galloped so happily after Margot, Diana, Norton and Ellen; they would have shone among the others when, brushed and slippered and smooth of dark hair, the quartette came down with Nurse to say good night.

Cam's brother and his family were in Germany: she must miss that visit. But Washington, in early December, seemed like a first step on the homeward trip. Cam was in wild spirits and gave John his first taste of jealousy at a White House dinner when, superb in olive-green brocade and pearls, she was not only the loveliest of all the lovely women, but when her hoarse sweet voice and the light in her blue eyes kept a circle continually about her.

The President and his wife left the group with formal good nights at about half past ten, and almost immediately afterward Cam and John went to their hotel, Cam still thrilling to the excitement and pleasure of the evening. When they reached their rooms she threw off her furred evening wrap and went to one of the windows, opening it to lean out into the balmy night, looking over her shoulder to invite John to join her.

"John, isn't a thing like that fun, once in a while? It would kill me every night. But wasn't that fun?"

Handsome in his full evening dress, a little pale, he came over to stand beside her and lock an arm about her. His cheek was close to her cheek.

"Cam, my darling, don't do that again!"

"Do what?" she asked, stupefied at his tone.

"Don't make me jealous, sweetheart. I've been in hell all evening. The first time we've not been seated together at dinner! You 'way up at the other end of the table! And then those men afterward. That damn ruffian from Baltimore who knew your brother——"

"Abner Johnson Kilgarif, you're not jealous!" she gasped, as he stopped short. She rubbed her cheek against his temple, her soft rich hair loosened into a cloud about her face. "Why, you consummate idiot!" she murmured.

"Oh, Cam, you do love me, don't you?"

"*Love* you? What *is* this?"

"When I see you among those fatheads and imbeciles, being so sweet and interested, looking from one to the other, I could kill them! You're mine, you know, Cam. Not one tiny fraction of an inch of you belongs to them; you're all mine."

"But of course I'm yours," she murmured, her head on his shoulder.

"You see, sweetheart, for two months I didn't share you, not with anyone. And then came that New York scramble, and I began to be unhappy there. Those mixed-up parties, with everyone screaming and coming and going, and everyone wanting to know who the new beauty was. Sometimes—you never saw it—but sometimes I'd come home with you ready to kill myself, or you, or someone. I know it sounds crazy!"

"Crazy!" she echoed significantly, with a little indulgent laugh. "It's worse than that."

"I know it. But it was such agony to me. I made myself get the best of it. But now, tonight, it's all come back. Oh, Cam, if we could only go on driving about the world together, without anyone else, not knowing where we were going, just you and I, it 'd be such heaven to me. I can't work when I feel this way. That was why I had to tear up the thing I tried to write in New York. I'm just humming, buzzing, pulsing, breathing *you,* and nothing else, and when I'm away from you—if it's only five feet!—I'm sick for fear someone else is interesting you."

'Why, you jealous little high-school nitwit!" Cam said lovingly. "Can't you see if other persons don't admire me, *you'll* stop? You'll say, 'She's lost something. She isn't as nice as she was, because there she sits in the corner, twisting that beautiful four-dollar handkerchief I got her in New York, looking down at those expensive slippers, and ignored by the fashionable yet unthinking throng!"

"Cam, I adore you," he said, kissing her neck.

"I want you to," she told him, raising the heavy upcurled lashes of her blue eyes to fix her look straight on his, raising the soft red mouth to meet his kiss. This hour she was all his; it was her glory to be. But after he and his jealousies were alike asleep she lay awake saying to herself a phrase that had magic in it for her own ears, that had been sounding in them all day.

"We start westward tomorrow—tomorrow—tomorrow! And I ought to be with you, my darlings, just eight days after that. Eight days, and you'll get your little new frocks and all your presents, and Mummy 'll fix your cereal for you at breakfast and have lunch out on the terrace or up in the woods with you! I can wait for eight more days and not one other minute!"

Well, it was all happiness. But eight days later did not find them at Cherry Ridge. Instead Cam was on a steamer deck, watching the clean, groomed beauty of the Panama Canal slide by on either side, strolling about in the unnatural December heat with John, charming, as she could not help but charm, a circle of new friends, and quieting with all the skill at her command the jealousies that would agonize him again and again.

"Fool that I was to plan this trip!" he would mutter. "But I wanted to surprise you."

"And you *did* surprise me." It had been almost too complete a surprise, the turning of the car's head northward on the morning of leaving Washington, the triumphant mysterious "You wait and see!" that had been the only answer she could get to her curious questions. A surprise, of course, but what sort? she had asked herself. He loved to surprise her, but why should they be going back to cold New York?

Perhaps, she had thought, in sudden ecstatic expectation, he had asked Mabel to bring the girls on, to drive back with them. For the last hours of the drive from Washington to the northern city Cam had been so sure of it that her heart had been fairly bursting for the moment when he should open a door into a bedroom adjoining her hotel room and should say to someone unseen, "Come in and say 'hello!' "

After this dizzy height of anticipation, it had been just a little hard to show the right measure of amazement and delight when, instead, they had not gone to a hotel at all; they had driven from the tunnel straight to a battered old dock, the blue car had moved steadily on until she had been actually upon a Panama liner.

If she had failed her own high ideal of acting, Cam at least had had the satisfaction of knowing that to John himself her surprise had been a complete success. He had recalled a hundred times, with all the conspirator's pleasure, Cam's face when she had realized that they were going home the long way.

"You actually got white, Cam," he would say. And he might add, "Ah, darling, you're such an adorable little girl about some things, and it's going to be such fun to surprise you all the way along!"

And then there were more presents for her: beautiful Spanish shawls, a black pearl and a creamy one as large as large peas, pottery for her California garden, small wooden shoes for the little girls. She and John swam in the warm sea shallows at Havana, roamed through the crowded old quarter of Panama City and looked up at the oily narrow balconies; took a jogging ride on livery-stable horses out to the point where Morgan's gold still lies safely buried. They got home on Christmas Eve.

CHAPTER XVI

AFTER THE PEAKS, even mountain heights seem lowered. Everything at home would presently be wonderful, and John was close beside her to help her solve them, but the problems that the farmhouse in Atherton presented swarmed about Cam's head like angry bees as soon as she was at home, and her senses and capabilities, weakened by too much felicity, seemed strangely unwilling and even strangely unable to cope with them.

Jane and Joanna, to begin with, met her indifferently. They were but scraps of girls, of course, and they had not seen her since September; a long slice out of their small lives. They clung shyly to Mabel. Cam, trying to smile through the tears that she could not keep back, had to woo them for a long ten minutes before they would come to her.

When they did, and when Jane's memory suddenly awakened, both burst into wild crying and clung madly to their mother, fairly screaming when she tried to put them aside to greet her mother-in-law.

"Girls, girls, she's home again now, everything's fine!" John said good-naturedly. He had been met by Taffy with a pleasant enough smile of affection and was already showing his son how to work a sand elevator. Cam felt a little ashamed of her own emotion and of her children's, and a little puzzled when both small girls insisted upon accompanying her as she went out to the kitchen to speak to the staff, went upstairs to change her dress, went down to dinner. They would by no means go to Mabel for nursery supper, although Toomey looked rather grim as she urged it. Cam had their chairs placed on either side of hers at the table.

"Just this once, you baby tyrants," she said, beginning even in these first hours to feel that she had quite a large and variegated family to manage. In Mabel's respectful martyred manner she had read trouble, and Joanna's shriek whenever Toomey came anywhere near her said little for the baby's feeling toward Taffy's nurse. Jane's exquisite skin had been roughened and reddened by some sort of wrong food; perhaps Mabel, who had more than once expressed the opinion that candy never hurt children, " 'cause look at Ma's children," had taken liberties in the mistress's absence.

Well, it would all straighten out. But it was a little disturbing to get home from a long trip on Christmas Eve to find the Tree still to trim and the stockings to fill, and to suspect that domestic ructions were already well developed and ready to break out. She must just go on from hour to hour and pray for the best. And perhaps someday they could find some other nursery eager to engage the perfect services of Toomey; two nurses were too much in any house, and Taffy was getting big enough to dispense with much of Toomey's care now. After the New Year excitements were over she would see about getting her house in order.

But Mabel would not wait for the New Year. On Christmas afternoon when on her way home to have turkey dinner with Ma and the family, Mabel firmly announced that she was giving notice.

"When you leave the children in my care, Mrs Kilgarif," Mabel said, "then it seems to me that other people should not have the privilege of spanking them."

Cam was conscious of feeling a little sick. She went on opening envelopes, glancing at Christmas cards. Her mother-in-law and Tids, escorted by John, had gone up to town to meet and if possible bring back with them an aunt who had chanced to arrived on that day from the Orient. The girls were asleep; the house was very quiet after the morning's exclamations and rejoicings.

"Did anyone spank Jane?" she asked, evenly, apparently absorbed in what she was doing.

"Tumor did. But it wasn't Jane," Mabel went on, in stolid satisfaction at bad news. "It was the baby."

"Joanna?" Forces were gathering in Cam's heart; she could not stop them. Fury thickened her throat and made her eyes see dim. To touch Joanna! That horse of a woman! Cam closed her mouth and heard the breath sing in her nostrils. Joanna's mother far away; Mabel, poor inefficient that she was, helpless; and that woman daring to touch Joanna! "What had she done, Mabel?" she asked.

"Why, it was my day in town. Mildew told me of it," Mabel explained. She was no more fortunate with the name of Mildred, old Mrs Kilgarif's personal maid, than with that of Toomey. "It seems Joanna wanted to go into your room, because she thought either I or you were there. Mildew said she kep' saying, 'Mummy!' and 'Maybe!' and crying, and she wouldn't go to bed. So Tumor come along and picked her up and paddled her real good, and so then she went to bed, but Mildew says she was crying for about an hour, and calling you."

Cam could not listen. Her breath came quick and shallow. Not for many years had she felt herself so angry. She would show Mabel nothing, of course; it was always a mistake to share emotions with simple, garrulous Mabel; but she would see to it that Toomey was dismissed at once. She would have her month's pay; that couldn't in any decency be withheld, but she certainly would not be allowed to remain in the family another week.

Her little Joanna, so gentle and timid and loving, crying for an hour and calling in vain for her Mummy! Where on earth had Tids and Mrs Kilgarif been? Placidly resting in their rooms, probably, quite sure that the children were safe and happy with Mabel and Toomey.

"You come back tomorrow, Mabel," Cam said, trying to bring her whirling thoughts into something like order, "and meanwhile I'll have a talk with Mr Kilgarif and then explain to you what we decide to do."

"You'll never fire her. You couldn't. Nor him either," Mabel asserted calmly, still packing stone blocks back into their box.

"That's a very silly way to talk, Mabel. Toomey is only a nurse like yourself. If we decided to tell her to go, of course she'd go, like any other nurse."

"Not that one," said Mabel. "The old lady thinks she's the only one can manage Taffy. He had to have peplum when he was a baby," Mabel went on, not very sure of the term, but definite enough as to the meaning of her words. "He had panocratic trouble, Toomey says. She's a practical nurse, and she gets a hundred a month, and lots of times she won't eat with Mildew and Dora and me."

Cam said nothing. Her manner indicated that she had somewhat lost interest in the subject. But inside she was boiling.

John, his mother, his aunt, and the aunt's tall awkward son all arrived in the late afternoon, and as the sunshiny Christmas Day had turned chilly and foggy there were fires everywhere in the house to greet them, and Cam, in Mabel's absence, found herself completely occupied in making the small girls lovely to go downstairs and greet their new kinswoman, and in keeping the machinery of the big farmhouse running smoothly. Aunt Maria Spaulding went upstairs with her to see the girls put to bed; Taffy, granted an extra half-hour, was capering about in pajamas and slippers; Jane and Joanna were exquisite in their delight over their mother's presence.

They crowded against her as she sat in a low chair; she was never, never, never going away again, they exulted. Toomey, in dignified and capable attendance upon the nursery party, was all amiability now, and Cam could not but be a little comforted when she saw how quickly her daughters had seemed to recover from anything they had suffered in missing her.

Mrs Spaulding, who had asked to share this hour, sat in a big chair by the open wood fire, approving the general happy excitement. Between Mummy's return and Christmas presents the small Sylvesters were completely content; Taffy, the great-aunt said, looked better than she had ever seen him.

"I guess his stepmother is pretty good to him," she said kindly.

"Well, I'm afraid it's just California," Cam answered honestly. "You see, we left on our wedding day and only got back yesterday. But I think Taffy's on the right road now; I think he'll go right ahead," she added, when Taffy had careened out into the hallway, blowing a horn, and followed by the girls banging on drums.

"That nurse of his is a remarkable creature; you're lucky to have her," Aunt Maria said in an undertone, when Toomey had gone out on the sleeping deck and was turning down beds with the air one servant always assumes when doing another servant's work. "She's had him since he was a baby, you know."

"I'm afraid she spoils him a little. I notice he's still a baby about his toys," Cam said.

"Well, I suppose she does, poor little fellow. Of course, when they lose their mothers——"

Mrs Spaulding was evidently highly maternal. She had two children and several grandchildren in Boston; her ship had been held in quarantine in Guam; she was missing Christmas at home for the first time in an ordered and prosperous life.

"My Mary's boys are just about the ages of your girls," she said. "It's unfortunate that my girl has boys and my boy girls—Leonard has four girls. One would like the name to go on."

Cam remembered some such sentiment expressed years before by Bob's mother. The Sylvester name. The Kilgarif name. What was the difference whether or not a name went on? It was only the women of the family who really cared about a name, and women lost their names anyway.

"You'll have a boy for John one of these days," the great-aunt said majestically. "You're the maternal type. As for my sister Lily," she added, "she never ought to have had children at all."

"John's mother shouldn't have?" Cam asked, amused.

"Of course she shouldn't. Lily was always a dreamer. John turned out to be a genius, just her luck. Geniuses are the nearest things to being completely cracked that there are," Mrs Spaulding pronounced.

Cam laughed joyously and could see that she pleased her companion, for the firm corners of the older woman's mouth twisted.

"And Amanda—Tids, as they call her—is—well, you know what she is," the aunt said eloquently, with a shrug.

"She seems like a child in many ways. I don't imagine that men or love affairs mean much to her," Cam ventured.

"Ah, my dear, you don't know her!" Maria Spaulding said forcefully. "Don't think there isn't a lot of passion wrapped up in that girl. She's a little furnace of feeling—and for men, too, for men. She's always dreaming of knights and cavaliers and all that sort of thing—she's like Who's-this in the poem, with her mirror and her spinning, who broke out and floated wide, or whatever it was!"

"The Mouse?" Cam said, amused.

"The Mouse. Ada may well watch that girl. Well, my dear, you've taken 'em all on," Mrs Spaulding continued, turning up her full silk skirt to let the fire's warmth reach her neatly stockinged knees, "and you'll have your troubles with 'em! But John's a fine fellow, if he has got the Johnson jealousy.

That was my father. Made my mother's life a hell for twenty-seven years and then, four months after she died, married and went off with a girl of nineteen. Oh, they're great lovers, the Johnsons, and he's all Johnson."

"Women like them jealous," Cam said, smiling.

"Yes, for a while they do." Aunt Maria departed, and Cam took the children to their beds. When she went into her own room fifteen minutes later John had already dressed and gone; the place was in the wild disorder he always created in the course of dressing—bureau drawers open, garments scattered about. Her poet was an untidy being. Cam straightened the room as she dressed herself; the maids were having a rather heavy day of it, she must save them what she could. She was already tired, and she would have the girls to get started in the morning. She must set her alarm clock for six; they might get into all sorts of trouble if they got up on their own responsibility. Cam stepped into slippers, ran a wet comb through her beautiful hair and brought it in two gold bands about her head, slipped into a black satin that John especially liked. The clock was striking seven. She must be downstairs in time to give at least the appearance of leisure for the half-hour before dinner.

There were cocktails and canapés and pleasant talk in the low-ceiled farmhouse parlor; the radio was softly sounding the Christmas hymns, played on some great organ, sung by fifty voices. A big fire was burning; the Christmas tree was lighted; it seemed good to be home for Christmas Night. Cam slipped into a chair beside John, and his big hand came out and gripped hers.

"I've been in a simple tantrum all day," he said, in a voice only she could hear. "But the minute I see my wife I'm all right!"

"You in a tantrum!" she echoed, amazed, anxious eyes on his face. They could say no more without being overheard, but she knew that it was not a joke, that something was wrong.

The Christmas dinner followed its appointed course. The Spauldings left at ten o'clock. Mrs Kilgarif and Tids lingered for a few minutes saying good nights, standing about the dying fire, and then Cam and John went upstairs and found themselves alone in their big bedroom.

By this time Cam, in her concern for Jack's disturbed mood, had almost forgotten her resentment against Toomey. In any case John gave her small chance to remember it. With a great bursting sigh, as if he freed his very soul of pent-up emotion, he flung his arms about Cam, crushed her to him, kissing the top of her hair, the fine thick line of her eyebrows, her temples, her wrists, the palms of her hands.

"Oh—oh—oh, I've got you to myself again! Oh, darling, hasn't this been hell! Mother calmly asking me to drive her into town because Mitchell had to have part of the day with his family; tea with Aunt Maria and a lot of talk about the Philippines—as if I cared a damn about the Philippines! And then home again, and no you—you were off giving the kids their suppers because Mabel had to have *her* day off, and then dinner, with nothing but talk of our grandparents and the dear old summer home on Buzzards Bay! I thought I would *bust* if it kept up another second! And full fifteen minutes of 'Good-by, dear, and all my love to Mary and the Leonards! Yes, I will. I'll tell her. Oh, do do that, Lily. And don't get too tired in that awful train, Maria.' And so on and on; I thought they'd never get through. Oh, Cam, I love you so, and you're so beautiful!" John said. "Why do we ever have to have anyone else around?"

She laughed. She was in her favorite low chair now, and he half crouching and half kneeling beside her, with his arm locked about her.

"We do seem to have stepped right into the midst of things!" she agreed. "Mitchell off from ten to ten, Mabel gone, Hing holding up the turkey waiting for the oysters, and Toomey never having ordered them, Mabel giving notice——"

"Oh, did she? Is she leaving you? Well, you can let Toomey get you the next one; she's awfully smart about that," John said absently, kissing her fingertips carefully, one by one. "She's really like a housekeeper, you know. My mother hates managing—she and Tids will be in their own place, anyway, and having Toomey here means that everything 'll run perfectly when we're away."

It did not seem the time to register a protest against Toomey.

"Sometimes I think she's a little *too* good a manager," Cam suggested mildly.

"Who? Toomey? Oh, she's a swell old girl—she's fine, really. She spoils the kid a little, but Lord, why shouldn't she? They all get over being spoiled. You know, Cam," John, whose attention had not been fully engaged by the subject of the nurses, spoke now with sudden feeling, "you know what I'd like to do? I'd like to get in the blue car again tomorrow and drive away, and never see anyone else again except ourselves! I'd like to get on little tramp steamers and simply go wherever they were going, and wait there for the next tramp steamer to come along. I'd like to get bicycles and go all through Spain, go places other people didn't go, and never try to meet anyone anywhere. Darling, let's have a picnic, just you and I, tomorrow. No, damn it, tomorrow I've got to get at all that proof," John broke off to say, reflecting. "But pretty near every week end we'll beat it somewhere, and get away from it all."

"Children adore picnics," she suggested.

"Oh, Lord, no; no kids!" he answered promptly. "They just fall into water or off things, and eat too much, and crawl over you! They're better off here with Toomey and Mabel."

Cam laughed, said nothing. The new life must be perfect for him; there must not be a crumpled roseleaf that she could spare him. John must be the first consideration; everything else must be adjusted to him if their marriage was to be all miracle, all success.

CHAPTER XVII

THE next morning after breakfast he went up to his study, a big back room above the kitchen that had been made over for him, and Cam took up the reins of government that Tids, the elder Mrs Kilgarif and Toomey had shared between them. She managed the transition as amiably, as pleasantly as she could and, as far as John's sister and mother were concerned, entirely without friction. Tids never had taken any responsibility at all, and the older woman was delighted to resign her very inefficient management to younger hands. What Toomey thought, Cam could only suppose, for Toomey accepted all her suggestions with a prim "Yis, medem," that was said quite without expression between lips drawn up into a severe buttonhole.

"I'd like to see the order books, Toomey, and the bills. They'll come here to this desk now, and the sooner I get them straightened out the better. Between the dogs' meat and the children's table and our table and the orders for the staff I certainly am going to have my hands full," Cam said.

Toomey, as Cam had half suspected, had not managed economically at all, and however serene she had kept surface matters, beneath her rule a very conspiracy of discontent had been simmering. Neither servant nor mistress, Toomey had exaggerated the rights of the family and had been ruthless in her claims on the staff. Hing's assistant, a small moon-faced nephew of the old Chinese, had been taken off salary entirely; Dora's wages had been cut. These things had been done with Mrs Kilgarif's consent, to be sure, but at the instigation of Toomey.

"And one English chop every day, thirty cents," Cam said, studying the bills from the market. "Who's that for?"

"That's Taffy's chop, medem."

"Oh? He has a chop always, at lunch? What about the chicken and steak and roast-lamb days? The children can't have stews or fried things, Toomey, but surely a special chop every day for a little boy of four——?"

"It's the only meat he will eat, medem."

"He won't eat chicken, or fish, or turkey hash?"

"No, medem. He'll eat nothing but the English chop. It's his doctor's orders for him."

Mabel's innocent eye met Cam's. Mabel went on folding clothes; Toomey looked neither to left nor right.

"Was that all, Mrs Kilgarif?"

"Yes, and thank you, Toomey." Cam glanced at grocery bills; taxi bills; drugstore bills; a florist's bill of more than a hundred dollars' worth of roses and young trees. She saw nothing. Taffy's nurse had a power to disturb her, to get her into a state of nervous irritation, that was inexplicable.

"What's more," Mabel said unexpectedly, when Toomey was gone, "you'll not get Taffy to touch custards or gelatine or baked apple or anything like that. Not him! He has to have his ice cream every day."

"Every day! Have the girls been having ice cream every day?" Cam asked, scandalized.

"No, ma'am. Tumor wouldn't leave them have it. They had to eat their prunes and apple sauce like they always done," Mabel answered, in a mincing, triumphant tone. "But *he* gets it."

"It seems to me if Hing is to go to the trouble of making it every day——" Cam was beginning, when Mabel firmly interposed.

"He doesn't make it every day! It comes from the drugstore."

"Ah?" Four house servants, not counting Mildred, and dessert for one child's supper coming daily from outside. Cam felt a prickle of irritation hot on her skin; she wondered in how many other details Toomey's dictatorship would eventually reveal itself.

The day was filled with confusions for Tids and her mother were house-hunting and betrayed a common helplessness where decisions were involved. Cam took the little girls, ecstatic and eager, in a family party to look at two possible places; one Mrs Kilgarif did not like because the "horrid woman who showed it talked so coarsely." But with the other Tids fell in love because it was on Windmill Lane.

"It will look so delicious on letterheads!" Tids said, in an uncomfortable girlish rush, and the children, who had completely wrecked their smart little dresses by seizing an unwatched moment to lie on their stomachs and try to drag an unwilling little dog from under the porch, spoke of this place as "the puppy's house" and voted eagerly for it later in the day when everyone was out on the terrace enjoying afternoon sunshine and discussing the move.

Taffy had declined to go on the house-hunting expedition, even though Cam had personally coaxed him to go. She had known, and had felt a certain discomfort in knowing, that he had been longing to go, but for some reason only attributable to childish perverseness he had decided to stay with Toomey. Toomey had taken an apparently neutral stand, saying evenly, "Go if you want to." But Cam had not felt that she was indifferent and had suspected that Taffy had known she was not, too.

Afterward, on the terrace, six-year-old Jane had exulted over him. They had seen a cow with a teentsy-weentsy baby calf, and a brown puppy that would not come out from under the steps. Taffy listened to these recitals jealously, finally proudly reiterated that he didn't care, he had not wanted to go. Cam felt sorry for him. He was a strange little boy. She attributed his strangeness entirely to Toomey. His fussiness about eating, his selfishness with his toys, his protest that he could not eat anything if it was also being served to the girls, and his unfriendliness to herself, she felt, were all Toomey's doing. Toomey had coddled, spoiled and talked him into feeling that Jane and Joanna were interlopers, pretty, golden-headed, good little girls whom his papa was certainly going to love very much. As for her own status as stepmother, Cam could imagine what Toomey would make of the mere word.

She would have felt quite sure of her eventual success with the child if Toomey had not been in the background, ready to carry him off for those murmured conversations which influenced him without his ever knowing their real significance. The children did not have their suppers together now, an elaboration of household detail which she found absurd. She determined to put an eventual stop to it, but she had to wait her moment to make the change; when John should be safely out of earshot, and Taffy sufficiently friendly to make it easy for her. But every day that found Toomey carrying the little boy's meal carefully upstairs on a tray, and the little girls being served in the pantry by Mabel, roused her to fresh impatience and dislike.

John fell into those erratic ways he called his regular working hours. He breakfasted late, started for his workroom at ten or half past ten and was invisible until two or half past two o'clock. Then he emerged tired and white, always affectionate and gentle with Cam, but obviously spent, and his luncheon had immediately to be served. Cam waited for him; it meant that four separate lunches must be served—five, indeed, for the oriental servants did not eat with the maids—but there was no help for it. That was the way a writer's life had to be.

Jane and Joanna had always been accustomed to a twelve-o'clock lunch, but Toomey had shifted it until thirty minutes later. Taffy, she told Cam, never was hungry at noon, and it meant baking potatoes and straining vegetables twice instead of once. The maids were served immediately afterward, and Tids and her mother had their lunch at half past one. Then came Cam's wait for John, and once again the table was beautifully set and the food must be freshly cooked.

It gave her free time to be with her children at their noon meal, and she liked that; it was almost the only time she could count on being with them, for John expected her to be in their room when, after a walk or ride or afternoon nap, he was dressing for dinner. And when they went down to dinner at seven, or a little later, the children were in bed. Afterward, if he worked, he liked her to come up to the study and sit there reading, where he could watch her and feel that she was near him.

Her getting the household into smooth-running order and her vague yet determined plan to get rid of Toomey were continually delayed by her husband's rapturous delight in carrying her off on Saturday at noon, taking her either to the city, to Del Monte or Santa Barbara, or even on longer trips.

"Pack your bag, darling, we're going somewhere!" he would announce at Saturday breakfast. Cam's responding smile and eager widening of eyes sometimes hid a moment of panic, hid the sudden thought: "Oh, my poor little girls, I promised them a picnic!"

And when he and she came back late on Sunday night, weary and sunburned and dirty, she would manage to creep into the nursery and look down on Jane and Joanna, sound asleep, and wonder if they had missed her during the two long days, wonder if they had cried, if there had been any troubles between them and Toomey or Taffy.

John often worked until one or two o'clock in the morning. Cam would grow chilly and sleepy over her book; she would curl up on the couch in the study and watch him working away, his typewriter keys clicking madly for a space; then the machine was pushed aside and John's handsome serious face, intent upon the scattered papers, came into view, his fountain pen making his beautifully accurate corrections and additions in the margins. She loved to see him so, gripping his pipe in his teeth, his hair disordered, his fine brows knitted, and he loved to look up and catch her eye.

"Sleepy, Beautiful?"

"Just comfortably so. A little chilly."

"Wait a minute, I'll put a log in the stove. There isn't a great deal more of this."

Perhaps as the clock's hands moved from twelve to one and one to two o'clock, she would doze, awakening cramped and chilled to see his big hand held out toward her and to discover all the lights out but one.

"Come on to bed, Sleepyhead. I'm dying. But that was a good night's work!"

Cramped, weary, his arm about her, they would find their way to their own room. Hing's orders were always to have a few sandwiches and a tall pitcher of grape juice there, and John never failed to enjoy a little supper the very last thing. Sometimes Cam had a sandwich; more often she let him eat his meal alone, while she fussed about with powders and cream and brushes.

"You keep fantastic and unnatural hours, John," she told him one night.

"A writer is a fantastic and unnatural creature, Cam. It seems to be the breed. Consider what writing women look like, and how they dress! To be odd-looking and odd-behaving is to be natural for a writer."

"Candace McBride," Cam said thoughtfully. They had met the poetess at Carmel.

"Exactly! Candace McBride. That—portière, was it?"

"A sort of mustard-colored drape. I'm sure she'd call it a drape—I hate the word myself. I think it still had the curtain rings sewed on it. And amber earrings the size of little ash trays. Perhaps they *were* little ash trays. And buck teeth."

"One woman who writes down in Hollywood says that she never can write anything unless she's in a tub half full of hot water."

"She doesn't!"

"I assure you she does."

"But does she ever write anything worth while?"

"Well—she makes a great deal of money."

"But she doesn't write a *Green Twigs,*" Cam said proudly.

"Nobody takes her very seriously. But then in a few years nobody may be taking me very seriously. And maybe I shan't care!" John said, his mouth full of rye bread and cheese.

"They always will. That man in New York was right. They can't ever write the history of letters in your generation and leave you out, John," Cam said proudly. "I look at you sometimes at night when you're working," she said, "and it seems such a miracle to me! One minute the empty page, and the next words that will always be alive."

"Ever think that there were ten minutes once in which Falstaff wasn't, and then was?" John asked. It was one of the whimsical little wandering thoughts that she loved in him. But then she loved him for everything he was and everything he was not, and these little side flights into his own deep musings and rich readings were just one more phase of delight.

They slept late in the mornings, sometimes lying and talking for an hour before they even mentioned dressing. Cam's head where she loved it to be, on his shoulder, his arm about her. The spring sun would come in through the farmhouse windows and fall upon Cam's magnificently appointed dressing table and upon John's riding boots and the children's photographs.

When they did finally decide to get up, two rings on the kitchen bell warned Hing that they would be down in half an hour. But often they rang three times, which meant that breakfast and the papers and the mail must be sent up as soon as ready, and then they might loiter for another hour or two, laughing, talking, wasting time. John would manage a shower, Cam brush her lovely hair. Presently, with his loose shirt open at the collar, and her beauty enhanced by the delicate laces and frills of a dressing gown, they would be falling upon their coffee and bacon, the laughter, the talk, the teasing still unexhausted.

Then there were the news and the mail to discuss, and if the latter was overwhelming, John telephoned his secretary in the village, and Gordon came up and went at the letters while John started to work. At this time Cam was free to fly to the children, to kiss them and make much of them, to explain that Mummy was so tired last night, and poor Uncle Jack had worked so late, that they had slept and slept and slept and not heard a sound this morning!

These hours were precious to her, for if she had any telephoning to do, any orders to give, letters to write, they must be gotten in now, as well as whatever she was to have of the children's company. They would perhaps be in the sandbox, busily digging and pouring when she went down; they always welcomed her with adoring affection, and she stayed with them for every possible minute until they went up for their naps at quarter past one. Then there was another brief interval in which she might do as she liked, and then John's shout: "Cam, Cam, come and eat! I'm starving."

Afterward he wanted her complete attention and was rarely willing to include anyone else, even his mother and sister, in his plans. Cam must be somewhere near, in the room if he took a nap. When he awakened they were going for a walk, or a drive, or into the city to see a very special movie or matinee. Or perhaps he was going to take her off for dinner and skip work for the evening, and in that case she must make herself look as well as she could, for his pride in her beauty was one of the things that made these city expeditions satisfying to him.

And always, and through everything, she felt the force of

his deep passionate love for her; every word, every look were hers; he wanted nothing else; his wife was his world.

The elder Mrs Kilgarif and Tids duly moved to "the puppy's house" in Windmill Lane; it was not far, Mabel and the girls could easily walk there on a spring afternoon, for Joanna and Jane adored Aunt Tids, and some previous tenant had built a playhouse there which was at once turned over to the small girls. Toomey and Taffy never joined them on these expeditions; they went every morning, coming back for lunch, and if, as the weeks went by, Cam hoped less and less for a serene adjustment between the two nurses and the three children, she was just as acutely conscious as ever of the discomfort of the situation. Toomey could have solved it with a change in her tone to Taffy; Toomey chose not to solve it. The old servant was perfectly conscious of her power; she had a nervous, indulged, impressionable little boy to handle, and she would not abate one jot of her influence.

Cam stopped the daily orders of ice cream and chops, and explained to Toomey, in Taffy's hearing, that desserts were not especially good for small boys anyway; Taffy could skip the custards and fruit for a while, and then if he wanted to he could have the regular desserts with the girls. Of the chops she spoke to Taffy herself. Wouldn't this be a good plan? He would eat what the girls did; cold chicken or peanut-butter sandwiches or toast and jelly, and Cam—the child had quite simply commenced calling her what his father did, and she had never stopped him—Cam would send a check every month to the poor hungry little boys in China from David Kilgarif.

"I want my own chops: I don't like boys in China!" Taffy said to this, in a sulky mutter. And at first the stoppage of ice cream made him ill. He was nauseated and pale, and said his head ached, and, his grandmother witnessing his collapse, Mitchell was at once sent for ice cream, and Toomey fed it to Taffy by spoonfuls as he lay languidly on his bed. But Cam held firm, and the daily order remained canceled.

He was much too young, he was really too fine and smart a

little boy, Cam would reflect, to be so deliberately and shrewdly perverse. He had charming moods, when he was affectionate, childish, amusing. But at the slightest sign of opposition he would become again the whining, stubborn, unmanageable child who haunted all her waking and sleeping dreams.

"Taffy, let Joanna have her bucket, and you use yours," she would say reasonably, pleasantly, out at the sandbox in the morning. There was a swing for the children, a long slide and a little slide, bars and a seesaw. And, this spring, men were busy building them a shallow pool for hot summer days.

Taffy would continue to sit in the sand, backed up against all three tin pails, his dark eyes mutinous.

"This afternoon I'll get him two more buckets, then he'll give theirs up," Toomey might say, not looking up from her knitting.

"You needn't stay here, you know, Toomey. I'm going to be with the children until they go in."

"I've nothing else to do, medem. And in case he gets into one of his tantrums it's better I'd be here."

"Toomey," Cam said once, when she and the nurse were alone, "I don't think it's wholesome for Taffy to have you speak of his tantrums before him. The sooner he forgets them and outgrows them, the better for us all."

"I doubt if he'll ever outgrow them, Mrs Kilgarif. After that one this morning he lay on his bed for two hours; he was exhausted, medem. They seem to go very deep with him; I wouldn't wonder would he always be subject to them."

"This morning——" Here was Cam justifying herself to Toomey again; she despised herself for her eternal explanations and palliations to the nurse, but she seemed unable to refrain from them. "This morning," she said, "I simply wanted him to wear one of his new linens. I got them at the smartest place in the city; they're what all the boys are wearing this hot weather; he says he doesn't like them. Well," Cam went on, "I'm not going to send back three-dollar linen suits just because a child of four——"

She knew from Toomey's expression that she was talking to empty air. Taffy, however, was presently wearing the suits, his little bared thin arms and legs looking twisted and pale beside the girls' round brownness, and Cam dropped the issue as concluded.

CHAPTER XVIII

LATER HER MOTHER-IN-LAW innocently reopened the subject, spoke to her admiringly of Toomey's marvelous handling of the boy.

"Do you know what she did about those new linen sun suits you got him, Cam?" asked old Mrs Kilgarif on an afternoon when she and Tids had come over to share his late luncheon with John, and the three women were sitting together in the garden afterward while John took a nap.

"No. She didn't tell me."

"Well, Toomey took him into town to see the dentist last week, and while he was with Doctor Sumner, she slipped across the street to the shop and returned the suits and had a talk with the saleswoman. Then when she brought Taffy out she suggested to him that they go look for some suits as much as possible like the ones she had sent back, so that you wouldn't know about the change. Of course that delighted our monkey, and he solemnly selected the very ones you did—with one exception, I believe, wasn't it, Tids? And ever since, according to Toomey's story, he's been wearing them and watching you out of the corner of his eye, wondering when you were going to find him out!"

Cam looked at her mother-in-law steadily.

"What a fool you are!" she thought. Aloud she said: "I would be afraid that she would rather mix up his small ideas of honor and honesty."

"Oh, she's marvelous with him," Mrs Kilgarif said, her eyes closed, her bloodless little silk-clad body basking in the sun. "Well, here's our boy himself, and Toomey, too," she added, as Taffy came out, smart in dark-striped linen and a linen hat, and snuggled up against his grandmother. "You look very nice," the old lady told him, approvingly.

"These are my new suits," Taffy said innocently, with a glance at Cam.

"Ah, they're lovely! It seem to me they're just the suits a little boy would pick out for himself," Mrs Kilgarif said playfully.

"Mrs Kilgarif got them for him," Toomey put in respectfully. "Come along, Taffy," she said, "and you can have the bicycle before Jane comes down."

"It's my bicycle, Grandma, and Jane is always using it!" Taffy complained.

"Well, then you go use it now, darling, while Jane's asleep."

"And who uses Jane's blackboard?" Cam asked. The moment the words were said she regretted them; they had come involuntarily; they hung in the air. A grown woman, arguing with a baffling scrap of a boy of four!

"You shall have a blackboard of your own, Taffy," Mrs Kilgarif promised him. "We know our own mind!" she added proudly, when Toomey and Taffy went away.

"Are all of you in a conspiracy to spoil him?" Cam asked, in her heart. Aloud she merely said that children grew out of these tyrannous moods.

"I thought your husband was to have *your* children sometimes?" Mrs Kilgarif asked quite naturally, opening her eyes to look at Cam. The question struck Cam like a blow. She had all but forgotten Bob, his claim on Joanna and Jane.

It was not the first time she had noticed the complete lack of tact that was the older woman's chief characteristic. Cam and John had more than once laughed at it—at his mother's innocent, "You have an unusually good appetite, haven't you, Campbell?" and at her frequent greeting to John, "Aren't you getting very fat, dear?"

But this was the sharpest shaft yet. For all the rest of the day, and for many days, it would recur to Cam, and always with an acute discomfort of spirit. She made herself answer serenely:

"He's living at his club, you know. His mother died. It would be hard for him to take care of them."

Tids, stretched in the sunshine—for May had been rainy, and this was the first warm day in several days—spoke lazily, not taking her face from her crossed arms:

"Mother, don't you know you ought not to talk about anyone's first husband when she's married to her next?"

"I love that 'next,' " Cam murmured.

"Nonsense!" said Mrs Kilgarif. "That's old-fashioned nonsense! Women marry as often as they like these days, and a sensible way to have it, too. If they have no religious scruples, that is."

"I suppose this is coming to me," Cam thought. "I've had it pretty easy, all my life."

"Well, if I were married to a second man, and anyone asked me about the first one, and I remembered that I'd gone on a honeymoon with him, and had children by him, it 'd make me feel queer!" Tids announced, thoughtfully and clearly, still not moving her hidden face.

"What's all that, Mouse?" John asked, coming out to tip up Cam's face and kiss her and to subside into a chair beside her.

"I say, John," Tids answered, rolling over, blinking at the sun, stretching her length on the warm red flags of the terrace, "that if I were Cam, and Mother talked to me about my first husband, I'd feel queer!"

"Did Mother?" John asked, lightly kissing Cam's hand.

"Your mother asked if the children's father wasn't someday going to borrow them for a visit," Cam explained, keeping it all as unimportant as she could. "That was all. Did you get to sleep?"

"I did. And now I want to know what's the plot."

"The plot is for us to go home," the elder Mrs Kilgarif said. "You're coming over to dinner tomorrow night?"

"But I have to come home right afterward, Mother. I'm working."

"I know. We'll let you go. But Tids and I go to Cousin Susan in Laguna on Friday."

"You wouldn't like to take Taffy and Toomey?" John asked suddenly. His mother's eyes met his in surprise.

"John, I don't see how we could. She's got that small place, and she's had a nervous breakdown."

"No, I was just fooling." He saw his mother and sister to the car, came back to find Cam staring absently into space, her brows faintly ruffled.

"Jack, why did you say that?"

"Say what, sweetheart?"

"About sending Taffy south?"

"Well, it occurred to me that it would ease things up here for you. Toomey was saying something about there being a scene almost every day; in fact, sometimes I hear Taffy yelling. I thought it might lessen the strain for you."

"What he was yelling about this morning was my not letting him take his little velocipede out into the highway. He can ride it around our roads here, or even in the upper lane. But when he gets down where the traffic is, it's quite a different story."

"I know, dear, you were quite right!"

"If Toomey would say one word to him about it, it would all be so much easier. But this morning she just stood by, with her face like granite, and said, 'You must do as your stepmother says, Taffy, you must obey your stepmother,' until I could have slapped her! Finally I said to her—and imagine how it weakens my position to appeal to her in this way!—'Toomey, would you let a boy of four take a velocipede out 'nto the main highway?' and she answered, 'I'm sure I shouldn't say, medem, it's for you to decide.' Anything rather than cross him!"

"Ah, well, you see, he's been ill a lot, and she loves him."

"I think she's the reason he's been ill, I really do, talking to him all the time about what he can eat and what he can't eat."

"Oh, come!" John said, laughing. "Joanna was doing some tall screaming herself yesterday."

"That was Toomey again. She gets them all into spasms of excitement. It takes a lot to get Joanna roused, but yesterday when Joanna was playing quite contentedly with Taffy's old sand machine, he suddenly wanted it. I said that he could have it in a few minutes, and Toomey said, 'Suppose you take her Crazy Jane, Taffy, until she gives you back your sand dump.' That made Joanna a little uneasy, but she didn't say anything until he gave Crazy Jane to the cat, and the cat jumped up on the shed roof with her. Then Joanna went into fits, and I went tearing after the cat, and it took me fifteen minutes to quiet her down."

"Well, I suppose Taffy thought the sand thing was his."

"Yes, I know, Jack, but we want the children to share things, and to play with them because they want to play with them, not simply to keep them away from each other."

John was not listening; his narrowed eyes were far away. He spoke musingly.

"I wish to God Mother hadn't brought that up," he said.

"Brought what up?" But she had no sooner spoken than she knew.

"Oh, Bob Sylvester. I hate him. I hate every bone in his body."

"Jack!" she said, shocked. He did not look at her; he was looking gloomily away.

"Well, I do. I've never said it. I've tried to forget the fool," he said harshly. "But you might as well know it. I hate him!"

"But you don't know him!"

"I know that you loved him, you belonged to him," John

said, in an almost strangled voice. "He could go into your room and kneel down by your bed and put his arms about you, as I do. He could wake in the mornings and see you asleep, all gold and apricot, with your eyelashes black on your cheek. You were his, as you are mine——"

"Oh, hush!" she said, putting her fingers against his lips. "All that's like a dream, like your life with Margaret, Jack. I never think of it unless something—like what your mother said today—brings it to my mind. Can't you be happy just in this very hour—now, when we're together on our own terrace, with our vine fig—or rather, prune tree—and our assorted Infantry, and when nothing can separate us?"

"God knows I'm happy, dearest!" he said humbly. And he told her for the thousandth time: "The trouble is, I love you too much!"

"But that's the way women want to be loved," she answered contentedly.

"Here's the thing that drives me crazy, Cam. When you love those children so, and when I see your lovely beautiful head down close to theirs, I wonder if you're thinking of him?"

She seemed to be drawing upon some unsuspected deep well of patience within her. She could smile, as she shook her head.

"A mother doesn't have to think of anyone else in connection with the love she has for her children, Jack. That's born with the children; it springs up like a fountain, it rolls over one like a wave. One could actually despise the father, I think. It wouldn't make any difference."

"But you don't despise him, Bob Sylvester, do you?"

"Why, no. I don't think of him at all. Whatever I felt for him was so mixed up with the fact that I was a girl, and visiting here, and engaged to the big footballer and golf player—all that belongs to another life, another me. The money crash came, and the children were born, and I had those lonely winters, those lonely summers at the Lake. It all changed me. And loving you changed me most of all."

"Can a woman tell, d'you suppose," he asked in a quieter tone, "whether she loves her children more than her husband, or how it is?"

"She loves them differently, Jack. You love Taffy, and you love your mother, but it would never occur to me that you were taking anything away from your love for me and giving it to them."

"You're not jealous, are you, Cam?"

"I don't think I am. Yes, of course I am," Cam said, very young and earnest as she analyzed it. "If the girls loved anyone else more than they do me——"

"You think of the girls first, you see."

"Jack, you idiot! I was coming to you. I was going to say that I could be horribly jealous of you if there were any cause. What makes me cross at you is that you're jealous without any cause. Half the time when I merely speak of the girls, or look down from the porch in the morning to see what they're doing, I feel as if you noticed it."

"Half the time!" he said. "Every time, and a thousand times when you don't mention them or look at them."

"Why, but that is dementia, my poor little fellow, and you will have to have your little head examined," Cam said in a motherly tone that sat oddly on her smallness and fairness as compared to his inches, his long legs and big hands.

"You little adorable darling, sitting there in your brown dress philosophizing!" Jack said. "I guess I'm crazy. How about taking a ride?"

"Is it pretty hot to ride?" she asked, widening her blue eyes. In her heart she said: "Oh, dear, why won't you sit quietly here on the terrace and let me see the girls when they come down? Jane had a sniffly sort of nose; she may have a little fever. It 'd be so reassuring to be here and see for myself that they're all right. . . . I'll go jump into riding things," she said, getting up, turning to meet his arms, feeling them big and strong about her, and raising her face for his kiss.

"You don't think I'm an utter fool, Cam?"

"Yes, I do. I know you are. But I like you to be a fool," Cam reassured him. He held her prisoner.

"Are you happy?" he asked.

"The happiest woman in the world. The proudest," she said. It was the question he had asked her from the very beginning of their engagement, on their honeymoon, throughout all the weeks since. She always answered it in the same phrases.

"And say that you wish that everyone else in the world was dead, and you and I the only people alive!" he added. Cam laughed.

"We have children, Jack, and when you have children——" she was beginning moderately, when he interrupted her.

"Ah, now, darling, that's just the way I hate you to talk! You'll make me jealous again."

"But, Jack, there are such things as obligations!"

"No, there aren't. At least not beyond seeing that they have good nurses, and plenty of fresh air and good food! I adore Taffy," John said. "I've always told Toomey that nothing should stand in the way of what he must have. But, Cam, you can't lead a child's life. We're a man and a woman who love each other, who are sufficient to each other! Why, looky," John went on, using the schoolboy word she had found amusing in his eager talk many times before this, "looky, Cam. You had the girls last summer, up there at the Lake, and you were damn lonesome and always wondering what your husband was doing, why you'd been shelved. Isn't that true?"

"Of course it's true, silly," she said, in a maternal tone of amusement. But in her soul she felt a certain surprise to realize that it was so. She had had the girls all to herself then. Nobody had interrupted their picnics, or laughed at her when foolish fears kept her beside one small bed or the other in the night. Cam had a fleeting instant in which to think how extraordinarily free she had been then; no Taffy and Toomey problems to perplex and irritate her, no adoring, insistent John to absorb four fifths of her waking time.

"So you see!" he was saying triumphantly. He kissed her

again, set her free and watched her as she ran off to get into her riding things.

"I'll have small help from *him,*" Cam ruminated, as they jogged along through the green forest. "He's like a happy little boy who wants his mama's entire attention every second. I'll have to work this thing out myself, manage to give the girls all I can of my time, keep Mrs Kilgarif and Tids happy, somehow win David's affection, and first and foremost—" her thoughts rambled on, "first and foremost I'll get rid of Toomey! At the next opportunity—and she's always giving me opportunities—I'll simply and definitely fire her. 'Jack, I've had to let Toomey go. Your mother 'll feel very badly, and I suppose Taffy 'll miss her for a few days, but it had to come sooner or later, and I couldn't stand her any longer. There can't be two mistresses in one house.' "

She rehearsed the sentences until she had them by heart. The only difficulty was to summon up courage enough to make them the truth. Toomey went her usual way and Cam hers, and if the nurse was purposely avoiding occasions of disagreement, Cam felt in her coward heart that she was avoiding them, too.

But the pricks were incessant. When Cam was suddenly seized and carried off by John for a trip to Las Vegas, to take a look at the big dam, she neglected to leave instructions for several various decisions that must come up in her absence. Mrs King's party for the children was one; Toomey, tacitly left in control, decided against it, hurting the little neighbor's feelings deeply. The swimming pool was finished, painted, filled during that week, but as Mrs Kilgarif had not expressly stated that the children might begin their wading in it, Toomey had not seen fit to permit them that pleasure, even on the hottest days of a hot July. Joanna had developed a severe case of poison-oak, and the competent Toomey had at once relegated her to a hospital room, where Cam, returning in a mood of felicity and serenity from a very honeymoon with John, was horrified to find her, homesick and frightened and ready to burst into frantic tears at the sight of her mother.

"How long was she there, Mabel?" Cam asked, when Joanna had been brought home, comforted, petted, and had dropped off to sleep in great happiness to the sound of her mother's voice.

"This is Thursday. She went Tuesday," Mabel reported.

"You and Jane saw her every day?"

"No, ma'am. Toomey said Jane might ketch something from the hospital, and she said we wasn't to go," Mabel said virtuously.

"Good heavens! You could have gone anyway. You knew what I would want."

"Mitchell don't take orders from me. It's Toomey tells him where we shall drive," Mabel reminded her, not without meek satisfaction.

"You could have telephoned for a taxi!" But Cam said it half to herself. She could not really blame Mabel. If she found Toomey difficult to outwit, how much more would simple Mabel be baffled by her! Cam could only tell herself that she would watch for the very first opportunity of bringing matters to an issue with Toomey, and after that hold tight to her resolution to get the woman out of the house. Mabel could easily do the little there was to do for Taffy; he should join the children at their meals as a matter of course, as all little brothers must; the atmosphere would clear as soon as Toomey was gone, and they would all begin to act more naturally and fall into more comfortable ways.

CHAPTER XIX

A FEW DAYS LATER HER opportunity came, and anger rose so quickly in Cam's heart, and she could speak with such feeling, that she was completely unconscious of making any effort whatsoever in the matter. She chanced to come upon Taffy at his supper, alone in his own room. John, who was not dressed, had suddenly remembered that a certain suit was hanging in the little boy's closet, and Cam, being dressed, volunteered to go for it. That was the cause of her entering Taffy's room unannounced; she had forgotten that Toomey always carried his supper upstairs to him at this hour, and involuntarily apologized when she found them together; Toomey knitting, Taffy playing with a saucerful of ice cream.

"Why *should* I apologize?" Cam's immediate uncomfortable thought ran. "After all, I'm mistress of this house." But the apology had been made, and the maddeningly serene Toomey had accepted it with a simple, "Oh, that's all right, medem."

Cam completed her errand, went back to John with the suit, got into her most exquisite array, to drive with him to a party in Burlingame. But the scene in Taffy's room lingered in her mind. It was ridiculous, when the little girls were enjoying their evening meal on the terrace, to have that smug nurse lead Taffy upstairs, sit over him while he ate. She was making a pompous little recluse of him; it was bad for him, and for the girls, and for the household! Taffy had been a delicate child, to be sure, but he was not delicate now, although his growth had been set back a little, and he was thin. He ought to be encouraged to lead as much the normal life of a child as possible.

Suddenly she remembered the ice cream. He had been eating ice cream! Cam's heart contracted on a spasm of pure rage; loosened again. She told herself she must be calm. Perhaps Hing had made it; perhaps all the children had had ice cream for supper tonight. Mabel would know. But if that woman was persisting in the absurdity of ice cream every night for a child of four——

Cam lost the thread of something John was saying; recalled herself with an effort and devoted herself to being as charming as she could for the rest of the evening. The occasion was a wedding and a supper; many of her old friends were there. She fancied—but then it was an easy thing to fancy—that a few of them deliberately avoided her. But most of them came up enthusiastically, and the bride herself accused "Aunt Cam" of running away with the show. She saw the Howards and the Fieldings and Aline and the Fords again, and Madeleine with her deep hoarse voice and talk of races. It was rather fun to see them all, even though she agreed with John, when they were driving home under the stars, that that sort of party didn't pay, and that such holidays as the cloudless visit to the Boulder Dam were much nicer.

"We did see people there, too, Jack—the Grovers and Doctor Merritt. But somehow engineers and scientists seem worth while, and tonight wasn't worth while."

They drove along in silent content for a while. Suddenly Cam was stirred to self-contempt by finding that her thoughts were with Toomey again. Silly fool that she was to let the woman influence her so! All the time that she spent in long, imaginary argumentative discussions with Toomey was time worse than wasted, and yet she could not seem to keep away from them. Well, tomorrow she would find out about this ice-cream thing, and if Toomey had been ordering it daily, in direct opposition to her wishes, that would be the end of Toomey!

It so happened that her bills were all waiting for her in the morning; she seized first upon the one from the drugstore. Her eyes ran rapidly over the various daily charges; everything else was there: camera films, poison-oak salve, chocolate bars, magazines, soap and murder stories, but no ice cream. Cam breathed anew.

"Mabel," she said, when Mabel happened to come into the room, "can you remember what the girls had for dessert last night?"

Mabel reflected.

"They had stewed blackberries and ladyfingers. Jane spilled a lot on her pajamas," she answered, after a moment.

"Taffy," Cam said simply, "was having ice cream."

"Yes'm. He has it every night," Mabel stated. "I told you that."

Cam slit envelopes, ruffled papers, her back to Mabel. A few minutes later, when Dora, the nice little dining-room maid, brought her a telephone message, she asked Dora to send Toomey to her. But instead of Toomey, a few moments later Dora herself came back.

"Toomey says did you wish her to leave Taffy alone at the pool or bring him with her?" Dora inquired.

"Wasn't anyone else at the pool?"

"No, ma'am."

"Well, let it go then, Dora. Any time will do." Cam worked along in the summer shadiness of the big room on a morning that should have been all sweetness and greenness, the flashing of birds' wings and the splash of water into the pool. But inwardly her mind and soul were a raging furnace of resentment; the imaginary conversation with Toomey had gathered fresh momentum; new phrases were battering about her ears like winged dragonflies.

When Mabel went by with the little girls, bonneted and barelegged, bound for the sandbox and the new fascinations of the pool, Cam asked her to say to Toomey that she would like to see her.

"Say that you will keep an eye on Taffy for a few minutes," she said. But even then she was not sure that Toomey would come, and awaited her with confused emotions that were at one moment dread of her defiance and at the next apprehension that she might really be on her way.

Toomey came in quietly, every inch the respectable servant, in her striped blue-and-gray percale, her knitting still in her hands.

"Toomey, sit down. There's something I wanted to ask you," Cam said, wheeling about in her desk chair. "I noticed that Taffy was having ice cream for dinner last night. Don't you remember that I said that I didn't want that to go on?"

"It's not being charged at Mullers' any more," Toomey answered composedly, her words thick with her German accent.

"Where does it come from?"

"I pay for it," said Toomey. Cam felt her cheeks grow hot.

"*You* pay for it!"

"Yes, medem. You said you considered it an extravagance, and I knew it was one of the most nourishing things he will eat." Toomey's fingers moved rapidly over a peculiarly dull shade of gray wool.

"Stop knitting!" Cam said, in a sudden passion. "Listen to what I say. I object to your interpreting my orders—my requests—concerning the children in this—this highhanded way. You have made everything as difficult as possible for me since I came here, and I know you're quite sensible enough to realize that this cannot go on. I've spoken to Mr Kilgarif——"

("How I do explain to this woman!" Cam thought impatiently. "How I do build myself up for her!") "I've spoken to Mr Kilgarif," she repeated, aloud, "and he agrees with me that Mabel is quite able to handle Taffy now, especially as Jane starts to school in October. And so I'm very sorry to tell you——" ("Well, *say* it, *say* it, *say* it!" she said fiercely in her soul.) "I'm very sorry to tell you that after the first of the month I want you to make some other arrangement. It's unfortunate that it didn't work better, since the child is so devoted to you, and you're naturally fond of him. But boys do outgrow nurses, and I think we'll all be happier when we've made a—a different arrangement. Perhaps I'm wrong in my ideas about the children," Cam added, gaining confidence as she went along, and speaking with something like gentleness, "but after all, I can only do my best. And I'm afraid what we're doing for Taffy isn't the best, isn't always wise."

Toomey rose, stuffing her knitting into a big chintz bag.

"You've never liked me, medem," she said, in her heavy Teutonic tones, meeting Cam's eye with her steady gray eye. "And you've always been jealous of the child. We'll not be afraid of words, we've hated each other from the first—I hated you from the day he took me to the Lake, to meet Taffy's stepmother. You'd a husband then, you'd children of your own; it wasn't enough for you. You'd no sooner come here than you tried to take the child away from me. I took him from his mother; I'd my hands on him before ever the doctor had. 'There's your baby, Toomey,' she says to me. 'His father 'll love him, but he'll marry again. You love him. You be always the person he's first with.' "

Cam gave her back her look.

"You've been wonderfully devoted," she conceded, coldly. "If you need a letter from me—a letter saying that with a very young child, or a delicate child, you are completely experienced and competent——"

"Was that all, medem?" Toomey asked, cutting brusquely across her words. Her eyes glittered: her breath came quickly.

"That was all. I hope you'll make whatever arrangements are convenient to you about going. I know Mr Kilgarif and his mother will want you to feel that in whatever you decide to do they want to help you."

Toomey was gone. The room rocked and shouted with words; words that had at last been said! Cam gasped, plunged into the business of bills and checks, halted, and heard the uproar about her ears again. Oh, it was over, she had said everything she had ever meant to say, and yet not too much—not too much! Toomey was fired. In a few days she and her trunk would be gone—gone—gone, and how sweet the house would be without her!

"Taffy darling," Cam could so simply say then, "will you have your supper tonight with the girls on the terrace outside the dining room, and serve the dessert like a real brother? We'll make it a little party, and go to the five-and-ten and get surprises. That 'll be fun, I think."

Of *course* he'd fall into line, once that malignant and possessive spirit had been removed! And then what happy days at Cherry Ridge, with children splashing and chattering at the pool, and Cam's cleverness gradually drawing John into picnics and holidays that included the boy and the girls!

That night, when he and she were taking a turn about the garden in the sweet early evening, she told John.

"Jack, I didn't have a chance to talk to you about it before. But now that she's gone off with Mitchell on some mysterious errand, and can't possibly overhear, I'll tell you the news. I've dismissed Toomey."

"Help!" he said, with a laugh. "You two been going for each other again? How that old girl does get your goat!"

"It isn't a question of 'getting my goat,' " Cam assured him with dignity; "it's a question of her usurping authority in every possible way, bossing not only the girls and Hing when we're away, but Mabel, too; decreeing that the children shall do this and shan't do that, but actually going straight against my orders. She's a *Hun!* You remember that I told you that I didn't like this daily chop and daily ice-cream business—oh, weeks ago? Well, Toomey simply took the law into her own hands, the ice cream is delivered every day, and charged to *her*."

She stopped, facing him, her eyes glinting in moonlight.

"For the Lord's sake!" John said, in proper amazement. "You cross little adorable beauty!" he said, catching his small earnest wife toward him for a kiss.

"No, but Jack," she persisted, speaking with some little difficulty against his lips, "don't you think that's outrageous?"

"Think what is outrageous, Beautiful?"

"Oh, Jack, please pay attention to me, and stop biting those little kisses off me! Life isn't all kisses," Cam said, laughing and struggling.

"Life *is* all kisses, sweetheart, kisses from little wives whose hair smells like heaven, and whose sunburned little necks taste like ambrosia," John answered, undistracted. "Cam, why are you so utterly gorgeous? Why am I so lucky? Life is all heaven with you, darling, mornings when we wake up together and nights when we have a little fire in the dining room, and the dinner table in front of the fire! So you fired old Toomey, did you? She won't care. She'll be right back on the job tomorrow."

"She will not!" Cam said on a brief mirthless laugh, as, with hands locked, they resumed their aimless walk. "I made that pretty clear. Paying for Taffy's ice cream indeed!"

"Well, you know really, darling," Jack began, in mollifying tones, "that was kind of touching of her, when all's said and done. I'm on your side, and if you say send her packing, why, I say send her packing, but there wasn't anything so criminal in that. Isn't plain ice cream on children's menus—doesn't Joanna have it?"

"Certainly she does. But it's going directly against my orders."

"She was boss for a long time. For four years she's done what she liked with Taffy. When the doctors said he couldn't live, she thumbed her nose at them. Many a mother isn't as much to a child as she's been to Taffy. And what's the difference if he likes ice cream? I like popovers, and Hing makes 'em every morning."

"Ah, but Jack, that isn't the point at all, dear. I'm really being reasonable about this, and she's in the wrong. She's gotten herself so entrenched with your mother and you that she thinks she can get away with anything, and she crosses me in everything. Every day, in one way or another, she manages to let me know that I'm not her mistress. You pay her to take care of a child that isn't my child; she never forgets it."

"Oh, she's a crank all right," John conceded good-humoredly, "but she'll be all right in the morning, you'll see. She has these blow-ups."

"But I don't *want* her to be all right in the morning! I've told her to go, and I expect her to go."

"Yes, but look here, Cam. That means a hell of a time with Taffy. He'll carry on like a troop of cavalry. You'll be exhausted; Mabel has no brains at all, and everything 'll be a mess. Then Mother 'll come sailing over and say that the child looks thin, and she thinks it was a dangerous change, and then where 'll you be?"

"Well, I'll expect all that," Cam said courageously, although her heart quailed within her at the prospect. "I'll expect things to go badly," she said. "I'll take that responsibility. For a little while we *will* have a hard time getting him reconciled. But he's only a child, and a smart and affectionate one. Within a few weeks we'll have him tamed; school will do the rest. She's a bad influence over him, Jack. I know it. I think she's one of those war-touched women; she's got it into her head that nobody else has the slightest rights over him. It's going to be heaven to get her out, once and for all!"

"How about waiting until we rush on to New York in October, and get back?"

"Why, Jack, that's months. This is only July! And I'm counting the hours until she goes."

"Well, you settle it," he said good-naturedly. But his tone

did not sound quite satisfied, and Cam felt that she had not made her case very strong with him. "I was going to work tomorrow morning," he said musingly. "I think perhaps I'll go over and have a talk with Mother about it. She'll be all upset, and I want to put your side of it to her before Toomey gets started."

"But you aren't going to interrupt your *work* for that!" Cam said, scandalized.

"I've come to a good stopping place," he offered.

Nothing more was said on the subject that night; the rest of their walk was what all their walks were, a time of memorable harmony and happiness. But Cam lay long awake that night still arguing and explaining in her thoughts with Toomey, or talking of Toomey with John's mother. And in the morning she was aware not only that her wearied thoughts were still milling about in the same grooves, but that everyone in the house except the children was perfectly conscious of what was going on.

John having kept his word as to going over to his mother's, she was free earlier than usual to go up to the pool with the children, to spend a contented three hours in their company, listening to their absurdities, watching the firm brown rounded little bodies doubled up in the sandbox or splashing in the clear water, and basking in green shadow under the big trees. Taffy elected to join them this morning and was at his sweetest, and Cam, in deep content, told herself that this happy time was only a foretaste of the serene days to come, after Toomey had gone.

"Don't you want to let Joanna get on part of the float, Taffy?" she asked mildly.

"Would it be generous?" he demanded, in an almost truculent voice. Toomey was nowhere within hearing; she had removed herself immediately, upon Cam's reaching the pool with the girls, and Cam fancied that her absence was already affecting Taffy for the better.

"It would be *very* generous."

"Then she can have it!" He was into the water like a frog. Cam sent him a heart-warming smile.

"Oh, sank you, sank you, sank you, Taffy," Joanna gushed, in sisterly gratitude.

"This couldn't be lovelier," Cam thought, the far-away dazzle of flower beds, the murmuring of bees, the rich tent-top of the oaks all contributing to the perfection of the summer morning. "It only takes courage," she mused, "to straighten out one's life. This time yesterday I hadn't talked to Toomey; this time tomorrow she may be gone!"

The children were all asleep upstairs when John returned in great spirits for a late luncheon. He and Cam could not very well talk while the meal was in progress, for the nursery windows were just above the terrace, but she did manage to whisper, "How'd your mother take it?" and catch his exultant answer, "Magnificently! Everything fine," before they went to other topics. Afterward, when they were driving to Palo Alto upon a host of unimportant errands, he told her the news.

"Mother's occasionally good for a brain storm," he said. "Or else this was Tids' inspiration—anyway they cooked it up together. Toomey and Taffy are going to move over and live with them! What do you think of *that* for a solution!"

Cam thought a great many things of it, but sheer shock kept her silent for a moment, and when she spoke it was with a tone of only natural curiosity.

"How do you mean? For how long?"

"Well—to begin with," John said. She could tell from his tone that he was pleased with himself. "To begin with, did you know that Toomey went over to see Mother last night?"

"She didn't!"

"Yes, she did. She asked me if Mitchell could take her on an errand, and over she went. She and Mother and Tids threshed the whole thing out, and Mother at once suggested her moving over to them. They've those two rooms, you know, that they're not using at all, and of course they idolize the kid. It settles the Toomey trouble once and for all. And the best part of it all is," John went on, driving down the hot village street now, and looking for a place to park the car, "that Toomey was so happy about it! I'll swear there were tears in the old renegade's eyes. She said to my mother, 'I'm very grateful to you, medem. I've always hoped I'd not have to be parted from the child.' And Mother of course began to alibi you: you had meant it all for the best, you had been most successful in bringing up your girls, all that sort of thing! 'I haven't the slightest feelings of resentment against Mrs John Kilgarif,' Toomey said.

"Did she really?" Cam asked, in so controlled and level a tone that John sensed in it nothing amiss and answered with a satisfied laugh:

"Indeed she did. So she's pleased and you're pleased, and Mother and Tids are pleased. It 'll all work out like a charm. I can wander over there every evening before supper if I want to see Taffy, and we'll often have him at the house."

"It's no solution at all," Cam wanted to say. "That smart old fox of a woman has fooled you all again. She's not fired; she still has complete control of Taffy, and she can give him chops and ice cream all day and all night if she likes! She's beaten me, and I know it, and *she* knows it. But that's not the end of the story!"

Aloud she said nothing. She and John went into the hardware shop and bought things for their new grill; they went into the five-and-ten for wrapping paper and ribbons, several family birthdays being imminent; they sat at the counter in the candy store and had cold sweet drinks. Then they drove home by a long circuitous back road upon which there were many beautiful homes under trees, with water sprinklers going in a blaze of diamonds against the sunset, and women in white sitting on shady lawns. A heavy summer fog was rolling like a wall of whipped cream over the line of the western hills, windmills were creaking, there was a delicious chill in the air. Wains laden with tomatoes were going along the highway; now and then there was a splash of the crushed ripe fruit under the motor wheels.

Cam determined to think no more about Toomey. The woman had destroyed enough of her life. She determinedly set herself to amuse and charm John, and succeeded so well that by the time they reached home both were in gales of laughter. Toomey, decorously ascending the stairs with Taffy's supper tray, looked at them blandly. She had won.

"Ah, well, let her win!" Cam thought. "Poor thing, she has so little and I have so much!"

But there was a sore spot left in her heart nevertheless. It had been part of her happy anticipations of marriage to John that his child should be important in the home group; when he counted up the joys of marriage to Cam, he must include that of having his son mothered again, a loved little boy in a happy nursery. Now that dream was shattered; everything had somehow gone wrong, and Taffy would be further away from his father than ever. It must be scored up as a failure, and Cam hated to fail.

"I mustn't let it seem important," she told herself. "The main thing is that Jack and I love each other and are closer together than ever. That's all that matters; the other things will all fit themselves into the pattern in time."

And she devoted herself to him with a completeness that dazzled him and caused him to tell her that, happy as the beginnings of their marriage had been, he had never really known how he loved her until now.

CHAPTER XX

ON THEIR FIRST ANNIVERSARY they had a family dinner party to which Taffy, at his sweetest and friendliest, and John's mother and sister came. The September evening was exquisite in warmth and beauty, and Cam had taken great trouble to have everything perfect. John's mother told her that it did her heart good to see how happy he was, and Cam felt happy, too. Taffy, she thought, did not look very well, but even that fact had its compensation; perhaps he was not so much better off under Toomey's undisputed sway as his grandmother had hoped he might be. At all events, he was charming with the little girls, and affectionate with Cam, and the evening went off with great harmony and happiness for everyone.

And immediately afterward came a fresh anxiety from an unexpected quarter. Bob Sylvester had married again, and his new wife, a quiet little mouse of a girl Cam had once known as Dixie-Belle Sunderland, wrote Cam a friendly little letter saying that she and Bob were staying with Mama in Oakland for the present and would like to have the children for a "real good visit."

The deepening devotion of Joanna and Jane to their mother had been almost an embarrassment to Cam for several months. Quite suddenly the children seemed to have grown up. They loved their mother, they wanted to be with her. Mabel's conversation and Mabel's company no longer satisfied them, fond as they were of the nurse. They wanted to follow Cam about wherever she went, and her continual absences were always a cause of great grief to them. She suffered terribly herself when she saw their lips trembling, when she heard them say, "Please don't go away tonight, Mummy, *please*." To console them, to try to give them some little philosophy, strained her nerves and burdened her heart; they were small and helpless and affectionate; it was unfair to leave them so much to servants!

More than that, she loved to be with them. She felt definitely cheated if she could not steal a few free minutes to go up to them in the evening before her own dinner, and see them finishing theirs, and get them into bed. Sensitive and intelligent, changing and awakening every day, their developing little natures fascinated her; it enchanted her to make them happy, to lift them from a dreary little vague morning mood to the heights of joy by offering to take them with her shopping, or to carry a picnic supper over to the beach.

It was a real sacrifice, even though what she did for love of John could not but be a delight, too, to give up so much of their time, so continually to close doors, evade them, put their small hands aside, break half-promises that meant joy to them.

She sat with Dixie-Belle's letter in her hand, wondering what on earth she could do now. Jane and Joanna were nervous enough already about brief partings from their mother. They would go out of their little senses at the mere idea of going away from her for weeks, living in a strange place with the father they hardly remembered. How could she break it to them, how make it seem right to them to shift their whole little scheme so completely? Suppose they said that they didn't want to go, as they very probably would. Jane would begin by pressing her small warm body against her mother's shoulder, as Cam sat in her low chair, tumbling her gold curls against her mother's cheek.

"Mummy, we'd much drather stay with you, if you don't mind."

"But think of Daddy, dear, he hasn't seen you for a whole year."

And then Joanna, following Jane's lead:

"Mummy, we'd *drather* stay with you."

Perhaps, this feeling of theirs tactfully represented to him, Bob would give up the idea of the visit. Dixie-Belle could not really want the children; she had been married before and divorced; she had never had a child. Why should she suddenly decide that she wanted to mother Cam Kilgarif's children? It was a pose, to impress Bob, and if difficulties were made she would probably be very grateful for them.

Cam discussed it with John, whose chief impression appeared to be that "Sylvester" was doing the whole thing to annoy Cam.

"No, he's not like that. He was always nice enough with the girls, the little they saw of him. But they've not seen him at all for a year now; they hardly remember him. It would be cruel to let him have them for weeks."

"Mabel would go?"

"Oh, certainly. He knows her, and she knows him, and that, at least, would be an advantage. But to turn the girls over to Dixie-Belle, who probably doesn't know anything in the world about children——!"

"Write her that you think they're too small," John suggested. Cam did immediately write to Bob's new wife, looking long at the name on the envelope; Mrs Robert Wren Sylvester. Her name for so many years! What would Dixie-Belle do when Bob began to be absent from home for nights and weeks together? Dixie-Belle played golf almost every day; they'd have that in common. Staying with her mother in Oakland, were they? That didn't sound much like Bob.

The answer from Dixie-Belle came promptly. She and

Robert were sure that "Jean" and Joanna were not at all too small to visit their father, and would send for them on October first, if that was "all right" with Cam.

It was bitterly all wrong with Cam, but after a talk with John, and two agitating telephone talks with the lawyer who had made all the arrangements for her divorce, she realized that she had no choice, and with a sick heart packed up the girls' small linens and white coats, mated their white shoes, rolled up scores of pairs of red and pink and blue socks, and when the day came put them into Bob's familiar car, in charge of Mabel and old Fred. Jane remembered old Fred, if Joanna was a little hazy about him, and observed excitedly, "Will Daddy let us see the monkeys again? Are we going to the Park?"

"Imagine her rememberin' that!" Mabel said, not displeased herself at this break in the daily routine. Mabel felt and looked important as she went off in complete responsibility for the little Sylvesters; she did not know anything about the Sunderland house, but if the staff there was not impressed with the Kilgarif name at first hearing, it would be before she got through!

Cam kissed Jane, kissed Joanna, clinging to the soft little bodies, pressing her hungry cheek against the firm brown little faces. She put them in the back seat, each at a window, with Mabel between them, and told them to be very good girls.

"You'll telephone me every evening, Mabel? And if there's a telephone in the room where they sleep, sometimes let them talk to me."

"I will, Mrs Kilgarif. I'll call you round eight every night."

"You're to be back in December," Cam said, in a lower tone. "But if for any reason you think they'd like you to come sooner, why, come straight home. It won't matter how things are here, *get* them here, and we'll straighten out the details afterward."

"Mummy, are you coming in 'bout an hour tomorrow this evening?" Joanna asked.

"Mummy 'll be waiting for you when you get home. All right, Fred."

Cam and John watched the car out of sight. The October morning was hot and still; there was not a cloud in the clear blue sky. Cam reeled a little and caught John's shoulder as they turned to go back into the house.

"I hate to see them go!" she whispered, very white.

"Why, Cam, sweetheart!" he said, amazed. "It's only for a few weeks!"

She sat down on a terrace chair and, half laughing and half concerned, he knelt beside her and held her cold hands.

"Oh, but I hate to let them go!" she breathed again.

"Why, you little silly, it's to their father, after all! And they'll love it. They're only babies—they don't feel things as grown-ups do!"

He talked along comfortingly in the crystal warm sunshine that was steaming on heaps of wet leaves and making the low eaves of the farmhouse twinkle, and she listened, her thoughtful blue eyes on his face, one hand resting against his cheek. Now and then she said: "Ah, you're quite right, darling," and when finally he went back to his work it was with the feeling on his part that she was completely herself again.

But Cam, passing the open nursery door, seeing the orderly little beds within, with Dora setting the white lamb and the woolly dog against Joanna's pillow, and Jane's last scrawled French lesson still chalked on the blackboard, felt an agony so acute at her heart that she put her hand there as if to stanch a wound. She went to her own room and looked about vaguely, pulled on stiff old gauntlets, reached for a shade hat and went out to dig somewhere, to get tired, to keep busy.

It was no use. There was no scent of baking potatoes coming out to greet her from the kitchen today; there was no disorder of blocks and paper dolls on the sheltered end of the terrace; there were no voices ringing out against the ripple of waters at the pool. A dreadful silence was everywhere, an emptiness that was like the aching emptiness of her heart.

At two o'clock, when John came out exhausted and hungry for his lunch, Cam was at her loveliest in something striped and blue and said that she was starving, too. She said that she had had a nap and a bath and had generally caught up with the demoralized morning. He did not notice that she ate almost nothing as they shared the delicious little meal on the terrace which was dappled with the thinning tree shadows of autumn. Afterward they took a long hard walk, ending up at his mother's house for a short call.

Home again for hot showers, they spent the late afternoon in their comfortable room, John dozing, Cam writing away busily at her desk. Now and then he awakened and watched her affectionately.

"Lord, I love to see you sitting there!"

"This is pleasant, isn't it?"

"Want a fire? It's getting dark early, and it seems cold."

"I don't think we need a fire. But we'll need one in the study tonight."

She glanced at the clock. Six. In two hours she would know how her confident little travelers, in their rough little white coats and hats, had endured the trip.

"What did you look at the clock for, darling?"

"Wondering if it was time for you to be stirring. But you have lots of time."

"God, I adore you, Cam."

Her eyes moved to him smilingly. She did not speak.

"You know it, too," he said. "When a man loves a woman the way I love you she has powers of life and death over him."

"How little power one has, after all, to order one's life," Cam thought, her blue eyes still lazily smiling, as she sat twisted about in her desk chair, looking at him over her shoulder. Aloud she said nothing.

"If we went into town in a day or two, what could I buy you?"

"Nothing. I'm smothered in presents!"

"Dress? Why not go to Hansaroff's and get you a gorgeous new dress? And that reminds me, Cam," John said, lying at ease with his hands locked under his head, staring at the ceiling, "Rand Bristow's on his way here—he and Mrs Bristow are going to China. That means we'll have to make a little effort to do something for them."

She was distracted at last. Her eyes widened.

"Not *the* Rand Bristow?"

"Sure. English."

"You *know* him?" The great writer's name had been sacred to her for half the days of her life.

"Yep. They weren't in England when we were there. They always go to Cairo for cold weather. Sure I know them. I lived in their house for six weeks. And damn it!" John added, thinking aloud, "I might get Bill Large to come up from Hollywood, if he isn't making a picture. He's crazy about old Rand. But that might mean Tara O'Kane, and I don't know anything about her."

"She has the reputation of being a perfectly lovely girl." Cam was excited in spite of herself. This sounded promising.

"Could we manage a house party, d'you suppose? It 'd be an awful pest, but I've got to do something for the Bristows. He may be all dated up; he probably doesn't know that I'm anywhere in the neighborhood. But I ought to give him a dinner at the club. Save me, Cam! What's the least we can to for 'em?"

"Why, you utter ingrate," she said. "We'll have to do *everything* for them! Have to! It's going to be the greatest imaginable privilege to have that man in this house. Burlingame will go mad over him; we'll be besieged for invitations. We ought to have a sort of garden party——" Cam mused, already beginning to make desultory notes on the sheet of paper before her.

"I wish people wouldn't break in on us. We're perfectly satisfied without them, why can't they leave us alone?" John muttered.

"Why don't the Rand Bristows stop bothering us, ha-ha!" Cam said ironically. "Chicken Maryland——" she added under her breath.

"You're amazing," the man said drowsily. "You're simply amazing. It appals me to think of even taking 'em to lunch, and you're already deciding when we'll have ham and when we'll have sand dabs. I simply marvel at you. Have you decided what room you'll give 'em?"

"Well, of course!" Cam said calmly, penciling away busily.

John could seem to find no suitable comment for this except the usual: "God, how I love you!"

With John, Cam called upon the distinguished English visitors at their hotel a few days later—an exquisitely groomed and lovely Cam, with gardenias pinned to her trim dark brown suit and brown furs loose on her shoulders. Little Mrs Bristow, wrinkled, pretty, friendly, with curly gray-brown hair, liked "Jawn's" wife immediately, and the great writer was captivated before Cam had said a dozen phrases. The four went downstairs to lunch together, and the next day the Bristows joined the Kilgarifs at Cherry Ridge. "My fawther's place in Cornwall was Cherryover House, so it seems like home," Ellen Bristow said.

Then Bill Large and the beautiful Miss O'Kane came up from Hollywood for the week end, and there was much loitering on the terrace, many games of amateur croquet, one happy picnic in the woods, morning rides and evening talks on the dimly lighted terrace. Cam engineered her garden party successfully, and Burlingame responded with invitations for one of the largest dinners ever given in one of its largest and most hospitable castles.

This was to take place the night before the dazzled Bristows were to sail for Yokohama. Cam and John came into town for the occasion and stayed at the big hotel on the top of the hill. Their suite had a roofed balcony on the east, below which the world of city and bay, waterfront and far mountains spread itself in magnificent panorama. The Bristows were to join them for a piazza breakfast on the morning after the party, and later John and Cam would take them to their boat and see them off, the most grateful and pleasure-sated old couple who had ever quite lost their hearts to hospitable San Francisco.

It had been a completely felicitous experience, their visit; not the least of its satisfaction to Cam lying in the proof it had brought her of John's importance in the world of letters, of the generosity with which the failing older writer had seemed glad to hand on his mantle to the younger man.

Even the comparatively quiet days they had spent at home had left their mark in pleasure and benefit. Such good talks of books and bookmakers, such happy cross references and so many stimulating games! Cam had felt herself shy and young in such distinguished company, but not so youthful but that she had managed her farmhouse perfectly, seen that delicious meals were ready whenever due, and kept the machinery of the place running smoothly. The young picture star and she had found much in common, and the great Bill Large had proved to be a clever and stimulating person and, for the moment at least, quite unspoiled.

So that Cam reached this last day of the Bristows' visit with a feeling of triumph. Since her second marriage, she had rather given up her friends and the claims of her social group; it had been pleasant to renew the old ties under these really distinguished auspices, to have everyone wanting Cam and John for all sorts of parties. Of course John declined them all quite casually and as a matter of course, and Cam herself had no special interest in them any more, but it was gratifying, on the rare occasions when one did step back, to step back with head held high and colors flying.

She had a new gown for the Burlingame dinner. She had told John that she really did not need a new gown, but they had wandered through a smart shop or two nevertheless, and finally a confidential saleswoman had taken them into a beautiful little gray-walled salon where evening lights were turned on, begging to show them just one dress and no more, one unique and extraordinary garment that had only arrived that morning, that the girls indeed had just unpacked.

Cam had looked at it—a thin silky velvet of a heavenly pale blue, with a heavy encrustation of pearls and silver and gold bullion embroidered upon the skirt, and a cunning cut to the low waist that wrapped it about her slender shoulders and firm young breasts as simply as a handkerchief might have been bound there. She saw herself coming down the great curved marble stairs at the Livingstons' party clad in this royal garment; she knew that nothing could keep her from being the loveliest woman on the floor that night, between John's adoration, Rand Bristow's open affection, his constant "I say, dear Mrs Kilgarif," and her position as hostess to the movie stars whom everyone was anxious to meet.

"Jack, it's first sight," she said helplessly. Jack laughed in delight, and the gown was immediately hers, and a fitter summoned to make it perfect.

John left her then. She would follow him to the hotel; they would have an hour or two of rest and idling and then get themselves ready for the dinner.

"Isn't he grand?" the fitter said simply, on her knees. "I'm so glad you got this dress, Mrs Syl—— Kilgarif, I mean. I was so afraid that some terrible dowd would get it. We girls are all crazy about it."

"I don't think I ever had a dress I loved so much." Cam's gold hair was in disorder, she had on low-heeled shoes, and the autumn sun, battering at the windows, had heated the little fitting room to suffocation and flushed her cheeks. But even so the mirrors told her what this dress, and herself in the dress, were going to look like tonight, and her heart sang with a natural innocent vanity that she was to be so openly beautiful and so beloved.

"You'll positively have it at the hotel before five, Miss Lucas?" she asked.

"I'm marking it special. It 'll be there by five. I'm going to put a girl on it this minute." Plain, kindly Miss Lucas, the glory of delicate blue velvet heaped on a twisted little shoulder, went her way, and Cam walked through the shop, glancing at beautiful things here and there: slippers, scarves, bags, jeweled clasps selected from the very cream of the world's crop and displayed with consummate cunning all about her. Brief dresses of every frail and exquisite fabric that hands could make; that one Jane's size, this one Joanna's—— But no, she wouldn't think of them!

She stood waiting for the elevator. It was early afternoon, and the shop was very quiet. And suddenly, like a thin knife slipped into her heart, not even hurting yet, and yet delivering a mortal wound, she heard small feet running, heard a little voice that had never quite left her ears in all these weeks of silence:

"Mummy! Mummy!"

It was Jane, looking somehow a little odd and thin and older, with a new haircut, who came flying toward her, who was in her arms, crying and laughing and clinging tight. Cam had dropped to her knees; she saw no one else in the world; she neither knew nor cared that watching eyes were taking in the little scene and that because of Jane's tears more than one pair of them were wet.

"My sweetheart, my little girl, my Janey-baby!" Cam said, trying to smile, with her lips trembling and tears running down her face. "My darling, where did you come from?"

"Aunt Dixie-Belle was buying me shoes, and she left me here with Mabel while she has her girdles fitted!" Jane said, still breathless and still strangling Cam with hard little arms. "Oh, Mummy, why didn't you come, and where were you? Joanna's sick. She's sick, isn't she, Mabel?"

"What's the matter?" Cam's tone was quick and sharp; she got to her feet, as Mabel came up, and stood facing the nurse.

"It's nothing but a cold. Mrs Sylvester thought she'd better stay in bed. But Nan—that's the colored upstairs girl—is with her, and we're taking her back a surprise," Mabel explained.

"Are they happy, Mabel? Jane seems well." Cam's arm was still about the little girl; she stooped now and pushed back Jane's hat and kissed her earnestly. They sat down on chairs at the edge of the millinery department, Cam occasionally glancing nervously toward the corset counters.

"Mummy, can't I go home with you?" Jane begged.

"Not today, sweetheart." Cam spoke composedly if a little thickly, dried the child's tears and her own. "But very soon you and Joanna will come home to Mummy," she said cheerfully, "and meanwhile I'll—I'll tell you what we'll do," she said, looking about. "Come over here with Mummy and we'll buy the velvet rabbit for Joanna to go to sleep on. She used to have one like that, do you remember? It fell into the lake from the launch. And you—which would you like? Are you too big for the pink one?"

"But, Mummy, I would drather go home with you," Jane said wistfully.

"Darling, you will in a very short time. But meanwhile you have to stay with Daddy, you know. Poor Daddy, we have to be kind to him, too."

"But why don't *you* come and stay with him?" Jane demanded.

"Well, I'll tell you all about that someday. And meanwhile I think Joanna would like the blue one best, I *think* she would, don't you? You know how I tried to find her one last Christmas and couldn't, and now here he is, popping up to say 'Hello, girls!' So you tell her,"—Cam's eyes anxiously sought the counters of the corset department again—"you tell her that in a very few days you and she are coming down to the farm again—and oh, the grill is all finished, and Mummy cooked lunch for twenty people there last Sunday, and you can help cook, too—and good-by, my precious, here's Mummy's elevator—tell my Joanny-girl to get well quick—— *Go on,"* said Cam to the operator in a hard tone.

The car shot down as the door closed. But not before she saw Jane's face: she was trying not to cry, the darling, trying to be good and brave, but with the little cheeks all in a pucker and the mouth trembling, with great tears brimming and spilling in the innocent blue eyes.

"Late, darling!" John said, when she entered the hotel room an hour later. "What did you do?"

"Took a walk," Cam said, going straight to the bedroom window. "How you been trying to sleep in all this light?" she reproached him, busily drawing shades, her back toward him.

"They kept you trying on that dress. You look all done in."

"I'm not. No; there was nothing to do to the dress," Cam said.

"Well, get some rest anyway, darling. I'm going to take a bath and then rap off a few letters. Do you love me?" John asked. Her face was not turned toward him, but he heard her completely reassuring laugh from her dressing table.

"Dearly, dearly, dearly, idiot!" she said.

"And are you glad you're going to be the prettiest woman at this jamboree tonight?"

"In that dress? It's the sort of thing every woman dreams of," said Cam. . . . "I can't go on this way, life *can't* be as mixed up and as hard as this!" she said in her heart.

CHAPTER XXI

THROUGH the beautiful clear days of October and November the farmhouse was at its loveliest. Cam and John breakfasted beside the snapping wood fire in their bedroom, loitered over newspapers and mail until almost ten every morning. Then John went whistling off to his work, and Cam devoted herself to the thousand small duties of house-managing, correspondence, beautifying that filled her time until the late luncheon.

At two they were together again, lunching either on the terrace if the day was fine, or in the low-ceiled dining room that had its own wood fire, and after that the horses came around, and they rode up into the carpeted rustling woods, on and on, through patches of thin shadow and strips of thin sunlight, with the hills dropping away below them and the little villages of the long valley twinkling in winter light.

Home again, John usually slept like a weary child for an hour before dinner, and after dinner there was the quiet of his study, with Cam comfortably ensconced on the couch among pillows reading, a fire turning the iron sides of the little stove clear pink, and the typewriter tapping, silent, tapping again.

On Saturday they almost always went on a "honeymoon." They went down to Hollywood, where Cam roamed about the big lots among pasteboard slums and castles, twisted French streets and Indian villages, while John held long conferences with directors; they went to Coronado and Agua Caliente, Del Monte and Yosemite. Finally they bought a cabin on a lonely strip of ocean shore near a little fishing village, and John liked that best of all. He bought her and bought himself leather coats and high laced boots; he was as happy as a boy as he helped Cam pack groceries and vegetables into baskets for expeditions to Halfmoon Bay; he would lie on the strip of strand basking in the winter sunshine, his hat over his eyes, his voice occasionally reaching her.

"Cam, this is heaven. I don't ever want anything better than this! You cooking me my breakfast, nobody else around, not even a servant—this is the way we ought to live, with the whole Pacific right in the front yard and no one else in the world but ourselves!"

The days went by and were weeks; the weeks slowly joined themselves into months, and it was December. Cam bought two dolls, soft dolls with nice faces, stiff bonnets and frocks of pink and blue organdy. She asked Hing to have sponge cake and ice cream for dinner; she went in and out of the nursery a dozen times, always with a fast-beating heart. It could not be that she really was the possessor of two adorable loving little blonde girls of four and six, and that they were coming home!

At five o'clock when John, who had worked far into the early morning hours, was sound asleep, suddenly they were there, small gloves, small cold rosy faces, small shy smiles broadening as they realized that they were with Mummy again. They did not understand why they had ever been anywhere else, but it did not matter; after a few rather bewildered minutes they were running and laughing again in the old way, and she close to them, down on the floor, kissing them, entering into it all. And for a little while the ecstasy seemed to wipe away even the memory of pain.

Now they were to be hers—hers—hers until sometime next summer. Dixie-Belle, in a nicely written letter, had asked that she and Bob might take them to the Lake next summer. But summer was far away, it was not even Christmas yet, and meanwhile Cam could say "the children," turning the words over and over again on her tongue, and forget that anything ever had been or might be different. Taffy had been specifically invited to come to supper with his stepsisters on this happy night, but he had not been very well, and Toomey had thought it wiser not.

"Well, if they want him to be run entirely by Toomey——" Cam had said patiently to this. She had trained herself to put Toomey out of her mind as fast as possible when the thought of Taffy's nurse came to her; she could afford to ignore Toomey tonight, with the old happy romping and laughing going on in the nursery.

"Is Daddy coming tomorrow, Mummy?" Jane asked, suddenly.

"No, darling, I don't think so."

"You know very well that your father has to go to New York," Mabel said mildly.

"I love Daddy," Joanna stated flatly.

"He was lovely to them, and she was, too," Mabel said, when she and Cam were alone and the children in bed. "You'd never know him, Mrs Sylgarif. He's different. He'd come up and play with them when they were going to bed at night, and she had a little party for them, and really they were perfectly sadisfied. I never thought they'd be sadisfied, but they were. Her mother is fond of children, and she'd tell 'em stories——"

"Mabel, that day I met you in Margin's, remember? When Jane cried? Did she cry very long?"

"I don't believe she did," Mabel said, reflecting. "It was Joanna that used to cry for you when she was sick. Every time the door creaked her head 'd come up, even if we'd thought she was asleep, and she'd say 'Mummy?' "

Cam was helping clear up the supper disorder in the nursery; she paused, a sticky silver bowl in her hands.

"Was she sick long, Mabel?"

"We kep' her in bed about two weeks, I guess. She wasn't ever very sick, but she didn't have any appetite, and she seemed to have a sort of cold or fever or something—I don't know what it was."

Cam thought of the little gold head, restless on the hot pillow, flashing up when the door creaked. "Mummy?" She put the silver bowl on the tray, took a damp towel from Mabel with hands that shook, began to wipe the sticky chair arms and table. She said nothing.

Mabel had news. She was going to be married. He was in the navy, but his time would be up in March, and then he was going to work with his brother in the Mission; his brother had a bicycle shop.

"I and my chum passed them on Market Street, and mind joo, Ethel thought he was the one she had met somewheres," Mabel explained, in pleased recollection. She accepted with only a vague polite assent Cam's dismayed reception of this announcement.

"Mabel, how on earth will I ever get along without you! Mr Kilgarif and I go away so much!" she protested.

"Well, you know how it is when you want to get married; it seems like not even your husband nor children nor anything makes much difference," Mabel reminded her blandly.

Cam gave her a keen look; exactly what did *that* speech mean? But Mabel was quietly straightening and ordering the room in the usual way and seemed entirely unaware of any special significance in her words.

Cam thought of them more than once that night and in the days that followed. It was quite true. Nature had so arranged matters that when one of her helpless children suddenly heard the call of love, he or she let nothing stand in the way. Fifteen months ago Cam Sylvester had calmly swept everything out of the way to come to her lover. Husband, husband's mother, children, even simple Mabel, if they had had any claims upon her, had been completely ignored; she had loved John too wildly, too deeply to allow any other considerations even to enter her mind.

Bob? She had reasoned, well, Bob hadn't really loved her. And what of his mother's claims? Oh, but she had been old, her game long ago played and lost. The children? Why, but they had been mere babies, to be satisfied with a sandbox and ginger cookies. It was easy enough to keep little children happy. And as for Mabel, casually switched from the employ of one man to that of another, transferred to a new home, addressing her mistress by a new name, it would have amused Cam immensely to have it put to her that Mabel was entitled to any thought in the matter at all.

She and John had gone off on a long honeymoon, had gone on a score of later, lesser trips, without worrying much about the augmented responsibility for Mabel.

Now Mabel was going to leave, and Cam felt a little hurt and a good deal disturbed. There must be another nurse. Rather disconsolately she assured Mabel of her affectionate good wishes and promised the bride whatever she fancied for a wedding gift. Mabel's modest answer of a parlor set rather staggered her, but, after all, that was the least of her troubles on this particular evening that had seen the delight of the girls' return.

She went into her room to find John awake at half past six, lying in his favorite position on his back with his arms crossed on the pillow under his head. He smiled at her affectionately.

"Circus get here?"

"Oh, yes—about five. They've been having a glorious time."

"I could hear some of it."

"It waked you!" She was concerned.

"No, no; it didn't matter. How do the ladies look?"

Cam sat down on the edge of his bed; their hands linked.

"Lovely. They grow so fast, you know, that even these few months seem to have changed them. Joanna's the same roly-poly, but Jane's shot up quite a bit. They appear," Cam said with a slight change of tone and a rather wry little smile, "to have gotten a pleasant impression of their father, and Dixie-Belle, as far as I can find out, has been extremely—even intelligently—nice to them. So!"

"Don't tell me anything nice about *him,*" said John. "He was too much of a boob to appreciate what he had in you, and he's probably trying now to win them away from you."

"I don't think that," she said, with a little twinge at her heart.

"I believe they can choose at fourteen," John said. "He's probably got that in mind."

"Oh, don't, Jack!"

"Why, you scary little thing, you, that won't be for years!" he said, laughing.

"I know. But I wish he didn't have anything to do with them. What terrific realities they are, John: fatherhood and motherhood," Cam said, musing upon the words as if she never had heard them before.

"I've taken my responsibilities for Taffy easily enough," he said. "Of course, Mother and Tids and Toomey have always been there. And he's not old enough yet to be a real companion."

"But that's exactly what I think they *are* old enough to be, Jack. Companions."

"Well, not at four and six."

"But exactly! I'd much rather be with them than with lots of grown-ups I know."

"Oh, come now, Cam! They're only little kids. Well, at that," John added, considering, "I don't know but that I'd just as soon be with them as most grown-ups. But they—well, naturally, all they need is sunshine and air and to be left alone."

She did not argue it. She presently began to dress for dinner, and they went down to it together, their hands linked. And that night Cam slept deep and happily with her children once more under her own roof, and her first thought on awakening was the wonderful thought that the girls were home.

A soft rain was falling; the clouds were low and heavy. There could be no going out this morning, but the girls settled down happily enough to the familiar blocks and paint boxes. Cam telephoned the other Kilgarif house to ask for Taffy for the day. But Taffy had a heavy cold, and his grandmother and nurse thought it would be wiser to keep him in one atmosphere.

Cozily established beside the nursery fire, Cam loved every moment of the dark hours, when the eaves of the farmhouse dripped and the wind whined, when rain ran in streams along the paths and the lamps had to be lighted at four o'clock. When John was safely off for a nap after luncheon, she and Mabel bundled the girls into old coats and rubbers and took them for a wet scramble. They went as far as "the puppy's house," and although Cam would not let them go in, dripping and rosy-cheeked to perhaps feel sudden chill and damp, they had a world of greeting from John's mother and Aunt Tids and saw Taffy looking down at them from an upper closed window. Liking Taffy as she did, feeling as she did very sorry for him, yet Cam could not but contrast her own glowing little red-cheeked daughters with the pale little housebound boy. She and the girls came home in gales of laughter, and Cam's face, when she laid it against John's face for a kiss a few minutes later, was, he told her, as cold as a corpse.

"Oh, we had a lovely walk!" She drew window shades in the warm bedroom, lighted a lamp, began to tear off her wet things.

"We? Who went with you?"

"Girls."

"You didn't take those infants out into this rain?"

"I did. They were kind of stuffy with being in the house all day, and it did them a world of good." Cam was in a warm wrapper now, combing her damp gold hair, pushing it into scallops against her forehead, humming as she watched herself in the mirror.

"It makes all the difference in the world to you to have them here, doesn't it?"

"Oh, well—Jack——" she murmured happily.

"What would you do if I got jealous of them?"

"Slap your little face for you. You jealous!" Cam said, in scorn. "Arter all I've did for ye? A-bustin' up my life, a-changin' of my name, there ain't nothin' I hain't did for ye."

"There hain't none of it I don't thank ye fur," John said.

"And you're happy?"

"God knows I am, darling."

"And not jealous?"

"I was only fooling," he said penitently. But it had not been quite fooling, and she knew it, and began from that hour to be conscious of a certain tendency to restrain her demonstrations of affection for the children when he was by. It was a hard thing to do, for by that innate perversity which is childhood Joanna and Jane chose such moments for special outbursts of devotion. She was their "little Mummy"; they wanted to kiss her; they wanted to know why they couldn't come into her room in the morning any more and wake her up.

" 'Member the mountains you used to make of your knees, Mummy, and Joanna always having a tent and being an Indian?"

"Mummy, if I feeled sick in the night could I come and climb in with you?"

"You won't feel sick in the night, silly," Cam might answer to such a question, but as the warm little bodies clung to her, and the gold curls were pushed against her cheek or tumbled on her shoulder, she was always conscious of John's eyes, and she dared not reply to the children in the old loving, impulsive fashion. They were too small to be given a hint; they had been too much loved all their lives to dream of anything but welcome and love and approval, whatever they did.

So when she and John were starting for a winter walk they would come tearing after.

"Mummy, wait for us! Take us, too!"

"Oh, but we're going 'way up to the Ridge, sweets."

"Could we go as far as the broken bridge?"

Cam would glance at Jack; he was always nice about it.

"Bring 'em along. But hadn't we better take Mabel, then, to bring them back?"

That meant that he idled with the little girls in the December sunshine, or it might be in the soft creamy dimness of the fog, until she went to find Mabel, until Mabel changed her dress, or at least her shoes, and got a coat. And that meant that conversation, for the first half-mile of the walk, centered upon Joanna and Jane, that the three adults were no more than an escort for Joanna and Jane, and that progress was so slow as to provide no real exercise for anyone except the little sisters.

When Cam finally made them turn back, it was with many kisses and much praising, and the promise to return to them speedily. Then she and John would be free to take their walk, but despite her best efforts to devote herself to him, to win him back to his usual mood, she would often feel that he was hurt and disappointed.

There was nothing for it then, loving him as she did, depending as she did for her own happiness upon his being happy, but to suggest something that might hope to dispel the last of his jealousy, for the time being at least. Breathless from the climb, sitting on a fallen great log, up in the chilly, sun-washed bareness of the winter woods, she would scrape mud from a gaiter, speak as if half to herself.

"I'll tell you what we ought to do someday, Jack."

"What?" From his own log opposite her he would bring his eyes from contemplation of the valley below them, a faint interest in his voice.

"We ought just to get in the car and go off to Mexico. You've never been there, and neither have I. It would only take us four or five days; we could have a few days there, and drive home. And no Claytons and no Hungerfords going along," Cam might add in an undertone.

"Just the two of us!"

"Yes. Anyone else makes it so complicated. 'Are you hungry?' 'Not a bit. But if you want to stop for lunch . . . No, I'm very comfortable here,'—that sort of thing!"

"It would be heaven, Cam. But you wouldn't do it! Oh, my *God,"* John might say fervently, "if I could have my wife to *myself!* If all these damn outsiders wouldn't come crowding in between us! If you loved me one tenth as much as I do you!"

It was always the same, and the phrases, the little kisses, the grasp of her firm small hand were always the same in comfort. She loved him too much ever to ignore his moods of unreasonable exaction; the sun could not shine for her unless it were shining for Jack, too.

CHAPTER XXII

BUT the time swiftly came when Cam realized that in her happiest times the three she loved could never be with her together. To be alone with Jack was heaven; there were many completely satisfied times when she could be alone with her children, too: morning hours at the pool, late afternoons when he was asleep. But the dream of combining them, the vision she had had of a united family, mother and father by the fireside, a sleepy sweet baby in the arms of each, were destined to remain only a vision and a dream. He would not share her, although he made a heroic effort to resign her to the children's claims now and then.

"Perfect love casteth out fear, Jack," she said to him one night. "If you really loved me, you wouldn't be afraid of anything!"

"I love you too much. I want to put you in a little garden of roses with a hedge all around it, and keep you for me, forever and forever!"

They were in his study; it was close upon midnight. John had stopped work and was idling in a deep chair, smoking a last cigarette before going to bed. Cam was curled up on the couch, her magazine laid aside, her sleepy eyes trying to keep themselves open until he should be willing to put out lights, thread the farmhouse's old passages, reach their room at last and let her tumble into her blankets.

She wore striped flannel pajamas of blue and white and a Japanese jacket patterned richly in maple leaves against cream and gold. Her blue eyes were dark and shadowy with sleep; the smooth peach of her cheeks was as soft as Jane's own. About the mobile mouth he loved to watch little expressions formed and disappeared again: a maternal half-smile, a stern little look of blame, a mused biting of the lower lip that showed white even teeth.

"It must be funny to be jealous," she said thoughtfully.

"Not so funny, darling. It's a horrid feeling."

"I can imagine being jealous," Cam mused aloud, "but not of a child. I can't imagine thinking that you were too fond of Taffy. I only wish we had him here so that you might see more of him."

"You aren't jealous, that's all."

"I would be of a woman rival!" Cam said, with a sudden flash of blue eyes in his direction.

John laughed, leaned forward to open the top of the cooling stove and rap his pipe against it. Rather to Cam's concern, he put two logs into it. The session was to be prolonged, then? Cam felt as if her very spirit were yawning. He had had two good hours of sleep that afternoon. She had spent that time in rather exhausting play with the girls.

"Do you mean to say," the man presently asked deliberately, feeling for his words, "that when you look at Taffy you never think of his mother?"

Cam's sleepiness deserted her, and the red in her cheeks deepened. It took her a full minute to get the meaning of what he had said, during which time she looked at him steadily, her brow faintly knit.

"What do you mean?" she finally asked, unwilling to believe that she knew.

"Well, I mean——" John began and floundered a little, as

if he were slightly ashamed of himself. "I mean, do you ever think of Margaret when you look at Taffy?"

"Of his *mother?*"

"Yes. Don't you ever?"

"But why *should* I?" she demanded patiently.

"Oh, well, I don't know. Often, when you're with the girls, I think of Bob Sylvester," he confessed, studying her face to see how the announcement affected her.

It impressed her unpleasantly, almost painfully, but she would not let him see it. Over a certain little sense of hurt and humiliation and a very real dismay, she laughed carelessly.

"Really, Jack——" she murmured.

"Yes, I know," he said quickly. "I know it's crazy! But I think of him loving you, and you loving him, and his going to the hospital when your baby was born—his having the right——"

He got up, his face red, his eyes averted, and began to walk the floor. Cam lay watching him in speechless consternation. For fully three minutes there was silence in the study, except for the sound of his footsteps, the crackle of wood in the stove and the occasional dreary hoot of an owl from the black winter woods outside.

"Jack, *dear,"* she said then. He came at once to drop down on the floor beside her, covering her hand with his hand, his elbow resting against her knee. "You *don't* torture yourself with such silly thoughts as that, do you?" she asked, unwilling to believe it.

"Sometimes I do. Sometimes I see nothing but him in the girls, his daughters in my house. A part of himself, eternally separating you from me! Wouldn't you feel it if it were Taffy, and if Margaret were alive?"

For a second she did feel a little twinge of pure jealousy at the thought that any living woman might have known Jack as she knew him, might have given him his first exquisite experience of husbandhood, of fatherhood. Might she feel differently toward Taffy if his mother were alive? She could not tell. Her immediate business was to comfort Jack, and she set about it.

"A mother's feeling for her children is entirely different from what she feels for the man she loves, Jack. You a writer, and don't know that?"

"I do know that, of course. I'm a fool," he said humbly. "I've been working too hard, and I'm all shot to pieces. D'you want to come out to the kitchen and make me a bacon sandwich or something?"

"Cook a little midnight supper for you? It's a privilege that about a thousand other women would envy me," she answered demurely, though her muscles ached at the mere thought. He laughed delightedly.

"You don't care a snap about my fame—what little there is of it," he said unbelievingly.

"It's all part of you. It's what made me first want to talk to you, at the Hunters' lunch," she said, reflecting, and drawing a soft fingertip down the center of his nose. He caught at her hand and kissed the palm gratefully.

"I'll tell you what," he said, "we'll go off somewhere tomorrow. We'll start at eleven. That 'll give me a couple of good hours, and we'll stop somewhere for lunch—Santa Cruz, maybe, somewhere."

"And not take the girls?" her heart asked. They would love it so, the exciting day with Mummy in the car, the beach and the tearoom sandwiches! Aloud she said: "That would mean that Friday I have to go in and get a nurse to take Mabel's place."

"Couldn't telephone?"

"Not very well. I thought I'd take Mabel and the girls in tomorrow and have their hair cut."

"After lunch?"

"No; I think we'd have to get started in the morning."

"Then I lunch all alone?" His face was panicky. Cam laughed, stooped forward to kiss him, settled back in her cushions.

"Well, it won't kill you, you big infant!"

"Couldn't send them in with Mabel to the hair woman, and have me drive you in right after lunch?"

"Well, let me see." Her mind ranged over the details. To send Mitchell in with Mabel and the girls meant small fun for them, for Mabel was a too-cautious guardian and so preoccupied with keeping them safe in city streets that she hardly heard their questions at all. Mabel could take them to the club for lunch, of course. She and John could join them—but then, if they were going to manage it that way, why join them at all? Certainly Jane and Joanna were not going to assist materially with the selection of a new nurse.

"I'll tell you what," she said, "if you and I are going off cruising tomorrow, why not send them in to get their hair cut at—say ten. Then they'll be home for their lunches and naps."

"Now you're being a darling!" he said enthusiastically.

"I'll leave a message for Mitchell in the kitchen while you're eating your sandwich."

"Cam, you're such a darling to manage it that way! And you don't mind, do you? I mean, it's really much more sensible to have them alone with Mabel than to have us all along, confusing them. The shorter and simpler we make it, the easier on them."

"Yes, that's true," she agreed, looking at him thoughtfully.

She pulled herself up and shook herself free of pillows and rug, and he steadied her on her feet, and they went down to the kitchen together. Here Cam found bread and bacon and butter, and John rounded up a frying pan, and presently, with the clock's hands creeping toward one, a good breakfast smell was in the kitchen, and John was enjoying his buttermilk and sandwich. Cam hesitated over the pencil and pad, finally wrote her message to Mitchell. It was a real disappointment, even though she knew she would be completely happy meandering in the car through the winter country tomorrow with John, enjoying occasional and spirited talk, enjoying long periods of peaceful silence.

"That looks like a nice little place to eat, Jack," she would say, watching the roads.

"You wait a minute now. There used to be a place in here —if I can find it——"

They would talk long over their meal, perhaps lock hands surreptitiously now and then. He loved these long talks that wandered everywhere, that were partly in the past, memories and dreams, partly plans and hopes for the future, that touched on politics and books and social theories and the beauties of museums in Paris and Florence and London.

And meanwhile her disappointed babies would be steered to the hairdresser by conscientious Mabel, steered back to the car, swept home for the routine of naps and lunch. No Mummy to make it a great adventure, and to love it—every instant of it—herself.

Just the glances that casual passers-by in the streets gave her small daughters were wine to Cam. Her pride in them, neatly buttoned into their navy coats with the brass buttons, their gold curls curving up against the lettered ribbons of their sailor hats, was one of the real assets of her life. It was wonderful to take them into the big bright music-flooded dining room of the Fairmont at half past twelve and sense rather than actually hear the "Ah-h-h!" that other women breathed when the small Sylvesters were helped up into heightened chairs, had their napkins tied under their round little brown chins, and fell upon chicken and mashed potatoe.

Not that the expedition with John would not be marvelous too. But why not have both? Why have to do so much sacrificing and adjusting, why suffer so many heartaches over it?

She could not answer her own questions. She could only tell herself that it was not an important or lengthy separation from the girls that faced her tomorrow; all of them would be home in the afternoon, and she could have her usual going-to-bed hour with them. Perhaps John would stop at a store somewhere and let her bring them surprises. She would promise them surprises when she told them in the morning that Mabel was going to take them to town, that Mummy couldn't go. That would help!

But after the sandwich was consumed and the note to Mitchell written, after the kitchen was darkened and when she was in bed with John sound asleep beside her, his hand, even in sleep, resting against her arm, Cam lay awake thinking, remembering what he had said, her face burning in the sheltering dark as it had burned when first she had heard him.

Did she ever think of Taffy's mother, or of the fact that he had had a wife before ever he met her, with jealousy and resentment? She did not seem to feel any emotion about Margaret at all.

But then suppose that Margaret were still alive somewhere, remembering the tones of love in that wonderful voice of his, a woman about whom his arms had often gone in those big embraces, a woman whose privilege it had been to pour his coffee and send his suits to the cleaner's, and to whom he had read his work whenever he was puzzled about it?

"John's first wife, who is living in Paris," she imagined herself saying. Or, it might be, "John's first wife who is right here in Burlingame." No, that really would be horrid. Divorce was always horrid, but then everyone knew it was. Nobody defended it or said it was ideal; it created infinite difficulties, and it gave a woman an abiding sense of failure. In the back of her head were always humiliating and nagging little memories of the first experiment. One always felt that one must in honesty explain to new friends, always on a note of apology: "Mr Kilgarif isn't their father. Their father and I, alas, came to the parting of the ways last year. They're very fond of him, and they visit him and his new wife."

And then what? One could not stop there. One always had to add in light, cheerful amelioration: "It's too bad it happens so, but sometimes it seems as if a man and woman could be better friends apart."

That was a miserable finish, too. That sounded as if the divorce had been gotten on very slight grounds; no real reason for it. And yet one could hardly say: "Mr Sylvester drank a great deal and neglected me frightfully. I did my best; I put up with more than almost any woman I know. But in the end it was no use!"

No, that was cheap somehow. The only thing to do was to ignore it, not mention it unless someone said: "Come here, you cute little Joanna Kilgarif, and say 'How d'you do' to me!" Then make the explanation as brief as possible.

Aline Chard had talked for years against Willie Chard to anyone who would listen. How her mother paid her household bills almost from the first month of her marriage, and how then Willie began to charge things to Aline's mother, and how, the instant she told him she was going to divorce him, he had had every drop of liquor moved away, although a lot of it had been hers, and although it had been the Prohibition era, when liquor had been terribly hard to get.

Cam would not descend to Aline's tactics. She would try to keep it all as sweet and charitable as she could. But what with Bob's new interest in his daughters, Mabel's going, the little girls' dismay when they were banished from their mother's company, and John's jealousy, she felt as if a swarm of gnats were buzzing about her ears.

CHAPTER XXIII

IN THE MORNING she braced herself for the changed program. Somehow she made it seem to the children that the most delightful adventure imaginable was going into town with Mablel; they were to be sure to have ice cream for lunch, and Mummy and Uncle John were bringing home surprises. She spent a quiet morning waiting for John to finish his quota of work and then got herself into sturdy warm tweeds, with a snug little tweed hat and thick warm gloves.

When he came out from his study at noon she and the small car were at the door. He did not dispute her place at the wheel as he pulled on the heavy coat and cap she had waiting for him. He was tired.

But after a few miles of driving he said suddenly: "Lord, this is fun. I adore you."

"Do we know where we are going, Jack?"

"Nope. Do we care?"

"I don't," she said on a contented note. They drove on through the winter day, Cam taking the less usual turnings, winding in and out of quiet back roads. And it was as if she could feel John tangibly relaxing, growing rested, his nervous fatigue falling from him like a cloak.

After a while they found Gustave's, which sounded, Cam

thought, like a good French table. John thought it sounded German. Either way, they were both too ravenous to pass it, and they went in to clean checked tablecloths, good Rhine wine and the expert ministrations of a Belgian cook. Three o'clock struck, half past three struck, and still they lingered on by Gustave's hospitable fire, filled to repletion by a lunch whose main dishes were fish adroitly flavored with mysterious herbs, kidneys disguised in a sauce which Cam tasted in vain a dozen times, trying to divine what was in it, and an apple roll made of spiced Spitzenburgs wrapped in a crust as thin as baked brown paper.

And John was utterly content. Cam's mind might wander to her girls, wondering if the hair-clipping took place on time, if they got safely home to lunch, if they were still asleep. But he never guessed it; he was happy, he had her in her loveliest and most confidential and affectionate mood entirely to himself and that was all he wanted in life.

"Do you realize," he asked her, "that we start for New York just three weeks from today?"

"Good heavens, I thought we went in February!"

"That 'll be February, darling. This is the twelfth. Look here," he said, half teasing and half serious, "what does that tone mean? Don't you want to go?"

"Idiot! But I can't realize that Christmas is over yet. Three weeks, and I've got to replace Mabel. And clothes—I've no clothes."

"Wait and get them there. We'll have to be there about six weeks. Here's what I was thinking, Cam. I'd like to go there and see Thomas and Russell, talk over a couple of propositions with them, and then run down to Havana with you—four days down, about a week there, four days back. That 'll give 'em time to think things over, and they can't telephone me and fuss me about it. How'd you like to see Havana again? It was quarantined when we came through last year, remember? We couldn't go anywhere but the club."

"It sounds wonderful. But, Jack, we lose a beautiful time

here if we go in February. Spring beginning, buttercups, fruit blossoms."

"I know it, but I have to go."

She would not tell him that she shrank from leaving the children with a new nurse. Wait and see what the nurse looked like first. If only she could get a nice one, but nurses were brittle material and were not often as satisfactory as Mabel.

"What you thinking about, Beautiful?" John asked, watching her.

"Thinking that I ought to go into town tomorrow and see about getting a nurse. If our time is so short we ought to give the children some chance to get accustomed to her. Suppose I go in at eleven and get back for two o'clock lunch?"

"I could go in after lunch and meet you, and we could see a picture?"

"No chance with the girls at all," she thought. Aloud she said: "Can you loaf for an evening?"

"If my wife asks me to."

"Your wife does ask you to."

"Then it's a date!" he said, pleased. "We have fun, don't we, Cam?"

"When a woman loves a man as I love you, Jack, everything's fun. I wake up in the morning and think that the whole day is going to be lovely, whether it's raining or foggy or hot or cold. I don't think," Cam said simply, "that there is in the world a woman who thinks her husband as wonderful as I think you! I like to hang up your old sweaters, I like to hear you whistling to the dogs on the terrace, I love the way you mount a horse and sharpen a pencil——"

"Shut up!" he said a little thickly. And she saw his fine eyes mist with tears, even though he was smiling.

"Isn't it nice to remember it all," she presently mused—"the garden luncheon, and you and I being casually introduced——"

"Our being introduced!" he echoed, struck.

"Isn't it funny? And you going off to that little table under the hedge, and our long talk!"

"I was blown to pieces, of course; it was all up with me. I was dizzy, Cam. The whole world was one whirl of you—one gold whirl of you."

"Remember the little girls coming across the lawn, and you calling them the blue delphiniums?"

"That's true—that's true, too. I'd forgotten them. But I remember going back to my club simply dizzied. 'Mrs Sylvester—Mrs Sylvester!' There wasn't anyone else in the world but a girl in blue, with blue eyes, sitting in the shade of a tall hedge. You, of course," Jack added, "didn't know I was alive."

"Yes, I did, really. I was tremendously—well, stirred," Cam confessed. "I knew that you had—liked me. And as you were quite the most interesting personality I'd ever met in my life I was—correspondingly impressed. I hoped you'd follow it up; I didn't quite know how. That it would all flame up and flash up and consume us both like a pair of little moths in a candle, never occurred to me."

"Less than two years ago. I hate the time to go by. I hate it to be years instead of just weeks that we've been married," John said.

"Funny, men seem to feel that. Now I," Cam said, with a little stress on the pronoun, "I wish that we'd been married for years and years. I wish that no one was talking about us any more—that we were just taken for granted. If we'd be married ten years it would be so much nicer!"

"The girls would be fourteen and sixteen, remember."

"Oh, horrors, so they would! But what I meant, I guess," Cam went on, feeling her way, "was that there's something wonderful in old marriage—marriage, I mean, that has lasted for years and years. Lasted until two persons have become really used to each other, really companions, liking to do the same things, and happiest when they're together."

"That time must have this compensation, that the man

isn't always afraid that every man who meets her is going to fall in love with his wife," John said meditatively.

"You mean to say that 'the man' is now?" she asked, raising amused eyes to his.

"The man is always in a state of panic about it."

"When we never go anywhere or see anybody, Jack!" Cam smiled.

"We go too many places and we see too many people," he growled. "By George, I can understand the old sultans who built harems and shut their beauties up in them!"

"You haven't much to complain of!" she told him good-humoredly when at last they went out to their car. He took the wheel now, and she rested her shoulder companionably against his.

"Let's go home Skyline, Cam," he said.

"You're the boss!" But even as she said it she remembered the little girls' promised "surprises." She had not wanted to stop for them on the way to lunch, for Jack had been tired and nervous and hungry. If they went home by the Skyline road there would be no chance to get them; there were no shops on the Skyline Boulevard. Her mind raced from one possibility to another; would they pass a drug-store? There were little perfume bottles and animal soaps in the drugstores. No, there was none between them and their own turning; in fact there was no sort of store at all. Nothing for it but openness, then.

"Jack," she said, "run right on down, when you turn, to Menlo. There's something I have to get at Barker's."

"What, for instance?" he asked, surprised. "It's nearly four. Don't you want to get home and have a bath and a rest?"

"Yes, but I really think I'd be happier going on to Barker's."

"We could send Mitchell; he'll be back."

"This is hush money, for the young ladies," Cam confessed.

"I thought so!" he chuckled. "Well, I've had one of the most perfect days of my life, so I don't grudge it. You've never been sweeter or more adorable than you are this minute! I'll never forget today."

That was the way to handle her problem, Cam reflected, as they drove along into the gathering winter dusk. To be everything he desired while she was with him, and to try to make up for the inevitable loss of the children's company by making them completely happy in the time she could give them. Jack's jealousy was only another evidence of Jack's love for her; perhaps there never was complete love without jealousy. When a man loved a woman he could not help being afraid that he could not hold her. Bob had not been jealous, but then Bob had not been an attentive or loving husband. His jealousies had been reserved entirely for men who made tennis and golf records.

Like herself with Jane and Joanna, for example. She loved them so that she imagined everyone else who came in contact with them was trying to win them away from her. Their radiant baby beauty, the peachy freshness of their faces, their tumbles of gold curls were all so dear to her that the added charm of the little personalities, the moments of confidence, of seriousness, of giddy gaiety were just so much superfluous charm—just so much value added to what had always been of incomparable value.

CHAPTER XXIV

SOMETIMES IN THESE DAYS Cam found herself remembering summers at the Lake only a few years ago. She had possessed Joanna and Jane in indisputed completeness then. She had been free to give them every hour of her life, to picnic with them today in the high woods, to keep them up this night or that, to toast their small feet at her wood fire and defy bedtime rules indefinitely. She could have their small friends in for visits, hear the enthusiastic little murmurs: "I think you have the wonderfullest mother anyone ever had!" She could read to them by the hour, arrange their trays with her own hands when they were ill, comfort them when they were hurt or sad, make all the arrangements that affected them unquestioned.

Now it was different. Now her children had been relegated to a different position, to what was perhaps their proper position. She was the important figure in the group now; and that was right. A grown person should naturally take a more prominent place than a child. But sometimes it did make living a trifle difficult.

Pinpricks were everywhere. It was only that night, the very night after their harmonious happy luncheon, that Jack interrupted his evening work to ask her suddenly:

"What did you mean when you said that, Cam?"

"What?" she asked wonderingly. She had been making household lists for the cook; she looked up innocently from her pencil and pad. "Asking you if you liked fried oysters?" she said.

"No, no, no!" He laughed in a little embarrassment. "I was talking right out of my thoughts," he said. "I meant what you said at luncheon today, about men always wanting time to go slow, and women wanting it to be years since they were married, all the novelty gone, settled down to routine. You said all men seemed to feel that. D'you mean that *he* did? I mean, was that one of the things Sylvester used to say?"

She hid the hurt it gave her, the touch of cheapness that it seemed to bring to the sacredness of their love. She made herself smile indifferently as she answered:

"No; Bob never went in for anything analytical—anything introspective. Nobody had to say that to make me know it. Every woman knows it. When she's exquisitely happy in love she wants to feel that it's proved, that it isn't going to change."

That quieted him. He was happy again. But she knew that the next day would bring another of these faint drifting shadows across the clear sunlight of their love, and the day after that still another.

She felt more than a shadow, she felt a storm brewing, when, a day or two later, she had a letter from Bob's new wife, Dixie-Belle. Dixie-Belle wrote to ask Cam two things: the first was if Cam and Mr Kilgarif would like Dixie-Belle's wonderful Nan as a nurse for the children? Nan, colored, forty years old, experienced, had been Dixie-Belle's own nurse, and the whole family loved her. She had gotten so fond of "Bob's girls" that she really missed them, and since Mabel had reported to Nan that Cam was having some difficulty in finding a nurse, Dixie-Belle wrote to make this suggestion. If Cam liked it, Nan would come down to Cherry

Ridge at once, and before Cam went East she would have a chance to see how she liked the nurse.

The second question was: Would Cam let Bob and Dixie-Belle have the girls while she was away?

"That is, let us have them without depriving us of our two summer months of them," the letter said. *"On account of my own expectations in November, Bob and I are not planning to get away at all this summer, except for a few visits. The doctor wants me to keep quiet, and as Mother's house is large and cool, and we have a big garden, we are counting on the girls as our only guests. They really seem happy with me, although I'm such a wretchedly sickly little thing, and my mother simply adores them. She misses them terribly, and she feels as Bob and I do, that while you and Mr Kilgarif are in New York—the paper said for six weeks—it will be a delight to have them here. Bob sends kindest regards with mine."*

Cam brooded for several hours over this letter before she spoke to Jack about it. It made her definitely uncomfortable and uneasy, this calm assumption, on the part of a woman she hardly knew, that Jane and Joanna were hers to dispose of as casually as if their mother did not exist at all.

The colored nurse would probably be the ideal person for the job. Indeed, Jane had frequently spoken with affection to her mother of "Nan, at Dad's house," and Joanna had even sat up in her crib and wept for Nan. But to surrender them to Dixie-Belle's nurse meant that they would be constantly in the charge of a strong partisan of Dixie-Belle; they would be weaned just a little more away from their mother.

The second proposition seemed to her cool. She could think of no other word for it except "cool." Pretty cool of Bob Sylvester to stipulate that he should have the girls for the two summer months of the original arrangement for them, and then ask for them for six extra weeks in the spring! A big shady house and three women devoted to them, and Cam out of it entirely. It angered her, even while she knew in her heart there was no cause for anger. They were, after all, Bob's daughters, and this second wife of his appeared to have tamed him to a point where he realized it.

The alternative, when she was away, was leaving them at Cherry Ridge to the new nurse, Nan, if Nan were indeed to fill the position, to Dora the maid, to Mitchell, and to the neighboring offices of Jack's mild little ineffectual mother, his vague ineffectual sister and the detestable Toomey. Certainly they would be much safer with their own father and with the three other women. But it was somehow maddening to resign them so soon again to Bob's guardianship.

Why could not Jack settle down here quietly to his typewriter, his wife, his little boy, his garden, dogs, walks, books, fires? Why must he be continually wandering, upsetting arrangements for the sole purpose of getting her away to himself?

Well, he was made that way. He was a genius, and they were all queer. He was so kind and just and balanced when he was happy that it was well worth her while to keep him so. Cam suspected, with a little wince at her heart, that he would think Dixie-Belle's suggestion a most acceptable one. She hated to admit it, but she found it acceptable, too. She would be easier in her mind about Jane and Joanna, knowing them to be with their father. But if her mind was easy, how her heart would ache, thinking of them as happy in the big old-fashioned Oakland house with the shady garden, with Dixie-Belle and her mother and Nan all spoiling them, and no Mummy in the picture at all!

When Jack had completely fulfilled her expectations by saying: "That seems to me a good idea, if you like it, darling," she suggested it tactfully to Jane.

"You know that Mummy and Uncle Jack are going to New York in a few weeks, Janey?"

The blue eyes widened with alarm.

"Oh, Mummy, why?"

"Well, business, dear. Uncle Jack has to see editors and things."

"Are we going?"

"Not this time. But someday we'll take you. This is what I wanted to ask you, Jane. You remember Nan, that took care of you at Aunt Dixie-Belle's house?"

"Oh yes, Mummy. That has the cat that has the kittens."

"Has she? Do you like her, Jane?"

"I like her the most of anybody 'cept you and Dad!" Jane said enthusiastically. "And Uncle Jack," she added a little doubtfully.

"Then suppose you and Joanna went to stay with Nan again when we go away?"

"We'd rather stay with you, *please,* Mummy," Jane said, troubled. She got up from her paint box and came over to dig her head against Cam's arm. "We feel so *lonely* when you go away," she said. "Joanna cries, and she won't stop cryin', and they think she's cryin' for something else, and they keep tellin' her they'll get her a new doll. Please stay with us just a little while!"

"I can't this time," Cam made herself say, "but I'll know you're having a happy time with Daddy, and when I come back I'll be here—oh, for months and months, and we'll go to the beach and have picnics, and have a wonderful time! And now listen, Jane," she added, with quick maternal adroitness, "if you and Joanna really are going to make real ice cream, I think we ought to get the chocolate and cream from Hing now, and get started. Joanna," she called, "we're going to make the ice cream now!"

So that moment was safely over, and there was no longer any choice of what she must do. The little girls would not be disciplined by Toomey anyway, and Dixie-Belle's delicate heath would mean that there was always someone near to stand back of Nan. And Bob, of course, *was* their father. She had to repeat it over and over again to reassure herself that his care for them would naturally be only a little less keen than her own. Bob *was* their father.

Then she liked Nan, and that helped to reconcile her to the fresh pang of parting. Nan was a quiet, stout colored woman who talked very little to the children's mother, but who apparently kept them splendidly amused when they were alone with her. Jane and Joanna seemed to quiet down happily in Nan's company; frequently they had to get up and go and press their radiant fair little faces against her black one to show her that they loved her.

So Mabel went her way, and Nan was installed, and presently the girls and Nan were off in the car to Bob's house, not without tears that seemed to fall like lead into Cam's heart, but soon to be comforted, of course. Soon to be comforted. They were small children still.

"But oh, who's to comfort me?" she asked herself, standing on the terrace as the car drove away. "Who's to comfort me, my children, my little girls? Your babyhood's running by so fast, and I'm missing you—losing you—and you'll never come back!"

Well, there was the immediate excitement of the trip East to contemplate. It was always thrilling, the way Jack managed it. They had a drawing room to which he always sent flowers and books for his wife, delightful packages to open and explore in the hour of starting. They had small packs of cards with which to play silly games in the train. They slept late, loitered out to a lunch-breakfast at noon, came back to their orderly little well-aired room to look out at flying prairies and snowy ranches, to endless idle, happy talk, to reading and resting and staring out of the windows again.

She loved the towns east of Chicago, so different from the straggling Western villages, with their straight streets, aligned trees, snowy barns and fences. And the arrival in New York was always a delight, for the few friends Jack really valued were there, and the Kilgarifs were met with enthusiasm, escorted to their hotel for breakfast, involved instantly in happy plans. There were always a few shows that they must not miss; there were special parties. Cam's warm bright hotel room would be filled with telegrams and flowers, and by the time she was bathed and dressed to accompany a group to some big hotel for a very gala luncheon, she would feel that she had been in the city for a week instead of a day.

Then there was always the fascinating Avenue with the new things in the shops, and the fascinating newspapers, and the general sense of having reached the hub of the world and of being in the immediate center of the group that kept it spinning. After months of country quiet, it was rather fun to go to the evening gatherings where all the writers, critics, musicians of the hour were on display, and to which the theater stars drifted in late, still with a little black about their eyelashes and a little grease about their ears.

Cam felt less shy now than she had on her wedding trip. She knew a few of them rather well, for one thing, and they liked her, for another. Then there was the undeniable asset of her beauty; she had never particularly valued it, as is the way with flawless blondes, but it was pleasant to be always exquisitely dressed and to know that quite a few of the persons about her were asking, "Who *is* she?"

The answer was satisfying, too. She knew what it must be, although she never heard it said:

"That's John Kilgarif's wife. You know, the man who wrote *What Fools We Mortals Be* and *Green Twigs.* Isn't she lovely?"

John was a source of infinite pride to her at these parties, too. He looked splendid in evening dress, handsome, serious, not too much in the spirit of the affair. He rather loitered about the edges of things, sometimes falling into talk with some older man or woman for a while, always quite obviously glad when Cam signaled him that it was time to go. Other men, with the confident audacity of their calling and their influence, told her that he was jealous.

"Oh, I know that; that's not news," Cam would answer, in the same mood. They all said everything they thought, and a great deal more; nothing was sacred to them, nothing in bad taste. Their frankness was only matched by their complete insincerity. "Insincerity," John said, "has become their only honesty. It sounds smart," he added, "but it really isn't. What you said is ten times smarter."

"What did I say?"

"You said that they were like a lot of ants walking around on the upper crust of a pie and trying to convince themselves that it was the good solid earth. Everyone's afraid of falling in, and yet no one will get off the pie crust. And they're all in love with you."

"They tell me you're my keeper, Jack."

"Who said that?"

"Corby."

"Corby 'd better keep his mouth shut. You wouldn't look at *him* if he was King of England."

"He knows it. Anyway, he's madly in love with Pat McGinnis."

"*She* wouldn't look at him, either."

"He knows that, too. But he wanted to take me to—oh, I think he said 'The Racetrack,' to hear Luisa what's-her-name sing, and when I said no, you wouldn't like it, he said you were nothing but a keeper."

"Would *you* have liked it?"

She looked at him patiently.

"Would I have liked to go to a night club with Corby?" she elucidated it.

John laughed guiltily.

" 'Shamed of myself!" he said.

And she thought he really was a little ashamed of himself,

and fancied that for a day or two he was more serene. But then came the occasion of the Marshalls' house party, and the whole ground had to be gone over again, and in a more serious fashion than anything that had happened since their marriage.

CHAPTER XXV

THE MARSHALLS had a beautiful place in New Jersey. They were a brilliant couple, the man a writer, the woman a portrait painter; invitations to their parties were rare and highly prized. On this occasion their guests would number about sixteen; there would be riding, walks, theatricals, there would be endless good talk and most stimulating society. Every one of the guests, with the possible exception of the lovely Mrs Kilgarif, would be a celebrity; the great English poet, Knowlson, would be guest of honor. Cam and John were to drive down with him on Thursday and bring him home on Sunday night.

They called for Knowlson at his hotel on a grim, snow-threatening afternoon and took him straight to the magnificent old brick house in the New Jersey college town. The Englishman was about John's age, somewhere in the middle thirties; they had never met before, but they formed an immediate liking for each other. Cam, sitting between them on the spacious back seat of the car, listened as they talked, moving her blue eyes smilingly now and then from one to the other.

That night he sat next to her at dinner. Sally Marshall was

an inspired hostess; Chouteau Marshall, one of the conversationalists of his day. There was no forcing, no effort; the magic words flew about on their own wings. After dinner the men and the women did not separate, but sat on, talking, talking, talking, and presently Cam, usually rather silent at this sort of gathering, found herself talking a little too, and felt that they were encouraging her and laughing with her.

Samuel Knowlson never took his eyes from her. She was wearing an odd shade of vital soft cherry red, a strange color with her flax-gold hair, but it matched the apricot fluctuating in her cheeks and made her eyes burn like sapphires. The fine taffeta of the gown spread about her slender little figure like the petals of an inverted rose; at the dip of the low bodice that showed the cleavage of her young ivory breasts there was a great flower in silver tissue. She wore ball earrings in Chinese filigree, and a chain of tiny filigree balls to match. She was excited and happy; she liked this house party, and to feel herself liked in return was a heady wine.

That night she was asleep when John came up to bed, for he had been drawn into talk in the smoking room. The next morning was all leisure and ease, and yet there was everything to do. They rode; Knowlson never far from her. They got off and walked their horses on a hill, Cam, rosy and picturesque in riding apparel, between John and Knowlson. At the buffet lunch that preceded their going off *en masse* for the dog show, it was the Englishman who filled her plate, who very pointedly seated himself beside her.

They had reached the big arena, jumped into different cars and attempting to reunite the party in the incredible confusion about the ticket offices, when she realized for the first time that John had not come. Her astonished questions to her hostess elicited the fact that John had not felt very well and had gone to lie down. He had been most anxious that Cam should not know, that she should have the fun of the races without him.

Sick with apprehension, she said that she must go back at once.

"There's never anything the matter with him! It doesn't sound one bit like him! He must feel terribly."

"I don't think it was anything but a headache," said Sally Marshall.

"John doesn't have headaches! I think, if you don't mind —I'm a fool about dogs——" Cam stammered in distress.

"I'll drive you back, of course," said Samuel Knowlson, beside her.

"Ah, but then you'll miss the judges!"

"Mrs Kilgarif," said her host, "suppose you stay for half an hour? That's all I'm going to stay for, for I'm expecting a telephone call from Washington at about four. I'll take you back."

"I'll drive Mrs Kilgarif back this minute," Knowlson repeated. But she would not let him do that. Distracted and preoccupied, she watched the crowd for half an hour, then Chouteau maneuvered his car from out the ranked lines, and they were off together under a cold unfriendly sky and in a steady wind that boded a storm.

Reaching the house, she ran up the stairs like a blown leaf, quieted herself outside his door, turned the knob noiselessly. The room was dark; she could see John's dark head against the white pillows. He turned instantly, and she saw a flushed and haggard face.

"Show over, darling? Did you have a good time?"

"No, they're not over." She flung aside her small hat, tossed off her thick coat and furs. "I came home; Chouteau was coming," she said. She sat down beside the bed and took his hot hand in hers. "What do you *mean* by giving me such a scare?" she said.

"Darling, I felt rotten," he pleaded. "I couldn't have gone."

"But why didn't you tell me? What is it? Did you eat too much lunch? What did you drink?"

"No; I couldn't eat any lunch at all. My head aches, and I feel rotten. I'm so sorry, Cam, to spoil your day!"

"You're not spoiling my day, idiot! What do I care about races, or about anything but you." Cam laid her fresh chilled cheek against his. "I don't think you're feverish," she murmured anxiously.

"No; there's nothing the matter with me. It's only that I'm so—so damn miserable, Cam!" he said.

"Miserable? What about, Jack? Is it business, dear?"

"No; it's just that—that they all see how wonderful you are, Cam. I couldn't sleep last night, thinking how they looked at you—how that Englishman looked at you! He didn't talk to anyone else at breakfast; he was right beside you while we were riding, and at lunch. I can't help it, Cam; I know I'm all wrong about it! But it seems to me that I simply can't get up and come down to dinner, watch him looking at you."

She sat quite silent, listening, holding his hand.

"What am I to do, Jack? Be rude to him?"

"Oh, I don't know." The handsome, intelligent face was dark with pain; his big hands held hers tightly.

"Aren't you getting any fun out of the party?"

"I hate it! I keep thinking of our little parties alone, our drive to Boulder Dam—all our parties—and that here I can't get you away from them; I'll never see you alone while we're here! Oh, Cam, I'm so afraid you don't love me the way I love you!"

"I love you better than anyone else in the world, Jack. You're all I care about," Cam said very earnestly, her eyes smiling while they filled with tears. "These people mean nothing to me. I never met most of them until yesterday. Would you like to run away with your wife and go back to New York? We'll be there for a late supper, and I'd give you milk toast and an aspirin tablet, and you'd wake up in the morning feeling like a two-year-old. Would you like to do that?"

"Cam, you wouldn't!"

"Ah, but I would! Why, you're all I want, and wherever we are, together," Cam said, her face against his now, and the soft mass of her hair loosened on his shoulder, "that's where I want to be! Samuel Knowlson has a lovely wife named Meggy, and she's going to have a baby; it's hardly likely he's going to break it all up just for me! But if it makes you unhappy——"

"I'm such a fool," he said, as she paused. "He's married, is he? You darling, did you race home just to see me?"

"I did. I wasn't having any fun. Seriously, do you want to make some excuse and go back to New York today?"

"No," he said, in a braced, sensible tone, as he abruptly left his bed and began a hasty brushing of hair and putting on of shoes. "You and I'll go off right now and go back to the show. I'm ashamed of myself. Your coming here has made me feel perfectly well, and I'll behave myself now, and see that you don't have to worry about me again! Chouteau's here, isn't he? He'll send us over, and you can sit next to Knowlson at dinner and wear your blue brocade and be as beautiful as you want to, and all I'll be is proud of my wife."

"*You're* the personality, you know, Jack; *you're* the one everyone wants to meet," she reminded him, delighted at his change of mood.

"Yes, I know. I see how they ignore you," he said.

"We're the Kilgarifs," Cam said, her gloved hand locked in his, her leather-coated shoulder touching his shoulder, as they were driven swiftly back to the dog show, "we belong together. When people like you, it makes me as proud as Lucifer, and you ought to be proud if they like me. How'd you like to be married to a drabby elderly clam like Mitzi Fitzgerald?"

"But she's got brains, honey. She did something with the fourth dimension or the undiscovered ratio or something."

"That's all very well. I don't notice the men jamming

about her, nice as she is! In my brainless way it would seem——"

"In your brainless way! You've got brains like a rapier, and you are positively the most beautiful woman God ever made. But more than that, you've got charm, Cam, a mean little insidious charm that's like rain on a roof or a baby Airedale going to sleep with his hairy little mug close to your face. You could look like a baked squash and still get away with it."

"There's something very *thorough* in the way you put things, Jack," Cam said approvingly. "You leave one in so little *doubt*——"

And the rest of that day was glorious. They arrived in time to see the blue ribbons given and the winners admired. Jack was in great spirits; Cam glowed and sparkled; everyone was happy. That night, at the animated dinner table, playing a game of "Hostess," there were gales of laughter, and the charades later were a triumph for Cam, who, as the draggled keeper of a third-rate boarding house, walked away with the honors. She and John went up to bed at one o'clock still laughing reminiscently at the absurdities of the evening, and if he felt any pangs he imagined that he showed no signs of them.

But the next morning, Saturday morning, he received a telegram from his broker. He brought it to Cam, idling with the others in the library.

"Chouteau just gave me this—he got it by telephone. Isn't it a plague?"

She read it, shrugged, leaned down to show it to Sally Marshall, who, with backgammon plaques and dice cups, was amusing her four-year-old daughter on the floor.

"Oh, *tiens!*" said Sally. She read it aloud: " 'Sailing for Florida tonight, important to see you first, sorry to bother you, Harold Nugent.' Who's he?" asked Sally.

"Broker. It probably means that we're ruined, Cam," Jack said.

"Oh, goody, I love to cook," Cam said.

"You must let me lend you ten pounds, Mrs Kilgarif," Samuel Knowlson said. "Now not a word, I love to do it! I've got it—I forget from whom I borrowed it—and you're entirely welcome!"

"You certainly don't have to pay any attention to this," Sally said, piling round little ivory disks.

"Well, I don't know. What would you wire him, Chouteau?" John asked.

"Simply 'bon voyage,' " Chouteau answered unhesitatingly.

"*You* don't have to go," John said to Cam, quickly.

"Isn't it worth a couple of hundred thousand to stay here?" she asked, and Knowlson laughed. John laughed, too, but a second too late. Cam's quick eye caught his expression, and fifteen minutes later they were upstairs packing, and off in a flurry of thanks and good-bys.

"And Jack," said Cam, in the train, peacefully lunching on club sandwiches and watching the snowy colonial towns go by, "the interesting thing is that Nugent doesn't know anything about that wire."

His stupefied eyes met hers. He could not speak.

"I sent it. I had the New York hotel send it," she said calmly. "I knew you were letting the general atmosphere get you again, and I said to myself, 'The poor creature's a poet; he's not all there; I'll have to do something.' So when we were all buzzing around in the hotel yesterday, I slipped over to the telegraph desk and sent Cameron at the hotel a wire. And here we are!"

John spoke solemnly, almost reverently.

"Cam, I'll never forget this of you!"

"I did it for myself, too. When it came to Knowlson inviting me to dine with him Tuesday night——"

"Did he? I thought you said his wife was having a baby?"

"She is. The first after eleven years."

"It doesn't seem to make sense."

"It doesn't seem to me to make sense."

"Well, anyway, here we are, and where are we going to have dinner tonight?"

It was worth it. It was worth it to have him praise her for it a hundred times, and remember it when they were going home to the girls and Cherry Ridge, and thank her for it again.

Then it was California, in the full flood of extravagant spring bloom, with banksia roses flinging wild streamers up into the air from the low farmhouse roof, and the thick high grass still hiding a thousand jewels of rain, packed with buttercups and poppies and the fine blue wild onion flower and delicate baby-blue eyes and the purple stars of the Indian sedge.

The blue eyes, the flowers Cam hungered to see, were in the picture, too. Nan, still adored and adoring, had brought the girls down to the farm in the morning. By the time their mother arrived at five o'clock, Jane and Joanna had had naps and baths and were radiant in new pink dimities and pink ribbons. And then what a feast of happiness, and what happy days to follow, with John working again, and morning hours and odd hours at all times free for Cam and her children!

"Ah din think yo' like 'em ez much ez yo' seemta," Nan remarked innocently one day. Cam laughed, pressing their soft little cheeks to hers, treasuring every word they said in her heart as if it had been a pearl of great price. They appeared to be in good health and spirits, but they had not forgotten their mother, and she knew that she still was first with them.

Early on the morning after the reunion, Joanna came to find her, small head tousled, small eyes bewildered with sleep, small body encased in thin summer pajamas.

It was only eight o'clock. Joanna had not had her breakfast yet. Cam was just awakening. She laughed the laugh of a conspirator, sprang out of bed, a finger on her lip.

"Quiet, sweetheart, Uncle Jack's asleep!" she breathed.

"No, he's not," said Jack. "Hello, Joanna McGinty. What are you doing up so early?"

Cam got back into bed, jerking pillows behind her to prop her into a sitting position, and Joanna climbed in beside her in the old way.

"I thought maybe Mummy wasn't here," Joanna explained. John, sleepy and good-natured, lay watching from his bed the two fair heads together, Cam kissing and snuggling her baby, Joanna trying to braid her mother's hair.

It was very pleasant on the airy porch, with tree shadows rustling green outside the windows, and the sounds of the farm coming through the morning stillness. After a while Nan came for Joanna, and immediately Jane was at the door.

"Mummy, can I come in and get into bed with you tomorrow like Joanna did? We always *used* to!"

"I think you may indeed. Come and give me a kiss and then go back to Nan, because I smelled breakfast, and I think you girls are going to be late."

Jane came flying over, fell bodily upon her mother.

"Don't I get one of those?" John asked. Obligingly, Jane went to him to give him an abstracted kiss, her eyes wandering as she did so. Then she was gone, too, and Cam and John could idle through the usual hour before ringing for trays.

Taffy had come to dinner with his aunt and grandmother the night before. Cam had something to say about him.

"I'm worried about Taffy, Jack. He seems such a nervous little fellow. He doesn't seem to grow up. He's getting round to five now, and yet he's still so dependent on Toomey."

"He's all right."

"It would be so nice if we could have him here with the girls."

"They go back to their father in June, don't they? It's April now."

How words could bite! How one's heart could shrivel away from them!

"Late June. That's—that's eight weeks. Well, why couldn't we have Taffy here for that?"

"Toomey, poor old tab!" John said indifferently. "She'd raise Cain with the girls again. Dora hates her; Mother told me that last year. Nan probably wouldn't fuss—she's quite a dignified old character in her way—but Toomey 'd high-hat Nan, and there 'd be the deuce to pay!"

"Toomey," Cam said significantly. John laughed.

"Yes, I know," he said.

"I have a feeling that if I could just get hold of that little fellow and have her completely out of the picture——" Cam began, and stopped. "If we could turn him loose here," she presently added, "with a few ropes and nails and a hammer, and if nobody made any rules for him, or paid him any attention at all, he might grow into——" She hesitated, not wanting to hurt the father's feelings. "He might be a much happier little boy," she finished simply.

"Boarding school for him sometime. That 'll lick him into shape. They're quite different from what they used to be, schools," John said.

"I don't think it's boarding school he needs," she said thoughtfully. "I wish we could all go camping into the Sierras."

"That 'd be kind of a swell idea," John said, glancing up.

"You've no idea how swell it is. You pack in on horseback and find a camp, and they usually put up a few boards for a platform, and drag in wood enough for a few days. Then the packers go away, and there you are, with trees and horses and bacon and matches, and nothing else for perhaps a month. I used to get more thrill out of washing our clothes in a cold swift branch of the King——"

"When were you there?"

She had paused, suddenly stricken by a memory of when she had been there, and with whom. She laughed.

"Oh, with Bob, with Bob, with Bob!" she admitted. "And if I could love it with Bob I'd be mad about it with you. But we'll cross out the High Sierras, and consider some beach somewhere by contrast. Or Lake Louise—but oh, dear," Cam exclaimed, interrupting herself again, "just as we got started the girls would have to go to Bob again!"

"How much do you like high mountains?" he asked her, two weeks later. "You were very enthusiastic about the High Sierras a little while ago. D'you really like mountains?"

"Jack, what are you thinking about?" she countered by way of answer. For his eyes were dancing, and he had come into her quiet noon hour suddenly, an open letter in his hand. This wasn't obviously his brooding jealousy. But what was it?

"It's Fitzgerald," he said. "Fitzgerald and the *Times*. They want me to do the Everest story. By gum, *that's* being picked out of the ranks and handed a commission! Everest! Nothing mean about us, darling, when we pick a mountain we pick a good one. Fitzgerald's starting from New York in September—September third, he says here. Mrs Fitzgerald —you remember her?—she's a scientist, too; she's going, and her maid—a colored woman, I imagine—goes along to take care of you women. Two young scientists, four press men, myself among 'em, and that's all until we get to Tibet! My gosh, what a chance! They'll pay me, and I'll get a book out of it, too. I'll get six books out of it—lamas, you know, Eastern philosophy. It seems they've gotten permission for the craziest reason you ever heard, but it holds with these priests . . ."

He went on and on. Cam listened, stricken. Only this morning Nan, noncommittal, gentle black Nan, had said to her that it seemed a pity to "roust" the children back and forth so often between the two households. "Miss Dixie-Belle she fixin' fur to have 'em all time," Nan had said. "But dey happier here. Dey like kittens 'at wants dey mama."

They would be going to Bob in a few weeks. And now—now—it began to sound as if they might stay with him—indefinitely——

"Everest, Jack! Isn't that the highest of all? Have they ever made it?"

"You smarty, how'd you know anything about Everest! Cam, this is going to be the adventure of our lives!"

No such adventure as going down scared and in pain, weak and bewildered and sweat-soaked, she thought, to the very gates of death, and coming back, all headache and boneache and weakness and ecstasy, to hear someone saying: "It's all over. You have a beautiful little girl."

Aloud she said, "How long would we be gone if we went, Jack?"

"*Would* we be, and *if!*" he echoed. "Ha! We'll be gone from September to—oh, I don't know. It takes months to pack in. We'll probably be gone about a year! Have you got a smart husband? There isn't a writer alive who wouldn't be glad to get in on this. Cam, sleeping bags and cameras and wool socks—but we'll get those in London. We'll stay with the Bristows! Tantara, tantara, tantara! Marching orders, Mrs Kilgarif!"

"Marching orders!" she echoed, straightening her shoulders gallantly.

CHAPTER XXVI

THE DAYS WENT ON and brought the rich fulfillment of young summer, and Cam moved through them, performing each hour what duty belonged to that hour, always smiling when John or her children saw her.

But she had never known pain like this pain. It bewildered her; it seemed to rise between her and the sunshine, and to sound between her and all the happy murmuring of life. It was like homesickness; yet she was at home!

The little girls, entirely unconscious of the changes that were coming upon them, splashed in the pool, laughed and chattered over their meals on the terrace, went sleepy and weary and still eager to bed on the sleeping porch about which the high trees waved and the last light of the long days lingered.

John was happy, too, studying catalogues, sending for information about boots and packing cases, sleeping bags and rubber pillows.

Their room, his room and Cam's, began to be piled with heaps of strange things; he made endless lists. For the steamer, for the land trip, for the camp in the great mountains.

"Cam, you'll have to have a lot of warm things. Three

suits of light fleece underwear, fleece-lined trousers to tuck into your boots, and a light coat of—wait until I look!"

"I'll look charming, I should think. Don't we get those things in London?"

"I'm writing London. We may have to go to Copenhagen."

"Oh, fun! I've never been there. What's a parka, Jack?"

"A jacket with a fur-lined hood. You'll have to have a parka."

"We won't need more than a couple of liners to get it all to Darjeeling, will we?"

"We leave trunks in London. If we come out the China way, we'll have 'em sent to Vladivostok, and down by steamer."

"It all sounds *crazy*. Darjeeling and Vladivostok. There *aren't* any such places, except in geography games. I don't believe it!"

"Sometimes," he would say, "I can't believe it myself. Of all the things I ever wanted to do in the world, this would come first! Lord, if we just don't *die* before September!"

She showed nothing. But sometimes she thought she herself actually would die of the agony of parting that faced her.

"Suppose we don't get back, Jack? Loads of Everest explorers haven't."

"It's different now. There's not much danger. Oh," he would say, rather relishing the idea, "there's always a chance of snow sliding—the camp getting buried. But they'll know how to look out for that. However," John added once, in a more than ordinarily serious moment, "we'd better get our houses in order. You've got a will, haven't you?"

Cam had a small property left her by her father. But she also held the responsibility of sole trustee for the girls' inheritance from their grandmother. This had been vested in her at the time of Joanna's birth, when Bob had been acting very badly and his mother had confided to Cam that she would not feel happy in leaving the estate in his charge. About this she did some serious thinking before consulting John.

"Jack, of course we'll come back. But I suppose there *are* chances that we won't."

"You bet your life there are!" John agreed happily.

"About the girls' property. The money Granny left them. She didn't change her will, you know, after Bob and I separated. I've still charge of it. I was wondering—who would you think should take it over—just in case, you know——"

"Oh, look here, honey," John said, diverting his attention from an elaborately pocketed wallet, "I was only fooling. We'll get back. Fitz knows the ropes, what to take and what to do, and one of the boys is a doctor. We take darned near a hundred pounds of medical supplies. You don't have to worry."

"Still, I think I ought to consider it."

He frowned; meditated a moment.

"I suppose their father's the obvious one," he said.

"I was thinking that."

"You can arrange all that through the lawyer. You don't have to see him."

"I wonder," she thought, "if there ever was a time when I wasn't arranging things through a lawyer!" Aloud she said, "Well, since they've been so nice, Bob and Dixie-Belle, I mean, perhaps it would be more civil to get in touch with them informally. After all," Cam went on, talking over a definite hard pain in her heart as she might have dragged a hurt foot over some log or stone, "they may have the girls for quite a while. She's going to have a baby, but she said—her letter said—that that was only one more good reason for having the girls. She must just—well, love children. And she did send us Nan, who's been such a success. Could I just write Bob, in a friendly sort of way, you know, and tell him that I'd like him to take over the responsibility if anything happens to me?"

"You manage it your own way; it's really only a matter of form," John said. "Look here, Cam, this is what I'll carry through the whole party. See, a flap for money, another here for passports, identification card, letter of credit—that reminds me, we've got to go up to the bank and go through a lot of fuss. What was it you said at breakfast you had to get?"

"Stockings. Woolen stockings, and they're not so easy to find as you'd think." He was so absorbed in the prospect of the trip that he never noticed anything lacking in her tone, anything forced in her enthusiasm. "And I was wondering, Jack, if I ought to cut my hair?"

"What for, darling?"

"Such a pest, traveling."

"But it's so gorgeous, Cam. Don't cut it. I could always bob it for you if necessary."

"Jack, I love the idea of what it would look like! I'd be taken for a lama and stuck in a cell!" She flung open three soft warm thin plaids to which price tags were still attached. "I love this one," she said, crumpling the silky wool of one of them against her cheek, "but it's pretty big."

"It won't seem big when you're wrapping it around you on the slopes of Kinchinjunga!"

He went on checking and inspecting, boy again, in a boy's dream of adventure, and she could slip away presently to write a letter.

"My dear Bob, Jack is going to Sacramento on the day the girls go to you, which is Thursday next," Cam wrote. *"He will be gone all day, and I am wondering, since it would be so much less conspicuous than a hotel lunch room and so much less disagreeable than a lawyer's office, if you and 'Aunt Dixie,' as the children call her, would lunch with me that day . . . "*

The answer came in a brief note. Bob would come, gladly, and bring the girls back with him, but Dixie-Belle wasn't awfully fit this summer, and wasn't making any trips. Cam said nothing about it to John. Time enough to explain later. One reference to any arrangement for the trip would happily distract him now; she could dismiss the matter of Bob and the girls with a few words.

On Thursday John left early for the flying field, and Cam spent a long restless morning with the children, conscious of nerves, conscious of heartache, wondering what she had ever considered trouble before this real sorrow of separation from her children had come to her. The girls were in bed and asleep long before one o'clock, when Cam, waiting on the terrace, saw a smart low-slung car come around the big bed of phlox and delphinium and verbena, and stop with Bob's usual jerk a few feet away from her.

Very brown and big and athletic he looked, his cream-colored clothes setting off his Indian skin, as he snatched off his cap and came smiling toward her.

"Cam, how are you?" he said. "My Lord, you look stunning!" And with all his old bold cheerfulness he added, "Do we kiss each other?"

She could not keep from laughter.

"I don't think we do." It was amazingly pleasant to see him, this man she knew so well, this stranger with whom the most sacred hours of her life had been spent. Memories of girlhood, of wedding presents in white boxes, of Bob dark and big and protective beside her at a reception that was scented with orange blossoms, were thick about her as she led him to the table that on this foggy cool July day had been set beside the dining-room fire. They sat down—as they so often had seated themselves!—opposite each other.

"What's the excitement?" he asked, when Dora's absence gave them an opportunity to speak freely.

Cam explained, sometimes looking away with a faint frown, when the words were too hard to say, sometimes raising her blue eyes to his.

"We're going on this long expedition, you see," she was

presently saying, "and there's always the danger of not coming back."

"He isn't an explorer, Kilgarif. How come he gets in on this?"

"You sound," she said with a smile, "as if you envied him."

"Well, by gum, I do! I've been reading about it in the paper. Lord, what a chance!" Bob's dark face was animated with interest. She found him, now that she had time really to study him, thinner, keener, altogether more vivacious than she remembered him, although Bob would always be of the bullock type. "How's it happen that Fitzgerald's taking Kilgarif?" he asked.

"Jack and Fitzgerald were in college together; they're very old friends; we met them at a house party last winter. Mrs Fitzgerald's a scientist, too—she's Dutch, you know, an older woman; she's fifty, I believe, and she's supposed to know more of those religious sects on the mountain than any other person alive. Fitz himself is quite young, thirty-five or so—Jack's age. He says he's always wanted to do it, and through some pull of her father, who lived out in that part of the world for half his life, she can get the necessary permissions. So off we go!" Cam ended cheerfully.

"Shall you like it?" Bob asked, with a keen glance.

"I hate," she said simply, "leaving the girls."

"That's what I was thinking. You never wanted to get ten feet away from them before."

"It's not an expedition for young ladies just past five and seven."

"I suppose not. Dixie-Belle's tickled to death to have them, you know. She's a motherly little soul. She and her mother run them like clockwork."

"And you'll manage their estate if anything happens to me, Bob?"

"Well, sure; but nothing 'll happen to you. It's a funny trip for a little thing like you to be making, but Lord, you'll be home before you know it. Why don't you name Pete Buckingham-Smith with me as executor? Pete's above reproach," Bob suggested, with his old grin.

"Shall I? It's a rather grisly business, whatever I do. I think of myself lying 'way out there under those eternal snows," Cam said, with a shred of rueful laughter, "and of my little girls growing up without Mummy, and it seems rather——" She looked at him smiling, surprised to feel hot tears prick her eyes. "It seems rather forlorn," she said thickly.

"Why do you go, Cam, if you feel that way?"

"Ah, he wouldn't go without me!"

"I suppose he wouldn't. Well, we'll give the girls a swell time," Bob said, "and round Christmas sometime they ought to have a nice little baby brother to play with. Dixie lost two babies in her first marriage, and she's tickled to death to think that there's going to be another."

"Do you still play golf a lot, Bob? It seems to me I don't see your name as I used to."

"Nope. I wrenched my leg, you know? I guess you were away; it was in the paper. Down at Del Monte, taking a perfectly good shot, and suddenly a muscle went haywire, and I had to be dragged in to the hotel like a beef. Harry taped it up, and I tried to play the Pebble Beach course that afternoon—no go. I had to drop out entirely for three months, and I'm just getting started again now. But I'll never play tournament golf again. And I don't want to," Bob confessed with a laugh. "I got kind of sick of that gambling crowd—Madeleine, that lot. 'Member the night she played roulette at Reno? Gosh, what a stinging! She never did get her emerald back. Cutter bought it for Edith. No, you wouldn't know me now, Cam. Domestic, that's me. I kind of like to fool round the garden, and when the girls are there Dixie-Belle and I have our lunch with them——"

She was listening so intently, her eyes so steadily fixed on his, that he broke off with an embarrassed laugh.

"What is it—am I saying anything queer?" he asked.

"I wonder——" she began musingly, by way of answer. But whatever it was she wondered she did not say. Instead she substituted suddenly: "Bob, if I don't come back, you'll spoil them, won't you? Spoiling doesn't hurt youngsters half so much as—as not being loved! See that there are picnics and birthday parties——"

Her throat thickened, and she sat looking at him with her eyes brimming with tears.

"Sure. We'll see that they get a break," he said, his own speech a little thick.

"I love them so, I want them so!" Cam faltered. She got up, unwilling to have him see her face, and walked to the fireplace and, putting an elbow on the low mantel, covered her eyes with her hand. "This means failure," she said in a low tone. "Failure with Jack's child—we rarely see him, he doesn't need us—and failure with my own! Girls need their mother, and mine may never see me after today!"

There was a silence, when she struggled desperately to get command of herself, and when he sat, as she perfectly realized, in red-faced consternation, staring blankly at her.

"Lord," he said at last, managing a laugh, "isn't it a shame that about sixty thousand fellers who'd give their eye teeth to go on this trip with Fitzgerald couldn't have your place, and you stay at home and play with the kids!"

Her grateful answering laugh was shaky. She found a handkerchief, wiped her eyes, came back to her place at the table.

"Coffee, Bob? Do you still drink so much coffee? No," Cam said, "I couldn't let Jack go without me. I've grown to depend on him."

"Love him, huh?" Bob asked simply. And again she laughed in spite of herself.

"Absolutely. He's a wonderful person, and he spoils me," she said. "But of course the girls *aren't* his, and his wife *is* his, and sometimes it makes for—a divided duty. Ah, here they are!"

With some bustle, and the chattering of young birds in bushes at morning, Jane and Jonna came in. They were fresh and dewy from naps and pleased in a bewildered sort of way to find their father and mother together. They went from one to another for kisses and finally were settled: Joanna sprawled luxuriously in her mother's lap eating a ginger cooky, Jane nibbling her own cooky as she leaned against her father's knee.

"Did you come to get us, Daddy?" Jane asked, placidly. Cam had hoped they would go quietly and happily; she had prayed that there would not be the old baby despairs at parting, but this was hard, too; this struck her very soul like a blow.

"Are we goin' to thee the dee', dee' l'il baby kitties?" Joanna inquired, raising in interest the little gold head that had been resting like a blossom against Cam's shoulder.

"They're all there. The bad black one, too."

"He can't help being bad, Daddy!" Jane said, in passionate defense.

"He hat to catch that wat!" Joanna added, excitedly. "It wath hith thooty!"

Bob, one big arm about his oldest daughter, proud eyes on the other, moved his gaze to catch Cam's look. She tried to respond, her heart sick within her. "Oh, little soft confidential friendly girls," her soul cried out, "oh, flesh of my flesh and bone of my bone, when will I have the sound of you, the sight of you, the sweetness of you in my arms again!"

Nan was like a shadow in the shadows near the doorway.

"Is the chil'ren an' me goin' back wid Mr Sylvester, Mrs Kilgarif?"

"Yes, Nan. You can ask Mitchell or any of the men to help you put their bags in the car. The trunks," Cam said composedly to Bob, "will go up with Mitchell tonight."

"Oh, Daddy, are you goin' to take us!" Jane said. "Can we sit up in front with you?"

"Yo' kin if yo' ack like yo's the Misses Sylvester, an' not trash offen the streets," Nan put in neatly.

It was still very foggy outside. Cam reached for a loose soft coat as they went through the hall. The girls were buttoned snugly into their blue reefers, their mother's hands lingering over top buttons, their mother's cheek against theirs more than once during the brief process of getting them ready to go.

"You wouldn't want them another week, Cam? It's pretty tough on you," Bob said, with unwonted concern for her set and colorless face.

"No. No, thank you. We leave in seven days, and that much time Jack will need, with the decks cleared for packing."

The three faces that had once been her world smiled good-by from the front seat. Jane and Joanna were sitting dutifully erect, on their very best behavior, but already bouncing with impatience to see all the kitties, and especially the bad black one.

Wheels grated on the gravel; Bob's brown car was swallowed into the silent, all-concealing fog. Complete stillness was upon the house, and the low shingled roof, and the mist-dripping trees.

"Mis' Kilgarif," Dora said, appearing with a corded and sealed and oilskin-wrapped box, "I reckon this is that stuff from Alaska. Anyway, it says 'Dobbins, Nome,' on it here."

Cam moved her eyes.

"Oh yes; I'm glad it's here. Mr Kilgarif will be delighted. It's fur, or it should be. He wants it made into—well, I'm not quite sure what, but I think it's boots."

"Mis' Kilgarif," said Dora, "Joe wanted to know if as soon as the girls went he could put a canvas over the sand-box, becuz when they water the nasturtiums they get the sand wet."

"Yes; tell him he can do that." They could take the sand-box away, for that matter. The girls would be too big for the

the sandbox when they came to live at Cherry Ridge again.

"Your head aches, don't it?" Dora asked sympathetically.

"It feels kind of heavy." Oh, horrors, here were these wretched tears again! Jack would see that her eyes were all tear-bitten.

"You can't have everything, can you, Mis' Kilgarif? That's what my mother always says," Dora observed.

Cam made no answer as she walked slowly into the house. Dora thought that she had not heard her.

CHAPTER XXVII

THE thin clear sunshine of an early winter day bathed the whole world in beauty. It turned old China into an exquisite faded tapestry whose very poverties were picturesque, whose teeming life held no more of tragedy than the ancient battles upon some dim drapery embroidered by a long-dead queen.

Peiping, in the late afternoon, basked in a long silence under the last of its red-and-gold and lemon-yellow leaves. It was a silence emphasized rather than broken by the clink of camels' feet as the long trains came in bringing loads of winter coal from the mountains, and by the ceaseless chatter and laughter of the irrepressible Orientals.

The long dusty lanes which separated the compounds were almost deserted, except for an occasional contented ivory baby playing in the dust and for the clean blue shadows. It was inside the lacquered red wooden gates that life went on, life that teemed and squirmed and laughed and cried, that chopped and sawed and sewed and cooked in the mysterious courts within courts within courts that to the Chinese say home.

Of some of the courts the foreigners had taken possession. From some of them barrow loads of filth had been taken away, buckets of hot suds had been introduced, whitewash had been ingeniously used, exquisite old carvings had been recovered;

ancient lamps had been set up to conceal modern light bulbs, and upon hard uncomfortable k'angs deep fleecy rugs had been laid. Every Moon Gate, every old stone passage, every latticed piazza and enameled flowerpot had been preserved. The American and English women who claimed the old places boasted of their very inconveniences as part of their charm.

One of the most beautiful of them all, even in beautiful Peiping, was the Chalmers place, decorated and restored and furnished by a charming Englishwoman, wife of one of the secretaries at the Consulate. It had been rented now by the American writer and his lovely wife, who had been ill for a long time.

All Peiping knew their story, as indeed all the world did. The echoes of the ill-fated expedition to storm the heights of implacable Everest were even now in the public mind, although the Kilgarifs and the half-crazed widow of the lost Fitzgerald had stumbled their way back to civilization many months earlier. Mitzi Fitzgerald had tottered on to England to sink deep into solitude and silence; the Kilgarifs, the man supposedly in a dying condition, had gotten as far as Peiping on their way to San Francisco when illness had halted them. The story of little delicate Mrs Kilgarif and her heroic nursing of her husband had been only the beginning of the sequel. She had written a book during those dreadful weeks, had actually gotten together her random and charming and poignant recollections of the fated expedition, and had substituted them for the articles that her husband had been far too ill to write, and they had had an enormous success.

For one more note of the dramatic, all this time, as all the world had known, there had been a baby coming to this wife of John Kilgarif, a baby born in a Peiping hospital almost at the cost of his mother's life. And ever since, she had been invalided, a helpless little figure in her lovely Chinese silks, resting under a willow and a persimmon tree in her Chinese garden, waited on hand and foot by the big husband whose adoration of her put a final touch upon the beauty of their story. John Kilgarif would go nowhere without her; he lived only for her. No dinner invitation would tempt him, no matter how distinguished the guests at the Consulate or how old the friends who tried to lure him to the hotel.

Mrs Kilgarif being unable to stand much social strain, the result was that they were all but buried behind their beautiful walls and courts and strips of clean green lawn and fountains paved with tiles. But they said they liked it, and the few intimates admitted always came away feeling that they liked it, too. In a world—and it is so especially the world of far-away ports and places—in which ugliness and divorce and unhappiness so often take refuge, the spectacle of the famous handsome devoted husband and the frail little wife perhaps was found rather refreshing. However it was, the Kilgarifs had all the company they wanted and never were made to feel themselves anything but loved and welcome in their strange adopted home.

Cam had lain in a long padded chair during the autumn days, simply resting. Every fiber of body, soul and mind had soaked itself in endless rest. There had been days, there had been weeks indeed, when she had felt herself too tired even to begin to rest; when the mere effort of relaxing had been pain. She had been tired when they had reached Darjeeling on the way out, she thought now—tired from travel. She remembered being a little scared, in all the strangeness of Calcutta's crowded streets and jabbering bazaars, to hear Jack say to Fitz: "Getting round to the start, old boy!"

The start! Why, many a long journey ended in Calcutta; that was an objective, not a springboard toward fresh impossibilities. Cam had felt overwhelming weariness and languor even there, but, for some reason she could not now define, she had not suspected the real reason for this sudden flagging of interest and energy, and when she did realize that there was to be a baby, that she was destined to be a clog instead of a help upon the trip, the expedition had been in Phari, and she could not retreat.

Phari, the high mountain village where the donkeys were waiting, stamping and wheeling restlessly in the snow, had been a nightmare. She told herself now that she had had a premonition of disaster then; she had asked herself in a sort of cold panic, when travel anyway was fraught with ordinary risks and dangers, why sensible men should leave the usual routes, should pack strange indigestible foods into cartons and cans, lay bales of preposterously clumsy garments upon donkeys' backs, weigh tents and test oxygen masks, blind their eyes with snow glare, skin their heels in long marches, sleep shuddering and cold in flimsy tents upon the inhospitable sides of giant mountains. What *for,* in heaven's name!

But gallant, determined, frightened, she had gone along with them, until her woman companion, the famous scientist Mitzi von Das who was Fitzgerald's middle-aged wife, had most fortunately found the greater part of the climbing too much for her. That alone, Cam felt, had saved her. Otherwise she must have asked John to send her back anywhere, to Kampa Dzong, Gyantse—any place where she would find living persons, fires, hot kettles, warm blankets!

"Get me a cave at Changmoo!" she thought she would say as fatigue and despair seized her in their talons and fear added the last touch of utter desolation. "Anything, to be *secure!*"

But Mitzi had broken first, and in making Mitzi comfortable in Base Camp Seven the men had made Cam reasonably comfortable, too, and she had determined to stick it out.

Twenty-one thousand feet up in the cold frozen air, with the sun eternally veiled behind thick white clouds, soft wet snows eternally falling, and constant winds attempting to snatch the very food from the women's hands as they ate, she and Mitzi had been established in "Seven Camp." There were to be six other bases above them; the final base, that chimera of which the men spoke so often and so fondly, would be "One Camp," on the very crown of Everest itself.

Seven Camp had been built against an ice wall; blocks of ice had fenced it on two sides; the women's tent had been double, its entrance but a few feet from the cooking tent. On certain of those incredible mountain-ringed days Cam had made no greater effort than to drag herself to the little table that had been spread three times a day with pans of hot canned meat and bowls of rice, blocks of Swiss cheese and tin cups of thick chocolate; to drag herself back to her bed again.

The altitude had snatched at their breathing, turned their limbs to lead, hammered at their hearts. But the men had had at least the excitement of inexhaustible planning. They had bent panting over charts, they had taken out their glasses and located the mountain, only a peak among all the other peaks, and not appearing to be by any means the highest, and yet to them daily more of a miracle, a mystery, an enchantment. They had been drunk and bewitched by Everest. She had floated above their heads untouchable and inscrutable and inviolate as in the days of Genghis Khan.

John and Fitz and two of the younger men had presently gone off, with ropes and guides and porters, to establish bases further up the slopes. After five days they had returned exulting. Because of a kindly glacier that cut off an expected descent and reascent, they could abolish two of the proposed bases: Seven Camp was really Five Camp. Two Camp, only on paper as yet, would be within two miles of the peak.

The next expedition had struck the first note of fear into them. The impregnable Himalayas had stretched down a warning finger. Young Bates and Brewster had come back with the guide, broken and exhausted, leaving Montrose up on the mountain alone.

Now it was terror! Now it was terror! Cam's heart had pounded on the words. "I knew this would happen. I knew this would happen. Now Jack will go out to get him," she thought, "and Jack won't come back. And I'm nine weeks along with my baby. O God, get us out of this horrible place—get us out of this!"

But Jack had not gone. Fitz, very grim and businesslike and confident, had started off with the chief guide and young

Dr Truesdell. And they had brought Montrose back—a handsome, brave, cheery fellow still, but he had had broken ribs and a bruised head now, and the women had had to nurse him. He was put into a sort of annex to their tent; they tended him faithfully, glad to have something to do.

Long before this, in Trieste, Mitzi's colored maid had left the party. The Billingses, of Morristown, New Jersey, had chanced to cross the party there—rich, fat Mrs Billings lamenting the desertion of the French maid she had foolishly taken back within scent and sound of Paris. It was suspected that black Etta, quietly deserting the Everest expedition, had as quietly joined the Billings forces. Mitzi and Cam had a big, quiet frightened Nepalese woman as a personal attendant, the wife of the head guide. She clung to them in a pathetic, childish way, and they were conscious of clinging in somewhat the same fashion to her, glad of any company in the dreadful whiteness and emptiness and blankness.

"Do you know what I do, Mitzi?" Cam had said, during one of the endless days that was destined so soon to be shut in by another black, wind-filled, endless night. "I project my mind into the future. I say to myself, 'There are gardens full of roses in California, there are long hot beaches, there are nice little maids in mauve moiré serving crab salad and peeled figs, there are sleeping porches where moonlight comes in through oak branches, there are libraries with big wood fires. You'll get back to them, don't worry—you'll find them again! This is only a dream.' "

"I wonder," the Dutchwoman had answered, "if det don't sometimes come in and get to be part of der dream."

"Oh, probably! I suppose we're all quite nutty by this time and don't know it," Cam had said calmly, and Mitzi and the sick boy had laughed joyfully.

The slightest and smallest of them all, she nevertheless did bring almost all the laughter they knew to the group, and they all adored her. Mitzi knew and John knew the secret she carried, but nobody else had guessed it yet, and the blessed time presently had come when she could think: "It's only a few weeks more, and then my baby and I will be gotten out of this, and never think of these accursed wicked Himalayas again!"

Four Camp, Three Camp, Two Camp had been duly planted higher and higher in the long draws of the glaciers, on the blue deep snows. Fitz and Jack had come back from these increasingly daring ventures sobered, breathing hard, but all the more determined to bribe the rebellious porters into line, to start afresh, to conquer the last peak and give a new story to the Old World. They had talked rations, apparel, fuel; only three of them would make the last assault, except for the four bearers.

The seven had started off in a winding fog on a grim May morning; it had been three days later that Brewster, who had been steadily watching the ascent through binoculars, had summoned the women from their tent. His voice had been low and grave, and yet it had already had a certain acceptance in it. What he had seen on the high slopes of the mountain peaks had not been unexpected. He had given Mitzi the glasses.

She had steadied her shoulder against his.

"Ja," she had said simply, "vun is det. Vich? Vun is det, all right."

Cam had felt her throat thicken and her limbs grow weak as she had taken the glasses in her turn. Far, far up against the sharp rise of the great mountain, men's figures had shown like black dots on the glacier. It had been impossible to distinguish them in the blaze of white light, but with the strong glasses she could find the unmistakable signal. Blankets, wisps of black against the flawless purity of virgin snows, were laid to form a tiny feather of a cross; that was what they had promised. Death was what it meant. One of them was lost.

Somehow she had dragged herself back to her bed, had felt someone putting warm blankets over her. Mitzi Fitzgerald had been quiet, she had not collapsed. But the landslide of the mountainside above her could not more completely have crushed Cam. Late in the afternoon the boys had reported that the party was coming down. One Camp had been destined to remain forever a dream.

"That means," she had whispered, holding tight to David Montrose's comforting strong young hand, "that it's either Jack or Fitz. Otherwise they'd go on. It was a crevasse. I could hear the ice cracking away from the mountain all night long. We have to wait, don't we, we just have to wait. What's today, David?"

"The third, Cam."

"They ought to be down by the sixth, oughtn't they? We'll know then, won't we?"

"They ought to be down tomorrow. They'll come fast. We'll be all ready for 'em. It might be a mistake, you know; they might have dropped some of the bags, or just chanced to put the blankets like that. Nimpan is going to have soup, hot blankets, everything. You'll see, it won't be as bad as you think."

Well, she was safe in her Peiping garden now, but sometimes at night that particular memory would come back upon her too strongly, and then Miss Fox would patter across the moon-washed courts to the kitchen and heat milk and mix into it the bitter grainy powders that meant blessed sleep. Cam was not to think of the return of the expeditionists from Two Camp: Bates with frostbitten feet, to go through life now lacking two toes from each foot, the porters frantic and jabbering, Jack, black-faced, raving, feverish, stumbling and tumbling along like a drunken man, not knowing where he went.

And no more of Fitz, ever. One of the many icy mouths of the mountain had swallowed him; the sharp lip of a crevasse had severed the rope as clean as the snip of a scissors; he had plunged down into blue echoing space with only one wild shout of protest.

The others had lain flat looking down into the pit for many

hours, hearing him call, madly splicing the ropes that might as well have been expected to reach a star. And then there had been an ice-slip, and the packed sledge and one of the bearers had quietly been swallowed down into the crevasse with one treacherous slide of the glacier face; had followed him down in a noiseless soft smother of aroused snow and surface smoke. After that there had been no sound from the depths and nothing to see but the enlarged gap in the whiteness, its revealed edges looking like glass teeth that grinned over their prey.

The survivors, their food and bedding gone, had started back to the lower camp. They had never dared stop, except for two-minute sleeps when five fell like clods in the snow, and the sixth, watch on wrist, watched them and hammered them awake. It had been a camp of madmen on that night when they had reached the women again; it had been only the following day that they could formulate a plan, could begin the slow escape from the fastnesses of ice. By that time the whole face of the mountain seemed to have slipped; had they been only a few hours later they must have all been lost, for the track, perilous and steep as it had been, was entirely lost now, and the grave of the explorer covered beyond all mortal finding. Beaten, now they could only go home.

Never leaving Jack's side, somehow Cam had weathered the long stages; had found ice for him in burning Calcutta, had set the fans going in their hot rooms on the Canal boat. At Shanghai the fight had seemed lost; but she had moved him by plane to the cooler airs of Peiping, had pulled herself day after day to the hospital, desperate, determined, never giving up hope.

Then he had been well again, weak and shaken, and with the pure silver at his temples making him handsomer than ever, and it had been her turn. They had taken the Chalmers house, waiting for the baby, and on a hot August day Cam's son, weak, tired, prematurely born, had come wailing into the world. She had tried to do her best for the baby before his birth, keeping her life normal and busy, amusing John, reading to him, taking long walks, distracting him during long convalescent days with her first adventure into letters. If he could not fulfill his contract with the *Times,* she could. And all this activity would be good for "Boo." But despite all that she did there had been grave doubt from the beginning that the little boy would live. He had been less than a month old when he and his amah had been sent "home"; the steamer that took him away had brought her first reviews: her book was a success. Cam had been too broken to know or to care.

She had kept her book simple, cheerful. She had tried to laugh at the memory of three half-frozen women eating English biscuit with strawberry jam and cream cheese piled on them, mixing greasy beef pemmican with their hot chocolate just for the warmth the fats put into their shaking bodies. And at the end she had paid a simple tribute to Fitz which lifted the book for a few minutes from the ordinary and made it poignant and unforgettable.

That America and England had devoured every word of it in the newspaper articles, that it was selling sensationally, had concerned her not at all. By the time a devouring, a devastating fatigue had enveloped her; she had sunk deeper and deeper under it until it had seemed to her and to those who loved and watched her that she would never rise above it again.

The tiny Edward had been sent to his doctor uncle in Baltimore. A fine gentle amah had escorted him. Cam had given the pulpy little wrinkled face but a quiet kiss for good-by, but she had felt that it was a long, long parting nevertheless. She had no children with her now; she was too ill to go to them.

It had not seemed important. Nothing was important. Just not to be so horribly tired all the time, that was what mattered! And never to have John very far away. She depended upon him for everything, and he never failed her.

He was working again now, getting his own book into shape—a graver book than hers—its serious handsome frontispiece a photograph of "Fitz," in his happy prime, with his woolen helmet on, his thick, light belted coat, his finneskoes and mittens. About his waist was the rope that had betrayed him; behind him a grinning ring of porters stood loaded, waiting for his leadership.

Jack still grieved bitterly for the loss of "the Owner." It seemed to him disloyalty to write the book that Fitz had meant to write. But Cam knew that every hour of work he put into it comforted him just a little more. It was to have been his chief's masterpiece; it would be his monument. Day after day it more and more absorbed him; she saw his color, vitality, his inextinguishable love of life come back into his veins as the work progressed.

She slept late on these strange idle mornings, usually having her breakfast and her mail at about noon. Jack always interrupted his work to come to her then; there was always news, sometimes trivial about the Pao-Machang races or new arrivals at the Grand Hotel, or sometimes the letters and cables that meant actual life to her. Dixie-Belle wrote every two or three weeks about the girls. Cam's brother Ned, in whose Baltimore home Cam's delicate baby was staying, reported regularly upon the baby's progress. There were details that wrung her heart; she would droop her tired head over the brief pages while bitter tears ran down her cheeks. But that, she would falter to Jack, was only weakness—only the silly helpless weakness that the illness had left. She was sorry!

The afternoon brought other moods. If the day was fine—and during that particular autumn the gritty winds held away and almost all the days had hearts of serene sunshine—she was moved out into the court and could watch the two gold-and-white parrots walking and tipping on their high perch, and the bright-eyed wirehair racing after the ball that was flung for him, and the mother cat he feared so deeply airing her little gold kittens.

Almost always in the afternoon she had callers, women

who loved to sit and gossip with her of American or English days; sometimes a Frenchwoman or a Dutch or Italian woman from one of the legations. The life they led as exiles was full of interest for them, and the news from home, wherever home might be, was discussed to tatters.

Then Jack would come back from whatever exercise that particular day had provided—golf, races, tennis, riding or perhaps only a tramp along the chilling gray dusty streets—and then they all moved in to the fire and had tea. Tea was the essential meal in Peiping, and the most social moment. Cam's servants served it perfectly; there were no such things as unexpected guests to their way of thinking. Whenever the guest came he was expected, and the bowing white figures with the trays were ready for him.

At seven she was carefully put to bed by her nurse and had books and magazines with her supper tray. Her diet was just what Jane and Joanna would be eating at home, she would think, when the toast and cooked fruit and soups and cereals succeeded each other day after day. John had his dinner alone, or sometimes asked in a man or two to keep him company; now and then he would go away to some dinner party, but he was always back at half past nine or ten, to see that Cam had her bitter powders in hot milk and was settled off for the night. And sometimes, after that, she would be lulled to sleep by the faint tick of his typewriter, across the moon-washed courts, and the sense that he was near her if she wanted him.

CHAPTER XXVIII

One winter afternoon she was alone by her fire writing letters, when the wife of the new American naval attaché was announced. Cam looked up with a smile of pleasure as the handsome blonde woman came in. She did not know Laura Reid, and thought it rather charming of the older woman to come to see her without the formality of a direct invitation.

"Alice Vivian said that she would bring you," Cam said, extending a rather white hand, as the amah placed a chair for the caller and carried away the writing materials, "and Jack and I hoped to have a few interesting persons here to meet you. But this is *so* much nicer!"

"I've heard that you were one of the most beautiful women in the world," Laura Reid said, generously; "now I believe it. Ivory and black and gold. *And* the silver and plum color and lemon brocade!"

"Jack finds me these brocades, and has them made up by a pattern I happened to have with me—a French thing I got in Paris, it seems ten years ago," Cam said.

"From what they tell me of him, I think you're a lucky woman," the caller said with easy friendliness. "Everyone is saying that if you wanted to live in the Summer Palace he'd manage it."

"We went by plane last week and saw it from the air. It's only an hour's flight. But I don't believe I'd like to live there!"

"Then you do get out sometimes, Mrs Kilgarif?"

"Oh yes; little trips. I'm really better. But it's so slow," Cam complained. "The doctors come, and they tell me I'm making progress, and if I stay up for three hours I'm so weak I have to cry!" She invited the other's sympathy with her appealing smile. "Did you ever have the sort of sickness when you eternally wanted to cry?" she asked.

"Once, after my second boy was born, I had a bad time. It only lasted a few weeks really, but I felt very melancholy. But you," said Laura Reid, "you've nothing to be blue about! You've had an adventure such as mighty few women in the world survive, and you saved your husband's life, no question of that. Then you dash off a little book that's selling the world over, and promptly produce a child. We were talking of you at Mrs Chase's dinner last night; they said you had everything. Looks and youth and money, the most devoted husband in the world, fame, two daughters and a son—and what else is there?"

"Health is important," Cam said, and as she said it tears of weakness came into her smiling eyes.

"Ah, well, that's only a matter of time and patience."

"Have you children, Mrs Reid?"

"I have three scrawny, freckly, red-headed boys, all exactly like my father. He's seventy, and he's coming out to see them this year. Yes, the Reids," the visitor said, apologetically, "always travel in caravans; we've always taken them everywhere—Rio, Peru, Costa Rica, everywhere."

"Fun!" Cam said.

"But now tell me, Mrs Kilgarif, are you writing another book? I don't know when I've enjoyed anything like that book of yours."

"Oh no, indeed. That was my one effort. You see, Fitz—our dear Dr Fitzgerald, who was the Owner—was gathering material for a book, and Jack had contracted for ten articles, and they used to discuss them together. Well, then, after Fitz's death, when we finally got back to Calcutta again——"

Cam stopped short, her eyes far away.

"When we finally got back to Calcutta again," she presently repeated, rousing herself from deep abstraction, "Jack was frightfully ill—in fact, they thought fatally ill. Fitz's newspaper people cabled Mitzi—that was his wife—to know if she wouldn't do some articles, but she was unable to do anything. Her brother came out from Rotterdam and took her home to England—she's better now, but she had a complete breakdown. So that left me, with Jack desperately ill and my baby coming. The doctors wouldn't let me take Jack home, so we came here, and then, as he got better and while the memory of the whole thing was fresh, it occurred to me that women might like to read a woman's side of the story—what we ate, and what we went through, and how scared we were. I thought it might amuse Jack, too, and it did. I couldn't touch Mitzi's stuff, nor Jack's either, so I took my diary and filled in the rest from memory, and there it was!"

"And he's working on the real work now?"

"Yes. And if I'm ever well enough to move again," Cam said cheerfully, "he wants to go home by way of London and have a few weeks there helping Mrs Fitzgerald with Fitz's notes. But this wretched little silly fever comes up at about six o'clock every night——"

"What is it—now, I mean? Now that you're practically well."

"They don't know. Personally," Cam confessed, her eyes serious, "I call it 'Everest fever.' The mountains, and the winds and the snows, and the poor porters huddling together like sheep to keep warm, and the rockets and signals and binoculars all seem to be in my blood. I've escaped them—perhaps that was cheating Everest; she's a jealous old thing. Perhaps she is going to haunt me forever, wake me up in the night thinking I'm back there, cold and nauseated and wondering about my baby! Only the other day the houseboy brought some

Swiss cheese in at tea, and the look of it went over me like an —well, an avalanche, and I stupidly fainted quite away. We used fairly to live on it.

"Well, I'm safe now, and warm and fed," she went on, as the other woman merely smiled at her with sympathetic eyes. "And I'm just like something with its back broken. I'm saying in my heart all the time, 'Oh, don't move me. Don't make me make an effort. Just let me lie here and watch the fire and hear the servants chattering across the court, forever and ever and ever!"

"I can understand that. But the time 'll come," Laura Reid said hearteningly, "when you'll want to see your children and home again. And that reminds me why I came today," the caller went on, in the stout woman's breathless, friendly voice. "I wanted to tell you about your little girls. You see, I've just got here from San Francisco, and I spent two weeks before I sailed with my cousin—that's Dixie-Belle Sylvester, you know, in Oakland."

Color flooded Cam's pale face; she breathed a little hard.

"You saw my girls then!" she said, in an electrified voice.

"I should say I did. Dixie-Belle's going to have a baby next month, you know, so she's not going out. She's a terribly delicate little thing, anyway, and she's keeping very quiet. So she and I and my Aunt Hattie May just fooled around with the children all day long. You knew there was going to be a baby?"

"Oh yes! We knew she'd lost her baby last year and that there was to be another."

"I don't think she ought to have children," Mrs Reid said decidedly. "But that's neither here nor there. The fact is she *is* going to have another, and the Duchess of York couldn't have a finer outfit! I never saw such gorgeous things. But it's really your girls I wanted to tell you about. I imagine that to have word from an eyewitness means a lot to you."

"You—imagine right," Cam said, her own wonderful smile moving her pale lips and lifting her black lashes. "We have letters, of course. But I've not seen them for fifteen months."

"Well, they're completely adorable," Laura Reid began cheerfully. "The moment I got there I fell in love with them—I've never had anything but boys, you know, and when these two golden-haired little princesses came downstairs I simply couldn't stand it! Tell me frankly, since we're alone," she interrupted herself to ask, "do you mind my mentioning their father?"

"Oh no."

"Well, he came in with one on each side, holding their hands. It was Thanksgiving Day, and they'd been riding with him. My dear—this isn't flattery—I never saw anything so charming in my life. Their little slim bodies in riding togs, and their hair all tossed about, and the red cheeks—I never saw such color in children's faces! They liked my boys, and the boys—really, for Siwashes of twelve and fourteen, they behaved very well," the mother conceded. "We had the most beautiful time with the lot of them, and whether I most envy your Jane or Joanna, or both, I couldn't tell you! That little Joanna—she's going to school now, you know, and studying French——?"

She paused on the interrogation, and Cam said faintly:

"She wrote me a letter in French."

"Well," Laura Reid said, "she is the duckiest little thing I've ever seen. But the other—of course you know that you have a rare child there?"

"Jane?" Oh, little baby born in a San Francisco hospital to such a proud little mother, is it of you that this strange kindly woman is talking in far-away Peiping! "I've lost so much of them," Cam said in a thickened voice. "Jane's almost nine. Nine. And is she lovely?"

"Dixie-Belle's had to put glasses on those beautiful eyes, you know. But just corrective glasses."

"Ah?"

"Well, anyway, she didn't have them on when I first saw her. And the young lady flattered me by liking me, and used to come into my room every night to do her home work. I'd be dressing—Captain Reid had come on ahead of me, and there was nobody about but the boys. And Jane. She'd sit there holding forth—she really is an exceptionally brilliant child; we all thought so."

"Dixie-Belle's been so kind to them."

"Ah, well, stepmothers aren't what they were. And Bob, of course, adores the children. He's not the type of man one usually associates with children, but somehow it's worked out that way. My aunt's delicate, and Dixie-Belle isn't strong, and it's ended in a real family group—lovely, too. It 'll just break their hearts to give them up again."

"That may not be for some time," Cam said, half to herself. She lay looking at the fire, and the other woman, eyeing her uneasily, saw that the thin hands that were linked together were shaking. "Anything you can tell me—anything you remember——" Cam presently said quickly, with an effort. Laura Reid began to talk.

"I wonder," her thoughts ran in an undercurrent beneath the talk, "if this is the moment to show her their pictures?"

She took them from her bag—a slim packet. Cam looked at one of the crisp little prints, looked at another; leaned back in her chair with her eyes shut, perspiration glittering on the pallor of her face.

"Might I have these?" she asked in a whisper.

"Oh yes; I brought them for you! Please—please drink your tea!" Laura Reid said anxiously, leaning forward. Cam smiled, laid the pictures aside, lifted her cup.

"I'll look at them later. They're lovely. I'm so deeply obliged to you," she said faintly. Before there was time for anything more the visitor heard a call from some place beyond the courts. "That's Jack," Cam said quickly. "Don't—don't say anything to him about the children. He knows I—I miss them. At least, I hope he doesn't, but he suspects it sometimes, and it makes him unhappy! If you just won't——"

Her color had come back; the visitor said to herself that the woman was completely changed. Snuggling back against the soft furs and brocades of her couch, she looked up like a rosy smiling child as the man came in. Before he so much as glanced at Laura Reid he leaned over his wife and kissed her, his hand clinging to her white thin hand. Then he was introduced.

"It's terribly nice of you to come to see this wife of mine. We left cards at the Consulate, but—did she explain to you?—she isn't up to much gadding about these days."

"We've been talking America," the caller said.

"And found a lot of mutual friends? By the way, I met your husband at the club yesterday," John said, "but Cam here hasn't had the pleasure yet. Well, what part of America were you in?"

"All over the place. Mrs Kilgarif," Laura said, rising, "has been good enough to include Whitman and me in your tea on Sunday. So I'll bring him and present him then."

He walked with her to the outer door. Mrs Reid was still new to Peiping and was traveling excitedly in a ricksha. Her boy, decently shod, as became the runner for the attaché, had been dozing in the cold. He came running up, and she went ricketing off down the muddy lane, laughing for sheer pleasure in her new mode of travel and waving her hand over her shoulder.

John went back to Cam. She had not dared to snatch another look at the snapshots that were hidden under her loose brocade gown. She smiled as he came in, and he sat down next to her and caught her cool fingers in his own warm big ones.

"That seems a nice woman, Cam."

"She's a darling. I like her. Whose house did you say they were going to take, Jack?"

" 'Member the house Doctor Monroe had?"

"Oh yes. Oh, that's a charming place. I used to walk by it on the way to the hospital on those dreadful days last September. Jack," Cam said, fingering his big fingers, her thick lashes lowered, "isn't it going to seem funny someday, I mean, supposing that we both live——"

"How d'you mean, 'supposing we both live,' you gruesome little crapehanger?"

"Well," she said, maddening tears of weakness in her eyes again, "somehow one doesn't feel as certain of it as one did."

"You and I'll survive the Fitzgerald Expedition, no matter who else doesn't," he said thoughtfully. One of the small reasons among many thousand big reasons that she adored Jack, Cam thought, was that he never adopted the nurses' favorite rallying cheerfulness with her. When she was depressed and doubtful he was always gentle, and sometimes just dubious and serious enough himself to help her to a more reasonable point of view.

"That's what I was starting to say, Jack. Do you suppose we'll get back home, and gather all our four children together someday, and talk about having people in for Sunday lunch, and do things—that old way again? Sometimes I wonder, if they started a new expedition to Everest or Kinchinjunga, whether we'd start right off with them. It's a sort of nightmare—remembering the high cold sides of the mountains, and the mules stamping in the snow——"

"Don't think about them, old sweet."

"Jack, in a way I like to," Cam said. "I love to remember how wonderful you were, how you wouldn't let any of us get depressed or discouraged, how the Chief depended on you."

"We all took the same chance he did. It was just something that had to be, that the mountain should destroy him," John said thoughtfully. "And it was a great experience, Cam. It was a great experience! For a while there—while we were getting out, and when I thought it was all up with me in the hospital here—it seemed rather expensive. You and your baby, myself a total wreck—it summed up pretty high. But now that I'm on my feet again, and you're getting there, it's something to remember always."

"If I could only get well *faster,* Jack. It's so dull, trying to push against a—a wall of weakness, and always dropping back. Health is like one of the mountains. You're always thinking you can make it, and always beaten back. Every time it's Amah's day off and she goes out to her son's place, I think, 'It *can't* be another two weeks; it can't be that I've been lying here in just exactly the same condition that I've been in for months—ever since Edward was born!' "

"You get better, Cam, but you're not conscious of it."

"Perhaps I'm going to be the little invalid woman of Peiping for the next thirty years."

"It's not likely." He glanced at a book lying near her. "How goes Mary Stuart?"

"I loathe her. She was a weak fool. All the men she loved were rotters, and she didn't love Scotland at all, or do anything for it. She was like Phyllis Rountree at home, Jack. She liked surrendering to weak men. But it's a fascinating book."

"Mrs Thomas has a copy of your book and wants you to write in it."

"Oh? Is she the woman who brought all the pigeons out with her from Honolulu?"

"Yes. She says she likes squabs once a week."

"Funny people out here, Jack."

"Or else one has a better chance here to know how funny they are. Maybe they're just as funny at home."

"Are you going to be good?" asked Miss Fox from the doorway.

"Yes, she's tired," John answered. His strong arm was about Cam as he and the nurse guided her across the cold fresh early darkness of the court and into her big, dim low-ceiled room. Here there was a fire burning briskly in an air-tight iron stove, and the air was soft and warm. Cam's big low bed had been opened, the linen sheets and fat soft comforters turned down, the white pillows heaped invitingly high. Her reading lamp was lighted; her nightgown and bed jacket of pale peach satin were waiting.

John disappeared, and the nurse went deftly about the routine of getting Cam ready for the night. The beautiful corn-gold hair was brushed; Cam had her alcohol rub. She was really weary when it was all over, and she could sink back into the delicious restfulness of the pillows. John came back then, and presently the tray came in, and he sat with her while she ate or pretended to eat.

"See if you can't get her to take an interest in that egg, Mr Kilgarif," Miss Fox said. "It was the smallest one I could find, and she's looking at it as if it were an ostrich egg at least."

"I had toast and tea," Cam pleaded.

"Well, suppose you did? That was at half past four, and it's after six—indeed, it's almost seven now."

The little nurse slipped out, and John took the spoon.

"Come on, now. I've seen you do this with Joanna. A big taste for Mabel, and a big taste for Mummy——"

She laughed, swallowing the food gallantly.

"Jack, do you know how much I love you! You're so wonderful to me, and I'm such a drag. You'd be home again—you'd be lecturing, perhaps, and having dinners given you, and instead you're immured in a Chinese garden, with a miserable invalid hanging on you."

"I've told you you're not to talk that way. D'you want a good smack in the jaw?"

"It would probably help me."

"I wouldn't be here at all if it hadn't been for you, Cam. It's all hazy to me, the trip down, and Calcutta, and the steamer. Nobody else could have gotten me through at all. They all know that! 'Member that place in Phari, and Truesdell telling you that it would be certain death to move me in a cart, and you pushing straight ahead? Why, I myself wanted to stay right there and die. Calcutta seemed as far away as the moon. But you wouldn't have it. 'Member the hot morning you wrapped me in a sheet, sweating right through it, and got me up on that load of skins?"

"Not skins. It was the tents."

"Well, whatever it was! That was the turning point in *my* life. And after that, on the ship, and Shanghai, so hot that even the natives dropped dead of it in the streets, and you close to your confinement, and still dragging me about like a log. 'We're going to Peiping, Jack, there's a certain doctor there——' "

She was listening, looking down at the big fingers that he was moving back and forth across her hand.

"And now you grudge yourself a few weeks' rest," he went on. "Why, just take it as a slice out of life, Cam. Just take it as a price for all the fun. London, and picking out coats in the Haymarket, and Paris and Cairo and Calcutta and all the rest of it! It's going to make us fascinating dinner company for the rest of our lives!"

"It's going to make us shocking bores, Jack. There's your dinner gong. Take all this away. Leave me the persimmon; I'll eat him later on. And the napkin, yes, and the knife. Thanks, darling. Is it just you and Foxy tonight?"

"Just the two of us. She'll tell me again about her sister's little boy in Akron. He'll repeat anything you say, and they had him in swimming when he was only two. Good-by for a few minutes, my darling. Do you——" His hard shaven cheek was against her own. "Do you by any chance love me?" he asked. She caught at his face and drew it hungrily against her lips.

"Did ever any woman love her husband as I love you!"

CHAPTER XXIX

THEN SHE WAS ALONE, and she could cross the floor swiftly to the big wardrobe, and with fingers that trembled find the little sheaf of stiff prints. She got back into bed, went through them slowly, turned back this one and that, reviewed them all again. And yet again, from the first to the last, finding new details with eyes that could not sufficiently devour them. Joanna's rounded bare legs and arms in the sun suit—ah, that was November on the Piedmont hills! Jane, beautiful and bold and straight in riding clothes. The two giving the puppy a bath. Cam could see the flushed little faces, hear the panting breath. Such a big wet slippery puppy, and such small determined girls, towels pinned around their little middles, their curls bunched on top of their heads.

Over and over and over. Cam trembled very much as she looked at them, but she did not let herself cry. To break down would be to betray herself to Jack, and that would never do.

She had many pictures of the girls, and the last mails from Baltimore had brought her four small snapshots of her son, held in the beaming amah's arms. A weazened little grinning fellow he was, with a high forehead completely bald and a toothless smile. He was collapsed in shawls; the one thin little claw of a hand that showed was still mottled, baby fashion, although his namesake uncle's writing on the backs of the pictures recorded him as "Edward Campbell Kilgarif, six weeks and two days old."

Cam could get no impression of him at all. Jane and Joanna had been bouncing, sturdy creatures from the first. Was this tiny scrap of babyhood in Baltimore really going to live, she would ponder, was he someday going to be walking about in a garden, trying for words, growing into normal childhood? He never seemed her own, somehow. She had been capable and active up to the day of his birth, taking walks, keeping busy and cheerful, rejoicing in John's complete convalescence.

But from the time that pain and confusion and stupor had descended upon her in the hospital, everything had been vague. She had seen the crumpled little monkey of a baby only a few times. They had told her that he had been born jaundiced; it was safer not to move or to tire him. And presently into her bewildered and exhausted senses, and over the weakness of her body and the dull constant aching of her head, she had been dully aware that Jack had been talking of sending him home. He had no chance at all here; he might have a chance in the care of the distinguished baby doctor who was his uncle in Baltimore. That was really all she knew of him, except for the disappointing scraps that got into letters. Everyone at home took it for granted that one knew everything; everyone was content with allusions to what supposedly had been explained in earlier letters, and that never had been mentioned at all. Jane would laboriously pen two pages about the little Ralston girl's birthday party, and end by saying "Joanna is back from the hosapittle now, and Daddy is not going to take us," and let Cam imagine the rest. Dixie-Belle wrote brief kind notes "just to let you know that our mutual girls are nicer than ever, and that I am sorry that I worried you in my last. It was merely one more scare." John's mother wrote long screeds lightly, in pale blue ink, careful page after page, perhaps dealing solely with the reasons for giving Tids the Gilbert Stuart portrait of Grandfather Moulton, an account of ants in the linen closet, and some sapient observations upon the political situation.

Tonight, when John brought his coffee in, as he always did, Cam showed him the pictures.

"That nice Mrs Reid is a cousin or something of Dixie-Belle, and she stayed there. Aren't they good?"

"They're lovely. Gosh, that is a darling of Jane."

"They've put glasses on Jane."

"Had to, I suppose. There's a cute one of Joanna. Growing up, aren't they? God help that poor dog they're washing!"

They often talked home news at this time of the day. He evidently, she thought in relief, had found it natural enough in her to keep the pictures until now. He took it quite simply, presently groped in his pocket for a letter, gave her his news in return.

"I'd a long effusion from Mother this morning, all agog. She's cooling a little on Toomey, says she wishes she could send her back to Alsace. And Tids is evidently going to marry her veterinary."

"Criticizing Toomey!" It electrified Cam; she sat up straight against her pillows. "What has happened?"

"She doesn't say. It's exactly like Mother."

"I thought you said she was all agog?"

"She is, but not about Toomey."

"Tids? She doesn't like Doctor Yelland? But he's not a regular veterinary, Jack! He's really a sort of cattle expert; that's different. And Buenos Aires—that's different, too. That's not like settling down to practise in Milpitas."

"No; I suppose it isn't, really."

"And your mother's upset about it?"

"Not about that, either. She dismisses Toomey with ten words. You can read it. Toomey, she says, she's afraid is being a bad influence for Taffy. She wants to send Taffy to nursery school. Her only reference to Tids is that she 'supposes' my sister will be married and gone long before we get back, and she trusts his children won't be black."

"But he's an Englishman, Jack! Isn't that ridiculous! And poor little Taffy in school! He'd hate it, but I suppose it has to come. And that devil-woman Toomey going someday! What a relief! She doesn't say why?"

John gave her the letter; she skimmed the closely written pale blue ink lines quickly, looked up in patient amazement.

"Jack, the entire letter isn't about some people who picnicked on the old gravestone, is it?"

"Apparently. She gives about six pages to it. She went out, it seems, and expostulated with them. She said that that was some family's old graveyard and that the stone was sacred. Later she and Mildred went out and found eggshells and oiled paper all over everything. Read on there; see what they did. They'll have my mother in jail if she doesn't look out."

Cam read, her face changing.

"They didn't gather up all the garbage and papers and mail them to the picnickers, did they?" she asked faintly, scandalized.

"Apparently they did. Isn't that exactly like Mother!"

"Pages of it," Cam mused, reading. " 'I then had Tids telephone Mullins, who is the deputy sheriff, and from whom I bought two dollar tickets last year . . . this impudent woman in the red cap then shouted at Mildred . . . this outrage to the helpless dead who cannot rise up and protest——' Oh, it's unbelievable!" Cam said laughing. "And three lines for Tids and her marriage, and two for Taffy. Poor little Taffy, being sent to a nursery school from seven to seven every day!"

"Let's hope he won't mind it."

She mused about it for a while. When she spoke, it was on another topic:

"You aren't going anywhere tonight, Jack?"

"I'm going to work."

"But I meant after that."

"Then I'm going to bed."

"Poor Adele!" Cam said.

"Ah, yes, poor Adele," John said somewhat grimly, over his pipe. "My heart bleeds for her!"

"Did she send you a chit asking you to dinner before the party tonight?"

"I see you read my mail."

"No, darling; but she told Fran Vance that she was going to ask you, and of course Fran couldn't wait until she bounded over here yesterday and told me."

"What a complete fool that woman is," John murmured thoughtfully.

"You're not trying to put me off the track, dear?"

He grinned unalarmedly.

"What are you trying to do, Cam? Build this up into something?"

"No. One only feels that it's the wife who is last to hear about it."

"Ah, I see, I see," John said nodding.

"Seriously, John, what gets into a nice little married woman like that, with a perfectly good army captain for a husband, and two nice children? She's making an absolute fool of herself."

"I suppose because she really isn't a perfectly nice little woman. She's just an extremely pretty case of arrested development that Mallon happened to meet ten years ago and think was perfectly wonderful. She has no brains, she has no charm, she's exactly today what she was when he married her. A cheap little romantic small-town girl who feels that flirtations are just too delightful, and out in China you can have all sorts of fun because nobody cares!"

"Well, according to Fran it's much deeper than that, and it's making Adele actually sick. She's lost weight. She hangs around places she thinks you're apt to be. Her mother knows about it, and her sister knows about it, and they're all frantic."

"Too bad!" John commented briefly.

"She came here, you know, to call on me, and I'm convinced it was for nothing else than to talk about you."

"You told me."

"I gave you a wonderful character."

"I believe you'd like to work yourself up to think that you're a little jealous of me," John said. "Unfortunately for you, however, it's never going to be that way. I may live to be ninety years old, but I'll never have enough of you. You're my world. I'll disappoint you in lots of ways, I'll drag you up mountains that just about kill you, I'll be jealous of people you like, and I'll beg off going to parties you really want to go to. But there 'll never be another woman, my dear. Not for a day—not for an hour. As persons, persons to talk to, and see at races and on steamers, they're all right. But as ever taking one instant of my love from you, touching you and me in that way—they don't exist. I suppose this poor little Mallon fool is bored with her husband, and picked me out as fresh new blood. I don't know, and I never will know, what she's got in her head, for I can't stand the woman and I avoid her. She writes me chits; I don't read 'em. She meets me—she met me coming out from that wedding last Sunday—and asks what she's done to offend me. Offend me! I don't know she's alive."

"Jack, that's such a nice thing to hear, after years of marriage," Cam said, her eyes glistening.

He looked at her unsmilingly, even with a little frown, as he packed his pipe again.

"Well, but it's so much less than the truth, Cam," he said. "That's not flattery; I'm not proud of myself. It's such a privilege to be with you, I'm so sick for the sight of you and the sound of your voice when you're out of my sight for five minutes, that life just goes—well, flat. I'm not looking round for the affections of other women; I'm wondering how the deuce I ever got you, and how the deuce I can keep you loving me. A lot of these women out here have the feeling that high school, dances, engagement, marriage, children, are all just preliminaries to the grand affair. All right, let 'em go on thinking so. But it's a game that makes me feel kind of sick. I don't get it. I'd rather come in here and talk, and then to go work, and turn in around midnight, than go to any of their parties. There! Declaration of—well, what? Dependence, I guess," John finished, getting to his feet. "I'm going to work. Be a good girl and go right to sleep. Is Foxy going to give you a powder tonight?"

"Not unless I need it. I'll lie here awhile. She'll look in when she comes back, and I can ask her then."

John went away, and Cam lay thinking. After a while Miss Fox did look in and found her trying to read.

"I think I ought to have a powder, Foxy. I hate to be such a baby. But I'm lying here thinking of my children, and of how far home seems, and it gets me all worked up inside."

"I'm going to wash your face, air this room, start a new fire and give you another alcohol rub, and if you aren't sleepy by that time you shall have your powder," Foxy said. "The doctor said that sleep was the great thing, and until you reach the point where you don't need them, there's nothing like a sedative. Now wait until I get off my coat . . ."

Foxy was a sensible, unalarming young woman, and Cam liked her. She acted—she had acted from the very beginning—as if Cam were quite certainly going to get well, which was somehow comforting. When Cam cried aimlessly, she encouraged her to cry. "The doctor I trained under," Foxy said once, "used to call crying 'white bleeding.' He said it did women good.

"You're getting better in spite of yourself," she used to say. "You don't see it, and you get discouraged, but that doesn't stop your getting better." And once she said: "You think I'm making too much effort lacing these high boots?

My dear, you'll be lacing your own this time next month," which made Cam cry weakly, even though she liked the idea.

Foxy and John brought in bales and bales of beautiful garments a few days later, from which Cam was to select Christmas presents for everyone at home. Or rather they guided into her room the old Chinese and the two young boys who had this merchandise for sale. For an hour the Chinese flung one exquisite robe, scarf, tapestry, fur-lined rug on top of another. Cam was dizzied with the beauty and the delight of it.

Prune color, gold, pale blue and deep blue, apricot and pearl brocades were heaped on all the tables and chairs. Cam chose small stiff wrappers royal in embroideries of bullion and tiny round mirrors and pearls. Her thin hands lingered over the rich stuffs that turned the room to a Sultan's storehouse.

" 'Oh, quivering lights, Arabian nights, Bagdad!' " she quoted to John. "Don't they say camels and jalousies and trains of elephants with fringes on their eyes!"

"We'll never really grudge this adventure, Cam. It's been such an eye-opener. We'll never do anything quite like it again, and you can't have everything, you know. If you're away from home you're homesick, and if you stay at home you're wishing you were traveling."

"John," she said, listening intently, her hands still buried in the rich silks, "I believe you're saying something that is quite true. I think one forgets that. You can't have everything."

He bought her a present. No day went by without its present. This one she knew she would love and keep near her all her life long. She had considered buying it herself to send to the kindly sister-in-law in Baltimore who was raising her delicate boy with her own sturdy nursery. But in the end she had decided to get a darker rug for Lucy—a brown fur rug lined with paler brown.

The rug John bought her was all white—white soft fur on one side, pure white brocade for lining. It was so flexible that it could be packed into the space in a hatbox; it was so warm that even fingering it gave Cam a sense of comfort in the hard China winter. Winds were moving in a steady wall in the unpaved lanes between the compounds now, and the bare, sore-crusted feet of the ricksha boys looked blue. But in the warm softness of furs and silks piled deep on her k'ang she was as snug as a hummingbird in a down-lined nest, and could lie dreaming through the gray, sunless days thinking of her sealed and corded packages making their way steadily across the seas, up to California, and to two little girls dancing in pajamas beside a Christmas fire.

CHAPTER XXX

ONE DAY IN LATE NOVEMBER John came home from the races in a state of excitement. There were some rather distinguished persons in the long, quaint, low-ceiled room that had been made into a parlor. Cam had company, and was looking particularly lovely as she dispensed tea from a low table by the fire. All the furniture in the room was of black teakwood, the floor was oiled and dark, the lamps lighted up spots of vermilion-red lacquer and the rich colors of old tapestries, and the whole made a dramatically beautiful setting for Cam's fairness and whiteness.

The unfortunate Adele Mallon was there, a thin, dark, pretty woman always trembling and paling and flushing from some devouring inner flame; the English minister and Lady Cluett were there; Dr Frederick Inges, the American scientist, had come with one of his tall, pretty, awkward young daughters. Cam knew, the instant John came in, that something was stirring him, and that it was not Adele's presence, but she had to wait until the guests left to discover what it was.

Meanwhile she went on talking to the Cluetts and the scientist, and amused herself by asking John if he would not show Adele the new chest in his study. Adele knew a lot about Chinese furniture; Cam wanted to be sure that she and John would not be cheated if he bought it.

"I could have slapped your little fool face for you!" said John later, referring to this incident. Like a sheep led to the slaughter he had dutifully gone away with Adele, and Adele had turned to him in the privacy of the study with the eternal: "What have I done, Killy? I need friendship—I need it terribly just now. I'm so horribly—lonely. Won't you tell me why it's all been so different since that wonderful first night at Marjorie's? The night we danced together, and you told me you hadn't had so much fun since before your illness? Please, I'll be so good. Whatever you say I'll—I'll accept. I'm really a terribly decent little thing. It's only that I like you so—so horribly, and I want so to steal just a little happiness if I can."

"It's the game they all play here; they like it," John said later to Cam, telling her about it. "But I think you were three kinds of a skunk to send me off with her. I could have killed you, and she knew it, too. Well, let's get out of here, honey. We've had enough of this. This is November. What 'd you say if we got away in—well, say six weeks if the doctors 'll let you?"

Her heart leaped, and the color rushed into her face. Oh, this was hope at last! This was the opening door after the dead dull weeks! Home—when would it be? Home in late February! Cam knew in that first wild moment of ecstasy that she had been afraid that she never would go home again.

"Here's the plot," John said, bringing his coffee and his pipe to a chair nearer her bed. It was evening now; he had had his dinner, and Foxy had settled her down for the night. "Now don't go ga-ga about this," he interrupted himself to warn her, "for everything depends on the doctors. But here's the plot. Remember Furlong? The man we met in Havana, and had dinner with?"

"On the Wickiup? Of course I do. A darling, too."

"He had more than half a crush on you, but let that pass,"

John said. "Well, he's here in Peiping, and he's coming to dinner tomorrow. Then he goes off to Harbin and Vladivostok, I don't know where. He's looking for old masks or something. Meanwhile they're overhauling the Wickiup, down in Shanghai. Now listen, he and I ran into each other at the club today, and we had a long talk. And in February—early in February, say eight or nine weeks from now, he's going to take the yacht to Europe through the Suez. He and an old doctor who's written two books about fungus and lichen and that sort of thing, and you and I! Cam, do you get it? That gorgeous boat! You never know she's moving, she's so beautifully built, no one on board but two men—and both of them decent quiet fellows who only ask to be let alone to read—a pack of perfect Chinese servants, the crew, and you and me!"

"You mean," she said, over a sinking heart and with a bright eager smile, "you mean that he's asked us to go along?"

"He's simply crazy to have us! Ask us? He fairly begged me, and when I hung back a little he began to tell me all the advantages. You loafing in a deck chair all day long. No tourists, no big dining room to go down to, a doctor on board, and three games of cribbage every evening. You could have an amah, or you could take Foxy. Think of it, Cam, Singapore and Bombay and Suez—just dawdling along, sails up most of the time, divine winter weather. Then at Venice we leave him, have a week at the Danieli, and loaf along up to Paris. London in—say April, and I have my powwows with Mitzi, get poor Fitz's stuff into shape, and take you to some shows at night. We'd just about strike the right season there, and we might see the sunshine once in a while. I've never seen it in London. Lord," Jack said, shaking his head as he looked at his pipe before putting it back into his mouth, "it does seem a break! I was wondering how I was going to bust you out of here, get started, and now here it is all fixed, and we wind up our big adventure with one more. It'll be something we never forget, Cam, just the four of us, talking nights, going into queer ports and having a look at them, and it 'll put something between the mountain and going back to everyday life. I'd just as soon make a longer break in there. What do you think?"

"I remember her as a beautiful boat, about the size of a small ocean liner," Cam heard her own voice saying. Her heart was lead.

"She's five thousand tonnage, he said today. Three baths and a sun deck and a library—remember the little library stuffed with books? Remember he had a mother dog and a bunch of pups in one room? Well, that.'d be our outfit, bath, lanai, everything. I've not been on many yachts, but I've never seen anything finer than his."

"Imagine!" she breathed. The tone sounded convincing to her.

"We're lucky, Cam; really we are. We got into a horrible jam last year, and here we are out of it and started off again. Well, this is just a plan, darling, and if for any reason it doesn't suit you, or if you're not strong enough in February, why, it's out! But Furlong will be here to dinner tomorrow, and Luce and Norwood want us on Friday, and then he's off to get his masks."

"Masks!" she echoed indulgently, fighting for time, glad to get off on a side issue. "What on *earth* does he want with masks?"

"He's completing a collection, it seems. Told me he'd been at it seven or eight years. He's got 'em from Bali and Pago-Pago and Jamaica and the Lord knows where else! Furlong, you know," John said, "has got so much money he doesn't know what to do with it."

"That spectacled, dark, quiet man? I thought he was a weary soul who had put all his money into the boat and simply lived at sea. If he's rich he's singularly unspoiled," Cam commented. In her soul the once-fascinating names of strange ports rang like funeral chimes. Singapore—Hong Kong—

Bombay—Port Said. Further and further away from the prunes and peppers and silences of a California hill ranch, further and further away from eager little voices calling "Mummy!"

"At Trieste I'll be getting nearer them again," she thought. "I must keep that in mind. After a long while, and lots of lunches on deck and games of cribbage, we'll be at Trieste, and then it's only overnight to Paris. A month in London, yes; but maybe Jack will cut it down to three weeks—maybe Mitzi 'll be ill, or something, and we can take the manuscripts home with us. It 'll pass, and New York will pass, and we'll be on the Overland, passing Omaha and Ogden and Reno——"

Reno made her remember the Lake and the round little sun-browned bodies splashing in shallow water, and she drew a quick breath.

"It sounds like escape to you, doesn't it, you poor kid!" John said. "I don't blame you for getting excited, you've been in prison long enough. But don't set your heart on it too much, Cam, because Paul von Mannheim may simply squash the whole idea. I don't believe he will, though. He was saying the other day that in a month or two you ought to take a sea trip—longer maybe than just home, down around Guam and Manila. This might be the exact thing."

"Two months here, every minute a year," she thought as she promised to be as patient as she could under the doctor's verdict, whatever it might be. "Two more months here, marking time. Then another month idling through oriental ports. They may decide to go to Siam and take a look at the Angkor Wat, or to Jamaica to eat sago and cane syrup. Talbot Furlong, it seems to me, is the man who talked about the Dutch 'reis-taffles' in Jamaica. Oh, my God, I don't see how I can face it!"

Aloud she asked the question the traveler loves to hear:

"What must we take, Jack? I mean clothes. Will it be hot already in the Suez? London will still be chilly, I know that.

You," said Cam, lifting the silky warmth of the new rug to touch it to her cheek, "you'll go to London, I promise you!"

He was happy; she had not seen Jack so happy since they had left Darjeeling for the mountain adventure. Again he could plan and make lists and talk to all and sundry about the proposed trip. Talbot Furlong duly came to dinner, and Cam liked him even better than she had before; a reserved, intelligent man whose wealth had been largely spent in foundation and research work; he made few friends, overvalued them gratefully, and had no other real home than his adored Wickiup.

Women, coming in to drink tea or cocktails and talk plans, were openly envious of Cam's new luck. Jack, working conscientiously in the mornings, and during many of the evening hours as well, was back at his beloved employment of getting ready to go away. The consideration of what Cam and he would need, of places that they would reach or leave at given dates, absorbed him.

Foxy could not go; she was going to be married. But there was to be a superb old amah on board who could do everything that would be necessary for Cam if her convalescence progressed as well as it seemed to have begun. John brought her more presents: a camera, a tall bottle of extravagant toilet water, a delightful English tea basket with white china cups and a butter box packed neatly in among fringed tea napkins and alcohol stove. Lovely Gwen Archibald, from the British Consulate, brought her a box of edibles.

"There's plenty of time; you'll not be starting for months," said Gwen; "but Don and I go on leave, and I wanted you to have the right things for any emergency—if you should feel rotten, you know, or want something simple. Chicken soup and biscuits and tinned plums. You've no idea how delicious tinned plums are when it's hot, or you feel a little sick of ship's food. I know it, because Don's uncle has a yacht; we took it down to the Mediterranean one year when I was frightfully ill, before Roger. I lived on hot clam broth and whole-bran biscuits and plums. Men on a ship do manage to eat so much thick, hot food—turbot and curries and pot roast. You'll get so sick of the sight of soda buns that you'll not want any food at all."

CHAPTER XXXI

THEY WERE ALL SO KIND! Cam smiled, and listened, and hated it all. Rose Filmore came and told her all about Count Rosencrans's divorce, and the Russian woman he had met in Shan Hai Quen and was going to marry. She said Cam had had an awful time, but she hoped Cam would always remember Peiping affectionately.

Mrs Van Wirt came and told her all about their cats, how valuable they were, and how hard they were to raise. She said that Cam must not forget Peiping. After all, she and Mr Kilgarif had both gotten well there after their terrible experience.

Lady St Maurice came and brought her daughter, Mrs Ross, and Mrs Ross had a good deal to say about Douglas's family in Scotland. They both said that Mrs Kilgarif had written such a charming book. Lady St Maurice's mother, fancy eighty-two years old, had thought it quite sweet.

Adele Mallon came and, finding Cam alone, said that there was something she must say. She said that she could not be sorry for anything that had happened, because John Kilgarif was in every way the finest and most wonderful man she ever had known, even including her father, who had been a king. She said she supposed Cam would think it very odd in her to come say this, but she felt it was squarer.

"I don't think it's hurt him," said Adele, very lovely and brave and strong, in her handsome new winter suit from Chez Marthe in Shanghai, "and I know it hasn't hurt me. I couldn't have you go without saying—just that much. I've always felt I did Fletcher Mallon a cruel injustice when I married him—I was only twenty, and I liked him. But that isn't enough. It's never enough. He thought the rest would come; it never came. I've made his home comfortable, I adore my children."

"And you adore the sound of your own voice," Cam thought, bored, impatient, amused all at once.

"What John's—you don't mind my calling him 'John,' when you're still 'Mrs Kilgarif,' do you?—what John's meant to me no one ever will know," Adele pursued, speaking in a steady, low voice, staring into the fire. "But I have to say this —and this is really what I came to say. I've not slept; for nights and nights I've lain awake, thinking that I must say this to you. John Kilgarif loves you, Mrs Kilgarif, with every fiber of that great heart of his. What he gave me was only friendship—the deepest, the most beautiful friendship I ever shall know, but that was all! That much I want to make clear to you. I can't excuse myself; I don't. But he never has betrayed by so much as a glance that he was anything but my good friend.

"He stopped our friendship short," she went on, as Cam merely continued to look sympathetically at her and did not speak. "Well, I think he was right. I think he was wise enough to see—sane enough to see—what I was too blinded to see. He said, 'Thumbs down!' And that was the end——"

"Oh, go take a running jump at yourself, Adele!" Cam said in her soul, as the lovely morbid voice went on and on. "John was right," she thought. "A lot of them do that sort of thing out here—the life makes for it. What a good time she's having!"

"So it only remains for me," Adele was saying, "to say 'Forgive me.' I didn't mean to hurt you—I never did hurt you—it was only myself that I hurt. Someday, I know, the pain will go away, and only pride remain, and when that day comes—oh, I know how far ahead it seems now, but it will come someday, and then I'll be glad of it, and stronger for it! You've everything in the world, Mrs Kilgarif, do you realize that? You've beauty and youth and wealth and children and fame, and your pride in him, and his love for you! I've only stolen a little of your sunshine for a few minutes. You can spare me that and forgive me?"

She was really in tears now as she got to her feet and turned, clasping her white gloved hands, toward Cam. It was just at this moment that John came in. And Cam knew that of all possible circumstances this was the one that Adele would have chosen to have happen, if she could have chosen.

Her instant rallying of her forces, the smile with which she greeted him, the light, cheerful tone she assumed, were all infinitely gratifying to that hunger within her, that devouring need for romance and drama and sacrifice and glory. Adele Mallon was only thirty; her life from now on would hold nothing, Cam realized, except these imaginary love affairs; she would go up and down the world at the side of her army-captain husband seeking them, embroidering them, dreaming about them.

After a while she would get a divorce from Fletcher Mallon for no particular reason, for the lover of the moment would have no intention of marrying her. Then she would drift about, identified as the woman who had so tremendously loved the Comte-of-this or Lord-Somebody-that, and that would be the end of her; caught by the swift-flying Forties and treacherous Fifties, she would go on into withered nothingness, betrayed by the eternal appetite she could neither control nor satisfy.

Watching her, standing there smart and straight, a sensitive, eager, beautifully gowned woman, looking right into

John's eyes, Cam felt a sudden flush of shame in her own cheeks. She herself had sacrificed everything for love; she had reached out for it and seized it when it came along. A certain pity for and understanding of poor Adele touched her, and she felt for the first time a kinship for the other woman. Children, parents, position, pride meant nothing to Adele; she and her love affairs were the laughingstock of the diplomatic circle in three cities. Cam had thrown them all aside, too; not quite as brazenly, but with the same hungry searching for love, the same consuming need to be beloved.

"No; don't walk out with me to the ricksha, John," Adele was saying. "I must go now—I'm late. We leave tomorrow, you know, and tonight we're going to the Rutherfords'. So—I may not see you again. Good-by. Good-by, Mrs Kilgarif."

"I'll go out with you, of course," John said sensibly. It prolonged the agony for the woman, Cam knew, but it was enchanting agony, and her look at John as he left the room beside her was the most eloquent that ever comes into a woman's eyes.

He was back in five minutes.

"She asked me for a book and I had to write in it," he explained. "Whew-w-w! I'm glad they're going. It's getting a little bit thick."

"She's enjoying it, you know, John."

"Are *you* telling me that?"

"She told me that you loved me."

"Oh, did she? Were you surprised?"

"Knocked off my feet. Despite your neglect of me, your ugly language, desertion, cruelty, nonsupport, she assures me that you love me, and that you and she have never taken anything away from me."

"If she had the nerve to get off anything like that——" John was beginning. Cam interrupted him with a laugh.

"My dear, it was your strength that saved you both from extremes. It was you who said, 'Thumbs down!' "

"She didn't say that!"

"She did."

"Poor little thing; she doesn't know what she wants. I don't know why a nice fellow like Mallon and the boy and girl don't satisfy her."

"She does know what she wants only too well. She wants life to be a continual flirtation. Jack," Cam said, in a different tone, now in the embrace of his big arm as he sat down beside her on the davenport and leaned back against her cushions, "how was I different from that a few years ago when you used to come up to the Lake and we talked about my divorce?"

He sat up to look at her in surprise.

"What are you talking about, Beautiful?"

"I mean, wasn't I hunting the same thing? Someone to love me, to make me feel important?"

"You're not putting yourself into the same class as this poor little bird-brain?"

"Shouldn't I?"

"Why, you poor girl, you've been in the Orient about long enough. You're losing your sense of values! It's a good thing they're getting the Wickiup in order. China's full of these half-baked little women who don't know how lucky they are to get one good husband, but who go wavering about looking for more love! And you—remain you, the superlatively wonderful woman of all time. Let's attempt to keep sane."

"Let's attempt to keep sane," she agreed. And then, with a little effort, "John, it seems to take a great deal to keep a woman sane. Would you think me perfectly cracked if I said that I don't feel up to the Furlong trip?"

He looked at her, stupefied.

"How d'you mean, darling?"

"I want," Cam said deliberately, "to stay right here until I feel stronger. Much stronger. And then I just want to go quietly down to Shanghai—I'll brace myself up for the boat trip, it's easier than the train, and it's only three days and two nights. And I'll get a steamer there for home."

"For California!" he said dazedly.

"Yes. And if you terribly want to make the Suez trip, Jack, won't you make it without me? You and Talbot, and perhaps one other man to make up the cribbage foursome? You wouldn't mind the trip up to Paris and the crossing to London; the mere thought of them makes my bones ache! And you'd have your weeks with Mitzi, and get that all cleared up, and then come back on one of the fast oceanic liners, and stay as short a time as you can in New York, and come home!"

"And where would you be all this time?"

"I'd stay here until I felt up to it, and then go home, and go down to Cherry Ridge and get——" Her throat thickened. "I'd manage it," she said.

"Get a cook and get the house running? Why, you poor pussy, you won't have strength enough for that for months! Cam, can you possibly think I'd let you go off alone, or even with Foxy, and face all that? Suppose you were taken sick on the steamer? Suppose you got there and found the house cold and deserted, and couldn't get hold of Hing or anyone, what then? Mother's given up her house; she's boarding somewhere until Tids gets married. There isn't a chance in the world of your managing it, darling, without killing yourself."

She rested against him, her head on his shoulder, silenced.

"Cam, don't worry about the Wickiup trip; it won't be until February, and by that time you'll feel like a new woman. I think just getting started on a trip will pick you up amazingly. Just forget it for a while and try to get well."

"I've forgotten so much, and I've been trying so long to get well!" she said with a long sigh. And for a while they were both silent, his arm about her, her fingers in his.

But that night she reopened the subject. She looked rather tired and white when he went into her room, carrying his after-dinner coffee cup, and signaled him to a chair that had been placed close to her bed. He sat down, facing her expectantly.

"Jack," she began at once, in a quick nervous voice, "I've been thinking, ever since, of what we said this afternoon. I mean, about your going on with Talbot and my going home the other way, the shorter way. I—I really meant it. That's what I want to do. I hate to say it—I hate to say it," Cam broke off to interpolate resolutely, "but you don't know how long I've been thinking about it, or what it means to me!"

He stirred his cup, looked at her thoughtfully.

"Don't want this trip the doctors think will build you up, sweetheart?"

Her eyes watered. It was so hard to go against him, lean and brown and persuasive, sitting there with his broad shoulders stooped a little and his head dropped on one side as he watched her!

"I—think—*no.*"

"Don't want to wait and see how you feel in a couple of months' time?"

She did not immediately answer. She lay for a few minutes with her lashes lowered, her small thumb moving against the big hand that held her own.

"You see, Jack," she presently began, a little thickly, "women are queer. They want—so much. I think God made women wanting everything. But most of all they have to be loved.

"Maybe, in the old days, if a woman's husband didn't love her, she just got along without it—she had children and garden and chickens, and fruit to put up. Or else they were so poor she had to think only of food and clothing. I don't know."

He was listening attentively, with the half-smile she sometimes loved on his face, that little smile that said: "This is my adorable little wife talking, and I'm all ears!" But just now, desperate to make herself clear, she wished he would not use it.

"But now it's different," Cam was continuing. "A girl marries for a set of emotions that don't last at all. She goes on, she likes it all—the new house, and being 'Mrs' Somebody, and years go by, and there are children.

"And then, gradually, creeping up on her, the hunger begins. The hunger for companionship, the need to be loved—oh, madly and completely and possessively—by some man! And perhaps, at somebody's Golden Wedding, she meets him. She thinks: 'Just to watch you, just to hear you speak, just to call you my friend would be enough to satisfy me for all the days of my life!' "

"Well," Jack said, as she paused. Tears stood in his smiling eyes.

"Well—if he likes her, Jack, if he reaches out for *her* friendship as she did for his, if he says things to her that dizzy her and make her walk on clouds—then everything that she's built into her life before just falls down like a house of cards, and nothing else is important except that they two love each other."

"And *is* anything else important, pussy?"

"Oh, lots of things, John. Lots of things, though she may not see it then! No," Cam corrected herself, "not lots of things. Only one. Her children.

"She can be—let's suppose for the sake of argument, Jack, that I *was*—everything a woman wants to be. Pretty, and with beautiful clothes, you famous and rich and adoring me, traveling, buying furs and pearls and things. Everything for happiness—and under it all, not happy. Under it all knowing that life isn't like that; knowing that I ought to be worrying about Joanna's cold or Taffy's lessons. That isn't living. 'That pretty Mrs Kilgarif——' "

"That beautiful Mrs Kilgarif," Jack corrected it, in a silence.

She smiled absent-mindedly, took it up again.

"A woman is sort of ashamed when she gets everything she ever wanted," she said, groping for the right words. "A woman likes, I think, to have to sacrifice herself a little, to do without something. Love is life to her, but I suppose one can get too much oxygen—one can stifle on it. No, I don't mean that!" Cam interrupted herself quickly, seeing the expression on his face. "I don't mean that, dear, and you know I don't! There isn't one hour in all the hours we've had together that hasn't been too short for me! The little suppers, the mornings in Paris when we've been off for the races, the nights in Venice with Leo singing—women all over the world dream of drifting into scenes like that, with the perfect lover. I've had it, and a thousand times a thousand hours of it.

"But what's keeping me here sick, Jack," she recommenced, as he merely sat holding her hand, looking at her without speaking, "is that I need—I need my children! They're nearer to me—they're more necessary to me than I ever dreamed! It isn't only heart and soul—though God knows they both ache for them day and night—but it's physical, too. I'm like something amputated—amputated away from them. I want to be useful to them, needed by them, I want to have something to say about them, as they grow up! My little boy, 'way off in Baltimore, may die, Jack—I'll never know what he looks like. If he lives, he'll need his mother.

"They've put—they've put glasses on Jane!" she broke out pitifully, in a whisper, as if speaking to herself. "Those beautiful blue eyes, and they've put glasses on her!"

"You can't mean, Cam, that if you had it to do all over again—our loving each other, our marriage—you'd do differently?" John asked seriously, as she stopped and groped for her handkerchief and hid her eyes.

"Oh no, no; not that! It's been all happiness for me, Jack—nothing but happiness! But there's something—something flat—in being a grown woman, being able to read and think and philosophize, and then flinging it all aside, everything one's done, responsibilities and affections, and saying, 'I must be happy! I've got to be happy!' "

She was so pale, was breathing so shallowly and swiftly, that he was alarmed for her and tried to stop the flood of passionate troubled phrases, tried to quiet her.

"My darling, you mustn't get yourself so excited. Give this convalescence of yours a little more time, rest for another month, and then we'll see where we are——"

"No, you mustn't soothe me, Jack, you mustn't put me off!" she said breathlessly. "I know how childish it sounds—I know you think it's partly illness! But it's not! It's that I've failed my children, failed yours, too, and taken only what satisfied me—what made me feel loved and happy and envied and on the top of the world! So complacent, at last! 'I've got what I wanted. He adores me. He's filled my life up to the brim with flattery and presents and lovemaking—everything else can go to ruin——!' "

"Stop it, Cam," he said sharply, in a tone she never had heard from him before, "you're getting hysterical. We found each other and we loved each other, as thousands of other men and women who've made one mistake in marriage are continually doing. We've had some perfect years—barring Everest, which of course almost finished us both as far as nerves were concerned! That experience, then the scare about me, then the baby, have all but wrecked you. But life will go back into its normal grooves, dear," John went on, watching her closely to see what impression he was making upon her. "We'll be home again, and you'll be well again, and you'll have plenty to do, I assure you, when all four children are home! But just now the main thing is to build yourself up and get strong, and it does seem to me that when a yacht like the Wickiup is practically put at your disposal——"

It was no use. There was a wild look in her eye as she rose up in her pillows and all but flung herself at him.

"You're talking me out of it!" she gasped, her face white, her voice dry and exhausted. "You're trying to delay it—to keep me away from them, and them from me! I can't—I can't, any more. I'll be lonely—I'll miss you every hour of my life, but I can't stand it! I can't stand it, Jack, I tell you! They'll grow up without me, lopsided, writing me their adorable little letters all over the world, staying with their father! I'll not bear it—I'll not bear it—I want to go home!"

She was sobbing the last phrase desolately to herself under her breath, "I want to go home!" over and over again, when John caught her in strong hands and put her forcefully back on her pillows. Her face was twisted away from him; tears were flowing down it; her fine gold hair was tumbled and hot against her face when Foxy came running in.

"I'm being so stupid!" she whispered, as the world went black again.

CHAPTER XXXII

CAM, VERY PALE STILL, but composed and inclined to laugh at herself, found the doctor in her room an hour later, lay talking comfortably to him for a little while. She confessed to being ashamed of herself; she could laugh apologetically when John came in, magnificent in evening dress, a little later. He kissed her, and she looked at him timidly.

"I was homesick, Doctor, and I behaved disgracefully. I don't know what possessed me! Jack, sit down a minute. I'm so sorry, dear!"

Jack sat down, holding her hand, drawing a deep breath.

"Whew-w-w, Doctor, she is a nice little Xantippe when she gets going!" he said, with the gesture of wiping his forehead. "I didn't know what to do with her."

"What was it all about?" the doctor asked.

"I want to go home," Cam said simply.

"Well, aren't you going home? What's this I hear about a beautiful yacht laid up in the Whang Po?"

"That won't be until February. They had to send to the Clyde for parts."

"And what makes you think you'll be ready for travel sooner than February? Here you are in the prettiest house in

Peiping, with this big man going all through the bazaars buying you things——"

"Look out, Paul," John said warningly. "That's the way to get her started!"

Cam laughed shamefacedly.

"I'll be good," she said. "Only—— But I'll be good!"

"Do you know that you are very lucky, young lady?" the doctor said to her reprovingly. "You're very lucky to have gotten through these last three months at all. When you landed here, and we took stock of you both at the hospital, I didn't think either one of you was going to make the grade. I remember saying . . ."

They all talked alike; they had been talking to her this way for weeks, she reflected, listening patiently, her beautiful blue eyes fixed steadily on the doctor's face. It did not matter much what he said. But Jack did matter. She could not speak to him freely before the third person, but when he came in from his party a little after midnight she was awake, and called to him to come into her room.

"Jack, dearest, I'm so sorry for that ridiculous outburst tonight," Cam said penitently. "It was nothing but nerves and fatigue. You haven't been thinking about it, have you? Of *course* we'll go with Talbot, and of *course* it'll be wonderful, and we'll do Venice and Paris and every other place, and have a gorgeous time! And Jack," she said, laying her face against his, locking her hands about his neck, as he knelt beside her, "don't think your wife doesn't love you first and last and always! You're all the world to me. It's only occasionally that I get these wild streaks of restlessness——"

He held her tight, his kisses against her cool temple, from which the gold braid fell back.

"Have you been awake all this time, you little imbecile?"

"No; I was asleep. I think I was! Or dozing, anyway. I wanted to see you, and to be sure that my ridiculousness hasn't changed any of your plans!"

"Nope. Plans all set," he said cheerfully. Cam rubbed her cheek against his.

"I love you," she said.

Still a little shaken from last night's storm, she lay wakeful long after he was asleep, and the next day was just awakening when he came in as usual at about one o'clock.

"Haven't had your breakfast yet, Cam?"

"I just woke up. How did the work go?" She sat up, pushing the soft gold bush of her disordered hair back from her white temples, smiling at him with eyes clear and blue and happy again.

"Fine. But I've just been uptown. Look here, Cam, could you get up early tomorrow?"

"Tomorrow? How early? What for?"

"Plane."

"Oh, somebody going to see the Wall?" She had made the trip in the plane before, floating low over Peiping, looking down at the narrow ribbon of the great Wall that rose and fell with the dips and heights of the long mountain range, looking at the checkered mud-colored squares that were the city, and the glowing red jewel at its heart that was the once-forbidden residence of a long line of emperors.

"Six too early for you?"

"In the morning? But why are they going so early, Jack?"

"We're going to Shanghai," John said.

"Shanghai?" Her eyes widened. "Did the doctor say it was all right?" she asked amazedly.

"You feel up to it, don't you?"

"Well, ye-es, of course. But they've been so discouraging?"

"The truth is I haven't asked them," John confessed, speaking in a brisk businesslike tone, feeling in his pockets for some evasive envelope. "The Hoover sails at four, and we ought to be in the city at one at the latest. We've got the cabin de luxe."

She looked at him, her mouth partly open, her eyes blazing in a suddenly colorless face.

"Jack!" she whispered.

"Yep; I think we've had enough of China, Cam. Today's the twenty-sixth—you ought to be having supper with your girls in Menlo Park about the tenth of December. How about it? D'you think you're up to it?"

He was sitting beside her on the bed; she clung to him as if in actual terror.

"Jack, you're not serious!" she said, in a shadow of her own voice.

"Well, take a look." He had found the envelope; now he opened it to show her yards of tickets, red passport books, identification cards. "They might go on telling you to be patient for another year," he said. "I don't believe you'll die on the trip, and if you do, it's my risk."

"Die!" she echoed, in a voice in which bells were ringing. "I'm alive—I'm aliver than I've been since Everest! Not—" Cam faltered, beginning to cry, clinging tight to his hand—"not *tomorrow?* On the ship, starting for home—tomorrow?"

"Well, don't cry about it and waste your strength before we get started. Yes, you and I and Foxy leave Peiping tomorrow morning at six. We'll be on the Hoover at one, and we'll get you straight into bed. Then Foxy 'll say good-by to you, and after that I'm your nurse. At four you'll begin to feel us moving——"

"Oh, no; I can't bear it—I can't bear it!" She was sobbing, straining her arms about him, laughing through her tears. "Oh, Jack, I can't believe it! Oh, darling, I'll be so good! I'll stay in bed, and I'll drink milk——"

"Remember now, if you die on me, I've killed you, and Adele will think it was all done for her."

"Oh, let her, let her!" Cam was beside herself, sobbing and laughing wildly. "Jack, you'll see," she said. "I'll be better the minute we get started. I'm better now! Oh, my girls—oh, Jack, I'll be home for Christmas!"

"Now, listen, take it easy, Cam. We don't know what we're going home to—things will be all in confusion, and if you get yourself exhausted it may mean a real parting with the girls! Just try to relax, dear——"

"I will, I will," she promised, lying down immediately upon her pillows. "But, Jack, we're going home!"

"Why, Cam, my sweetheart," he said, reproachfully, "you could have told me this long ago. You needn't have broken your poor little heart over it. I've just been realizing that all this time, while I've been in heaven going about with you——"

She put her hand over his mouth.

"Nothing would have kept me from going with you to Everest. And all the rest followed without our having any choice at all. No, you shan't ever say that again! But, Jack, I am so completely, so insanely happy I've got to say it. And no matter what sacrifice it is for you, it's giving me new life again."

"It's no sacrifice for me," he said, almost bewildered at the violence of her emotions. "I love those girls of yours, you know, and what of my boys? I've got two sons in America; more than once I've lain awake at night, thinking about them, and the raw deal we've been giving them. Now you lie still here, and I'll ask for lunch," he went on, in a different tone. "Foxy and the amah are coming in to pack—we've got a lot to do. The man's coming up here to check on our baggage, a lot of it 'll have to follow us . . ."

She did not hear him. Her eyes, mystical with joy, were fixed on space; her hands were clasped over her heart. And it seemed to Cam that in all the happy hours she had ever known, there had been none so wonderful as this one.

CHAPTER XXXIII

THE S. S. HOOVER plowed her way steadily past the low-lying port of Kobe, past Yokohama's jumble of junks and barges and strange craft, on and on and on through the eternal channel of the blue waters. And to Cam the ecstasy of it was not only in that she was going home; it was that she was moving back to health and strength and high spirits, too.

The sleep that came to her in her gently rocking bed was the best sleep she had known since those first nights on the great mountain, before nausea and fear and cold had had their way with her. The meals she shared with John at the little wall table in the big dining salon tasted to her as no food had tasted for a long time. To walk the deck with him, to feel the fresh salt air in her face, was to live again. At first she was timid, looking for signs of fatigue, going obediently to her cabin to rest long before she felt tired. But presently she knew that she was well, well in mind and soul and body, and after that the trip became one long delight.

Hawaii sent them a great breath of flowers from its sun-washed waterfront; they were getting home now, they were getting home now, Cam's heart sang. Honolulu was a sort of front garden to California; it was only days now! John had sent cables; the family knew that they were coming. Fundamental things would be ready for them, and what was not fundamental could be easily added.

Day after tomorrow—tomorrow—today, the passengers reiterated, walking the decks in the cooler air, finding warm coats and old caps for the deck promenades. And actually, miraculously, it was San Pedro at last, with Cam trembling now with excitement that she could no longer control.

During the six-hour stop they went in to Los Angeles, to the big hotel. And there were telegrams there; a little sheaf of them held with an elastic band. John tore one open, and the burdens and responsibilities that he had ignored for more than a year reached out clawing fingers and seized him. He read a second telegram and Cam heard him say "My God!" under his breath.

"Not bad news, Jack?"

"Sad news. Poor kid, you have come back into a good deal of a mess. I wish I could spare you, Cam. I wish I'd left you quietly in your Peiping garden."

"But what *is* it?"

"Bob Sylvester's wife died three days ago. December seventh, my mother's telegram says, and the girls have been sent to the Menlo Park place. And Taffy's ill."

"Dixie-Belle dead! Of the baby, I suppose. Poor little thing, poor little thing! She simply wasn't destined to have her baby. But Jack—where's your mother, and where's Taffy, and what's the matter with him?"

"Mother isn't very definite. Thank God we'll be there tomorrow. Fever, she says. Evidently she and Taffy and the girls and Toomey are all at Cherry Ridge. 'Impossible to get cook,' she says. They must be having a nice time! My poor little fellow, he's sick, is he? Well, Toomey 'll know what to do with him. And we'll straighten it all out. The little girls probably don't know what it's all about, and I suppose Mother's doing the cooking for them. Gosh," John said youthfully, slitting open another telegram, "they've gotten themselves into a mess!" His face shadowed. "I guess he's pretty ill," he said soberly. "This is from some doctor, later than Mother's. 'Your mother wishes you advised son's condition not satisfactory.' Ah, my God," John added in a lowered tone, as if speaking to himself, "I'm sorry. I'm sorry. What have they done to the poor little kid?"

Cam had crossed the airy big hotel bedroom and was thumbing the telephone book.

"Write out a telegram to have them meet us at Mills Field," she said. "We'll be there for lunch!"

"Cam, my darling," he said. "Let *me* go! You go back to the ship, take it easy, get to San Francisco tomorrow and go to the Fairmont and get into bed. You can't plunge into this. I'll see Taffy in the hospital, or get him moved into a hospital——"

"Jack, Jack, Jack," she interrupted, her arms about him, "can't you see that it's just that that I want!"

Three hours later they were at Cherry Ridge.

It was all oddly flat, oddly disappointing. She would not let Jack see it, but her heart sank strangely during the first hour at home. Cam, for the first time in the more than sixteen days since their hurried departure from Peiping, felt weary and chilled and discouraged, felt that there really were left, as a legacy from her long illness, limitations upon her strength.

They had left December sunshine hot in Los Angeles, flown north to fog and bleakness. The farmhouse looked shriveled and shabby somehow, after the mellowed heavy beauty of oriental walls and towers; no one was in sight when they arrived; their telegram came some hours later. Attempts to telephone it had been made, but no one in the house was paying any particular attention to the telephone.

Jane and Joanna received their mother without enthusiasm. Joanna was still the golden-headed little loving baby Cam remembered, but Jane had grown tall and weedy, her beautiful mouth disfigured with gold teeth bands, her eyes hidden behind large dark-rimmed glasses. Nan was in the kitchen struggling with the wood stove; the gas had not been connected yet; a Japanese schoolboy was sweeping the porches. Upstairs in a bedroom that looked desolate and dusty Jack's mother was lying flat on an unmade bed, an ice bag on her aching forehead, a hot-water bottle at her cold feet; in the next room Toomey stood guard over Taffy, who was tossing in a fever.

The house was cold, drafty. There was a sense of fog and soot and chill and the strong smell of boiling onions over the place; the furniture looked scared, huddled into corners of the rooms. Bread and a paper bag in which it had come, butter still in its quarter-pound wrappings, an empty milk bottle stood on the end of the dining-room table.

John went straight up to his son's sickroom; afterward he went into town in his car; presently there were two nurses and a doctor at the farm, and the Japanese boy had been removed from his senseless sweeping of leaves and was firing the furnace. Heat began to percolate into the cold rooms, where boxes and barrels, half-unpacked trunks, dusty furniture still in summer covers, heaps of books and mummied queer crates from the Orient were set about on tracked and dirty carpets in the wildest confusion.

Cam dug out a working apron somewhere, rolled up her sleeves. She went to and fro busily, attended by the whining Jane and Joanna, who wanted to go to "little Sarah's" house.

"Where *is* little Sarah's house, Nan?"

"Up'n Piedmont, Mis' Kilgarif," the colored woman's voice said lifelessly, heavily. Her heart was grieving for the little mistress she had seen laid in the wet winter earth the day before. She was bound to these two new little charges now with bonds that only death could break, but her spirit was still sore and sick, and she could not lift her voice.

"But you girls must know that with poor Taffy so sick you can't go to Piedmont!" Cam said sharply.

When Jack came downstairs she met him eagerly.

"How is he, dearest?"

"I don't know, Cam. He—he wanted me; I know that. Stretched out his poor little pipestem arms." Jack spoke thickly; there was no shred of color in his face. "I've been lying down beside him; they say he's quieter than he's been at any time," he said. "The minute he saw me he seemed to pull himself together. He whispered, 'You came, didn't you, Dad?' He went to sleep with his head here."

Jack touched his shoulder briefly with his hand; his eyes did not meet Cam's eyes.

"I'm going back," he said. "I told him I'd sleep in the next room, but he pulled me down and asked me to have a cot put up right near his. The nurse says it's not necessary—Doctor Pierce says that there's no immediate danger. But I'm going to stay with him for a while. Cam," John said, drawing her aside in the hallway that was beginning to smell of oiled furnace pipes, "I don't know whether he's going to pull out of this or not. If he doesn't, it's going to mean—it's going to mean lifelong remorse for me. Lifelong remorse. But whether he does or doesn't, you brought me home to give him his one chance. That's the only comfort I'm ever going to have—that I got here, and he had been wanting me, and he knew it. My mother—my poor mother moved in here five days ago, under the impression that she could get the place in order for us. Of course Toomey and the boy came along; they've been trying to get a cook, to get someone to clean, ever since. When poor little Dixie-Belle died, Bob Sylvester shipped the girls down here, that was three days ago. Poor fellow, I don't suppose he knew what else to do! If we'd been traveling through the Suez——"

"Don't think of it," she interrupted briskly, steering him kitchenward with a firm, small, dirty hand. "You come out here and have something to eat. You've had nothing since breakfast, and it's three o'clock. Nan's telephoned a cousin in San Francisco, and she says she'll send down two girls to take hold right away. By dinnertime we'll have things in some sort of shape. I've sent for chops and bread and oranges—everything down here 'll be all right."

"It 'll kill you," he whispered, clinging tightly to her.

"It 'll not kill me at all. The only thing," Cam said, with a jerk of her head upward and backward to indicate Taffy's sickroom, "the only thing that will kill me is to have anything happen to *him*. Left here with his grandmother and nurse—it *sounded* safe enough——" she mused. "What started it, Jack? Did he get a cold? Has he been ill?"

"They seem to think it's a nervous condition, mostly."

" 'Nervous'! A baby that age! Eat that, John."

"That was just what I wanted, Cam," John said, finishing his hurried little meal and setting down an empty cup. "Children can have nerves, seemingly. The doctor who telegraphed me yesterday evidently is an alarmist, and he and Mother had the child dying," he went on; "but we'll have another opinion. Only—only there's something about it I don't understand. He seems so weak. I'm going back."

Hours later, when she crept to bed sore in every fiber of her body, with her hands cracked and stiff from manipulating cords and keys, trunk trays and packing, he was in Taffy's room, lying on the extra bed that had been set up there, reading. Taffy was asleep.

Cam crept in quietly, her gold hair braided severely away from her face, her cheeks shining with cleansing cream, her old blue wrapper belted warmly about her. She went noiselessly to Taffy's bed and laid her hand gently on his forehead.

"Rather hot, little boy," she breathed.

"You must be exhausted," John said, as she came over to sit on the edge of his bed. "You're turning in? He seems to me quieter."

"I'm sure he is. He was quite wild when we got here, and the room was cold, and the whole thing was dreadful," Cam said, in a soft, small shadow of her usual voice. "Your being here made a difference instantly. I didn't know," she continued musingly, "that he had missed us so much."

"No; nor I," John said quickly.

"Well, we'll get them all straightened out," she said, courage rising above the deep weariness in her voice. "I'm off," Cam added, getting up to go away. "Miss Fargo comes on at one, and I've left her a little supper downstairs in the kitchen."

"He keeps whispering about Toomey. 'Toomey, Toomey, Toomey!'" John said, with a glance toward Taffy's bed. "Maybe we ought to wake her."

"But she's *dead* with fatigue. She's had the whole responsibility since your mother collapsed. Except for Nan, of course, who is a perfect tower of strength. I gave Toomey a powder and she went to bed at eight o'clock—two hours ago. Miss Fargo 'll be in, and then you come get some sleep. I hope Toomey 'll sleep the clock round."

"Ah, you're wonderful, Cam! To come home to a mix-up like this and get things in line."

"He's all that worries me." She had laid her fingertips lightly on Taffy's flushed little dry forehead again. The house was warm now, and the fine colored girls who had come down from San Francisco at Nan's request had put her bedroom into something like order; her bed was turned down, the pillows piled invitingly. Cam tumbled in, too tired to know or care what problems were awaiting her in the days to come, only grateful for rest and sleep.

CHAPTER XXXIV

JANE and Joanna came in to her in the early morning. A cold winter dawn was rosy on the western hills; the bare garden trees were cased in frost; a bitter wind was whining over the stark and shriveled world.

But the radiators were clanking with a heartening insistence, and Miss Fargo, coming in to report, had said that little David's fever was decidedly less, and that Mr Kilgarif had gone off at midnight for a long night's rest. Matters were all on the mend.

Cam's daughters seemed more her own in this hour than they had since meeting her on the afternoon before. They were sociable and sweet in their pajamas and slippers, full of small gossip, and growing easier and more confidential with her every moment. Jane was not wearing her glasses now; to Cam the beautiful sky-blue eyes looked perfectly strong and normal. She seized this as the first opportunity to warn Jane that at any sacrifice of reading or study she was not to wear spectacles. Joanna had developed as amazingly in a mental sense as Jane had physically; Cam had to take them gradually, watch and study them, to feel that she recognized them again. She told them that someday she would describe to them the whole experience with the big mountain and the snows, but their real interest was in the mention of presents in the trunks which were coming by steamer up from San Pedro, and delighted questions kept them occupied all the time that they were dressing with her by her fire, and during the breakfast which Asilda and Mamie served so nicely.

Confusion and dirt were everywhere, but the maids managed to create little oases in it here and there, and Cam could hope that in a few days' time the worst of the moving in would be over.

She went upstairs at eight o'clock to send John down to his breakfast. Toomey was still asleep; the night nurse had left; the day nurse was enjoying her fruit and coffee downstairs. Cam took a chair by Taffy's bed and sat watching him. The child lay in a light uneasy slumber, but her touch on his temples had assured her that the fever had been broken. The dark hair against his white skin was moist; his whole body looked relaxed and comfortable, sunk into the whiteness of the sheets.

The room was very still on the winter morning. Now and then the wind rose to a fretful chafing at the window, or she heard branches click in the frost; muffled far-away sounds indicated where the breakfasters were clinking silver and talking in subdued voices. Taffy sighed a little and murmured something unintelligble. Cam sat very still, looking about at the dust on the chairs and the half-packed boxes of toys and clothing. She must get Mamie and the other girl in here to clean the room just as soon as it was safe to move him.

Presently, glancing toward him, she saw that his beautiful sunken dark eyes were open and fixed upon her.

"Aunt Cam," he said in a whisper. Cam felt herself tremble a little with fright; sometimes children had these lucid periods just at the end, she thought wildly. "Grandma is a liar because she tells lies," Taffy said, simply.

A little lightheaded still, she thought. She smiled: she was near enough to him to put out her hand and lay it on his.

"Isn't she?" he said, with surprising spirit.

"I'm sure she doesn't mean to be, Taffy," Cam said soothingly, completely at a loss.

"You know what she said?" he demanded.

"I know that you're much better this morning," Cam said, in a cheerful, quiet voice. "And I know Dad and I are home to stay this time. And we're going to get you out in the sunshine in a few days, and you'll have your bicycle and maybe a pony, and ride all around here."

"Grandma said," he persisted, with a sudden anxious air of hurry and stress that infinitely distressed her, "that if Toomey said that again, she'd fire her. And she didn't fire her!"

A little fear, a certain sick reluctance to hear what she thought she might be going to hear, touched Cam's spine with ice. She tried to smile.

"What did Toomey say? I don't think it could have been very dreadful," she began.

"It was 'bout the President," Taffy explained.

"Oh?" Cam said, relief in her heart. It had not had anything to do with him, then? Just a political argument; she had heard Toomey and the old lady idly and ignorantly arguing politics before this. "What did Toomey say?" she asked, humoring the small, thin, eager creature whose face looked so pinched against the pillows.

"Gram said that if Toomey voted for someone she wouldn't love her any more, and Toomey said, 'Then I won't tell you who I'm going to vote for in 'lection,' and then Gram said, 'All right, if you say that again I'm going to fire you,' and they all laughed," Taffy explained. "But then Toomey *did* say it again," he went on, excitedly, "and Grandma just laughed when I told her that she said she was going to fire Toomey. And then," he added, sinking his voice to a whisper now, holding tight to Cam's hand and glancing cautiously toward the door as if he were afraid of being overheard, "then, you see, that made Toomey *mad*."

Her heart was lead.

"Toomey wouldn't be mad at you, darling? That wouldn't make her mad."

"But it *did,*" he said.

"Did what, sweetheart?"

He had closed his eyes.

"She was *mean* to me," he said pitifully. Cam knew that the little phrase would be graven upon her heart forever and forever. She made her voice quiet and natural.

"Toomey was mean to you?" she asked simply.

Taffy opened his big dark eyes.

"She was always mean to me," he whispered. "And I told Grandma so, and I said that Grandma was a liar, and then I began to scream, and Toomey said it was my nerves, and she took me upstairs. And I hate that room, I hate that room!"

"Did she whip you, Taffy?" Cam asked, very gently.

"No. But she said she would make me go to bed for days and days, and she said if I made Daddy send her away she'd come creeping back up the stairs—some night when I was all alone—and get a scissors——"

"Do you know, Taffy," Cam interrupted quickly, her face as pale as his now, but her tone all amusement and reassurance, "that was just silly talk! That was just like Jane saying last year that she was going to get wings and jump up on the roof. Do you remember that? Wasn't that funny?"

"She couldn't!" he said, in a child's rich tone of protest.

"Of course she couldn't! And that's a silly way to talk. But did Toomey ever whip you?" Cam asked.

"No, because she said then my grandmother would know it. But she would read me sad stories," the child said simply. "Stories about Indians stealing babies, and people being mean to them. And then she would ask me if I loved her most in the world, and then she would be kind to me again. And you won't tell Dad, will you?" he asked quickly. "Nobody must ever tell Dad, because then she says he'd try to send her away, and she wouldn't go! But don't you," Taffy added, snuggling confidentially nearer to Cam, clutching her hand tightly with thin little fingers—"don't you ever let her be alone with me at night, any more, will you? And by and by," he concluded, with a spirit that seemed to Cam as heartbreaking as any other element in the whole heartbreaking affair, "by and by I'll be grown up and I can get a ticket and go away on a ship where she won't ever know where I am!"

" 'By and by?' " Cam echoed. "Why, you won't have to do that! You see you're getting bigger and stronger all the time, and you're going to sleep right out on the sleeping porch with Dad, with the girls and me on the next porch, and—did you know this? You're going to have a dog, a real bulldog, you know, the kind whose jaw sticks out in the pictures? Well, tomorrow I'm going to buy you a little tiny baby bulldog, who'll be gentle until he gets used to you and the girls, and he'll be with you all the time. Every minute. And you know how fierce they are!"

His eyes were flooded with tears of joy.

"Oh, I would love him!" he said, shakily. "He'd be mine, wouldn't he?"

"Yours. Of course we'd all love him. But nobody else could feed him, and he'd sleep right on your bed, on your feet. And if anyone took any chances coming up on *that* porch," Cam said, with a great air of bravado, "he'd find himself running away pretty quick!"

"But if you and Dad went away again?" Taffy asked, his face clouding.

"But we're not going, dear. It was only because Dad was so ill, and then I was ill, and then your bad little Chinese brother came——"

"My dog will take care of my brother, too!" Taffy said, in a loud, defiant voice.

"Well, of course he will! But now, what are we going to name him?"

" 'Poodle,' " said Taffy, his eyes shining.

"Well, I don't know. He won't be a poodle, you see. I

should think 'Buck' would be better, or 'Bingo.' Or, I'll tell you, we could name him 'Pete.' "

"We could name him 'Caruso' for Gran's canary." Taffy lay back, panting a little, his forehead beaded with sweat, but joy in his eyes. "But Toomey said you couldn't ever have a dog in boarding school, and maybe she won't let me," he offered, after thought.

"But that's what I meant to tell you, Taffy. Toomey's going 'way back home."

There was a moment of electric silence.

"To be with her sister?" Taffy gasped then, amazed eyes on Cam's face.

"I think so."

"For a visit?"

"No; to stay."

"Now?"

"Today."

"And not coming back?"

"Never."

He tried to take it in, his eyes never leaving Cam's face. Presently his mouth pursed anxiously.

"Is she mad?"

"No."

"Dad didn't know she was mean to me?"

"Oh no."

"If she came back I might be big," Taffy said thoughtfully.

"You would be. And then you'd have the dog, you know."

Cam was still trembling, hardly conscious of what she was saying. But her voice was cool.

" 'Lion,' " Taffy said. "I'm going to name him 'Lion.' But maybe," he added doubtfully, "maybe she won't go."

"Oh yes; she'll go." Cam was conscious of a moment of actual terror as she glanced up and saw Toomey standing in the doorway.

CHAPTER XXXV

SHE spoke above a quaking heart. "Did you have a good rest, Toomey?" she managed to say.

"I thought you might like to go down to breakfast, medem."

"I've had my breakfast, thanks. Things are still so upset that we have to take them as they come. Toomey, will you please go downstairs and tell Mr Kilgarif that I want to speak to him?"

"Would you prefer to leave me here with Taffy, medem? Then you'd be quite free, for I've had my tea."

"No; I'd rather you'd go, please."

A moment when the eyes of the two women were riveted together. Cam's color rose, as the nurse's perceptibly faded.

"I usually help the nurse give him his sponge bath at this time," Toomey said, quietly but boldly; "those are Mrs Kilgarif's orders, medem. I don't like to go against them, as if I'd two mistresses."

It was with a sense of being rescued that Cam saw John's head in the doorway.

"How's my boy?" he asked.

"I'm going to have a bulldog, Dad!" Taffy said weakly, beaming.

"Will you stay with him, Jack?" Cam asked. "I have to speak to Toomey. Don't leave him," she said, as she passed him.

She and the nurse went out into the hall; walked to the doorway of Cam's room.

"You're leaving today, Toomey," Cam said flatly, without preamble. "I've been talking to him. He's only a baby; he doesn't know what you've done to him. But if his father and I can make it up, we'll give all our lives to it. You pack your trunk and get out. Get out before lunch, or I'll have the authorities here. It might be that a doctor might find out that what you told that child—the terror you've kept him in—would mean that you're the sort of person they shut up. I don't know. You've never become a citizen; America could deport you, send you back to where you came from. But that's not my business. All I care about is that you get out, now, today!"

Toomey was looking at her steadily.

"Not so fast, medem," she said coolly. "It's the other Mrs Kilgarif who pays me. She's the one to tell me to go or stay. I'll take no orders from you, no, nor the child's father, either! I'll talk to her."

Swiftly, while speaking, she had crossed the hall to Mrs Kilgarif's door, and Cam, following, saw the old lady seated in her bed, with a breakfast tray before her. Her bewildered eyes met them as they came in, but before she could speak, Toomey opened the conversation passionately, in a breathless voice.

"I've come to tell you, medem, that Mrs John Kilgarif has just given me the sack!"

"I don't—why, what's the matter? I don't understand you, Toomey," John's mother said in a frightened voice. "Cam, what's wrong? We've all been in a state of confusion—my headaches——"

"Toomey has been frightening and bullying Taffy for a long time," Cam said, in a voice as excited as Toomey's had been. "I've just found it out! I won't stand for it! She's going today."

"Not today, Cam," faltered the old lady tremulously. "We know he's always been a nervous, delicate child——"

"She's made him one!" Cam interpolated hotly.

"And he's ill now," old Mrs Kilgarif went on placatingly. "He really isn't in a condition to tell us anything, poor dear little soul! I'm sure that when we're all rested things will straighten out."

"You don't know what's been going on," Cam said, desperate to make her point. "She had him sick with fright—— What is it?"

This was to Mamie, who appeared in a state of incoherence and tears in the doorway.

"Asilda and me is goin'," announced Mamie.

"Oh, not now! With nurses and sickness in the house!" Cam stammered, every unwashed dish, undusted chair, unpacked trunk seeming to leer at her as she spoke.

"Mah brother Willy hurted hisse'f this mornin' in Oakland," Mamie explained. "We-all will be back tom'ow. But we got to go now——"

"Jack," Cam said, seeing him behind the maid's black head. "Come in here. Who's with Taffy?" she broke off to ask, with a glance for Toomey, who had given signs of being ready to slip from the room.

"Miss Fargo. She's going to fix him up for the doctor's visit. But he's better," John said. "What's the matter?" he asked Mamie. "What's the matter with everyone?" he added, glancing in alarmed perplexity from his wife's distressed flushed face to the pale countenance of his mother, who was now inaudibly praying.

"The matter is Toomey," Cam said directly. "The trouble with Taffy is that she has been bullying him, terrorizing him, for months! He couldn't complain. We were on the other side of the world, and his grandmother didn't see anything wrong. Oh, listen, Jack," Cam said, catching at his arm, "don't think I'm crazy. She frightened him. She warned him that if he told us about it she'd come back and punish him. He's afraid of her, can't you see it? Can't you both see it? He thinks we don't dare send her away! Jack—Jack—you must believe me, no matter what she says——"

"Well, but darling, he's in a fever," John said, his arm bracing her, but his tone remonstratory and unconvinced. "Children in fevers have those delusions——"

"John, I really cannot stand this," his mother murmured. "I've had one of my wretched migraines——"

"Mummy, where are our paintboxes?" Jane asked, advancing from the porch door. Cam caught the small warm hand and held it, but she hardly glanced at the child and did not answer her.

"What's stirred all this up, Cam?" John demanded.

"Something Taffy said to me. I said I wouldn't quote it; I promised not to tell you, and I have!" Cam reproached herself. "But it's too serious to mind that! Poor little fellow, we all seem in a conspiracy to betray him!"

" 'A conspiracy to betray him,' medem!" Toomey, gaining confidence every second, repeated roundly. "Why, I have been with the child since he was born. What object would I have in harming him? If I'd tell him in fun that his grandmother couldn't dismiss me, he knew it was only that I loved him!"

"You're the one I'm worrying about, not Taffy," John said solicitously to Cam, noting her pale face and agitated manner.

"Jack, can't you hear her admitting it? She has convinced him that none of us can get rid of her! She has frightened him into thinking that she is stronger than any of us!"

"He *has* a little fever——" his grandmother began anxiously.

"If Toomey's been teasing him, Toomey 'll stop," John said pacifically.

Cam spoke quickly, with deadly seriousness:

"She is never to see him again, Jack! That's what's been the matter all this time. Her keeping him away from us, her convincing him that he couldn't do anything without her—it explains it all! It's all clear now. He won't get well unless he knows that he's not to see her again. I promised him, and I wish you could have seen his face!"

"You arrived unexpectedly only late yesterday, medem," Toomey said, in a tone of strong scorn, "and you naturally find things in a state of disorder. If you'll consider for a moment what was put up to Mrs Kilgarif and me, you'll see that we're hardly responsible for the condition of affairs."

"This paritcular occasion has nothing to do with it," Cam said quickly. "It's been going on for a long time. When this child tells his father what you've done and said—and I'll see that he does!—I suppose you'll deny it. But it's your word against his, and no child of six could make up what he told me this morning! That you'd come into the house some night when he was all alone, if we sent you away, and come creeping up the stairs! Enough to make any child a nervous wreck——"

"I would never do such a thing. It was just a manner of talking," Toomey said hotly, beginning to break and to show signs of nervousness. "It was a sort of joke. I've been the only nurse he ever had, I've always had a joking way with him. But if it's a question of devotion, I'm free to say that you cannot buy what I've given the child. My entire life is bound up in him——"

"But look here, look here," John interrupted, his arm still tight about Cam, his own face paling a little, as hers had done. "You never did—as a matter of fact—you never *did* tell him that we would not dare to send you away, and that if we did, you'd come back and punish him?"

Toomey looked about, flustered. She flung up her head.

"One 'll often say things to children that mean nothing at all!" she asserted, with a glance for support in the direction of the distressed old lady in the bed.

"But what he said was true?" John asked, in a quiet, reflective voice that Cam did not know. "You *did* tell him that if you were sent away, you would come back?"

"I don't know what I told him or what I didn't, sir," Toomey said civilly. "A small child! It's usually the nurse that has the right way of handling him. It seems to me there's no call for any such investigation, one way or the other. It's no secret in this house," she added bitterly, "that Mrs John Kilgarif is against me and would be glad to see me go! And that 'd be to give him no chance at all, what with you both here one day and off the next. If you'll excuse me, I'll not apologize any further——"

"Don't go into his room," John said in a quick warning tone, his hand on her arm. She turned, furious.

"What I've said to him or made him do was to keep him mine!" she said, in a sudden burst. "I took him when his mother died. I'd lost my own girl. I'd nobody else. Give me five minutes with him and I'll tell him that all I ever said was only to keep him mine."

"You shan't have one minute with him; you shan't see him again!" Cam said in breathless fright. "You *have* been good to him—you *have* lived just for him—but he's outgrown you now! You shan't see him!"

"You'll never keep me away from him!" Toomey said, at white heat.

"Jack, don't let him see her! It will set him back; he'll go into a fever again!" Cam begged.

"This all seems to me so unnecessary," the old lady said plaintively. "Please can't we leave it until my head is better and I can talk to Toomey quietly?"

"Don't go into his room at all until he's better and I can talk with him," John said, in a low tone. "You can take a few days off if you like; go up to the city. He'll tell me the truth, and until I know the truth there's no use in these scenes. Mrs Kilgarif is tired from her trip——"

"You're all crazy! You're all a lot of monkeys!" Toomey said loudly, with an angry laugh. "I know that. I've known for a year that you're all a lot of monkeys! Why, damn you all——"

The quiet middle-aged woman was metamorphosed. Her face was flushed and dark, her eyes wild; the sudden coarseness and frenzy in her manner told their own story. Toomey had been a sane enough young wife in a little village on the Alsatian frontier in 1914, expecting a first baby. But that was a long, long time ago. All that the years had stored in her heart was poured out now; they could not stop her, and she could not stop herself.

Finally, with a quick movement she was at the porch door.

"Don't let her go out, Jack!" Cam shouted. "Mamie—everyone, stop her!"

Still holding to the bewildered Jane's small hand, Cam ran in the other direction and across the hall to Taffy's door. She was vaguely conscious that old Mrs Kilgarif, with amazing agility, had sprung out of bed and that Jack had dashed through the door to the sleeping porch. But all the world seemed to be rocking and roaring with danger and monstrousness, and there was no reason or safety anywhere. Toomey had gone mad—she had gone mad—and Taffy was in danger!

She was so quick that as she entered Taffy's room, almost upsetting Miss Fargo and an armful of linen Miss Fargo carried, Toomey was coming in by the window. Cam let go Jane's hand then, stumbling against Joanna, who had joined the mad rush in the hall. She was first at the bedside and had dragged Taffy from it as Toomey made a lunge for the child. Cam heard her own voice screaming.

"Hold her, John! Don't let her touch him! It's all right, Taffy! It's all right, dear! Hold her, don't let her move!"

Then she was leaning against the wall, panting, and protecting Taffy, and Nan and John and Antone, the Portuguese gardener, were holding Toomey. There was a moment of silence when they could hear each other breathing, and then a confusion of low quick voices.

"Help me get him back into bed, Mamie." . . . "But what *was* it, Mummy? What was it?" . . . "Get the police, Mother—call the village and get the police." . . . "Keep quiet, there." . . . "Don't let her arm go." . . . "You're all right, Taffy; just lie still, dear." . . . "We'll have to get her into her room and keep her there." . . . "Nobody's going to hurt you, Toomey, everything's all right."

And then Mrs Kilgarif's voice, quavering at the telephone:

"Oh, dear—I know it says what to do on the cover, but I haven't my glasses Will you please send someone—there's been a robbery, I don't mean a robbery . . ."

"Just lie still, Taffy," John said. "Dad will be back in two minutes and explain it to you. Everything's all right."

"We'll want the doctor," Miss Fargo said in a low tone, her fingers on Taffy's pulse. Taffy did not speak; his face was colorless, and there were beads of sweat on his white forehead. He lay quite still, brilliant dark eyes moving in terror from face to face.

"Me an' Asilda 'll stay," said Mamie. "For a while anyways."

"We want you just to go to your room, Toomey," John said; "that's right—she'll go with us——"

"He'll tell you he doesn't want me to go!" Toomey's deep voice said heavily.

"We can talk about all that later," Cam said soothingly. Her one anxiety was to have this horrible scene over, to have all these frightened persons quieted, to have Toomey taken away out of their lives forever. As they came out into the hall she saw the figures of two policemen in the garden and for the first time in her life realized what their protection meant. With a great gasp of relief she looked across Toomey's shoulders at Jack.

"We're all right now, Jack!" she breathed. Toomey was quiet; she seemed dazed. She walked along quietly enough between John and Cam; Antone, Nan, Mrs Kilgarif, the colored maids in their hats and coats, and the two little girls forming a scared and watchful escort. The policeman, stuffing gloves into their belts, had been admitted by Nan, who followed them upstairs.

"Nan," John said, "telephone for the doctor, will you?"

"Dare's a doctor here," Nan said.

"Oh, thank God! Which one?" Cam demanded eagerly.

"He jus' 'rive; I don't know his name," Nan answered. "He ask for you; he got lady widdum."

She turned as she spoke, and Cam saw coming around the turn of the stairs a stout, square man of thirty-five with a fine thoughtful face, followed by a well-dressed woman who looked eager and smiling. In the man's arms, carefully carried, was a baby. Cam stared at them dazedly.

The two adult newcomers stared back in equal stupefaction. They saw, amid the litter of boxes and trunks in the upper hall, besides the three colored maids and two fair-headed little girls, a Portuguese gardener in his shirt sleeves, an elderly woman rocking and wringing her hands, two policemen, and a stout German woman held firmly by the arms by John Kilgarif and Cam. The man who carried the baby hesitated, looking quickly from face to face for an explanation of the scene.

"Campbell!" he said.

"Edward!" Cam answered weakly. She let go of Toomey's arm and sat down on the stair top. "But who—where——" she stammered. And then, in a faint, incredulous voice, as he put the baby into her arms: "But this isn't—this can't be——?"

"That's your boy!" the strange man said triumphantly. "What do you think of us for baby-farmers!"

Cam rested her cheek against the rosy little face, her face wet with swift tears.

"I'm asleep," she said, quietly and rationally. "This is all a dream. This must be a dream!"

One of the policemen, at a nod from John, had pinioned the arm Cam had been holding. The two men held Toomey securely.

"Well, you've got your wish!" John said. "The children are all together under one roof at last!" Cam, sitting on the stairs, disheveled and exhausted, began feebly to laugh and then to cry. Miss Fargo spoke sharply from the hallway.

"Did somebody telephone for the doctor?"

"I'm a doctor!" Edward Bayne went up to her quickly. Somebody helped Cam to her feet; she went slowly to her room, with Jane and Joanna beside her.

"Mother, whose baby? Is it our baby?" the little girls asked.

Cam's sister-in-law questioned bewildered old Mrs Kilgarif:

"What is it? The policemen—has something happened?"

"Cam," John's mother said faintly, "I think I shall have to lie on your bed! I really—I *really*—cannot stand—at my age——"

"Go ahead, Mamie, go find out how your brother is," Cam told the colored girl. "We'll get along. What is it, Nan?"

"I was fixing the spare room for yo' company," Nan said. "Shall I bring the crib downstairs fo' this boy you got?"

"Cam," said her sister-in-law, "what has happened? What on earth is all this about?"

"It's simple enough, I'll explain it!" Cam said. And she began to laugh and cry quietly again. And for a little time she could not stop.

CHAPTER XXXVI

BUT THE HOURS WENT BY, and the air slowly cleared, and she could get control of herself. Edward Campbell Kilgarif took his bottle like the good baby he was, and went to sleep in his half-sisters' crib as if he had been used to excitements all his life. Taffy had a pill from "Uncle Edward" and went to sleep, too. Miss Fargo had a bath and put on a clean uniform. A closed car imposingly marked "M.P.P.D." came and took Toomey away. The policemen flashed off on their bicycles, a heavenly peace and quiet began to knit together the torn edges of the household calm. Antone lumbered regularly downstairs to the furnace; Dr Bayne and John brought in great armfuls of wood, and the open fires sparkled and crackled and sent long tongues of flame up the blackened old chimneys. The day went its course, and Nan and Edward's nurse and Cam and Lucy got together some sort of supper at six o'clock.

They sat talking a long time over their sardines and scrambled eggs, their tea and cheese and bakery chocolate cake. Cam was still pale, but her eyes were bright. Gentle Lucy Bayne was still trying to get it all straightened out in her mind. The little girls had returned from naps. The elder Mrs Kilgarif, shaken and pathetically appealing, was present and ate, Cam noticed, a reassuringly hearty meal.

"But why did you keep her if she was murderous and insane?" Lucy asked more than once.

"Toomey? But she wasn't!" John's mother almost wailed. "She was perfectly *fine* with him. He adored her when he was a baby. It was only lately——" She stopped short, glancing timidly at Cam.

"Since I came into it," Cam said, in assent rather than question. "That was the trouble, wasn't it?"

"Well—that began the trouble——" the old woman faltered.

"She was wonderful while you were away. But as soon as we began to get the cables to say that you were coming back I noticed a change. It was just the time Tids was getting married and going off with Alonzo, and I couldn't exactly think what was wrong. But she would say things about losing Taffy, and about Cam not understanding him, and it did make me a little nervous. And then—a few nights ago, before we came here—she was decidedly—well, queer," Ada Kilgarif went on unhappily. "She told me a lot about her own child that she had lost, and about the war, and the bombs and star shells. She was only eighteen, and she was alone with her father and brother when they were both killed——"

"Edward!" Cam breathed, reaching out quick fingers for his own. She had never known any relative except a brother.

"And she was crazy all the time, I suppose," Lucy said.

"No; she wasn't crazy," Edward Bayne asserted. "We've had hundreds of those cases since the war. She was cheated out of her own life, her own man and child and home and country, too, and she comforted herself with this little fellow; he was everything she had. When you came in, Cam, she knew her day was over. You had not only the authority, but had what might charm him, youth, and young motherhood, that sort of thing. She began to pity herself, poor soul!"

"What will they do with her?"

He turned his eyes toward John. They had gone with her to police headquarters, but no charge had been made.

"Nothing. John promised to send her back to Alsace, and she wants to go. She has a sister and a brother living there in the old village. She'll stay awhile and get rested."

"And he's all right?"

"David? Oh, he's all right. Excitement and fear and worry are all that's the matter with him. He'll come out of it, when things settle down. You can easily convince him that it was all affection—all joking. She's not the only person who ever spoke so to a child. 'All right, you send poor Toomey away and she'll come back!' That sort of thing. But Cam," her brother said, "you were the one we were worried about. What were these reports from Peiping that you'd had a breakdown, that you weren't able to walk?"

"Well, I decided, when I arrived here yesterday, that I'd have to put off the next breakdown," Cam said.

"I should say so!" Lucy Bayne said. "We should have let you know we were coming," she apologized. "But it all came up so suddenly. Edward was asked to read this paper on bone treatments at the San Diego medical convention next week, and I did want to come, because my mother has been in Pasadena since October. But we didn't know quite what to do with Boo."

"My Edward is still 'Boo'?" Cam said, smiling.

"Well, you called him that in letters: the children have always called him that. And he was our problem. He'd been getting along so beautifully that we didn't want to make any change. And yet we knew you were on your way home, and it seemed silly not to personally escort him——"

And Lucy Bayne laughed comfortably, as became the mother of five husky children who had had every imaginable illness and accidents many times over.

John looked tired and grimy; he had gone over to the police station, had come back to open crates and try to extricate linen and pillows and other special things for Cam.

The day had been full of exhausting efforts and anxieties; Taffy was still seriously ill. But when he spoke it was with a broken, reluctant sort of laughter.

"You certainly came home to a nice rest cure!" he said.

Cam put her elbow on the table and her forehead in her hand and began to laugh feebly. And suddenly they were all laughing. Jane and Joanna, looking in bewilderment from face to face, laughed uproariously, too, without any idea of what was causing the half-hysterical mirth.

"You two holding onto the woman!" Edward Bayne said.

"And the two colored women just going, with their hats on!" John added.

"Two policemen—and the children crying—and Miss Fargo in the background patiently demanding a doctor!" Cam said faintly. Her whole body shook with her laughter, but the hands that covered her eyes were wet with tears.

"And we coming up the stairs neatly and promptly like a play with the baby held out!" Lucy Bayne said, and for a long moment they all laughed helplessly again.

Then John, magnificently waving aside arguments as to table-clearing and dish-washing, took Cam upstairs to bed, and when she was in bed her brother mixed her a sedative and made her drink it. She complied obediently enough, but when the men had gone downstairs again she slipped into Taffy's room and looked at him, peacefully asleep, had a word with the colored nurse at the baby's bedside, went in to talk quietly for a few minutes with John's mother.

A deep peace, an unfathomable restfulness seemed to envelop the old farmhouse, despite dust and disorder, invalids, children, guests; despite the fact that two of the servants had gone, and the cook's and the waitress's places were empty. Cam went back to her bed, climbed into it, and was almost instantly deep asleep.

Some months later she and John happened to have a talk about it, and about many other things. Spring was glorious and green over the Western world now; shadows were deep and sweet in the woods; the reclaimed garden was a glory of bloom.

Above the orchard, on the west side of the farm, there was a little footpath through dried meadow grasses that led straight into the woods. A stream, fretted on pebbles and winding about many a fallen log and jutting tree root, rippled and sang through it, and beside the stream Cam had brushed a table clear on the top of a fallen boulder and had set out the basket luncheon on a fringed red square of Perugian linen.

The baby made one of the party today. He had had his special menu earlier than the others and was asleep in his basket, fine beads of perspiration showing on his forehead, for the day was hot. At ten months he was still something below the average of weight and length that was expected of him, but he was a gay, talkative baby, and nobody found anything amiss with him.

Jane, learning to get along without glasses, and Joanna, all blonde beauty, were sturdy in linen shorts and sandals; Taffy, growing browner, harder, stronger, taller by the minute, was nude except for his brief white trousers and sandals. All three were busy in the creek bed, hauling rocks, damming water, digging; they were panting, soaking themselves ecstatically as they worked.

Down the hill and across the new green of the orchard beyond them, Cam could see the silvery gray low roof of the farmhouse; the blazing lines of orange light were marigolds in the garden; pale green feathers of the rose vines, spouting above the porch, were striped with pink and red. In the shade of the great line of eucalyptus trees along the barnyard, the three Jerseys were standing, not moving in the warm noon.

Overhead stretched the oak boughs, infinitely interlaced, spread in a thick screen against the sun. Light filtered graciously through them and fell in blots upon the rich pattern of the rocks and the water, the delicate under-foliage of hazel and young madrones. It was a day in which to rejoice in life alone, a day humming with the delicate sounds and sweet with the odors of early summer. Gnats wove and spun in little columns against the light; birds hopped in the woods; chipmunks flashed their clean-striped little bodies against the fallen logs of the forest and chattered at the chattering children. Now and then, in a dreaming moment of silence, the note of an owl came with a woodeny sound from the heart of the forest.

John lay flat on the leaves, his eyes closed. But Cam knew that even in half-sleep he was conscious of the rippling sound of the waters and the children's voices, the slow, soft sweep of a spring breeze high up in the new leaves. Now and then he turned his head, opened his eyes and smiled at her.

"Nice," he said after a while.

Cam had set forth boiled chicken and vegetable salad, brown sandwiches and fruit. She glanced at the creek; the children were still absorbed; they were in no hurry for luncheon. She came and sat down beside him, and their hands linked.

"What an hour, Cam! Somehow these last weeks seem to be getting more and more wonderful."

"I suppose it's Boo's going on so splendidly, and Taffy getting well. But it seems to me there never was such a June! Every day of it better than the last."

"That's what I meant. We've come such a roundabout way to it, Cam. A year ago——"

Her thoughts went to Everest and the eternal snows; the camp against the sharp white rise of the mountain's shoulder; the native porters stamping beside their fire; the howling of the desolate high winds—were all with her again.

"Only a year!"

"And we might so easily not have come back, Cam, and so have missed all this!"

"Ah, don't."

"Maybe I'm getting old," he said. "I'm forty. But I have

a feeling that all this is going to satisfy me for a long time. I don't want to go away any more, Cam. Perhaps it was the mountain that cured me."

"No, it wasn't that. It was finding out that they need us, that our being here really makes a difference in their lives. Jane would never have stopped wearing glasses if I hadn't come back."

"And I might have lost my boy," John said. "My God, Cam," he added, under his breath, as he watched the brown little active figure splashing and busy down by the creek, "I never would have believed what Taffy's come to mean to me! It was Toomey and my mother, I think, who were always between us, and then his being only a baby, and having lost his mother——

"But now," he went on as Cam did not speak, "now I'm sorry when he goes to bed at night, because we lose him. I'm planning already to take him riding with me—he's up to it now, only your brother said to go slow for a while. I've never known a finer mind, or a quainter way of putting things, than he's got. The other day, when I had him in town with me, I was continually laughing at him. Now that loafer," John ended, with a jerk of his head toward the baby's basket, "he's a cute little monkey. But I don't know that I'll ever be as crazy about him as I am about David!"

Cam spoke over a faint deep prick in her heart.

"David sounds cute for him."

"Well, it's a beautiful name. It was my father's name And if he starts to school this autumn——" John paused, musing, suddenly roused himself to glance at her smiling. "You won't mind my taking him off on a spree now and then?" he asked, half seriously.

"Mind you two finding each other! After the way we'd failed him?" Cam demanded. "We've got a lot to make up to Taffy," she said.

"We're making it up. He's not a nervous kid," the father said, watching him.

"I don't think he is. I heard him boasting to the little Pomeroy boy the other day that he had had a nurse who frightened the wits out of him. The poor little Pomeroy simpleton asked him if there really were lions and tigers under his bed, and Taffy said he thought there were but that he wouldn't care if there had been, he'd have killed them all!"

"I believe he's going to take it that way," his father chuckled.

"I think he is. Most of the time, except for those nightmares now and then, he seems to me one of the most normal, boylike little boys I've ever known," Cam commented. "And as for invidious remarks about Neddy-Boo," she added, "I'll give you another year to be his slave."

"I suppose so. But it's richness, Cam, to find this other little fellow so affectionate and eager and intelligent, and to feel that our peerless delphiniums have a brother they really can love."

"Love! They can't let him alone. And he is wonderful with them," Cam mused contentedly. "Look at him now, letting Joanna have the blue trowel. She's so mad for that fifteen-cent trowel that I gave him the other day that she was talking about it in her sleep last night, Nan said."

"Couldn't we acquire another blue trowel?"

"I like them to have to share. Aren't they beautiful down there, with those speckles of sunshine on them? I'm glad, Jack," Cam added thoughtfully, "that you took Taffy to see poor old Toomey off on her ship. Much better to have things friendly, to have her sending him postcards and feeling kindly toward us all. With the money she has she's bound to get a warm welcome from the brother—he has a houseful of motherless grandsons, and she'll soon have another favorite, and probably be quite sane about it. Was he cute with her?"

"Adorable. He stood squarely on the deck, asking questions of various ship's officers, and he finally raised his face for her to kiss him, and promised her a picture of his dog."

"Not mentioning that the dog was originally intended to be a protection against her?"

"I believe not," John laughed, shaking his head. "Good Lord, what a day that was!" he said.

"It was living, Jack. And I love to live! I want people to need me, and to miss me if I go away!"

"You get your wish," Jack said dryly. "You're in for running a three-ring circus now!"

"But it's running. We've made mistakes," Cam said under her breath, as if she spoke to herself. "It was a terrible mistake ever to let a woman like Toomey——" She stopped, musing.

"Yes; I'll pay for that all my life," Jack agreed seriously. "I'll be only too thankful to God if Taffy doesn't! But I think we've caught him in time. And looking back," he added, "it only seems to make a time like this more wonderful! Oh, we'll travel again," Jack said, "but we'll take them with us, the whole pack. We'll not find ourselves off on the side of Kinchinjunga again, wondering what's going on at home. We've reached peace now, and we'll hang onto it."

"I've made mistakes, too," Cam said half aloud; "and I'll pay for them. But I've learned through them—or I hope I have! And this is a wonderful little happy time, isn't it?"

"How d'you mean little?" he asked in his turn. "It's always going to be like this, Cam, from now on. Us and our kids, and the garden and the swimming pool, Taffy learning to ride and the girls growing up. What's going to stop it?"

"Nothing's going to stop happiness," she said, "for we've learned where to look for it. But there are going to be breaks, Jack. It isn't always June. Bob"—she hesitated a minute on the name; went on piling creamy stiff little oak leaves together and did not meet his eyes—"Bob Sylvester will marry again," she said. "Perhaps he'll marry another girl like Dixie-Belle, now that he's not playing golf any more, and perhaps she'll want to borrow the girls, take them to Europe maybe. Perhaps they'll have their first ocean voyage with her instead of with me. And as they grow older they'll wonder why Mummy and Daddy stopped living together, they'll love him, and they'll love me, and they won't understand. I'll have to pay that, too. I'll have to pack them up and send them off—not owning them, as I own Edward, not feeling that they're wholly mine. Always a little jealous when they say 'Dad.' Not—not the way it ought to be."

He lay flat on his back, his eyes closed.

"And how ought it be?"

"Not a divided duty," Cam answered, after thought. "Duty ought always to be perfectly simple and clear."

"And was it worth it, Cam?"

"Was it worth it!" Her voice was so astonished that he had to open his eyes and laugh in a little shame at himself. "You mean—you mean you and me?" she asked.

"Well——" he began, embarrassed. And in an apologetic tone he added, "I wanted to be sure."

"Do you mean the love that you and I have for each other, Jack, the wonderful, wonderful years we've been together? Do you mean those first months of—of heaven, when we drove to Banff and Lake Louise, and went down to New York and walked up the Avenue? Do you mean that you think I could think—— But no, you're not *quite* fool enough for that!" Cam said. "Imagine our lives without each other!!"

"I love you," he said, dreamily. "I'll always be a fool about you. I'll want special days with Taffy, but it 'll be only because I can come back to you. I'll hate Sylvester until I die because he has the power to make the woman I worship unhappy. I'll always be afraid that you're liking Jane and Joanna better than you do me. You'll have to tell me several times a week for the rest of our lives that the miracle hasn't lost any of its glory. I mean the miracle of our finding each other at the Hunters' party, the miracle of those times when I went up to the Lake, and you came walking under the pines to meet me. I can see it still, the blue water and the low flowers, all a tangle of Queen Anne's lace and Michaelmas daisies, and the great stalks of the pines going up high and bare and red into the sky!"

"When I don't think that that's the living glory and crown of my life I'll have to be dead, Jack," she said. And in a scornful whisper she echoed: "Was it worth while!"

There was an interruption. The children shouted from the creek.

"Mother!" It was Taffy calling. "Every time Joanna splashes water on me he growls! Watch, Mother! Aw, Daddy, please watch!"

John sat up, dry leaves tumbling from his shoulders. Truly enough, as the joyously laughing Joanna splashed Taffy, the tiny tan lump that was Lion emitted a faint baby growl.

"Aw, he loves me, he knows I'm his master, he loves me!" Taffy exulted, fondling Lion. John got up and went down to the creek, and Cam saw him, man fashion, begin to borrow the children's tools, begin his own spattering and digging.

CHAPTER XXXVII

SHE SAT ON, her smallest child sound asleep in the basket beside her, her back braced against the bole of a great oak. While she watched the workers at the creek, and the pattern the noon sun made through branches and leaves, her thoughts went on, happy thoughts, yet with an undercurrent of that soberness that is the inevitable fruit of life.

It was true, what she had told him. She must always pay for the choice she had made; now and in the years to come her daughters would be less her own because she had taken them away from their father. They would grow to beauty and understanding, and they would go to him for weeks at a time, for contacts of which their mother would know nothing, and they would come back, bound to be silent about them, bound to seem to sympathize with her in what she had done, just as they showed him sympathy and kindness when they were with him. Yet all that only made her daughters dearer. Even mistakes and stupidities had their gain.

John would never quite forgive himself for the blindness that had come close to costing him his firstborn son, but as a part of that remorse, Taffy meant to his father now what a firstborn son should mean. In that richness of discovery it was inevitable that Cam's claim should suffer, if only by a fraction of a degree. John's firstness with her was impaired, too, now that the little girls and the two boys were beginning to be so knitted into their lives; he could never be anything but supremely important, but other elements were important, too. Well, it was right that it should be that way, Cam thought, watching the splashing and listening to the laughter that were going on down by the creek.

A woman could not have everything. The care of four small children, even with good help, even with sufficient money, was an absorbing thing. Between the problems of their meals, their clothes, their laundry work and sleeping arrangements, their small illnesses, accidents, vagaries, moods, Cam's hours were filled to overflowing. Her conferences with Nan, now installed as sole nurse, sometimes lasted for a whole precious hour in the mornings.

"If the linens are too small for him, Nan, there's nothing for it but sending them back to the White House. Wait a minute," Cam would say, "I'll make a note of writing them. . . . The Magnin people didn't send slips with the girls' dresses? Stupid! I'll make a note of that, too. . . . They can't go over to Grandma's today—oh, why not? I like them to go in the morning. . . . What's the matter with the car? . . . Oh? Well, then let them walk over, and I'll call for you all and bring you back. . . . Ask Asilda to come in here a minute, will you, Mamie? Some friends of Mr Kilgarif are coming Friday night. . . . That chair didn't come back, did it, Nan? . . . Does anyone know if the man came about that tanky, tinny smell upstairs in the hall?"

And so on and on. During the morning hours, when John was working, Cam was working, too. Her baby's special nurse had long ago departed. Edward's hours, usually from seven to seven, with a long afternoon nap in between, were exacting and tiring. His linens, his crib, his sterilized bottles and carefully strained vegetables, his bath and powdering and pinning were all part of a ritual that could not vary even in the smallest particular. Asilda and Mamie, obligingly